The Lone Hunt

by

L.L. Raand

2013

THE LONE HUNT

ISBN 13: 978-1-60282-860-5

This Trade Paperback Original Is Published By
Bold Strokes Books, Inc.
P.O. Box 249
Valley Falls, NY 12185

First Edition: March 2013

Credits
Editors: Ruth Sternglantz and Stacia Seaman
Production Design: Stacia Seaman
Cover Design by Sheri (graphicartist2020@hotmail.com)

Applause for L.L. Raand's Midnight Hunters Series

The Midnight Hunt
RWA 2012 VCRW Laurel Wreath winner *Blood Hunt*
Night Hunt
The Lone Hunt

"Raand has built a complex world inhabited by werewolves, vampires, and other paranormal beings…Raand has given her readers a complex plot filled with wonderful characters as well as insight into the hierarchy of Sylvan's pack and vampire clans. There are many plot twists and turns, as well as erotic sex scenes in this riveting novel that keep the pages flying until its satisfying conclusion."—*Just About Write*

"Once again, I am amazed at the storytelling ability of L.L. Raand aka Radclyffe. In *Blood Hunt*, she mixes high levels of sheer eroticism that will leave you squirming in your seat with an impeccable multi-character storyline all streaming together to form one great read." —*Queer Magazine Online*

"*The Midnight Hunt* has a gripping story to tell, and while there are also some truly erotic sex scenes, the story always takes precedence. This is a great read which is not easily put down nor easily forgotten."—*Just About Write*

"Are you sick of the same old hetero vampire/werewolf story plastered in every bookstore and at every movie theater? Well, I've got the cure to your werewolf fever. *The Midnight Hunt* is first in, what I hope is, a long-running series of fantasy erotica for L.L. Raand (aka Radclyffe)."—*Queer Magazine Online*

"Any reader familiar with Radclyffe's writing will recognize the author's style within *The Midnight Hunt*, yet at the same time it is most definitely a new direction. The author delivers an excellent story here, one that is engrossing from the very beginning. Raand has pieced together an intricate world, and provided just enough details for the reader to become enmeshed in the new world. The action moves quickly throughout the book and it's hard to put down."—*Three Dollar Bill Reviews*

Acclaim for Radclyffe's Fiction

In **2012 RWA/FTHRW Lories and RWA HODRW Aspen Gold award winner *Firestorm*** "Radclyffe brings another hot lesbian romance for her readers."—*The Lesbrary*

Foreword Review Book of the Year finalist and IPPY silver medalist *Trauma Alert* "is hard to put down and it will sizzle in the reader's hands. The characters are hot, the sex scenes explicit and explosive, and the book is moved along by an interesting plot with well drawn secondary characters. The real star of this show is the attraction between the two characters, both of whom resist and then fall head over heels."—*Lambda Literary Reviews*

Lambda Literary Finalist *Best Lesbian Romance 2010* features "stories [that] are diverse in tone, style, and subject, making for more variety than in many, similar anthologies…well written, each containing a satisfying, surprising twist. Best Lesbian Romance series editor Radclyffe has assembled a respectable crop of 17 authors for this year's offering."—*Curve Magazine*

2010 Prism award winner and ForeWord Review Book of the Year Award finalist *Secrets in the Stone* is "so powerfully [written] that the worlds of these three women shimmer between reality and dreams…A strong, must read novel that will linger in the minds of readers long after the last page is turned."—*Just About Write*

In **Benjamin Franklin Award finalist *Desire by Starlight*** "Radclyffe writes romance with such heart and her down-to-earth characters not only come to life but leap off the page until you feel like you know them. What Jenna and Gard feel for each other is not only a spark but an inferno and, as a reader, you will be washed away in this tumultuous romance until you can do nothing but succumb to it."—*Queer Magazine Online*

Lambda Literary Award winner *Stolen Moments* "is a collection of steamy stories about women who just couldn't wait. It's sex when desire overrides reason, and it's incredibly hot!"—*On Our Backs*

Lambda Literary Award winner *Distant Shores, Silent Thunder* "weaves an intricate tapestry about passion and commitment between lovers. The story explores the fragile nature of trust and the sanctuary provided by loving relationships."—*Sapphic Reader*

Lambda Literary Award Finalist *Justice Served* delivers a "crisply written, fast-paced story with twists and turns and keeps us guessing until the final explosive ending."—*Independent Gay Writer*

Lambda Literary Award finalist *Turn Back Time* "is filled with wonderful love scenes, which are both tender and hot."—*MegaScene*

By Radclyffe

Romances

Innocent Hearts
Promising Hearts
Love's Melody Lost
Love's Tender Warriors
Tomorrow's Promise
Love's Masquerade
shadowland
Passion's Bright Fury
Fated Love
Turn Back Time
When Dreams Tremble
The Lonely Hearts Club
Night Call
Secrets in the Stone
Desire by Starlight
Crossroads

Honor Series

Above All, Honor
Honor Bound
Love & Honor
Honor Guards
Honor Reclaimed
Honor Under Siege
Word of Honor

Justice Series

A Matter of Trust (prequel)
Shield of Justice
In Pursuit of Justice
Justice in the Shadows
Justice Served
Justice for All

The Provincetown Tales

Safe Harbor
Beyond the Breakwater
Distant Shores, Silent Thunder
Storms of Change
Winds of Fortune
Returning Tides
Sheltering Dunes

First Responders Novels

Trauma Alert

Firestorm

Oath of Honor

Short Fiction

Collected Stories by Radclyffe

Erotic Interludes: *Change Of Pace*

Radical Encounters

Edited by Radclyffe:

Best Lesbian Romance 2009–2012

Stacia Seaman and Radclyffe, eds.:

Erotic Interludes 2: *Stolen Moments*

Erotic Interludes 3: *Lessons in Love*

Erotic Interludes 4: *Extreme Passions*

Erotic Interludes 5: *Road Games*

Romantic Interludes 1: *Discovery*

Romantic Interludes 2: *Secrets*

Breathless: *Tales of Celebration*

Women of the Dark Streets

By L.L. Raand

Midnight Hunters

The Midnight Hunt

Blood Hunt

Night Hunt

The Lone Hunt

Visit us at www.boldstrokesbooks.com

Acknowledgments

I have enjoyed sci-fi/fantasy since I was young. Ray Bradbury's *Martian Chronicles* is one of the first I can remember reading. Marion Zimmer Bradley's Darkover series was among my favorites and likely influenced the writing of the Midnight Hunters series in ways I never realized until I recall how fascinated I was by her ability to create endless new stories in a world filled with magic and romance. Despite my love of the genre, I never seriously considered writing a fantasy until the hybrid genre of paranormal romance exploded onto the scene in the late twentieth century. Paranormal romance "weds" my long-standing love of gothic romance with the limitless possibility of sci-fi/fantasy. Writing an entirely new world is a challenge, but as in every book I write, character is key. The Weres and Vampires and other Praeterns in this series may be driven more by primal urges than "civilized humans," but the traits that create heroes remain unchanged. Loyalty, passion, honor, and love are at the heart of every story. I am thankful for all the pioneers who helped create this exciting genre and to the readers who support it.

Thanks go to Sandy Lowe, for creating the space I need to write in countless ways; to Ruth Sternglantz for friendship and editorial expertise; to my first readers Connie, Eva, Jenny, and Paula for reading the early drafts and providing support and feedback. Cindy, Sheri, and countless others keep the wheels at BSB turning, and their skill and expertise are greatly appreciated.

And to Lee, who shares my enthusiasm for all things fantastical—*Amo te*.

Radclyffe, 2013

For Lee, for the love of words

Chapter One

Lara stalked the human servant down the silent corridor into the depths of Liege Jody Gates's lair. Hunger forced a flood of feeding hormones into her mouth. Her canines lengthened and throbbed. Her clitoris tensed in anticipation of having Zahn Logan, head of security for the Night Hunters—Jody's Clan and one of the most powerful Dominions in the world—helpless beneath her. Lara envisioned the blonde submitting to her, imagined inducing the arrogant human to writhe in the throes of bloodlust, of driving her to orgasm with her bite. Her predator instinct surged. She growled, her wolf rising, eager for the claiming.

"You should cage that wolf," Zahn said without turning, her stride nearly as sensuous as the glide of a Vampire. "You dishonor your master with your lack of control."

"I am no one's slave." Lara leapt, her claws slicing the back of Zahn's tight black T-shirt before the human twisted aside, surprising her with her speed and agility.

Zahn spun to face her, the blade she carried in a sheath strapped to her muscular thigh now in her right hand. Silver glinted in the double-edged weapon—a Were killer. "I will feed your Vampire with pleasure, but your wolf will die on my blade."

Lara crouched, her wolf eyes glinting amber, her bones and muscles sliding, shifting, morphing. "I will take what I want, when I want it."

"No," Zahn said softly, "you won't. You are more than Were now. You are Vampire."

Lara shuddered, caught in the dark swirls of Zahn's russet eyes. Her nipples tensed, and tawny pelt streaked down the cleft between the rigid columns of her abdominals. The deep glands surrounding the base of her clitoris filled and she wanted to fuck. Fuck and feed. Instincts laced with pain and mindless need. "Get away from me."

"No. I do not fear you." Zahn smiled, her mouth twisted in arrogant challenge. "I want to feed you."

"Why?" Lara growled, her vocal cords thickened with the change.

"Because I can. Come with me, Warlord." Zahn turned and walked on. Her flesh was scored with shallow pink gouges beneath the torn black shirt, but she was nearly healed. She wasn't immortal like the ethereal Vampires she served, but her raw power and sexual allure were nearly as potent.

Warlord. The word cut through the frenzy clouding Lara's senses. She had once been *centuri*, one of the elite guard protecting the wolf Were Alpha. Now she was a Vampire's general, the commander of an army on the verge of war. She had lost her Pack, her station, and her honor when she had died and been resurrected as a Vampire, but she could still fight. She could still kill the enemies who had taken everything.

Lara gathered her will and forced her wolf to withdraw. She would not let Zahn witness her loss of control, would not let Zahn have the satisfaction of goading her into sex frenzy. Zahn might be faster, stronger, more resistant to injury than an ordinary human, but she was still human. And Lara would not let a human hold power over her, even when the human offered her blood and sex, all that she now craved. "You will not need your blade, *Capitaine*. It is your blood we will spill."

A fine shudder ran through Zahn's muscular body. The pleasure of the Vampire's bite was magnified a thousand times for those of her line. She had been born to answer a Vampire's call, the urge to sustain her master's lineage with the unique chemicals in her blood a primal instinct. And Lara was of her master's blood. She ached to feed her. She slid the blade into the leather sheath with a flick of her wrist, so fast only a Praetern could have followed the motion. "Come, Vampire. Take what I offer."

Lara was beside her in an instant, her claws pressing into Zahn's lower back. She smelled Zahn's need, rich and verdant. She sensed the beat of her heart, strong and seductive. "Hurry. I want you in my mouth."

Zahn's hands trembled as she opened the door with a key she withdrew from a pocket in her leather pants. Lara followed her into one of the many chambers in the underground stronghold where Gates and her consort, and Gates's Vampire soldiers, spent the daylight hours guarded by their human servants.

The dim room was warm and windowless. A large bed filled the space, centered on the wall opposite the door. Silky dark-chocolate sheets covered the surface, and a row of matching satin pillows was piled against the mahogany headboard. A royal blue brocade settee, angled in one corner as if waiting for a third participant to arrive, was the only other piece of furniture. The room held no dressers, no night tables, no armoires. Just the bed and the empty settee. A space for feeding—for blood and sex and pleasure-pain. Lara's thighs tensed as her wolf surged again, long denied but still strong. Still eager to hunt.

Taking a breath, keeping a short leash on the prowling predator raging to chase, to capture, to take, Lara closed the door behind her and forced herself to wait while the human walked to the side of the bed and methodically began to disrobe. As humans went, Zahn was attractive—as elegant and beautiful as any of the Vampire guard who answered to her, although Zahn was blond, and most of Gates's Vampires were black haired and blue eyed. Strange that a human should hold such a lofty position as head of a Dominion's security forces, but Lara did not know all the political nuances of the Vampire world in which she suddenly found herself. Wolf packs were controlled not by politics, but by power alone. The Alpha ruled through sheer force of will, cunning, and physical dominance. Before she was turned, Lara had succumbed on occasion to the seductive thrall of a Vampire's power and experienced blood ecstasy herself. Like many Weres, she enjoyed the intense pleasure accompanying a Vampire's bite, but she had always distrusted the Vampire alliances that shifted as easily as a battle won or lost, where trusts were betrayed for fleeting advantage. She walked on the side of the Vampires because she had no choice. She was one of them now, and better to fight where she had a place than to die a slow death every day among the Weres, where she no longer belonged.

Lara locked the door.

Zahn stripped off her tattered shirt and turned to Lara, her high breasts gleaming in the slanting glow of lights tucked away, unseen, in corners. Her nipples were two tight, dark disks on the pale flushed beauty of her breasts. Her muscled abdomen rose and fell in shallow bursts. Her arousal skated over Lara's tongue and flooded her throat with pheromones. Lara's canines jutted, elongating, scraping the tender inner surface of her lower lip. She tasted her own blood, subtly changed.

A metallic undertone tingled in her throat. Her sex glands bulged, full and ready, forcing her engorged clitoris to extrude. The red haze of bloodlust curtained her vision. It would be easy, so easy, to surrender and take what had been offered. The host had come willingly, agreeing to feed her, making no demands, giving no restrictions.

She was free to take—to plunge her canines into the etched column of Zahn's throat, to drink her ferrous-rich blood until her cells were empowered, until her sex throbbed, full and potent. Until she was satisfied.

"You should have a second," Lara said. Her wolf rose to the call of blood just as her Vampire parts thirsted, and she could not hold her back completely. Zahn was not safe without a guard of her own if Lara lost control.

"I need no second." Zahn unstrapped her knife sheath and tossed it onto the brocade settee, out of reach, a deliberate show of confidence and superiority. "I can meet all your needs."

Lara leapt and dug her claws into Zahn's naked shoulders, forcing her down onto the bed. She straddled Zahn's hips, pressing her torso to the bed with extended arms. She didn't draw blood yet—once she did, she wouldn't stop. She dropped her head over Zahn's face, the curtain of her own chestnut hair framing Zahn's high cheekbones and arched jaw. The pulse of Zahn's blood beneath the unblemished skin of her throat was a siren's call. She flashed her canines and Zahn gasped. "You don't know what I need."

"You're wrong." Zahn gripped Lara's black BDUs and tore them down the length of her thighs on both sides.

"Am I?" Centering her hand on Zahn's chest, Lara raised up enough to pull off the shreds of her pants. Her sex throbbed in time with her heart, driving all thoughts save one from her consciousness. *Take her. Take her.* Lara rumbled a warning.

"Yes," Zahn whispered, sweat beading in the hollow of her throat. She reached between them and peeled the leather from her hips. Bowing beneath Lara, she angled her hips and rubbed against Lara's lower body. She was wet, her flesh hot and open. Fingers digging into the hard muscles of Lara's ass, she arched her neck, exposing the great vessels that pulsed vibrantly beneath the surface of her slick skin. "Take my blood. Take my body. I am ready."

Lara snarled. This human sought to control her by offering what made her weak. She needed blood. She craved sex. She ached to lose herself in the taking. And if she did, she would give up what little power she still had. She gathered Zahn's wrists in one hand and pinned her arms above her head, the skin beneath her fingers as delicate as porcelain against the rich chocolate sheets. As strong as Zahn was, she was stronger—she could rip her throat open, tear her heart from her chest, bleed her dry. Slowly, body quivering with the effort to control her bloodlust, to contain the sex frenzy, Lara lowered her head until the points of her canines indented Zahn's skin but did not break through.

"Beg me," Lara whispered. *Don't let me kill you.*

Zahn struggled for sanity in the cloud of pheromones seducing her senses—rich wolf Were stimulants flooded her blood, Vampire thrall enticed her very cells. Every inch of her screamed for the Vampire bite that would transport her, for the Were body that would release her. Never had she ached so much to be bitten, to be drunk, to be filled. To be fucked.

"Oh God." Zahn groaned and wrapped her legs around Lara's hips, forcing her tense clitoris against Lara's. "Please. Bite me. Fill me. I need. Oh God, I need."

Lara's eyes glowed the amber of her Wolf shot through with flame as she drove her Vampire canines into Zahn's throat, releasing the erotostimulants that turned pain into pleasure, transformed sacrifice to scorching satisfaction. Zahn cried out and orgasmed, her sex throbbing against Lara's.

Lara swallowed, her cells expanding with the rush of life, her clitoris taut, swollen, pounding for release. She thrust her hips and slipped between Zahn's drenched folds, sliding easily into her cleft, lodging there, tight and hot.

Zahn thrashed, another orgasm crashing through her. She scored Lara's back with her nails, the distant pain a grace note to the agonizing pleasure. Lara thrust and swallowed, thrust and swallowed, taking life with every swallow, releasing her essence with every thrust, the *victus* thick and rich with borrowed life. She shuddered, close, so close to the final shattering release her wolf craved. Her skin burned, her breath tore from her in tortured sobs. She couldn't empty, couldn't find the ultimate satisfaction without—

Lara's need called to Zahn as her masters' had called to those of her line for millennia. She tightened her grip on Lara's shoulders and jolted upward, sinking her teeth into Lara's shoulder, breaking the skin, drawing blood.

A shaft of pain arrowed into the deepest reaches of Lara's sex and she exploded, her glands emptying, her clitoris spasming in the depths of Zahn's flesh. Zahn sucked at the bite she'd made and came again.

Lara pulled her head away, yanking her shoulder free from Zahn's mouth. Zahn moaned, nearly unconscious, deep in the thrall, mindless with pleasure. Lara's clitoris still pulsed under Zahn's, a tender knot forming mid-shaft. Zahn's bite had triggered her wolf's instinct to join. "No!"

Lara staggered to her feet, Zahn's blood and hers running in rivulets down her chest, over her breasts, matting the dusting of pelt down the center of her abdomen. Somehow Zahn had known what her wolf needed. What *she* needed. More than blood, more than sex. A joining that could never be hers. Empowered with Zahn's blood, her wolf did not recognize the truth. She would never mate. Weres mated for life, and she was already dead. Lara threw the sheet over Zahn, paced to the door, and flipped the lock.

With sunfall still an hour away, she should be tired, but she wasn't. She was Vampire, but she was Were, and she needed more than blood. Needed more than the bite of the human she did not want. She spun around, pulled the door open, and bounded into the corridor, her wolf breaking its chains at last. Her vision grayed into the sharp lens of the predator. A human guard. By a door at the end of the hall. She smelled sunshine beyond that door. Beyond that door a staircase led to the outside, led to freedom. Naked, covered in blood and sex-sheen and *victus*, she leapt the length of the hall toward the guard. His eyes widened and his dark face turned ashen, but he stood his ground, his automatic weapon still holstered on his thigh. Brave man.

"Step aside, Human, or you will die."

"I have orders that no one leaves until moonrise, Warlord," he said, his voice raspy.

"You will obey me, soldier, or you will die this day."

"The sun has not yet fallen. Zahn ordered—"

Lara grasped him by the neck and tethered him to the wall, his feet ten inches off the floor, his face less than a breath from hers.

"I am the Warlord of the Liege's armies. I am your master. You take your orders from me."

"Yes, Warlord," he wheezed through the thin column of air she allowed him to suck in. "But the sun—"

"I am not afraid of the sun." She wasn't sure how she knew, but she did. The daylight was not her enemy. "While I am gone, you will see that no one approaches Liege Gates's quarters. No one enters the Liege's chambers except Zahn until I return. Not for any reason. Do you understand?"

"Yes, Warlord."

"Open the barricades." She let him down, and he nearly fell but regained his feet and snapped a salute, fist to chest.

"Yes, Warlord."

He punched numbers into a keypad, pressed his palm to a plate on the wall, and stared into a retina scanner. Locks ratcheted open and the reinforced steel door slid soundlessly aside. She bolted through, up the stairs, and into another long corridor. A soldier at the far end held another door open as the last shafts of sunlight flickered outside, refusing to surrender to the night. For the first time since she'd been turned, Lara felt her Wolf ascend, body and spirit, and she let her come. By the time she soared through the camouflaged exit and out into the street, she was in full pelt and ready to hunt.

CHAPTER TWO

I feel fine," Chris said, looking as if she was about to jump off the examining table. "I need to get back to the labs."

"I'll decide when you're ready to return to duty." Drake folded her arms in front of her chest and deliberately moved into the young lieutenant's personal space. Chris, naked except for her jeans, still showed signs of injury despite having shifted to pelt after being caught in the explosion that had leveled the research wing at Mir Industries that morning. Her right shoulder and neck were bruised and swollen, and traces of debris remained embedded in a latticework of lacerations that trailed down her bare arms. Her shift had been too short or the damage too severe for her wolf to heal completely. Chris was the head of security, and she had to be feeling responsible for the explosion. She wasn't at fault, but try telling a dominant wolf she couldn't control everyone and everything within her sphere. A fruitless task. Drake ought to know, she was mated to the Alpha wolf. She dealt with the challenge of trying to reason with a Were driven by instinct on a daily basis. "You're not going anywhere just yet."

Chris rumbled low in her chest, not a challenge, but a sign of displeasure and irritation. Drake could live with that. After all, she could hardly expect a wolf like Chris to roll over and give her throat at the first sign of a harsh word. She eased back an inch, giving Chris's wolf room to stretch. "Now, let me see you raise your arm."

"Really, Prima," Chris said, her tone a fraction more conciliatory as she lifted her injured right arm. "I just twisted it. I've had worse on a hunt."

"That may be." Drake slid her palm under Chris's elbow and grasped her wrist with the other hand. She'd learned very quickly after her transition from human to wolf Were that the one thing every wolf understood and accepted was the law of the Pack. And, as the Alpha's mate, she was at the top of the Pack in rank and power. "But since I'm the doctor here, let's let me make the decision."

Chris sighed. "Yes, Prima."

Smothering her smile, Drake ranged the shoulder, elbow, and wrist. Chris—blond haired, blue eyed, chiseled and muscular like all of Sylvan's soldiers—sat implacably, but Drake felt the thrum of tension streak through Chris's frame as she stressed the shoulder gently. "You've got a tear in the tendons around your shoulder."

"It's just a little sore," Chris muttered.

"I imagine that it is." Drake carefully released Chris's arm and walked behind the table to look at her back. The skin over the broad muscles was shredded. Not serious, but painful. The shoulder was a different story. "You'll need to shift and stay in pelt the rest of the night to heal these wounds and get your shoulder back in shape."

"But, Prima," Chris said, twisting on the table to look in Drake's direction, "I need to get back to the lab to secure the area and begin our search. We're not even sure there aren't more devices in the rest of the buildings."

Chris's eyes rose to Drake's. The challenge was unintentional, but Drake growled nevertheless. Without iron discipline, a Pack of Weres ruled by primal instinct would splinter into chaos. Chris immediately ducked her head.

"If you delay your healing," Drake said, "you may have permanent damage in the shoulder. I doubt the Alpha would be pleased to find her lab's head of security functioning at less than a hundred percent."

Chris's chin shot up, but she wisely did not meet Drake's eyes. "I would never give the Alpha less than my best."

"Of that, I have no doubt. And that's why I want you in pelt, in your quarters, until morning." She put command in her voice, her tone sending the same message a curled lip and lowered ears would have if she was in pelt—the warning of a dominant wolf to a lesser member of the Pack to mind her place.

Chris sucked in a breath. "Yes, Prima."

Drake slipped her palm behind Chris's neck and squeezed, the comfort of her touch reminding Chris that she was an important part of the Pack and important to Drake. "You did well today. You guarded the Alpha's back, and you saw that your Packmates were safe. You've done your duty, and in a few hours, you can resume."

"Thank you, Prima," Chris murmured, shivering slightly under

Drake's touch. Wolves needed the physical comfort of their packmates, especially their leaders. At first, Drake had found the casual physical affection disconcerting, and on occasion, when it involved Sylvan, more than that. Sylvan was her mate, and even though Sylvan constantly reasserted her authority and her dominance by touching her wolves, no one, Praetern or human, would touch Sylvan without Drake's permission. *Sylvan.* A wave of electricity rippled over Drake's skin and she stepped back.

"The Alpha is coming," Drake said, sensing Sylvan's approach through the unique bond all mated Weres shared. Her pulse quickened and her body readied. "I'll be sure to let her know you'll be back on duty tomorrow."

Chris jumped down from the table and picked up her shirt, not bothering to put it on. Most wolves rarely bothered with clothes when in the Compound. "Thank you, Prima."

The door swung open and Sylvan strode in, bringing with her a surge of power that washed over Drake's skin like the heat of a furnace. Muscles danced beneath the sleek surface of Sylvan's naked torso, her bronze skin gleamed with a sheen of pheromones, and gold shimmered in her blue eyes. She was more wolf in skin than many lesser Weres in pelt. Her gaze skimmed Chris.

"Alpha," Chris said, her tone a salute.

"How are you, Lieutenant?"

"Fine, Alpha."

Sylvan's attention moved to Drake, a question in her eyes.

"The lieutenant's on the mend, Alpha," Drake said. "By tomorrow she'll be fine."

"Good. When you return to duty," Sylvan said, "organize teams and begin the search through the rubble. It's doubtful we'll find any physical clues as to who planted the devices, but any remnants of the bombs might help us identify them in the future. I've suspended operations until we can examine all the wreckage."

"I could get started sooner," Chris said, "with the Prima's permission, of course."

Drake shook her head.

"As the Prima commands," Sylvan said, her tone leaving no room for discussion.

"Yes, Alpha," Chris said, a sigh escaping as she departed.

Sylvan grinned as the door closed behind the security chief. "I take it she's not happy about being stood down?"

"She is your wolf," Drake said. "She's not happy unless she's in the thick of the hunt, but she's not yet fit for duty. She will be."

"Are you all right?" Sylvan murmured, skimming her hand under the back of Drake's T-shirt and up between her shoulder blades, tugging Drake tightly into her body.

Drake slid an arm around Sylvan's shoulders and kissed her. She hadn't seen her for over an hour, and even a few minutes' separation was intolerable now that she was pregnant. Even before she'd been pregnant, with their mate bond so new, she was physically uncomfortable whenever Sylvan was out of sight. The constant need to touch her was all-consuming. And only hours before, Sylvan had been in mortal danger. They hadn't been alone since the explosion—she hadn't had time to reassure her wolf that her mate was safe. Drake rumbled and rubbed her cheek on Sylvan's. "I'm all right now that you're here."

Sylvan grazed Drake's neck with her canines and buried her face in the curve of Drake's shoulder, drawing deeply of Drake's midnight-and-oak scent, absorbing her heat, tasting the pheromones that coated her skin—centered by the unique chemicals that called only to her. Drake was her mate, her strength, her life. "I love you."

Drake slid her fingers through Sylvan's hair and tugged her head up until their eyes met. "I love you…and you're going to need to learn to be more careful, Alpha."

Sylvan grinned her infuriating grin, the cocky lift at one corner of her wide, generous mouth that said she'd do exactly what she wanted because, after all, she was the Alpha. "You don't need to worry."

Drake nipped at Sylvan's lip hard enough to taste the potent pheromones Sylvan released when she was aroused. "Do you think I can't make you?"

Growling low in her throat, Sylvan lifted Drake and turned her until Drake's back was against the door and Sylvan's hips were tight into her crotch. Drake wrapped her legs around Sylvan's ass and her arms around Sylvan's shoulders, tilting her head back to give Sylvan her neck. She wasn't submitting, she was inviting.

"You think you can control me?" Sylvan grumbled, her voice thick and heavy as her wolf rose to her mate's challenge. She licked Drake's neck and bit lightly. Beneath her, Drake's abdomen pressed against hers, and inside, Drake carried their young. Sylvan worshiped her as the mother of her young and exalted in a mate who challenged her in every way.

"I would never want to control you," Drake said, fisting both hands in Sylvan's tawny gold hair. "I would only ever want to love you."

Gold eclipsed the blue in Sylvan's irises and the bones in her face shifted until the elegant arches and curves became lethally sharp, brutally beautiful. Her canines lengthened, and the press of her sex grew heavy and hard between Drake's legs.

"I would take you back to our den," Sylvan said, "and take you slowly, all night long. I'd show you how much I love you. But—"

"I know," Drake said, pushing one hand between them and hooking her fingers inside the waistband of Sylvan's jeans. She slashed the denim open with her claws and pushed her hand lower, closing around Sylvan's distended flesh. "But you have time to take me."

She stroked and Sylvan threw her head back, eyes wild, canines gleaming. Sylvan was already hot and hard in her palm, and if she kept stroking her, she would make Sylvan come. She loved having that kind of control over her mate, the most dominant of all the Weres, but she needed Sylvan closer. Her wolf raged at her to join, shredding her control. She needed Sylvan in every part of her. "Inside. I need you."

"Hold on to me," Sylvan growled, her words so guttural they were barely recognizable. Drake clamped an arm around Sylvan's shoulders but kept her fingers closed around Sylvan's clitoris—squeezing, tugging, preparing Sylvan for what she needed. Sylvan tore Drake's pants away from Drake's hips and shoved her own jeans lower. "Release me."

"Not yet," Drake whispered, shuddering as her clitoris tensed and she readied for her mate. She stroked Sylvan, feeling the furious beat of her blood and the slick wash of sex. She fingered the tender undersurface of Sylvan's clitoris and dipped inside her. Sylvan's hips jerked and she snarled, a dangerous, lethal sound that made Drake's nipples tense and pelt flare down her abdomen. She was so, so ready but she wanted more. She licked the mate bite on Sylvan's chest and Sylvan spasmed in her hand.

"No more. I can't…" Sylvan grasped Drake's wrist and pulled her hand free. Surging forward, she slotted her distended clitoris below Drake's. Their flesh, their spirits, bonded, sealing their union. The hard knot of need between Drake's thighs exploded, and she coated Sylvan with her essence, marking her. Sylvan roared and buried her canines in Drake's shoulder, coming with her. Drake scissored her legs around Sylvan's hips, keeping Sylvan inside as Sylvan thrust through her orgasm.

Sylvan held Drake tightly as her legs buckled and she went to the floor, cradling Drake in her lap. Sylvan's chest heaved and her belly rolled with pleasure. Gasping, she twisted until her back was against the door. "You take everything."

Drake curled into Sylvan's arms and kissed her throat. "I know."

Sylvan sighed, and for that brief moment, she was free from the burden of rule. She was only Drake's. "Thank you."

Drake murmured contentedly and caressed Sylvan's breast. "For what, Sylvan?"

"For giving me a place to rest."

"Always."

Sylvan rubbed her cheek in Drake's hair. "I talked to Niki and Sophia."

"How is Niki?" Drake asked.

"Healed, she says. Sophia agrees, and I trust her assessment."

"Niki's lucky. You both were." Drake kissed Sylvan's chest. "I imagine Sophia is having the same talk with Niki that I had with you."

"Niki is my general. She was born to fight. Sophia knows that."

"I know, but love changes perspective sometimes."

Sylvan nuzzled Drake's throat. "It does."

"You need to eat and get some sleep, love."

"What I need I have—you."

"You have me." Drake stroked Sylvan's face and kissed her. "But the Pack needs you strong, and if you're going to face Francesca, you need to be at your strongest. I don't trust her."

Sylvan laughed. "You don't like her."

"You're right, I don't. And not just because she's touched you. She's the Chancellor of the City and Viceregal of the Eastern Vampire seethe because she's clever, self-serving, and powerful. Don't underestimate her, Sylvan, and don't believe her at her word."

"I don't intend to." Sylvan paused. "There's something else. Something you need to know."

Drake tensed, hearing the distress in Sylvan's voice. "What is it?"

"Sophia told me something tonight that her parents have kept secret ever since they joined the Pack when Sophia was a young child."

"Something about Sophia's transformation?" Drake had known subconsciously all along that the Pack medic was no ordinary *mutia*. No ordinary turned-Were. Sophia was different than other Weres, just like Drake.

"Sophia wasn't bitten, wasn't turned by a Were—rabid or otherwise. She was…created by an experimental virus that was being studied in a human laboratory."

"Studied? Developed, you mean." Bitterly, Drake thought of Gray and Katya, two of their female young who'd been held captive in a laboratory and studied, their bodies biopsied, their blood analyzed, their sex glands stimulated to force emissions. Cold rage spread through her chest. "Why? What were the experiments supposed to do?"

"The Revniks thought they were working on a cure for Were fever, but what was really going on was an attempt to create Weres or at least replicate Were traits. Obviously, they were only partially successful. Most of the subjects died, but Sophia didn't."

"Sophia was only a child. She shouldn't have lived," Drake pointed out.

"That's what makes her unique. The Revniks think the experiments are still going on."

"That might explain the infected humans you liberated from the lab. And the dead girls who appeared to die of Were fever," Drake said, dread settling in her depths.

"Yes," Sylvan said quietly.

"The experiments, the partially turned humans, the viral contagion—it would explain me," Drake said.

"Possibly," Sylvan said.

"The Revniks need to study me," Drake said.

Sylvan growled. "I know you want to do whatever you can to help those girls, but—"

"I'm not thinking just about the girls." Drake pressed her palm to Sylvan's heart. "If I am Were because of a manufactured virus, we can't know that the mutation is stable. I'm pregnant, Sylvan. We have to know what this will do to our young."

Sylvan shook her head. "I already know. I can sense them, so can Sophia. They're healthy. Trust me."

Drake nodded. She trusted Sylvan with her heart and her future, and whatever fate their young faced, she would protect them with her life.

Chapter Three

Lara emerged from Jody's lair and headed toward the river, skirting the edges of Washington Park, crowded with late-day dog-walkers and parents pushing strollers. Keeping to side streets and alleyways, she slid into the shadows whenever a passerby gave her more than a cursory glance. Humans saw what they expected to see—a four-legged, furred creature with a tail and a canine face was a dog, despite her wolf's larger-than-average size. She was faster than a dog, more agile, and, unlike dogs, able to assess and strategize as well on four legs as she could on two. Her wolf wanted to run, to hunt, and knew where she needed to go. Within minutes she'd reached the banks of the Hudson and turned north. The land bordering the river as it wended into the Adirondack Mountains was largely undeveloped, edged by woods, prime farmland, and the occasional waterfront summer cottage. Farmhouses sat well back from the river, above the floodplains where the river dumped its rich silt when it overran its bank after a heavy rain or spring snow melt. Trails—deer, fox, wolf, and cat—threaded through the woods and pastures, invisible to most humans but as familiar to Lara as the highways she traveled by car. She ran as she never could in skin—her limbs stretching to the rhythm of the earth rippling under her paws, her mouth open, tasting the air, the trees, the undergrowth—absorbing the world through her pores, clear and clean with no artificial barriers to isolate her. Her wolf, unleashed after weeks of pain and imprisonment, ran with an unfettered joy and fierce desire for freedom.

Every instinct drove her north, toward Pack land, toward home. Home, but no longer sanctuary. The Compound, the Alpha's walled haven in the heart of Pack land, was closed to her. She had petitioned for her freedom, asked to be released from her oath to the Alpha in order to serve another, and the Alpha had granted her request. She was no longer the Alpha's *centuri*—she was Gates's warlord. Although she hunted in pelt, she was more than wolf, more than Were now, and she skirted the borders of Pack land, hundreds of acres of dense virgin forest patrolled only by a network of Were *sentries*. A doe crossed her path, hesitated at the scent of the predator close by, and, with a wild roll of her eyes and flick of her snowy tail, bunched her muscles and bounded deeper into the forest.

Lara's wolf took notice but didn't give chase. She wasn't hungry. Her blood didn't rise to the call to hunt. Confused, but unprotesting, her wolf let the deer go and pushed on. Acid burned in her muscles, breath scoured her lungs. Her tongue lolled, her chest heaved. And still she ran, desperate for freedom, wild to purge the pain that lacerated her heart. Weak sunlight flickered through the trees, thinning filaments of gold that laced her pelt as she passed in and out of shadow. Fingers of heat trickled through her fur, but she did not burn. Just as the fire she'd driven through to rescue the Alpha and the Liege had failed to touch her, the sunlight had no effect on her. Lethal to Vampires, the UV radiation seemed powerless to damage her. Not Were, not Vampire. She didn't fear true death, but death refused to claim her.

She stopped once by a stream coursing down a ravine to drink cool, clear mountain water from a shimmering pool. An owl hooted from deeper in the forest, rabbits and squirrels rustled in the underbrush, and once she scented a whisper of wolf—one of the *sentries* on patrol, guarding the Alpha's land. The dark, spicy aroma of Pack teased her senses, stirred an answering surge in her cells.

Ignoring the call, she struck off again, staying downwind of the *sentrie*'s location. She wasn't sure of her welcome—a dominant wolf on Pack land, an ally, perhaps, but no longer *of* the Pack. Her presence might be seen as a challenge to the Alpha, and if challenged, the Alpha would show no quarter. That was the law of the Pack. She had not come to give challenge, and soon she would have duties elsewhere. Jody would rise at sunfall and feed, first from her consort Becca and, if the injuries she'd sustained in the raid on the human labs were not totally healed, from Zahn or another of her human servants. The warlord needed to be there when Jody was ready to convene her forces. Lara was not a guard—Rafaela was in charge of Jody's Vampire guards, and Zahn oversaw Clan security. But all Jody's soldiers, human and Vampire alike, were Lara's to command. She would not have left the lair, even for her wolf's fierce need, if she thought Jody might be in danger.

In the last few minutes of daylight, she climbed an escarpment, scrabbling over loose rocks, pushing through underbrush, struggling to reach the pinnacle, needing to see the forest stretching endlessly before her, longing for a glimpse of the majesty that had always been her home. Crouched on a boulder on the very edge of a cliff, she watched the sun set and the moon rise, twin hearts destined to share the universe, always separated as they passed on the edges of the day.

The first glimmer of moonlight silvered through the gray twilight, and Lara's blood stirred at last. She raised her head and howled, pierced by the primal beauty. Her cries tumbled into the river valley below, echoed to her, mournful and solitary, from the mountain peaks surrounding her. When silence was all that remained, she padded down the steep slope the way she had come. If she ran all the way back, she would reach Jody's town house only a little after full nightrise.

As she skirted the underbrush toward the water, a sound sliced the still air. Hackles rising, she stilled, her ears pricked, her nose testing the air. She'd heard the cry of a cat. The Catamount cat Weres' territory was a few miles to the east, and occasionally their raiding parties forayed into Pack land. In pelt, the cats resembled huge mountain lions—tawny-gold coats, four-inch canines, thick muscular haunches, and powerful shoulders. More feral than wolves, the cats were sworn enemies of the wolf Weres. The cats had never been well organized and, as a result of their infighting and lack of a united military presence, had never been considered much of a threat to Pack security—which explained why Sylvan had not wiped them out. But the Alpha's leniency only extended so far. Cat hunting parties were known to attack wolf young and solitary soldiers, and the standing order to all wolves was to attack on sight, and attack to kill.

Lara hunkered down and slunk through the underbrush in the direction from which she'd heard the sound. The wind had shifted, and she scented nothing she couldn't recognize—no foreign markings that didn't belong. She swung her head from side to side but heard nothing unusual. Sound carried in the mountains yet was just as easily distorted and redirected. She might be chasing a ghost, but she needed to be sure. She might not be *centuri*, might not even be wolf, but her duty remained. She would not turn away from an enemy.

The riverbank narrowed into a rocky stretch bordered by a steep cliff crisscrossed with narrow ledges, outcroppings of scraggly underbrush, and jumbled piles of boulders. Narrow crevices seamed the rock face, providing perfect cover for attack from above. Lara slowed and scanned the lengthening shadows. She perked her ears, heard nothing. Raised her muzzle, sniffed the damp air. Nothing. Across the water another owl hooted. She flicked her ears. Perhaps that's what she'd heard. She padded forward slowly, searching. A small shower of stones trickled down the slope. One bounced off her shoulder. She froze.

Something moving above? She could see nothing. Scent nothing. But instinct told her she was not alone. She crouched, eased forward. One step. Another. A screech of fury sliced the air, sharp as a blade. Lara froze an instant. An instant that cost her as a crushing weight landed on her back and slammed her to the ground.

Rocks scraped her muzzle, gouged her chest.

Jaws clamped onto her neck, teeth tore through the muscles of her shoulder. Claws raked her flanks. Pain exploded in a dozen places at once.

Lara growled, claws slashing and canines snapping. Unable to reach the vulnerable belly or throat, she rolled to dislodge her attacker. The beast rode her back, limbs wrapped around her shoulders and hindquarters, shaking and twisting her neck in powerful jaws. Fire roared through Lara's chest, rained down her back, and she snarled and thrashed. Her wolf was a seasoned fighter, and now, she was more than wolf. Stronger, faster. Spinning with Vampire speed, she caught a leg in her mouth and locked her jaws, twisting and tearing. Warm, rich, potent blood filled her mouth. Her clitoris tensed, her sex filled. Her teeth met bone.

Another scream tore through the night and the pressure on her neck relented. Her hind legs made purchase on the stony bank, and she levered her body into a sharp curve, snapping the bone between her jaws. Claws tore through her side, slashed through muscle, and she released the leg, snarling wildly. She arched her back and the weight disappeared. Spinning quickly, she faced her attacker. A huge mountain lion, ears pinned back, green eyes nearly black with rage, screamed a challenge. She was a beautiful beast, sleek and muscled, her jaws wide, lethal canines gleaming, covered in blood. Lara's blood. Lara was smaller but quicker, and she leapt, hungry for blood, primed for the kill. She buried her teeth in the cat's throat, pressing her body close to the cat's underside. If she exposed her belly to the churning limbs and deadly claws, the cat would tear her innards from her and rip out her throat while she strangled on her own blood. A cat this big might even be able to kill her, but not today. Today the kill was hers.

Lara squeezed the cat's windpipe closed and dug her claws into the cat's sides, tethering herself, refusing to be dislodged even as the cat screamed and rolled, thrashing, slashing, a whirlwind of furious power. But even the strongest enemy could not fight forever without air. Lara's belly burned, her shoulder gushed blood, but she held on. The cat grew weaker, fell, and didn't rise. Howling triumphantly, Lara straddled the prone form, shaking the cat's giant head in her jaws. Her sex pulsed, verging on release. Her belly quivered, tight with need. She sensed the cat's heartbeat slowing, tasted the life leeching from the blood that poured down her throat. Another few seconds, and she would have her kill. Another few seconds and she—

A foreign sound cut through the fury of her bloodlust. A weak cry, thin and forlorn. Lara stilled, listened. The cry came again, was joined by another. Lara released her hold on the cat's throat, raised her head, peered into the darkness. Another shape materialized, coming fast, silently—another wolf. Lara sprang off the cat and crouched beside the bloodied, motionless body, facing the intruder. She growled a warning. Her kill. *Hers.*

The wolf, a slender gray-and-white female, hesitated, ears back, tail straight, hackles raised. Snarled a challenge. A *sentrie*, a young one, and one Lara knew. Lara glanced at the cat. Barely breathing, barely alive. She sniffed the air again, caught another scent beneath the blood and pheromones clouding her mind. Young. The cat had young.

Wait, Lara signaled to the *sentrie*. *Guard her. If she moves, kill her.*

The younger wolf crouched, growled softly, eased forward an inch at a time. Preparing to spring. Refusing an order. Lara snarled. She should kill this wolf, but...something was wrong. She shifted, stood upright. "Misha, stand down."

The *sentrie* quivered, whined, and shook. An instant later Misha crouched on the rocks, head lowered. "I'm sorry, *Centuri*, I didn't...I don't know why...I didn't recognize you."

"Never mind that now," Lara said. "Guard this..."

"Lara!" Misha warned, dark eyes wide.

Lara spun around. The cat Were had shifted as Weres often did when dying. Her hair was the same wild tawny color as her pelt had been, lying in tangled curls around her shoulders. Blood still trickled from the slashes in her throat and long sloping belly. Teeth marks scored her full breasts. Bone protruded from her right forearm. She had fought ferociously, even when dying, and she was still beautiful in death.

Lara stared. She had vanquished an enemy and all she felt was crushing emptiness. Inside, her wolf howled with pain and fury. Lara knelt beside the fallen female. *Who are you?*

Eyes the color of spring leaves, shimmering with pain, met hers. Blood trickled from the corner of her wide, generous mouth. “Please.”

Lara leaned closer, not sure she hadn’t imagined the sound, barely a breath. *Who are you?*

“Kill me, not them. Please not them.”

“No,” Lara whispered, the words an oath. “Not them.”

CHAPTER FOUR

Raina stared up into the face of her enemy, struggling with her last ounce of strength to stay alive. *Weak. So weak.* And everywhere, the pain. So little left after she'd fought so hard, for so long. Never once had she begged, never once had she bargained. Her pride, her honor, her fury wouldn't let her bend. And she'd almost won. Almost. Until this enemy had come out of the mist broadcasting such deadly power she'd had to stand and fight. She'd fought to the last and lost, and now her pride meant nothing. Just as her life meant nothing. She had nothing left to give except her life, and even that was not enough. Raina waited for the final blow, the last searing agony.

Her enemy's eyes were twin fires, crimson flames dancing in an amber blaze, endless depths that caught and held. She'd die a captive in those eyes. Raina's vision dimmed and she forced herself to move. Instantly, rivers of pain flooded her consciousness from every direction, driving off the creeping fog of death. Beyond her own silent screams she heard nothing, a silence so absolute she almost smiled. The cubs had learned, almost too late. They would be hiding now, as she had taught them. Wary, vigilant, motionless. Waiting for her to return. The pain in her heart was worse than anything her body endured.

"Find the young," the *centuri* ordered, never moving her gaze from Raina.

"No." Raina gasped, the slightest movement unbearable. But she forced her head back, gave her throat even as she felt the blood from her wounds pouring down her chest. "My life…in exchange for theirs."

"I already have your life," her enemy growled. Her gaze never faltered. Hard, merciless eyes. Hard, cold, deadly beauty.

Raina shuddered. She had nothing left to offer, but for them she would sacrifice her honor. "I know things. Tell your Alpha—"

"Who are you?"

The words echoed in her mind as if she had heard them before. But they were only the echoes of the question she'd asked herself as she'd hidden alone in the mountains, hungry, hunted, homeless. "I am Raina. Alpha to the cat Weres."

Her enemy, with the burning eyes and chestnut hair, grabbed her by the throat. "I should kill you now."

Raina groaned, tears of anguish leaking from her eyes. She couldn't use her right arm. The slightest motion pushed her to the brink of unconsciousness. Weakly, she used her left to grip her enemy's arm. No honor, no pride. "Sanctuary. I seek sanctuary."

The *centuri* swung her head around and spat out an order. "Call Callan and Niki. Tell them we have a prisoner." The stony face, utterly cold, achingly beautiful in its remote austerity, turned back to her. "If you die, Cat, I will feed your cubs to our pups."

Raina snarled. "One day, Wolf, I will claw your heart from your chest."

The cool beauty smiled and she tightened her hold. "You're welcome to try, but I am hard to kill."

Raina gasped, fighting for air. Her chest constricted, her vision clouded. If she died, this wolf would kill her cubs. She tried to sit up, failed. So weak. And the blood still gushed from her wounds.

"Centuri," a young female said, "they're coming. Elena too."

"Good."

"I'll get the cubs."

"No!" Raina thrashed. *"No."*

"Lie still," her captor snapped. "You need to stop the bleeding. Can you shift?"

"Too weak," Raina lied. She could shift, but the energy to transform would sap her last reserve and she'd probably lapse into unconsciousness until she healed. She could not trust these wolves with her cubs.

"What kind of Alpha are you?" the wolf said derisively.

Raina's eyes blazed. "Alpha enough to—"

"Don't struggle. You're no match for me at full strength." The haunting eyes narrowed. "If you bleed to death, your young will die."

"When they are safe—"

"You don't have that long. Don't fight me."

Raina tensed as the wolf leaned over her, strands of chestnut hair falling across her breast, ghosting over her cheek. Something deep inside her stirred, came to life in a way she'd never known. "No."

Be still. The words, a sensuous command, reverberated inside her head. And then she was running through golden meadows under a summer sun, her cubs at her heels. They were young and strong, frolicking, tumbling, filled with life and wild spirit. Wind ruffled her fur, and she breathed sunshine and sweet clover. Warm lips slid over her neck, a luxurious mouth caressed her skin. Raina shivered. Heat flooded her body, curled in her depths. Her loins filled, pulsed with life and power.

She roared and she was running again, free and strong. Her limbs stretched, her muscles soared, and the calls of her young, vibrant and beautiful, filled her senses. Her nipples tensed. Her belly tightened. Tendrils of pleasure skated over her skin, teasing and tormenting, promising unbearable excitement. A second of piercing pain in her neck made her tense, and the fire returned, burning her to cinders. Raina cried out as the orgasm consumed her.

Lara licked the rents she'd made in Raina's neck, sealing the wounds with the feeding hormones that filled her mouth. Raina arched beneath her, warm and alive—so beautiful, so tempting. Lara's breasts brushed Raina's and her nipples tightened. The cat's orgasm flooded through her, and Lara drank her pleasure, struggling not to drink her blood. Raina had none to give—she teetered on the brink of death, and Lara did not want to let her go. The cat was the enemy, but she had fought valiantly, and she was still fighting. Fighting to live, to protect her young. Her eyes, glazed with pain, had been filled with strength and endless loneliness. Lara recognized the soul-deep sadness. Growling, she forced the image of Raina's wounded eyes from her mind. The cat Were might be useful to the Alpha—the only reason she needed to keep her alive.

Lara bit her, infusing Raina's system with the healing essence unique to Vampires. She refused to feed, but she could not refuse the call of Raina's flesh. The rising tide of Raina's passion ignited her bloodlust. She kept herself from drinking with the last tethers of her control, but she could not deny the need kindled by the hunt and fired by Raina's allure. She had to release. Straddling Raina's thigh, Lara relinquished Raina's neck and pierced Raina's breast with her canines. Raina, lost in thrall, clawed her back, the pain as exquisite as a bite. Lara came in a torrent so fierce she could barely keep from collapsing on Raina's still form. Panting, drenched in blood and sex, she pulled her mouth away and braced herself on outstretched arms. Her muscles quivered and her sex pounded. She groaned.

Raina's eyes, clouded with pleasure, roamed over Lara's face. "Who are you?"

"I don't know," Lara murmured.

Becca sat on the side of the vast four-poster bed, naked except for the cream silk sheets, a few shades lighter than her skin, draped over her thighs, and finished the meal Jody's servants had brought to the door not long before. She hadn't gotten used to sleeping during the day yet and had awakened before sunfall. She hadn't waited to share the meal with Jody. Jody did eat and drink, but when she woke, she wouldn't be hungry for food. She would be ravenous to feed, lusting for blood, especially as she'd been so recently injured. Becca had sent Jody's blood servants away, even though Jody would not be happy to find Becca alone in the bedroom. Jody was recently Risen, and most Vampires couldn't control their bloodlust so soon after making the final transition. Jody worried she would lose control when she fed from Becca and take too much blood.

Becca wasn't worried. Jody had the control of a much older and stronger Vampire. She pushed the service tray away and turned on the bed, leaning on one arm to watch Jody wake. She lived for and feared this moment every day. While asleep, Jody was lost to her, so deep in daylight somnolence she was barely breathing, her heartbeat so slow and subdued as to be impossible to feel. Becca was still terrified Jody would not wake and she would be helpless to reach her. Jody was so beautiful—her porcelain skin flawless, her bold features carved from ivory, her hair as dark as midnight. Becca leaned over and kissed her, and when she pulled back, Jody's obsidian eyes were fixed on her face. Where once Becca had seen only endless night in those eyes, now scarlet shards cut through them, an ever-present reminder that Jody was Vampire.

"Hi," Becca said.

Jody smiled. "Hello."

Her incisors glistened against her lower lip and her eyes were suddenly more flame than obsidian.

"Becca—" Jody murmured, half warning, half invitation.

"I've been waiting for you." Becca took Jody's hand and tugged as she lay on her back, drawing Jody over her. "Wanting you. Needing you."

Jody's hand came into Becca's hair and tightened, guiding her head back, exposing her neck. Becca wrapped her legs around Jody's slim hips. Jody's body was cool and smooth as marble against the heat of Becca's flesh. Becca's heart thundered in her chest, but she felt no answering pulse from Jody. She gripped Jody's shoulders. "I need all of you. Take what you need. Take me."

Jody was at Becca's neck so fast all she felt was the quicksilver flash of pain as Jody pierced her skin and then only unbearable pleasure.

"Oh God," Becca cried out, digging her fingers into Jody's shoulders. Her orgasm exploded through her, exquisitely raw, unspeakably intense. Jody rode between her thighs, drawing life from her life, coming with her. Their bodies, their heartbeats attuned with every pulse of Becca's blood into Jody's cells.

Deep in bloodlust, Jody's throat worked convulsively, her hips pumping to the rhythm of Becca's blood flowing into her. She wanted only to drink, to stave off the cold, dark emptiness from which she'd just emerged. Becca was warmth and light and life. Becca. Her consort. Her *human* consort. Jody dragged her mouth away, severing the exquisite connection—choosing love over blood. "I love you."

Becca's eyes were glazed, her mouth swollen. She smiled lazily and ran her hands up and down Jody's back. "Mmm. I noticed that."

Jody laughed and kissed her on the mouth. Her clitoris pulsed against Becca's center. Filled with blood, Becca's blood, Jody was potent, strong. She framed Becca's face and kissed her again, rocking against her. "How do you feel?"

"Like I want more." Becca brushed Jody's hair from her forehead, tugged a lock between her fingers. "Like I want your mouth on me again. Like I want your bite."

"Do you?" Jody asked, sliding slowly up and down between her thighs.

"You know I do." Becca arched, rubbed her breasts and belly over Jody's. "Now, Vampire."

"With pleasure." Jody kissed her way down Becca's body and, settling between her legs, took her into her mouth. Licking slowly, sucking gently, she drank her essence as she had her blood, feasting on her.

"You're going to make me come," Becca warned breathlessly.

Jody caressed Becca's abdomen and cupped her breast, squeezing gently as she closed her lips around Becca's clitoris and sucked her into readiness.

"Oh yes…you are." Becca's legs trembled, twisting restlessly against the sheets. "Soon, darling. Please."

Jody caressed Becca's breasts and, at the instant Becca climaxed, carefully pierced the flesh on either side of Becca's clitoris. Her hormones tumbled Becca into a crescendo of orgasms, spiraling higher and higher until Becca cried out and went limp.

Jody gathered her into her arms and kissed her. "Better?"

Becca laughed softly. "Better…hmm. Yes." She pillowed her head on Jody's shoulder. "How are you feeling?"

"I'm healed. I'm fine. Are you—"

"Wonderful. Stop worrying."

"No headache, no weakness?"

Becca made a fist and lightly punched Jody's shoulder, earning a raised eyebrow from her elegant Vampire lover. "I told you. It doesn't hurt me to feed you. Not at all."

Jody's brows drew down. "If I didn't know better, I'd think you were born to this."

"Maybe I was. It's possible, isn't it? That there might be human servants that don't even know they have the capacity? Just because they've never been with a Vampire?"

"I suppose it's possible," Jody said, rolling over onto her back and drawing Becca into her arms. "We've always assumed that Vampires and our servants have been together since the beginning—linked genetically. There's very little crossover among servants in different Clans, and as a result, our lines have evolved together. But there could have been humans who never served, and their lines remained… dormant."

"Perhaps certain humans have the genetic capability, and it's expressed differently in some generations or is triggered in some individuals," Becca mused. "I'm not an expert on that sort of thing, but I know someone at the university—"

"Becca," Jody said, her voice suddenly flat and cold. "There are reasons we don't expose ourselves to humans. Remember, we have been hunted nearly to extinction. We must be careful what we allow the humans to know."

"I understand," Becca said, appreciating that until very recently, all the Praetern species had lived in utter secrecy, hiding in plain sight for millennia. But for her, information was not just knowledge, it was life. And if there were things she could discover that would help keep Jody safe and strong, she would find a way to get the information. "I promise, I'll be careful."

"And you'll tell me what—"

A knock sounded on the door, and Zahn called, "I'm sorry, Liege, but an urgent call."

"Come in." Jody drew the sheet over Becca.

Zahn, dressed in a black silk shirt and trousers, carried a cell phone to Jody and held it out. "Alpha Mir."

Jody took the phone. "Gates."

"You need to come to the Compound," Sylvan said.

"What is it?"

"Lara is here, and there've been developments."

"I'll be there within the hour." Jody ended the call and stared at Zahn. "Why is Lara at the Compound and not here?"

"She left, Liege. Shortly after she fed." Zahn grimaced. "I'm afraid I was…incapacitated, and she ordered the guards to open the barricades."

"Before sunfall?"

"Yes, Liege."

"Tell Rafaela to gather my guards and bring a car around."

Zahn inclined her head. "Yes, Liege. Do you need to feed?"

Becca raised her head from Jody's shoulder and smiled at Zahn. "No, Zahn. Thank you. Jody has already been taken care of."

"Leave us," Jody said.

"As you wish." Zahn bowed slightly to Jody and left.

"You have no need to be jealous," Jody murmured.

"She's very beautiful."

"And you are my consort."

Becca sighed. "I know. Give me a century or two and I'll get used to it."

Jody laughed. "Take as long as you need." She pushed the sheets aside. "I must go."

"I'll come with you."

Jody hesitated, unused to sharing her life with anyone.

"I'm your consort, Jody. I belong with you."

"Yes. You do." Jody held out a hand. "Come."

"Lara went out during the day?" Becca asked as she gathered her clothes.

"Apparently."

"How?"

Jody's jaw hardened. "I don't know."

CHAPTER FIVE

"*Sentrie*," Lara called.

Misha moved up quickly beside her. "Yes, *Centuri*?"

"Warlord," Lara said.

Misha ducked her head. "Yes, Warlord."

"How far is your weapon?"

"Only a few hundred yards. I wasn't far when I heard the struggle and waited to shift until I was close."

"Good. Get it and guard the prisoner."

"Yes, Warlord." Misha sprinted away.

Lara crouched beside her prisoner. Raina's bleeding had stopped, but her wounds had not healed and wouldn't until she could shift again. All but the strongest of wolves would need hours if not days to heal from injuries as bad as Raina's, but Raina was an Alpha and sure to heal faster than any other cat. The effect of the infusion of Vampire hormones was uncertain too. If Raina regained her strength and challenged again before the other *sentries* arrived, Lara would have to kill her. A cat that powerful could not be allowed to live, even if she had invoked sanctuary. Her voluntary imprisonment should last until the Alpha pronounced sentence, but cats couldn't be trusted to keep their word—unlike wolves, the felines were lawless and without honor. If Raina could escape, Lara had no doubt she would.

"Where are your guards?" Lara asked Raina.

Raina's jaw tensed, her direct gaze a challenge.

Lara stared her down. "Don't make me hurt you again—I just saved your life."

"I'm alone."

"Why?" Lara shook her head. "No Alpha travels without guards."

"I'm alone."

"Alone in Pack land, with cubs?"

Raina's eyes narrowed and she growled.

Lara almost smiled. The cat was helpless and still she challenged. "Where are they?"

"Let me get them," Raina said.

"You're too weak to go anywhere."

"I think I know what I am capable of, Wolf," Raina said, a snarl underscoring her words.

"You forget, Cat, you are a prisoner. Even if you weren't as weak as one of your cubs, you aren't in charge any longer. I am your new master."

"I am no one's slave." Raina's canines flashed, and her eyes darkened to the green of the forest after a hard rain. Her cheekbones arched, sharp and bold beneath her tawny skin. A flare of gold burnished her belly. She verged on shifting, no matter she could never stand to a challenge.

"Cage your cat, Raina," Lara murmured, her blood stirring at the unmistakable tang of power in the air. Raina was barely conscious, but her call was strong. Not the wild burn of the Alpha's call, but a dark, seductive caress that promised secret pleasures. Lara had never tangled with a cat, no wolf would, and the tightening of her clitoris infuriated her. "You're in no shape to challenge me."

"Leave them alone."

"You'd rather have them die?"

Pain flashed across Raina's face. She was fearless for her own safety, but frantic for her young. Lara crushed a surge of sympathy and rose as Misha strode up, automatic rifle at the ready. "If she moves, shoot her in the heart."

Misha's chin jutted and she snapped a salute, fist to heart. "Yes, Warlord."

Lara stalked away. The cat might be beautiful, but she was still an enemy. Lara skimmed her fingertips over the pelt line that bisected her abdominals and disappeared between her thighs, swallowing the pulse of feeding hormones coating her tongue. Her nipples were tense, the deep glands beneath her clitoris throbbing. She still tasted Raina's blood, still scented her musk. She wanted to howl. She wanted to feed. From her.

Ever since she'd awakened to discover she had died and been

resurrected Vampire, sex and blood had been all she'd craved. Anyone's blood. Anyone's body. Raina might be a cat, but her blood was that of an Alpha—potent, erotic, addictive. Maybe she should have killed her. The cat was dangerous. Lara slid her hand lower, brushed the swollen prominence at the apex of her thighs. Soon, she'd find another to feed from. Soon.

Lengthening her stride, Lara forced thoughts of Raina and sex and blood from her mind. She needed to find the cubs before the area was flooded with wolves and the cubs were killed on sight. Once she was far enough away from Raina that the cat's distinctive mountain scent was just a lingering note teasing her senses, she stopped and extended her awareness outward into the craggy canyon. After a second, she detected the crushed-leaf aroma of cat and felt the twin heartbeats, fast and frightened. Silently, she followed the vibrations upward, gliding over the rock face as quickly in skin as she had in pelt, faster in either form than when she'd been wholly Were. Three-quarters of the way up the cliff she reached a narrow ledge less than a foot wide that ended in a blind turn. She guessed the cubs were sheltered around that bend, probably in a niche in the rock wall. A highly defensible position. Raina had chosen well. Lara eased along the ledge and crouched at the bend, gripping the rough stone surface with one hand and leaning out to peer around the corner.

Four bright eyes glinted in the shadows.

"Hello, little ones," Lara murmured. The echo of their heartbeats escalated in her blood. She reached around and tiny claws raked her forearm. Laughing, she gripped the cub by the ruff and hauled it out. Four tiny limbs thrashed and miniature teeth flashed. A fighter. After tucking the cub between her hip and the wall, she retrieved its littermate. They were practically newborns, barely bigger than the palm of her hand. Raina must have just given birth—no wonder she'd been too weak to fight. Their pelts were feather soft, the fur finer than their mother's and dotted with faint brown spots, whereas Raina's pelt was an even tawny gold. Their eyes were hers, though, a distinctive brilliant green. One had shards of gold ringing its irises, like she'd noticed in Raina's eyes when Raina dropped her guard. Lara held the scrabbling young up in the air, one in each hand, and examined their soft round bellies. One male, one female. The female with the green-gold eyes bared her teeth and swatted at Lara's wrist with a paw the size of a pea. Lara shook her gently and growled. "Like your Alpha, foolish but brave." She rose, tucked them both into the curve of one arm, and started down. A moment later she stood over Raina. "They're just whelps."

Raina's gaze shot to her cubs. A protective rumble rose from her chest. The cubs mewled and struggled harder. Lara tightened her grip.

"A little over a week," Raina said at last.

"You gave birth to them out here, didn't you?" Lara shook her head. "Why? You had to know how vulnerable you'd be with two helpless cubs and you not at full strength." Lara knelt, watching Raina for any sudden aggression. "Why? Who are you running from?"

Raina's mouth set in a tight line. "I will speak to your Alpha and no one else."

Lara heard the sound of vehicles approaching fast. Soon Raina's fate would be out of her hands. The idea of anyone, even the Alpha, taking charge of Raina and her cubs made her snarl. Raina tensed, flashed her canines. "Save your energy. You'll have your chance to face the Alpha soon enough."

"Let me have the cubs."

Lara laughed. "You're in no condition to take care of them. Besides, I might want to play with them."

"You bastard." Raina half sat up, and Misha leveled the automatic at her.

Lara smiled as Raina relented and dropped back to the ground. "Have you forgotten the rules of war, Raina? You lost. You have no power here."

Two Rovers pulled to a stop a few yards away, and the doors of both vehicles flew open. Lara expected to see Callan, the captain of the *sentries*, leading the retrieval squad, but to her surprise, Niki, the Alpha's second, jumped down from the first armored vehicle. A half dozen armed soldiers exited the second and spread out into the forest. Shirtless in camo BDUs, Niki, a muscular redhead with an automatic rifle slung over her back, strode forward and nodded curtly to Lara. A swath of barely healed burns crisscrossed her chest and left shoulder. Hands on hips, she stared down at Raina, her lips drawn back and canines gleaming. Aggressive pheromones clouded the air. "I didn't believe it when I heard. A cat Were. Why isn't she dead?"

Lara's canines dropped and her pelt line flared. She slid between Niki and Raina and rumbled a warning. "She has information for the Alpha."

"So she says. How do you know it isn't a trap?"

"Look at her. What kind of trap could she spring?"

"How do you know she's who she says she is?" Niki snorted. "An Alpha would never let herself be bested—of course, this one is a cat, but still." Niki prodded Raina with her boot. "Who are you, bitch?"

"Niki," Lara whispered, "she's *my* captive."

"You're on Pack land," Niki said, pushing into Lara's space, her tone issuing a warning. "You have no rights here, Vampire."

Lara fought her fury. Niki was the Alpha's second, and if she decided Raina was a threat, she had the power to order her execution. She understood Niki's instinct to protect the Pack, but Lara was no longer bound by Pack law—she was Warlord to the Night Hunters first. Their long friendship, the times they'd tangled—both desperate for release and some semblance of connection—meant nothing now. This was a war zone, and they were soldiers. "We don't know what information she may have, but I stand for Liege Jody Gates, sworn ally to your Alpha, and under the terms of our alliance, I claim jurisdiction over this prisoner."

"You can't—"

"Niki," a soft female voice said, "no one is going to fight over her now. Move out of the way so I can attend to her."

Lara glanced at the golden-haired medic. "I thought Elena was coming."

"She was," Sophia said, "until Niki decided she had to be the one to assess the situation." Sophia pressed a delicate palm to Niki's chest and pushed. "Give me some room here, *Imperator*."

Niki rumbled but stepped aside, glaring at Lara.

"What have you got there?" Sophia gestured toward the cubs, who squirmed against Lara's chest.

"Hers."

"At least let me throw them in the river," Niki muttered.

Raina roared and pushed up, trying to get her legs under her. Niki leapt and buried her claws in Raina's shoulder, pinning her back to the ground.

Instantly in a rage, Lara looped an arm around Niki's neck and dragged her off, crushing Niki's throat with her forearm. "Stand down! She's mine!"

Niki coughed and raked Lara's arms with her claws, twisting to get loose.

"That's enough!" Sophia crouched over Raina and glared at the struggling dominant wolves. "She's *mine* now, and both of you need to get back. Lara—take those cubs to the Rover. Niki—you stand guard while I examine her if you're worried, but don't touch her."

Lara drew a deep breath and her vision cleared. Sophia was Omega, neither dominant nor submissive, and her empathic powers calmed even the most aggressive wolf. She was also Niki's mate, and Niki's instinct was to please her. Lara eased her hold when she felt the tension diminish in Niki's shoulders. The cubs she'd clamped against her side protested her tight grip with indignant cries.

Raina struggled weakly, blood trickling from the claw marks Niki had put on her chest. "Are they hurt?"

"I have them," Lara snapped. "Sophia, she's bleeding and she's lost a lot of blood already. She probably has internal injuries. She can't shift."

"I'll take care of her." Sophia opened the med kit she'd carried from the Rover. "Take the young to the vehicle and wrap them in a blanket. They should be kept warm. There are clothes for you in there too."

Lara gave no thought to her nakedness. She only cared about protecting her captive. She held out the young to Sophia. "You take them."

Sophia shook her head. "I need to see to her. Go on, the cat will be safe until you return."

Lara glanced at Niki. She didn't trust Niki with Raina, but Sophia, like all medics, was ferociously protective of her patients. "Don't touch her."

Niki lifted a lip, her eyes flashing as she stared at Raina. Raina struggled to push herself up onto her elbows, her lips drawing back in a snarl. She was badly hurt, but she was an Alpha and would not back down from a challenge.

"Stop it." Sophia held Raina down with a hand on her shoulder. "You don't have the strength for this."

"You don't know me," Raina growled, her attention fixed on Niki.

"No," Sophia murmured, pressing her fingers to the pulse in Raina's throat. "But I know dominant Weres and just exactly how stubborn they can be. Now hush and let me see to you. You have cubs who need you."

Raina shuddered, too weak to hold herself up, and fell back, her gaze traveling to Lara.

"I'll secure them," Lara said gruffly. With a last warning growl to Niki she loped to the SUV and jumped into the back. After emptying one of the equipment drawers, she lined it with a blanket and put the cubs in. Kneeling, she said, "Stay here."

The tiny golden cubs pressed close together in one corner, their eyes wide, their soft coats stiff. High-pitched growls reverberated in their chests. They were frightened, but they were ready to fight, both of them. Lara smiled. "Your mother would be proud." She lowered her face and snarled, teaching them who was in charge. Their ears flattened and they crouched farther back in the corner. "Don't move."

A sound behind her had her spinning around, ready to fight. Misha stood in the open door, watching her. "Do you think they understand you?"

Lara pulled a pair of black BDUs from a pile on the floor and stepped into them. The wounds Raina's claws had made in her sides were healed. "I don't know. They understand who's in charge. Some pups that young are sentient. The Alpha's pups usually are, and Raina is an Alpha."

"Yeah, but she's a cat. They're not as strong as us."

Lara thought of Raina's ferocity and power, despite her weakened state, and wondered how well the wolves really knew the cats. "What are you doing out here alone?"

"When the labs were attacked, Callan doubled the patrols. Most of us are out here." She climbed in and knelt by the cubs. "What if they shift to skin? Will they be okay?"

"I don't think they will until their mother calls them to shift. Our pups don't even shift to pelt until they're older and stronger. I suspect Raina wanted them in pelt because they've been outside so long."

"What is she doing here?"

"I don't know." Lara glanced over to where Sophia was injecting Raina with something from her med kit. "But whatever she's running from, it must be deadly if she risked coming here."

"If I'd seen her first, I would have shot her."

"As you should have."

"They would've died." Misha stared at the tiny cubs who watched her warily. She held out a finger and one swatted at it. She laughed. "A pup would have tried to bite."

"Cats fight with their claws first—we fight with our teeth." Lara regarded the cubs and refused to think of Raina outside, bleeding, entrusting them to her. "They don't belong here. This is Timberwolf territory. She violated Pack borders. Your orders are just."

"Yes, *cent*…Warlord." Misha straightened. "What's going to happen to her now?"

"I don't know. She shouldn't be here, but she is. We are at war with humans. And I…" Lara shook her head. "Nothing is as it was before. The Alpha will need to interrogate her."

Lara jumped out of the Rover and headed for Raina. She wasn't letting her out of her sight. No matter what the Alpha decided, Raina was hers.

CHAPTER SIX

Dr. Veronica Standish regarded her bodyguard with a resurgence of desire as the Vampire drove the Town Car toward Nocturne along the industrial highway adjacent to the Hudson. Luce's chiseled profile was perfection, like that of every other Vampire she had ever known. Luce's beauty—coal-black hair, iridescent blue eyes, sculpted features—would have been disconcerting if Veronica was the least bit intimidated by anyone under any circumstance or less than supremely confident in her own beauty and ability. Vampires were beautiful and clever—even, in some cases, intelligent—but at the core, they were still predators, controlled by primal urges. Uncontrollable urges were weaknesses and, once understood, susceptible to manipulation. The very things that made Vampires so very interesting—their sexual power and seductive lure—also proved very useful tools for those who knew how to take advantage of them. Like her.

They'd only just left her bed. Luce had appeared at her door, hungry from the day's sleep and radiating such sexual compulsion Veronica had skyrocketed to the brink of orgasm without a single touch. She'd come the instant Luce's incisors pierced her neck and hadn't stopped until Luce released her. When in the thrall of Luce's bloodlust, she was forced to cede control, and those moments of excruciating pleasure were all the more addicting for that wholly unfamiliar experience. But she didn't intend to let Luce or anyone else believe they held true power over her.

"You don't approve of this little visit, do you?" Veronica asked. Nothing of what Luce was thinking about their impromptu trip to the Vampire blood club showed on her face, and that supreme control both fascinated and annoyed. Veronica leaned over and slipped her hand between Luce's thighs, letting her palm rest high on the inside of Luce's leg. She lightly scraped her fingernails over the black silk trousers and was rewarded with the barest flicker of muscles beneath her fingertips. She smiled to herself. Not so imperturbable after all.

Luce cut her gaze from the highway to Veronica, her blue eyes alight with fire. Flames that telegraphed her need. "Does it matter what I think?"

Veronica laughed. "I'm curious."

"Nocturne is not a safe place to sightsee."

"Don't you fear for your job? That if you annoy me I might have you replaced?"

Luce glanced back at the highway, her shoulder lifting in an insolent shrug. "I can think of a dozen reasons you might have me replaced. I thought you would prefer honesty."

"What I prefer," Veronica murmured, cupping Luce lightly, "is keeping you in my bed and by my side."

Luce hissed softly. "When I woke, I wanted you. The taste of you was all I could think of."

"And did you think of me while you were sating your hunger those first few minutes?"

"I didn't," Luce murmured. "I took enough from a blood slave whose name I don't even know to keep my sanity. Then I came for you."

"I love when you come to me hungry." Ordinarily she would have been irritated if a lover took satisfaction elsewhere. She did not share her possessions and wanted her lovers focused on her, and her alone. The reverse was not true, of course—she never allowed anyone to make a claim on her. But the idea of Luce feeding out of desperation while wanting her made her instantly wet. "I love when you bury yourself in me."

Luce smiled, slid one hand from the wheel, and covered Veronica's. Her skin was cool, smooth, and when she pressed Veronica's fingers to the cleft between her thighs, heat blossomed beneath Veronica's fingertips.

"Do you?" Luce murmured.

Suddenly Veronica was back in her bedroom, spread-eagled naked on her bed, arms extended and wrists tethered with silken ropes, thighs splayed around Luce's shoulders. Luce's mouth was on her, bright points of pleasure piercing her clitoris, tethering her as Luce fed and she came and came. Harder, longer, so intensely that every thought was wiped clean from the surface of her mind.

Veronica gasped, feeling as if she was unmoored, in danger of being dragged out to sea. Jerking upright, she looked around. Luce was just pulling into the parking lot of a building she would have passed without notice had she not known their destination. A single-story, flat-roofed, windowless building, painted matte black—some kind of abandoned warehouse, most likely. The enormous parking lot, despite being crowded with vehicles, was completely dark. No lighting, no valets, no visible security. No indication of any kind that this was the most popular Vampire club in the state. She was sitting in her seat, her hands in her lap. Her clitoris tingled, and she wondered if her orgasm had been remembered or real. She'd never experienced the Vampire thrall quite so blatantly, and if she hadn't been so excited by it, she might be angry. Luce took dangerous advantage, something she would have to deal with when the time was right. Veronica took a steadying breath.

"Do you feed here?"

"Sometimes." Luce stopped the car, turned off the engine, and swiveled on the seat. Scarlet completely eclipsed her brilliant blue irises. "But right now, all I want is you."

"Again?" Veronica purred, certain of herself once more. Luce might have momentarily enthralled her, but Luce was the prisoner of their passion, not she. *She* didn't need to feed to live. Her very existence wasn't tied to sex. Oh, she enjoyed sex—sex was very often the ultimate power, and never more true than when dealing with Vampires—but she could walk away. Any time she chose. But Luce, Luce would literally die without the blood exchange that was an integral part of Vampire sex. "Take me inside, and if you're hungry again, I might even feed you."

Luce ran her long, supple fingers through Veronica's hair, twisting one of the soft dark waves around her fingers. "You'll have many to choose from."

Veronica's nipples tightened. "Will I?"

"You're very beautiful." Luce leaned closer and kissed her, the tips of her incisors pressing into Veronica's lip.

Veronica's clitoris jumped and she opened her mouth to deepen the kiss. She heard a moan, realized it was hers, and steeled her mind to avoid losing herself completely to Luce's powers again. She pushed away with a hand on Luce's chest. She broke the kiss, but she couldn't escape the haunting vibration of Luce's heartbeat slowly drumming under her fingertips. Life—her blood had given Luce that. Her head swam with a rush of power so thrilling she almost cried out.

"I can taste your desire," Luce whispered against Veronica's mouth.

"You'll have to wait," Veronica said, keeping her voice even with effort. If she hadn't learned at an early age to contain her emotions with ironclad control, she could easily find herself completely helpless with Luce. But she'd had plenty of practice maintaining the upper hand with all kinds of adversaries—first her father, who had been so easy to manipulate once she'd gleaned his barely contained and quite unpaternal obsession with her, then the men and women she'd seduced and discarded as she'd climbed the professional ladder, and now those gullible ones, like Nicholas Gregory, whose egos prevented them from seeing she only *allowed* them to believe they were in charge. Vampires might be seductive and strong, but in the end they were still vulnerable to their needs. Unlike her. "I have business with your mistress first."

"Whatever you say." Luce settled into her seat.

"Be sure you remember that, my dear Luce." Veronica slid a hand behind Luce's head and tugged her closer, unwilling to let Luce dismiss her. She brushed her thumb over Luce's mouth, slowing to press the fleshy pad against Luce's incisor. Luce growled and Veronica laughed. "Now take me inside and let me see who I might want to play with tonight."

Raina slowly tested the straps holding her to the stretcher as the vehicle bounced and rocked over the wild terrain, gauging the strength of the leather bindings. Her cubs were nearby—their heartbeats a constant refrain in the undercurrent of her awareness—but she couldn't see them. They didn't seem frightened, only wary, as she had taught them. But they were defenseless as long as she was a prisoner. The restraints across her bare chest and thighs were five inches wide and at least an inch thick. Even in her weakened state, she could snap them if she flexed her muscles hard enough, but the vehicle was filled with wolves, and the one watching her from a few feet away clearly wanted to kill her. She might not be able to immobilize all of them before they overpowered her, and this time there would be no second chance.

She knew the redhead, the one who'd threatened her cubs, by reputation—the Alpha's second, Niki Kroff. The Pack *imperator* was reportedly as fierce as the Alpha, and she lived for the kill. Raina looked forward to killing her for the threat she'd made to her cubs, but she'd need to choose her time carefully. She couldn't risk their lives by attempting an escape. Not yet.

Then there was the other one—the one she'd fought, the one not quite wolf but something else, something even more powerful—who knelt beside her, one hand steadying the stretcher. Lara, they called her. Lara didn't look at her with the same flat, deadly stare as Niki, but Raina wasn't foolish enough to trust her, either. Any of them would kill her and her cubs without a second's regret if they thought she had nothing of value to offer.

If she couldn't escape, she might have to sacrifice everything she had left, but before that happened, she would fight. She hadn't ruled three hundred half-feral cats for over a decade by being lenient or afraid to risk her life. She ruled by cunning and might. But she hadn't had her cubs to think of, those times she'd defended her rule by tooth and claw. And because of them, for the first time in her life, she knew fear.

One thing a cat was born with was patience. She could lie motionless on a tree branch all day, waiting for a deer to amble into range, or hunker down in the grass and watch a flock of geese for hours, picking out the slowest. She'd wait to make her move, and in the meantime, she'd assess her enemy. Every enemy had a weakness.

And she was growing stronger by the second. Her wounds were healing—slowly, but more rapidly than they would have ordinarily without a shift. Something had broken inside her when Lara had dragged her down—she'd felt the blood filling her belly, known she was dying. Now the pain had receded, the pressure in her relenting. Lara had done something to her, something she'd never experienced before. When Lara had taken her throat, she should have died, but she'd dreamed of being free instead. She'd been fevered, like she'd been in heat, but she'd never burned like that before. She'd coupled when her body overruled all thought and reason, when the fire burning in her loins drove her to accept any available cat until the insanity released her. She hadn't taken a mate—she'd submit to no male, and none would submit to her. The females she might have wanted submitted too easily, and after a coupling or two, her interest disappeared along with the challenge. Coupling was a biological imperative, and pleasurable enough, but none of her Pride had ever ignited her the way Lara had.

She wanted to ask what Lara had done to her, but not with the others around. Whatever had happened, it was something unusual, something she might be able to use to gain her freedom. She needed an ally, and she'd use anything at her disposal to gain one. She drew a breath and relaxed beneath the restraints.

"Thank you," she murmured.

"For what?" Lara replied just as softly. She'd pulled on pants, but her chest was bare, her small breasts a surprising softness against the chiseled muscles of her chest. Not a scratch marred her golden skin, even though Raina knew she had scored her deeply.

"You saved my life."

Lara's eyes were amber again, a beautiful golden brown. The fire that had leapt in them when she'd loomed over her, before she'd brought her mouth to her neck, before she'd done whatever it was she'd done that filled her with such pleasure, was absent. The arrogance, though, remained. "I would have killed you if you hadn't claimed sanctuary."

"Would you?" Raina said, taking a chance that she'd been right when she'd sensed the smallest bit of hesitation earlier. She'd been helpless, unable to fight any longer, and Lara had not struck the killing blow. Another wolf—probably any other wolf—would have. "Then I am in your debt."

Lara's eyes narrowed and her canines flashed against her full lower lip. "You may not think I've done you any favors before long."

"I know. Your Alpha may not be as merciful." She glanced at Niki, who leaned against the side of the vehicle, no weapon in sight, but claws and canines extended. Fury clouded the air around her. "She wants me dead."

"And if you found a wolf in your territory? Would you be any different?"

Raina huffed. "Who knows what any of us might do now? The cats did not want the Exodus, but we were not consulted. Your Alpha spoke for all the Weres, but he did not ask us what we wanted."

"The cats have never been organized enough to have a voice."

"That's what you believe." Raina sighed. "It's done now, and we all must live with the changes."

A shadow darkened the amber of Lara's eyes. "Yes. We all must live with change."

The pain in Raina's chest flared, and she slid her hand over the one holding the stretcher. Despair, heavy and bleak, flooded through her. Lara's anguish struck at her heart and she blurted, "What have they done—"

Snarling, Lara jerked her hand away. Niki bounded forward and pressed a knife to Raina's throat.

"Let me gut her and save everyone the trouble of listening to her lies."

Lara shouldered Niki aside, enraged at the threat to Raina, furious at her own weakness. Somehow Raina had glimpsed her shame. "Leave her alone. We don't kill helpless prisoners."

"She's a cat."

"I said leave her." Lara shoved her face into Niki's, her teeth bared.

Niki growled.

Sophia rose from her seat on the other side of the SUV. "She's not going anywhere and she's no threat. We'll be at the Compound in a minute." She edged over to Niki and stroked her abdomen. "The Alpha will want a report. Then you'll do what she orders."

Niki looped an arm around Sophia's shoulders and rubbed her cheek against Sophia's hair, her gaze still locked with Lara's. "This isn't done."

"Fine," Lara snarled.

Niki eased away and Lara knelt again. "You all right?"

"Yes." Raina nodded in the direction of her cubs. "If I am executed, will you get my cubs to safety?"

Lara laughed. "Why would I do that?"

"They're innocent."

"Are they?" Lara stared at the two cubs, wrapped up in one another in the corner of the drawer, motionless, eyes the color of their mother's, wary and watchful. "Is anyone ever innocent?"

"You can have the pleasure of the kill yourself," Raina said. "In exchange."

"You think you have something to bargain with. You don't. Your fate is no longer something you can control."

The lion who lived in Raina's soul screamed in protest, ferocious and proud. Raina growled, defiant, a dominant cat who would not be declawed.

Lara laughed again and traced a finger over the stark curve of Raina's jaw. "If you fight back, you'll only bring more harm to yourself." She tilted her chin toward the drawer a few feet away. "And them."

"I'll kill anyone who touches them." Raina's claws broke through her fingertips. Pelt shone over her torso. Even in the dim light of the Rover she was golden, a gorgeous animal.

"There's nothing you'll be able to do." Lara resisted the urge to stroke her. "You are a prisoner. You're going to have to accept that."

"Would you?" Raina panted, struggling to subdue her beast.

Lara smiled grimly. "I already have."

Chapter Seven

Francesca sensed the commotion outside her boudoir and mentally transmitted her annoyance to Michel.

Whatever it is, it can wait.

Michel had been her *senechal*, her enforcer, for over eight centuries and should know better than anyone not to disturb her during her first feeding of the evening. The older she became, the less she had need of sleep, but more and more of late, when she awakened after even a few hours' somnolence, she was plagued by an inner hollowness, an ever-expanding void that threatened to consume her. Her hunger grew more ferocious with each passing week, assuaged by neither blood nor sex. No matter how many hosts she brought to her bed, or how much blood she consumed, or how many orgasms she incited in her blood donors or experienced during the depths of her bloodlust, she could not completely erase the foreboding that haunted her. And today she wanted to lose herself in the burning forgetfulness of bloodlust even more than usual. She needed to blunt her anger with pleasure. Today, she fed alone, and not by choice. Michel had been moody, withdrawn, since their visit to Sylvan's Compound, but she steadfastly denied being troubled. She also denied her new and obvious predilection for feeding from young female Weres. This evening, when summoned, Michel had opted to feed upstairs in the club rather than with Francesca, and she was undoubtedly sating her hunger with yet another Were.

Francesca kept her incisors buried in the young Were's neck, ignoring Michel's rapid approach. She was far from satisfied, and the male sprawled beneath her, buried to the hilt inside her, was far from empty. His brown eyes were glazed with pleasure, his canines extruded, his rock-hard abdomen covered with soft, red-brown pelt. His cock was as rigid as his heavy jaw and nearly as immobile, the thickened core wedging him fast. She drew on his vein and felt him jet again. Her own orgasm flowed languorously, a continuous wave of release that grew stronger as her cells revitalized, drawing nourishment from his blood. She'd barely taken notice of him at the Compound, but when she'd caught his profile on the security camera at the entrance to the club, she'd known he was one of Sylvan's soldiers and sent for him. She liked the idea of taking something Sylvan would not want her to have. There was no edict against Sylvan's Weres feeding Vampires—in fact, the number who visited Nocturne for exactly that reason seemed to be increasing—but Sylvan would not approve of one close to her inner circle being so vulnerable.

He was enjoyable, but he would only be the first of the night. No Were, and certainly no human, male or female, came close to providing the raging rush of power an Alpha's blood carried. Sylvan had never allowed Francesca to bite her, but she'd allowed Francesca to taste her, and that had been enough. Now Sylvan had a mate and no longer needed anything Francesca could provide, and all other Weres paled in comparison. This male had nowhere near the potency or power of his Alpha, but his stamina was admirable. As she fed, pulling deeper and harder at his throat, he emptied with powerful thrusts and showed no sign of slowing. She didn't worry about draining him as she might if he were human. He could shift and replenish himself within hours.

I'm sorry, Regent, Michel telegraphed. *I must speak with you. It's urgent.*

Francesca withdrew from his neck, sealed the punctures, and sat back, still straddling him.

"Come in."

The ornate wood doors to her bedchamber swung open, and Michel slipped inside, pulling the doors shut behind her. The sitting room beyond was already prepared for Francesca's bath and tea. Michel, rapier thin in black trousers, a black silk shirt open between her breasts, and gleaming knee-high black boots, surveyed the tableau on the bed. She was pale, and Francesca suspected she had not fed much. Her Adriatic blue eyes smoldered as she took in the stunned young male, the blood streaking his heaving chest, and the thick cock captured by Francesca's slowly churning hips.

"What is it?" Francesca questioned languidly, running her fingers through her hair and arching her back to lift her naked breasts. She cupped them and thumbed her nipples, a reminder to Michel of exactly what she had declined, sighing as another orgasm slowly climbed through her belly and spread outward. She smiled as waves of lust poured off Michel—after all these years, they were so attuned her orgasm would stir Michel no matter how strongly Michel barricaded herself.

Across the room, Michel's mouth tightened and her hands closed into fists. Her eyes flared crimson and her incisors glistened, but her finely carved features registered nothing. "Veronica Standish is upstairs. I've ordered our soldiers to keep her away from the clientele, but she seems bent on hosting someone."

Francesca threw back her head and laughed. "Really? And it only took Luce a few days. Veronica might have wanted you, darling, but she didn't resist Luce's charms for long. Is Raymond with them?"

"No. He reported that Veronica dismissed him just before Luce arrived for her night duties. He's in the parking lot if we need him."

"Good. Tell him to wait."

Francesca slid off the male beneath her and stood, ignoring his incoherent groan as his body spasmed at her sudden withdrawal. "And have someone move this to another room until he is recovered enough to leave."

"And Veronica?"

"Dr. Standish is a very clever woman. She pretends to be our confidant, but her work in Nicholas's secret lab suggests she wants to control, perhaps eradicate, the Weres." Francesca drew on an ivory silk gown and tied it loosely at the waist. "She is human—and we are Praetern, like the Weres she regards as less than animals. Maybe she's here to spy for Nicholas."

Michel laughed shortly, her burning gaze following Francesca's every movement. "Not so very clever if she believes she can come into our territory and best us."

"Mmm." Francesca slowly crossed to Michel and kissed her. Michel tensed and Francesca scented her hunger. Tracing a sculpted fingernail down Michel's cheek, leaving a faint blood trail behind in the shallow cut, she murmured, "You should have joined me earlier, darling, we could have had so much fun. He was really quite tireless."

"I had business with some of my soldiers." Michel pulled Francesca close and kissed her again, the wound on her face already closed. Her hand slid down Francesca's back and over her ass. "Standish is a high-profile scientist with a national presence. She will be hard to contain."

Francesca tasted Michel's need, but the distance was still there. She rubbed against Michel until Michel's nipples hardened and her thighs tightened. Satisfied she'd gotten the response she wanted, Francesca stepped away. "Dr. Standish is in the unique position of being able to tell us what's going on in Nicholas's laboratories, and Nicholas's other plans as well. We lose nothing by allowing her to satisfy her curiosity here." She glanced at the Were, who had not yet emerged from his postorgasmic torpor. "But we need to keep her safe. She thinks she has control, and we should let her continue to think that. Send someone you trust to play with her. Someone who will be careful not to injure her."

"Will you speak to her?"

"If she requests an audience, yes. For now, let her believe she is in charge."

"I can send Henry."

"Yes, Henry would be a good choice and…Daniela. She can use the experience, and Standish seems to like mixing her playmates."

Michel nodded. "As you wish, Regent." She turned for the door.

"And, Michel?"

Michel looked over her shoulder. "Yes?"

"I don't like you absent from my bed."

"Forgive me."

"Of course." Francesca smiled, her incisors glinting like diamonds against her blood-red lips. "This time."

"We're almost there," Lara said as the stockade gates in the twelve-foot high fence surrounding the Compound swung open. Raina growled, her pelt flaring and the musky scent of aggression pouring off her pheromone-drenched skin. The sound of Raina's racing heart pounded in Lara's head, and her chest tightened. Centuries before the Vampire-Were wars, millennia before this new human threat, the cats and the wolves had fought for supremacy over the territory and game they all needed to survive. Now Raina, an instinctual predator, was trapped and threatened by an age-old enemy, and her primitive drive to fight ruled her reason. "Cage your cat, Raina. The Alpha will not make a hasty judgment, but you cannot fight her. None of us can."

Raina panted, her claws extruded and her eyes narrowed to glimmering slits. "I will willingly serve you if you stand for us now. Anything…"

Lara wanted to say she already owned her, but she knew that was not true. Raina was her captive, but she was no one's slave. The cat was afraid, not for herself but for the cubs, and willing to sell her soul for them. Lara remembered a time she had done the same for the one person whose life meant more than her own. Raina's panic, and her bravery, reawakened Lara's protective instincts, but she resisted the urge to comfort her. Raina and her cubs were not her responsibility, *could not be* her responsibility. A Vampire owned what was left of her soul.

"I can't."

Raina thrashed and the leather bindings creaked, the metal rivets securing them to the stretcher screeching in protest. Niki was beside them instantly, her automatic rifle trained on Raina's chest. "Break one strap and you will never leave this vehicle."

The Rover slowed. Only seconds left. Lara's heart seized. If Raina didn't submit, someone would hurt her. "Raina—"

Sophia pushed between Lara and Niki and pressed her hand between Raina's breasts, over her heart. "Raina, it's all right. I'll look after them, I promise."

"Get away from her," Niki snapped. "She's dangerous."

"Niki," Sophia said quietly, brushing the damp hair from Raina's face with her other hand, "she's helpless. I'm fine. Please, just…" She looked up at Niki, smiling gently. "She's no threat to me or anyone else. If she is, you'll take care of it."

Jaws rigid, Niki backed away. The Rover stopped, and Niki pushed open the rear door and leapt out into the Compound. Blazing fires lit the group of log and stone buildings that ringed a central courtyard carved out of the forest. Lara smelled Were, and the remnants of game left from the last meal, and home—she smelled home. The reflections of the fires filled the back of the vehicle with tongues of flame. The Alpha and her mate, flanked by the *centuri*, stalked from headquarters across the open expanse of ground. Lara edged between the stretcher and those outside.

Sophia said from behind her, "I'll stay with the cubs until the Alpha gives permission to take them to the nursery."

"They'll need to feed," Raina said, her voice strained and rough. She'd started to shift and her cat still prowled near her skin.

"I'll talk to the Alpha," Sophia murmured.

"Don't make promises you can't keep, Sophia." Lara watched Niki reporting to the Alpha, her words inaudible but her body language angry. When she spun around to face the Rover, her face was contorted with fury. "Your mate seems to have other plans."

Lara jumped down, blocking the rear compartment as the Alpha and her party strode forward. She had no plan—she only knew she wasn't going to let them drag Raina out and execute her, the laws be damned.

"Warlord," Sylvan said, her eyes wolf-gold, her call so strong Lara struggled to stay standing. "It is customary to seek permission to enter Pack land."

"My apologies, Alpha," Lara gasped, fighting to keep her head up. She wouldn't look Sylvan in the eye, but she would have to stand her ground if she hoped to keep Raina safe. "I went for a run and meant no disrespect."

"Where did you find the cat?"

"At the northeast border with the Catamount territory."

"She was inside our borders?"

Lara tensed. She had never lied to the Alpha, and even considering it went against everything she had ever been. But she was not what she had been. All the same, she knew there was no way to hide where Raina had birthed her cubs or where they had fought. "Not far inside, but yes, within Pack land."

Sylvan glanced past Lara into the Rover, taking in the restrained female, the scent of aggression, and Sophia sitting next to the two cubs, her expression nearly as protective as that of the mother cat. She switched her attention back to Lara. "How is it she survived an encounter with you?"

Lara grinned. "She's fast and quick."

"And yet you overpowered her?"

"Yes, probably because she was weakened by the birth."

"And your estimate when she regains full strength?"

"She is an Alpha and powerful." Lara shrugged. "She'll be strong, but she's still a cat."

Sylvan watched the flames flicker in the depths of Lara's eyes, sensing her wariness and something she hadn't expected—protectiveness. Lara had not killed the cat when she'd had every opportunity to do so. Any other wolf would have finished her. "Jody's on her way. You can wait for her at headquarters."

"I claim the cat as my prisoner," Lara said. "I want to be present when she is questioned."

Sylvan growled softly. "I've given you more leeway than you deserve, Warlord. You trespassed on my land and now you stand for an enemy?"

"I claim the right to take part in her sentencing."

"My *imperator* wants to challenge you for your disregard of Pack law."

"I'm ready," Lara snarled and Niki took a step forward, her canines flashing.

Sylvan rumbled softly and brushed Lara's cheek with the backs of her fingers. Niki fell back. "I have not forgotten that you were once mine, and I have not released you from your oath to me, no matter that your first allegiance is to the Vampire. You are still my wolf, and as long as that is true, you are welcome on Pack land. But next time, let me know."

Lara shuddered as the heat and power of Sylvan's touch raced through her. She leaned into the Alpha's hand and rubbed her cheek over her fingers. Some of the darkness in her heart receded. "Yes, Alpha. My word."

Sylvan nodded. "Niki, Dasha, Jace—take the prisoner to the holding cells."

Lara stiffened. "Raina says she has information—it would be wise to hear her out."

"Raina," Sylvan murmured as the *centuri*, armed with stun guns and a restraining collar, clamored into the Rover. "She was just coming into power during my mother's rule. I never met her, but my mother thought Raina might bring order to the cats. And yet, here she is, running for her life."

"She's no coward." Lara trembled at the waves of fury pouring from the vehicle. Her wolf clawed and bit at her psyche, demanding she answer. She ignored the gut-wrenching urge, denying her wolf the claim she had no right to make.

Sylvan watched the prisoner being dragged into the infirmary. "We'll find out soon enough what the cat is made of."

CHAPTER EIGHT

Drake watched the *centuri* unload the prisoner from the Rover. Andrew gripped one arm and Jace, a young blue-eyed blonde and one of the newest of Sylvan's guard, the other. A restraint collar embedded with silver encircled her neck, tethered to a short, stout baton that Niki used to control the stumbling female as the group moved toward the infirmary. The open wounds beneath the collar oozed blood and fluid. She had to be in pain, but the only sound she made was a low, steady rumble of anger, not distress.

"Is all that necessary?" Drake said quietly to Sylvan.

"She's an enemy, encroaching on our land, for reasons we do not know." Sylvan clasped the back of Drake's neck and squeezed gently. "Most of my soldiers and all of my *centuri* would prefer she be killed with no discussion."

"She's obviously badly injured."

Sylvan smiled thinly. "You are one hundred percent Were, Prima, but you have not lived in the shadow of the enemy all your life. Wounds like that would not stop me from seeking my freedom, no matter how many captors I had to fight or how much blood I shed."

Wrapping an arm around Sylvan's waist, Drake rubbed her cheek against Sylvan's bare shoulder. "She is not you."

"We don't know who she is."

"You're right. You must look to the safety of the Pack first." Drake kissed the side of Sylvan's neck. "I'm going to the infirmary to take a look at her."

Sylvan stiffened. "No, you're not."

Drake shook her head. "Somehow your vocabulary has become extraordinarily limited in the last week or so. Do you realize that most of your sentences start with the word no?"

"I don't find anything humorous about this." Sylvan glowered, the harsh bones in her face standing out beneath her bronzed skin. She was almost always in half-form these days, her wolf so close to the surface she was operating on instinct more than reason, and she was always a breath away from fighting anything or anyone she perceived as a threat to her mate. She was glorious in her fury, and ordinarily Drake would have soothed her by dragging her away where they could be alone. She'd learned to calm Sylvan with her body and, even more importantly, by offering Sylvan a safe place to voice her fears—the one thing no one else could ever give her. Today, she didn't have time for privacy or slow assurances. She pressed closer, letting Sylvan feel the heat of her body. "She's harmless right now. Niki will be there. I'll be perfectly safe."

Sylvan's canines flared, long and heavy. The shadow of her pelt line extended and thickened. Drake traced her fingers through the soft silver trail bisecting Sylvan's belly. "Sylvan, you have other business. Jody will be here soon, you have another prisoner, and Lara—Lara needs you."

Sylvan gripped Drake's wrist, pulled her into the shadows of the stockade, and backed her against the rough wooden posts. Pressing the full length of her body to Drake's, she covered her mouth in a hard kiss. When she eased away, her teeth scraped Drake's neck, her breath scorched Drake's skin. "I'll tell you what I need. I need you to go home with Dasha and stay there. I need you to take care of the young in your belly. The cat and her whelps are not your concern. They'll probably be dead by morning."

Sylvan's breasts were tight, her nipples hard knots against Drake's chest. Her thighs were columns of stone pinning Drake to the barricade. Sex pheromones streamed from Sylvan's skin, coating Drake, forcing her sex to swell and pulse. Drake's stomach tightened, and she wanted nothing more than Sylvan between her legs. Sylvan was so very good at making her want, and if she let her, Sylvan would rule her with pleasure.

Drake gripped Sylvan's hips and dug her claws through her denim pants, burying them in Sylvan's ass. "I will give you anything you need, but I cannot always give you what you want. Elena and Sophia are medics, and I would trust their assessment of any wolf, but this is a cat, and there are young involved. I'm a doctor. I want to see them. And"—when Sylvan started to protest, she scraped her claws higher, making

Sylvan grumble deep in her chest—"I don't want you to interrogate her until I've had a chance to be sure she's stable."

"Why do you care?" Sylvan growled, her voice barely audible through thickened vocal cords. Even in the dim firelight, her eyes glowed brilliant gold. Her wolf ruled her.

"Because we are not lawless animals, Sylvan."

"No?" Snarling, Sylvan jerked Drake's shirt away from her shoulder and pressed her mouth to the bite on Drake's shoulder that branded her as Sylvan's.

Drake arched, her mate's bite flooding her system with pheromones. Her orgasm was swift and intense and left her gasping. Still riding the crest of release, she gripped Sylvan's hair and yanked Sylvan's head away. Pushing away from the wall, she spun until Sylvan's back was against the rough-hewn logs and slid her hand between Sylvan's legs. She bit Sylvan's lower lip and Sylvan tightened beneath her, muscles rigid. Drake caught the heavy prominence between Sylvan's thighs in her fist and slowly squeezed. Sylvan's hips bucked and she threw her head back with a roar. Drake kissed her throat, the soft skin between her breasts, the darkened shadow of the mate bite above her heart. Sylvan shuddered and sighed.

"You tame me, Prima," Sylvan grumbled.

"Hardly," Drake murmured. "Jody will be here any minute. Go take care of business. I'll be fine."

"Ten minutes. That's all you have before I come for you."

Drake smiled against Sylvan's chest. Sylvan's heart slowed and steadied, the waves of aggressive hormones receding. She was settled for the time being. "Yes, Alpha."

Sylvan's arms came around her, and Sylvan buried her face in Drake's neck. "Be careful. I love you."

"I know." Drake stroked her hair. "I will be."

❖

Raina lay still, waiting for her chance. The room looked like an infirmary, with glass-fronted cabinets filled with drugs and equipment along one wall, a counter covered with boxes of gloves, bandages, and stacks of IV bags, and bright lights hanging from the ceiling, but it was really a prison cell. She was naked on a cold stainless-steel table, her wrists shackled with metal handcuffs to the table's sides. The restraining collar, a leather and metal affair, was locked to her neck.

Her skin burned under the cuffs and collar. Silver. She held back a snarl—even the slightest sign of aggression and the redhead who stood a few feet from the table with the control baton in her hand tightened the noose on her throat.

"Take that thing off." The small black-eyed brunette called Elena stood by the table, her arms folded across her breasts, her expression furious. She pointed a finger at Niki. "I'm telling you, she doesn't need that and I can't appropriately examine her while it's in place. Take it off."

Niki scowled. "No."

The door opened and another dark-haired female strode in. This one had midnight eyes, and unlike the submissive medic who wanted to touch her, this one was dominant. Very dominant. Even the hard-eyed guard who wanted to shred her heart couldn't summon that much power. Raina's cat thrashed, growling in challenge until the silver bit into her neck.

"Niki, please," Elena said.

"She's dangerous," Niki snapped. "Look at her. She'd go after the Prima if she could."

"I understand what you want to do, Elena," the dominant one said as she stroked the medic's hair, "but we can't let you endanger yourself."

"Look at her," Elena said. "There's nothing she can do to me. She's already restrained."

Prima. The Alpha's mate. Raina expected her to tear her throat out, but she stepped up to the table and met Raina's gaze instead. Even though she radiated command, her eyes lacked the cold, hard enmity of the guard's.

"Niki, loosen the neck restraint so she can speak."

Raina's cat coiled within her, a challenge roiling in her throat.

"Prima—" Niki said.

"It's all right. Let her speak."

The burning pain in Raina's throat eased.

The wolf said, "I am Drake McKennan, Prima of the Timberwolf Pack."

"Raina," the female said. "Alpha of the cat Weres. Where are my cubs?"

Drake glanced at Elena.

"Sophia has them in the nursery."

"They're safe," Drake said.

"Why should I trust you?"

Niki growled and Drake sighed. "Because you are not dead yet."

Raina tilted her head back as far as the collar allowed and scented the air. The Alpha's mate had an oaken, almost intoxicating aged-wine scent, but woven through it was a strand of cinnamon and burnt-leaf tang. Complex and compelling. "You're pregnant."

Niki hissed and jerked on the collar. Raina arched and clamped her jaws shut. She would not give the wolves the satisfaction of hearing her scream.

"Niki," Drake said softly. "Take off the collar."

"Prima—"

"It's all right."

Niki hesitated and Drake growled. "Now, Niki."

Raina's pelt streamed, the dominant tone a challenge.

"Yes, Prima." Rumbling, Niki unlocked the collar and separated the two halves, drawing it off Raina's neck.

"Where are you injured?" Drake asked.

Raina shook her head. "I won't talk to anyone about anything until I've seen my cubs."

"As soon as we've determined that your injuries are healing, you can see them." Drake glanced at Elena, who nodded. "What do we know so far?"

"I've drawn blood. She shows signs of infection, probably postpartum—antibiotics should clear that up. Her wounds aren't healing, but at least they're not bleeding any longer."

Drake studied Raina. "Why don't you shift?"

Raina's jaws bunched but she remained silent.

Drake looked from Niki to Elena. "Would the two of you step outside for a moment?"

"Of course," Elena said and turned away.

"Absolutely not," Niki said.

"Niki, don't make me repeat myself again."

A fine shudder passed through Niki's frame and she tucked her head. "Yes, Prima."

A second later Raina was alone with the wolf Prima.

"Now," the Prima said. "Tell me why you haven't shifted to heal your wounds."

"The cubs," Raina said after a long moment's hesitation. "They've been in pelt for a long time. They need to shift, and if I'm in pelt, they won't."

"How long have you been out there?"

"A week."

"And they've been in pelt most of that time?"

Raina sighed. "Yes."

"Let me examine you, and I'll take you to them." Drake paused. "I'll see that they are safe."

"Your Alpha may not agree."

Drake smiled thinly. "The Timberwolves do not kill children."

"That's not what the stories say."

"Perhaps," Drake said softly, "none of us know as much as we thought."

"My ribs are broken. I thought my lung was punctured, but…" Raina might be able to trust this one's word, but she did not want to mention the strange infusion of power she'd felt when Lara had tended her. "But my breathing is better now."

"As soon as Elena finishes her examination," Drake said, "I'll take you to your cubs. But…I want your word you won't attempt anything in the nursery that will endanger our young. If you break your word, I'll lead the hunt for you myself, and I will not be as merciful as Lara."

Raina had never expected to trust a wolf, but for the second time that day, she had to. "You have my word."

❖

Lara paced in the huge meeting room on the first floor of the Alpha's headquarters. A fire burned in the massive fireplace, the hearth as broad as a highway and as tall as a barn. Her skin prickled with urgency, and a searing unease clawed at her insides. She wanted to comb the Compound for Raina, to see that she was safe. She hadn't been this agitated when she'd been in heat. Not even the Vampiric bloodlust that could drive her to madness created such relentless compulsion. The door opened behind her and she spun around. Sylvan strode in and slammed the door.

"Where is she?" Lara demanded.

"Have you forgotten everything?" Sylvan roared. "What were you doing out there?"

Lara prepared herself for Sylvan's onslaught, already feeling teeth at her throat, dragging her down, Sylvan's claws raking her gut. "I had to come."

Sylvan snarled and circled, her gold-shot eyes slanted and hard.

"You cannot flout our laws—I cannot make exceptions, not even for you."

"I know, I'm sorry."

"Sorry." Sylvan shook her head and cradled Lara's cheek in her palm. "So am I. I miss you. We all do."

Lara grimaced. "Niki wants my blood."

"Niki wants you to be as you were." Sylvan sighed. "I'm sorry for the price you paid."

Lara closed her eyes. Sylvan's touch flooded her with fleeting peace. "I would make the same choice again."

Sylvan drew her close, slid an arm around her shoulders. "I know. How is it—with the Vampires?"

Lara rested her cheek against Sylvan's shoulder. "I don't know. I am with them, but not of them." She sighed. "Not yet, but more each day."

"Your wolf seems healthy."

Lara laughed ruefully. "Happier. I didn't even think about holding her back. She needed to run, to run here, and…we just did."

"You must have started out before sundown."

"Yes."

"How—" Sylvan whirled toward the heavy double doors. "Your Liege comes."

The doors swung inward, and Jody and Becca, flanked by Sylvan's soldiers, swept in. Jody's personal guard followed.

"Liege Gates," Sylvan said.

"Alpha Mir," Jody said brusquely. "Lara, wait outside."

Lara stepped away from Sylvan. She might not know who or what she was, but she knew her duty. She straightened. "Yes, Liege."

As she strode toward the door, Zahn joined her at a signal from Jody. They stepped into the wide stone hallway, and the doors closed, leaving them alone.

"How are you?" Zahn asked.

Lara's vision wavered and the hunger struck. She gritted her teeth. She would not let Zahn see her weakness. "Fine."

Zahn moved closer, her breasts brushing Lara's. "It's a long run here from the town house. You need to feed."

Lara's canines punched down and the feeding hormones erupted. "Yes."

Zahn smiled, the pulse in her neck bounding. "Well then, I arrived just in time."

CHAPTER NINE

As the door closed behind Zahn and Lara, Sylvan signaled to Jody to walk with her away from the others. They stood by the open windows looking out across the Compound toward the dark forest. The scent of prey and pine called to her, and she wished she could leave the threat of war behind and run with her mate in the moonlight. She thought of the wounded cat and her cubs, and her chest ached at the thought of her own young in peril. She sympathized with Raina, but her duty demanded she put her feelings aside. Drake would probably say she would make a better leader if she let her feelings guide her, but Drake's instincts were not born of millennia of fighting to survive. Even though she had inherited her father's mission to unite the Praeterns in the struggle for freedom, she couldn't afford to ignore her instincts with the welfare of her family and her Pack in the balance.

"Are you well?" Sylvan asked at length. Jody had been badly injured while aiding Sylvan in a raid on a secret facility where her wolves had been kept captive. Another debt Sylvan owed her.

Jody's pale, cool face was unreadable as usual, but a faint smile softened her carved features for a second. "Worried about me, Wolf?"

Sylvan rumbled, irritation rippling over her skin. "I have no use for an ally who can't stand up in a fight."

"I could fight in full sunlight as well as any wolf."

Sylvan snorted. "You wouldn't last a round, in or out of the light."

"Someday, perhaps we'll test that."

"Perhaps, when I'm in need of amusement."

Jody laughed. "You would make an interesting pet."

Sylvan's concern eased. Jody was fine. "Lara trespassed on Pack territory tonight."

"Does she need permission to enter?"

"She knows the law." Sylvan growled, her wolf still unappeased. "When she chose to be your warlord, she made herself a lone wolf."

"Meaning?"

"Meaning she forfeited the right to come and go unannounced."

"Even considering who she is?"

"Especially because of who she is." Sylvan clenched her jaws. "As my *centuri*, she was dominant over most of my Pack. They would follow her orders without question. Her status has changed, and the Pack needs to see what that means. Without laws, we have chaos."

Jody smiled thinly. "And what is it you think we have now?"

"Now more than ever, we need to preserve order. Our laws have served us well for centuries. The Praetern species have survived in peaceful coexistence by respecting boundaries—and enforcing them when violated."

"There have always been territorial disputes," Jody pointed out, "both inter- and intra-species. I can think of half a dozen Vampires who would be happy to see me turn to ashes."

"Not surprising," Sylvan muttered, and again, Jody smiled. "We're predators—we'll always have to fight to hold our rule. And as long as more than one predator species survives, we will always challenge each other for dominance."

"Not necessarily," Jody said. "At one time, Vampires ruled the Weres, and everyone had enough prey. A very workable situation."

Sylvan laughed. "The Weres will never be the slaves of the Vampires again. Those times have passed—we might offer you our blood, but not our servitude. Besides, now humans are voluntarily prey for the Vampires—do you plan for them to become your slaves?"

Jody gazed out the window, the night fires reflecting red in her eyes. "You ask questions no Vampire would answer."

"And yet we are more alike than not," Sylvan said quietly. "Sometimes I think all that lies ahead for us is destruction. Our path may not be one we can change."

"But you will try."

"I will do whatever I must to protect my wolves."

Jody nodded. "As will I, for my Clan."

"We are no threat to the Vampires," Sylvan said. "We do not hunt your prey."

"No, but the time may come when our prey becomes your ally, and we become the hunted."

Sylvan turned from the night. Across the room, Jody's mate, Becca, sat in front of the fire, facing them. A circle of Vampire soldiers flanked her on the left, warily watching Sylvan's guards. Two groups of lethal predators, and all that might stand between the Praeterns and those who would destroy them. "You have my word, the Weres will never hunt the Vampires except in retaliation for an attack."

"You do not speak for all the Weres."

Sylvan thought of Raina and the cats who lived in near anarchy in the neighboring mountains, of the smaller enclaves of coyotes who roamed in the north, and the scattered others who lived in even deeper hiding. Alone, leaderless, they would be easy prey. United, they would be protected. "I plan to change that."

"I believe you might," Jody said quietly. "But that assumes, my friend Sylvan, that you survive long enough."

"And as long as I do, I will count you my ally."

Jody let out a long breath. "If I must have an ally, I can think of none better."

Sylvan laughed softly. "A compliment from the Liege. I'm honored."

"Why did you want me here tonight?"

"Lara is a Vampire, isn't she?"

"Yes."

"Then why was she on Pack land well before sundown?"

"Lara is Vampire, but she is also a dominant wolf, and she was turned in an unusual way." Jody shook her head, hesitated. In a rare show of emotion, she frowned impatiently. "These are not things usually discussed with outsiders."

"These are not usual times."

"No. They're not." Jody looked over her shoulder to where Becca waited, still protected by a cadre of guards. Then she turned back to Sylvan. "I never expected to have a consort. Or a Dominion to guard. Or an ally I counted as a friend."

"Be careful, Vampire," Sylvan said softly. "You'll spoil me."

Jody grinned, her incisors flashing. "I was hoping for a taste."

Sylvan snarled and Jody's grin widened. "What about Lara? I'll keep your counsel."

"I know." Jody grew serious. "Ordinarily, turning is a deliberate and controlled process. The Vampire RNA is carried in the blood and hormones and injected into the host slowly, allowing the mutation to take hold in the marrow and ultimately replace the host stem cells with

Vampiric progenitors. The host benefits from longevity to the point of virtual immortality. The downside, of course, is the defect in the blood cell itself, requiring the infusion of oxygen carriers through feeding."

"Is anyone compatible with the process?"

Jody sighed.

"I give you my word the information remains with me and my mate," Sylvan said.

"No. In some hosts there's a rapid immunological response that destroys the introduction of the Vampire RNA, preventing the mutation from establishing itself. In essence, those hosts are resistant to turning." Jody stared out the window. "In many cases, the host is so depleted of their own natural cells that they die."

"Is there any way to tell beforehand?"

"Not that we've been able to discover. That's why we agree to turn so few hosts, even those who petition for it." Jody sighed. "Until now, before human blood hosts were so plentiful, we also resisted turning for practical reasons—we didn't want too many newlings competing with us for prey."

Sylvan leaned against the open casement window. "Why are some hosts so susceptible to the Vampire essence that they become rapidly addicted?"

"The feeding hormones are usually eliminated from the host's system slowly, over a few days to a week. In some, they're so rapidly broken down the host suffers withdrawal without a new infusion and then experiences extreme pleasure with each new exposure—causing an addictive cycle. And again, impossible to predict."

"And what about Lara?"

"Lara's blood volume was completely replaced with mine—like a bone-marrow transplant, only under rapid, traumatic circumstances. My guess is her Were genetic sequences fused in some unanticipated fashion with the Vampire genes. That might explain why she doesn't respond to ultraviolet radiation the way most Vampires do."

"I'm not sure that her Were characteristics haven't been altered as well," Sylvan said, remembering the strange transformation she'd seen when they were trapped underground. Lara had taken a half-form, ordinarily something only an Alpha Were could assume. "She may be stronger than ever now."

"It seems we both have something new and potentially dangerous to contend with."

"You still claim her as yours?"

Jody smiled. "She *is* mine."

Sylvan growled softly. "And mine."

"What of the prisoner?"

Sylvan grumbled. "We have more than one. A human we caught when we raided the research facility who swears he is a friend but will not reveal who else he works with, the two human females with Were fever, and now this damn cat."

"Tell me about her."

"I don't know much. An Alpha with newborn cubs, hiding in Pack land. It makes no sense at all."

"I'm surprised she's still alive."

"Ordinarily, she wouldn't be. But she says she has information for us and…" Sylvan shook her head. "Lara has claimed her as her prisoner. She is within her rights, as she represents you, but there is still the issue of Lara being on Pack land without official sanction."

"Let's see what the cat has to say, and then we can decide what to do with her."

"Then we can decide what to do with all of them."

❖

"You're right about the healing," Drake said to Raina, hanging the stethoscope on the IV pole next to the treatment table. "There's evidence of blood in your chest cavity, probably from a punctured lung. However, you aren't showing the symptoms I would expect. How do you feel?"

"The pain is almost gone." Raina had been wary about submitting to the examination, but the wolf had been thorough. And gentle. By the time it was over, she felt stronger. It no longer hurt to take a deep breath. The pressure in her belly had disappeared. The weakness was starting to wane too. Her cat prowled nervously, fretting to be free. They'd taken the collar off, but her hands were still cuffed. She ought to be able to slip out of them if she shifted, but once she did, she would have to attack swiftly and lethally. She would not attack a pregnant Were, even if she was a wolf, unless she had no other choice.

"I wouldn't have expected you to heal so quickly without shifting," Drake said.

Raina said nothing. She *shouldn't* have healed so quickly even if she had been able to shift. Lara was the cause. She shivered lightly, remembering Lara's mouth on her throat, Lara's body moving over hers—reliving the heat, the violent, excruciatingly pleasurable release.

Drake frowned. "What else happened out there?"

"Nothing," Raina said.

"That's not what your body says."

Raina glanced down. Her pelt had thickened down the center of her torso, her skin glowed, slick with sex-sheen. Her cat paced and hissed, wanting a joining. Deep inside, she felt a call, different than she had ever known. A tearing, gripping drive to mount and join and claim. Her breathing grew ragged, and she leashed her cat before she broke her bonds and clawed her way out of captivity. "It's nothing."

Drake was silent. She couldn't force Raina to tell her what had prompted the physiologic response, but the nature of the response was unmistakable. Something had stirred the cat's mating instincts. Even she could feel Raina's urgency, and her wolf stirred, despite being mated and pregnant. "If you have a mate out there, one who will try to find you—"

"I don't."

"Another cat on Timberwolf land will be killed on sight."

"No. No one is coming." Raina's limbs trembled, her belly tight with need. "I need to see my cubs."

"Remember your promise—"

"My word."

"All right." Drake took the key Niki had left, unlocked the cuffs, and slid her arm behind Raina's shoulders. "Let me help you sit up. I'll take you to them."

"Why are you helping me?" Raina shuddered from the power pouring off the wolf, but it was not her she craved. The bite on her neck flamed. Her cat screamed in rage, and she closed her eyes, holding her beast down.

"I'm helping *them*," Drake said softly. "They're innocent in this struggle."

❖

Lara grabbed Zahn's arm and pulled her across the huge stone-floored ground level of Sylvan's headquarters to the massive front doors. She shoved them open with her shoulder and dragged Zahn out onto the plank-floored porch.

A *sentrie* appeared out of the dark, his bare torso illuminated by the fingers of flame thrown by the fire pits in the courtyard. He blocked their path, a rifle canted across his chest. "My orders are no one leaves the building."

Lara snarled. Zahn's rich citrus scent filled her nostrils, the iron in Zahn's blood a potent lure, inflaming her. Her mouth filled with the tang of feeding hormones. Hunger throbbed in her belly and her sex. She could enthrall him, but the assault would be a breach of Jody's treaty with the wolves. She could take him along with Zahn—she was hungry enough to drink them both dry. If he didn't yield—

"Warlord," Zahn murmured, her tone a quiet warning.

Wordlessly, Lara yanked Zahn down the long porch to a corner beyond the reach of the firelight, into the dark recesses of the night. Zahn opened her shirt, exposing her breasts and the elegant column of her throat, her heartbeat a loud, seductive pulse in Lara's head.

"Feed, Warlord," Zahn whispered, slipping her hand around Lara's nape, drawing her ever deeper into the shadows.

Lara shoved Zahn against the wall, pinning her to the rough logs with her body. She skimmed her canines over Zahn's breasts, almost breaking skin. Zahn moaned, her back arched. Lara sucked at the hollow of Zahn's throat, the promise of blood so close driving her to a frenzy. Sex-sheen misted her skin. Her clitoris readied. The need was so great she shuddered, bloodlust and frenzy warring in her guts.

Zahn groaned and shoved her fingers into Lara's hair, pulling Lara's mouth to the pulse in her neck. Her hips thrust against the rough fabric of Lara's BDUs. "Drink."

Lara managed to hold back long enough to slide her hand between them and open Zahn's trousers and her own. In seconds, she was naked between Zahn's legs with her canines buried in Zahn's throat. Zahn whimpered once and orgasmed, her head thrown back against the wall, her fists clenched in Lara's hair. Lara swallowed, the electric heat of life pouring through her. She rocked between Zahn's legs, the slick essence of Zahn's release hot and thick on her swollen flesh. She groaned, her ass tightening. She swallowed and thrust. So much power filling her, so much need. Her wolf clawed and snarled for freedom, wild to tangle, to join. Lara set her claws into the firm muscles of Zahn's ass and yanked her closer still, riding her, ready to come.

Her strength magnified with every swallow, but her hunger grew. Pleasure taunted her, elusive and cruel. She needed to come. She needed to empty her mind and body of fury and desire, of anger and want. Her claws broke skin, her hips churned. So close.

Zahn cried out and came again. Lara drank deeper. Zahn's blood was rich, potent, honed by centuries of breeding for this unique destiny. Prey—Zahn was prey. *Her* prey. She would drink her, drain her. Her wolf would feast. The agony would end.

Lara yanked her mouth away and blood flowed down Zahn's neck and over her chest. Lara howled in rage and need. All around her she sensed wolves. Pack. And one scent that twisted inside her above all the others. Cat.

Lara's wolf roared and she exploded, her mind a merciful blank.

Chapter Ten

"This way," Drake said, leading Raina through the infirmary toward a rarely traveled hallway that jutted off the central corridor at the far end. Niki walked close behind them, her weapon trained on Raina. Drake doubted Niki would even need a weapon to subdue the cat at this point—Raina was healing rapidly, but she showed signs of malnutrition and chronic blood loss. Weres were extremely resilient and long-lived, but they weren't invincible. Raina looked as if she had been living under duress for some time.

"When do you expect your young?" Raina asked.

"A few weeks." Drake punched in a code on a security panel next to a reinforced door. The nursery was one of the most highly guarded areas within the Compound. Weres had so few young that each was a precious gift to every member of the Pack, and everyone protected them. The Compound hadn't been raided in years, but at one time, when the Timberwolves had been establishing their territory and bands of marauding rogue wolves and feral cats would make clandestine strikes at their encampment, the young had been frequent targets. A few had been lost, and even one loss was more than the Pack could bear.

Maternal wolves and dominant soldiers frequented the nursery, caring for the young, guarding them, and providing the nursing mothers a peaceful and quiet place to attend their offspring. Pups stayed with their mothers for a few weeks after birth and then, if healthy, moved to the nursery where they could be socialized with their littermates and other Packmates, and where their training could begin. Most of the young spent the majority of their time in skin, although the offspring of the most dominant wolves would frequently shift unexpectedly for brief periods of time.

Drake felt a stirring in her belly as her connection to the young lives milling about in the nursery energized her senses. She and Sylvan would keep their young in their den longer than most young spent with their mothers. They expected their young to shift earlier than most, and if the pups tried to explore and escaped the confines of the nursery, they might get hurt. Drake smiled, thinking about their young inheriting Sylvan's strength of purpose. She had no doubt they would want to run as soon as they could.

"Your first?" Raina asked.

"Yes. You?"

Raina nodded. "I would not have had them now, when the future is so uncertain, but my heat was strong and the time…" She shrugged. "The time was right."

"You have no mate?"

"No."

Drake couldn't imagine life without Sylvan. She would have to survive for the sake of the Pack and for the young she bore, but she doubted she could exist very long without her mate. Her life force, her very essence, was bound to Sylvan. She shuddered inwardly, unable to conceive of the loneliness Raina must endure. "Sophia, one of our medics, has been tending the cubs. She'll let you know if she's found any problems, but you'll know better if something is amiss."

Raina quivered, scenting her young so close. "Are there wolf pups inside?"

"Yes, but not in the same unit as your cubs." Drake wanted to assure her that she and her cubs were safe, but she wasn't sure she could offer that. She didn't know who Raina was or what she'd done, or why she had crossed into their territory. Sylvan had yet to question her, and until the Alpha had come to a decision, she would not offer false hope.

"We won't have much time this visit." Drake nodded to the *sentrie* who stood post at the mouth of the corridor. "Evan. All quiet?"

"Yes, Prima." He ducked his head to Niki. *"Imperator."*

Niki stepped around Raina and Drake and surveyed the long, quiet hallway. Another *sentrie*, a young female, came to attention at the far end near the exit. Niki growled, "Keep this hallway clear. No visitors until I say so."

"Yes, *Imperator*," both *sentries* replied.

Drake said to Niki, "Wait outside the care unit. Too many wolves in the room will frighten the cubs."

Niki snarled silently but marched ahead of them to the last door and took up a station next to it. "I'll be right outside. If you need me—"

"We'll be fine." Drake brushed Niki's jaw with her knuckles, a silent acknowledgment of Niki's loyalty. Niki was bonded to Sylvan in a way she never would be to Drake, but she still needed the connection to Drake, the Pack's Prima. "Thank you. I can't think of anyone I'd rather have looking out for Sylvan's young."

"No thanks are needed," Niki said gruffly.

Drake gripped the knob and said to Raina, "I'll need to stay with you."

"I understand." Raina smiled grimly. "Lara? Where is she?"

"At headquarters, I believe."

"She is an enforcer?"

Drake considered what she might say without breaching security. "Lara is an ally of the Pack. And a friend."

"She is more than wolf."

"Perhaps."

"She promised to stand for my cubs."

Drake sighed. "I hope that won't become necessary. Come on. Let's go see them."

❖

Sylvan bounded over the railing at headquarters into the center of the Compound, and leapt onto the porch of the infirmary with one powerful lunge. She could smell her mate, sense the life force of her young, and feel the weight of the protective mantle of the Pack surrounding them all. But under the pulse of the familiar beat an undercurrent of something foreign—something dangerous. Foreign hormones, foreign power. Cat. Her wolf didn't care about politics or alliances or treaties or war. Her wolf knew only her devotion to Pack and mate, her need to protect all she loved with her last breath. This cat was too close to her den, too close to her mate, too close to everything she was sworn to protect. Sylvan's pelt pushed at the undersurface of her skin as her wolf pushed for ascendency. The *sentrie* on the infirmary door stepped aside, and Sylvan strode to the treatment room and glanced in. Elena turned, a question in her eyes.

"Where are they?" Sylvan rumbled. Drake should have been here. The cat had been here, she could smell her.

"The nursery."

"By whose permission?"

"The Prima, Alpha. She took Raina—the cat—to see her cubs."

Sylvan's vision morphed to monochrome and her wolf looked out, searching for prey. "Where is Niki?"

Elena shuddered under the onslaught of Sylvan's fury. She gripped the counter behind her, her eyes lowered. "She went with them… Alpha…I—"

"Never mind," Sylvan roared, spinning around and bounding down the hall to the nursery wing. A *sentrie* jumped out of her way as she shoved through, a soft whimper escaping him. Niki stood blocking a door halfway down the corridor. Sylvan leapt to her side. "Where are they?"

"Inside, Alpha. The Prima—"

Sylvan gripped Niki's shoulder, her extended claws breaking skin. "Why is Drake alone with her?"

Niki's pelt flared and her canines extruded, but she kept her eyes at the level of Sylvan's jaw. Her wolf bristled at the physical onslaught, but she would not challenge the Alpha's might. "The Prima instructed me to wait outside."

"You know I don't want her alone with that cat. What's wrong with you, *Imperator*?"

Niki's chin shot up. "She is my Prima. I obey her orders in your stead."

Sylvan threw back her head and howled. Niki was right, but she didn't care. Drake could be in danger. She half-shifted, her jaw elongating, her pelt thickening on her torso, her hands tipped with lethal claws. "Stand. Aside."

Shivering in the wash of the Alpha's power, Niki backed against the door. Her legs trembled and her stomach cramped with the effort of standing in the wake of the Alpha's wrath. But her mate was inside. "Sophia is with them. Alpha, she is innocent. I am responsible."

Sylvan thrust her face close to Niki's, her eyes flaring gold. Her voice was gravel on stone. "Don't you think I know that? You think I would harm Sophia?"

"I don't know," Niki whispered, sweat running in rivulets down her face. She couldn't fight Sylvan's call any longer. Whining softly, she tilted her head, exposed her throat.

Niki's submission calmed Sylvan's wolf, and she drew a breath, the haze clearing enough for her to think. Sliding a hand to the back of Niki's neck, she squeezed and rested her forehead on Niki's. "Your mate is safe with me. I trust you to keep mine safe. I need you, Niki."

Groaning, Niki pressed against Sylvan, her naked torso hot against Sylvan's. Her skin was slick with stress pheromones, her body vibrating with tension and sex. "I swear on my life I will protect her."

Sylvan rubbed her cheek against Niki's hair. "I know. I thank you." Sylvan dragged her wolf back from the edge of frenzy and shivered, waiting until the heat of temper cooled enough for her to contain her fury. She eased Niki back. "Let me pass."

❖

Veronica stood with her back to the long, polished onyx bar, sipping a glass of champagne and taking in the scene in the cavernous room, trying her best to contain her excitement, to maintain the façade of nonchalance, while all the while, her body heated with piercing arousal. In contrast to the bleak exterior, Nocturne was surprisingly opulent inside. Broad leather couches and chairs wide enough to accommodate two or more individuals defined seating areas interspersed between massive brick columns, giving an aura of privacy. Muted light pierced the murky darkness from cleverly directed spots tucked into the recesses between the labyrinth of heating ducts and pipes that crisscrossed the ceiling. She didn't need the subtle illumination to make everything happening before her sharply visible. Even if she hadn't been able to see clearly, she would have had no doubt about the activities.

Despite the background music that thrummed like the heart of a great beast, the sounds of erotic pleasure were unmistakable. Ecstatic groans, orgasmic cries, and low breathless pleas for release surrounded her. Her skin prickled as if iced, but she was hot, burning on the inside. *Pheromones*, her mind registered.

She was breathing in the chemicals released from dozens of Weres in the throes of sex frenzy as they fell willing prey to their Vampire hosts. Her nipples were tight, her pussy throbbing, her clitoris so tight she thought she might orgasm with the faintest brush of tongue or fingers. The pulse in her throat beat demandingly beneath her skin. The memory of Luce's bite was nearly enough to set her off. Her hand trembled, and she feared she might spill the champagne. Turning casually, she carefully set the glass onto the gleaming bar. "What happens when you want to feed?"

Luce ran her fingertips over the soft skin above the collar of

Veronica's pale silk shirt, lingering over the column of blood that raced along her throat. Her incisors ached with the need to drink her, but she held off, waiting for instructions. She knew better than to feed from her here without the Regent's permission. "When I see someone I want, I take them."

Veronica turned, gave Luce a hard stare. Luce's arrogance was just the antidote she needed to the overwhelming crush of Vampire thrall infusing the air. "Really? Just that easy? And what if they decline?"

Luce smiled. "They rarely do. Why else would they be here?"

Veronica skimmed the edge of Luce's perfect jaw and kissed her. Luce was beautiful, sexy and alluring, and Veronica loved the hunger in her eyes. Hunger for her, a taste she intended to cultivate by making her wait. "Well, I can't imagine anyone turning you down."

Luce cupped Veronica's breast and brushed her thumb over the prominence of her nipple through the layers of silk.

Caught off guard, Veronica moaned but caught Luce's hand and pulled it to her waist. "Not yet, darling."

"No? Are you certain?" Luce kissed the pale triangle exposed by Veronica's open shirt. "I can taste the desire on your skin."

Veronica drew a shaky breath. "Are you sure that's not your hunger you taste?"

Luce laughed and leaned back against the bar, breaking all contact. "Feeding will be all the sweeter for the waiting."

Veronica's head swirled with the scent and sound of sensual pleasure. Luce's teasing had her body humming with excitement. "Tell me—"

Beside her Luce straightened, her attention diverted from Veronica by a pair of approaching Vampires. They might have been brother and sister, they were so alike in their beauty and their bearing. Both with thick, wavy dark hair, both dressed in formfitting black shirts with loose billowing sleeves, tailored black pants, and polished black leather boots. Ivory complexions, dark arching brows, aquiline noses, and full elegant mouths. They were elegant predators who moved with the sensuous grace of dancers. Both above-average height, the woman had full breasts, a narrow waist, and subtly flaring hips. He was slim, nearly delicate, but his stride and taut physique suggested hidden strength and masculine power.

"Who are they?" Veronica asked, having no doubt they were coming to join them.

"Daniela and Henry," Luce murmured. "The Regent's handmaiden and a favorite of her court."

"Did she send them?"

Luce considered her answer and then felt a mental pull from the shadows. Michel emerged from the dark on the far side of the room, out of Veronica's line of sight.

Give her what she wants, but see that she comes to no harm.

"Yes," Luce murmured, nodding to the others. "It seems the Regent wants to be sure you enjoy yourself."

The Vampires stopped in front of her, and the male took her hand, brushing his mouth over the tops of her fingers. "Good evening. I'm Henry."

Daniela leaned close, her breasts brushing Veronica's arm, and kissed her cheek. Her lips were cool and soft. Her mouth lingered against Veronica's ear. "I'm Daniela."

Veronica fought the haze of lust rapidly consuming her. She wasn't foolish enough to forget she was surrounded by animals who ensnared their prey with sexual thrall. She intended to take her pleasure with them, but on her terms. She was not the plaything they were used to. She was stronger than that. She caressed Daniela's cheek and let her hand drift lower until her fingers slipped inside the dark silk to her breasts, while pressing against Henry, kissing him on the mouth. His cock went hard against her abdomen. She let her tongue play over the surface of his incisors until he hissed softly. Daniela leaned closer, pushing her breast into Veronica's hand.

Veronica pulled back and turned to Luce. "Take us somewhere I can enjoy these two."

"I can show you to a private room," Luce said.

"Good," Veronica said. "And I want you with me, darling. I promised I would feed you."

Fire leapt in Luce's eyes and her lips drew back into a feral smile. "Come with me."

Chapter Eleven

The wolf Prima held the door open, and Raina stopped just inside the room and quickly assessed the space where they'd put her cubs. Fifteen feet square, plain whitewashed walls, wide unpainted plank floors, small windows near the ceiling. The single-paned windows weren't so small a cat in pelt couldn't get through, but easily defensible if an attack came from the outside. A counter ran along the back wall, stacked with supplies. A rocking chair, still gently moving, sat next to a big rectangular box with solid wood sides, rough-hewn timber legs, and wheels. A simple portable crib. The cubs must have scented her while she was still in the hall—they both stood with their paws on the top edge of the crib, yowling indignantly. Two sets of deep green eyes fixed on her as if she were the only one in the room.

The blond wolf medic, Sophia, stood a few feet away, an indulgent smile on her face. She glanced at Raina with more friendliness than anyone in the wolf stronghold had yet afforded her. "I'm pretty sure they're hungry."

"They are," Raina murmured.

"I offered them milk but they didn't want a bottle."

"They won't take food from a stranger." Still, Raina remained motionless. Hers were the only young in the room. She'd promised the wolf Prima she wouldn't endanger any wolf pups, but she'd never promised she wouldn't do whatever she needed to safeguard hers. Her cubs waited for a sign from her. They both looked unharmed, strong and sturdy, even though they quivered with anxiety over the strangeness of the place and her absence.

Tessa, as usual, was louder and more demanding to be freed from her confinement. As large as her brother, she was also turning out to be more dominant. She'd been the first to explore the boundaries of the small cave where Raina had hidden them. She'd been the first to show stalking behavior. And she rarely ended up on her back when the two of them play-fought. Eli was more deliberate, content to stay in one place while Raina was out hunting. Even now, he was watchful and wary. One day, Tessa would be the Alpha and Eli would prove to be her irreplaceable general, calm and steady and ever loyal.

Beside her, the wolf Prima said softly, "Is there something you need for them? Something we can help you with?"

Raina studied her, seeing only genuine concern in her eyes. "Why do you care what happens to a pair of cubs?"

"Whatever you've heard about us, you should withhold judgment until experience proves the truth."

"Can I expect the same of you?" Raina slid her hand over the lingering burns on her neck from the silver-impregnated restraining collar.

"I won't pretend we are merciful with those who threaten our Pack," Drake said, "but one thing I can promise you—the Alpha will be fair."

"Then she is rare indeed."

"Yes."

Raina wasn't ready to let down her guard, even if so far they had treated her better than a wolf taken captive in cat territory would have been treated. Cat troopers would have tortured a prisoner for information and, when no more was forthcoming, executed them. Still, she would be a fool to trust any wolf, and she would take whatever opportunity she had to escape with the cubs. "Let me hold them and I'll call them to skin. They're old enough now to share in a kill, but I have not been able to hunt for them."

"Will they eat what we hunt?" Drake asked. "We often take our pups with us when we hunt—to teach them the scent of prey and the order of the kill. We could take the cubs too."

"I don't know if they'd share your prey," Raina said, surprised again. "If I were there when the kill was offered, they might."

"I can't promise you that. You'd have to be guarded, possibly chained, for security while we hunted."

"And who will look after the cubs when they're surrounded by wolves?" Raina challenged Drake with a look. "Some of your wolves would see us dead just for being cats."

"The cubs will need to eat. If we take them on a hunt, we can assign someone to look after them"—she shook her head at Sophia when Sophia started to speak—"but not one of our medics. They might be needed elsewhere."

"You expect a fight, then?" Raina asked.

Drake raised a brow. "What do you know of the recent attacks on us?"

"Not much," Raina said. "I've been in hiding for almost two weeks."

"Why?"

"That's something I'd rather tell your Alpha."

"Of course," Drake said, knowing Raina would hold back any information she might be able to bargain with until she met with Sylvan. "You should see to your cubs."

Sophia pushed a wooden stool next to the crib. "Sit here."

Raina lifted the cubs by the scruff, one in each hand, and sat, securing them in the curve of her arm. The two of them squirmed and fussed, trying to climb over each other in their bid for attention. She brushed her cheek over their blocky heads, closing her eyes at the exquisite softness of the deep golden fur. She waited while their heartbeats settled into rhythm with hers, faster, but with the same cadence. When their physical and spiritual connection with her deepened, she extended her power to them, calling their life forces to shift. As she expected, Tessa, ever the leader, shifted first. Eli followed a second later, and she heard a small gasp from across the room. The medic watched intently, a look of almost sadness in her eyes.

"They're beautiful," Sophia murmured, handing Raina a blanket. "I've never seen hair that color."

"Cat cubs are almost always golden haired like this. Some will darken to brown as they grow." Raina wrapped the twins in the warm blanket. When she tried to ease Tessa against her to feed, Tessa struggled. Like a true Alpha, she wanted Eli to eat first. "Don't worry, I won't forget about him."

Raina settled Tessa and brushed her fingers over Eli's soft halo of sunlit hair. His blue-green eyes fixed on her face, calm and steady, unafraid, and she could see the Were he would one day be. Valiant, brave, a stalwart second to his sister. If he lived. The protective urge exploded in Raina's chest, bringing her cat to her feet, wary and alert. Her skin prickled and she searched the room for danger. Not the medic. Not the wolf Prima. They were no threat, but a threat was nearing. She growled.

Drake's head came up and she glanced at the door. "Sylvan is coming."

Sophia hurried to stand between Raina and the door.

"No," Drake said. "Give her space. Stay on the far side of the room."

Raina rumbled softly. A dominant predator was on the hunt. Her canines punched down, her pelt streaked beneath her skin, and the urge to shift, to fight, was an ache in her bones.

"Raina," Drake said firmly, "don't challenge. She's not going to hurt you."

Tessa fretted, sensing the danger, and Raina moved the twins to the other arm, leaving her stronger arm free to fight if she had to. If only she'd had a little more time to heal and be sure they were strong enough, she could have shifted and fought her way to the window. But she had run out of time. Her cat crouched, ready to spring, to defend. "I'll submit."

"Good," Drake murmured as the door flew open and a wave of fury flooded the room.

❖

Lara sagged against the side of the building, her legs still trembling from her last forceful release, but her hunger sated for the moment. She supported Zahn with an arm around her waist while the blood servant recovered. Despite having fed, Lara's wolf still paced, agitated and unsettled, as if caged behind invisible bars. The sky was inky black, punctuated by silver flares of starlight. So much purer than the sky in the city, where lights washed out the heavens and diluted the beauty. She'd been called to run under that moon from her first breath, had hunted beneath that starlit canopy all her life, and never had she seen a night so beautiful. Never had she felt so alone.

Zahn, her head resting on Lara's shoulder, stirred against her side. "We should go back. The Liege may need us."

Lara stroked her bare shoulder, grateful for the strength Zahn had shared. "Yes. Are you all right?"

"Another minute, I will be." Zahn kissed Lara's throat. "It's a pleasure to serve you, Warlord."

Lara laughed softly. "That's not what you said earlier."

"Now you are more Vampire."

Lara stiffened. "What do you mean?"

"You're changing. Your thrall is stronger. Your essence is purer." Zahn stroked Lara's abdomen. "You feel like Jody when you fill my blood. Nearly as pleasurable."

Lara eased away and closed her pants. "I don't care if you like feeding me or not. It's your job, isn't it?"

"Feeding a Vampire as powerful as the Liege is an honor." Zahn buttoned her shirt and tucked it into her trousers, slowly closed her zipper, and did up her belt. Her voice was coolly disdainful. "You're the job."

Lara snarled and pressed Zahn back against the building with the weight of her body, scraping her canines down Zahn's throat. Zahn's breath caught in her chest and she moaned.

"Just a job," Lara murmured. Zahn trembled, and Lara stepped away. "I don't think so. After all these centuries, maybe you're more of a blood slave than—"

"Be careful, half-breed." Zahn shoved away from the wall, faster and more forcefully than a human should have moved. "You aren't as strong as you thi—"

"That's enough," Jody said quietly, misting out of the shadows. She ran a finger down Zahn's cheek. "Go get some rest. Feeding her twice in one night is demanding. Even for you."

"I'm fine, Liege—"

"I know. Go on," Jody repeated. "Becca is inside. See to her."

Zahn nodded. "Yes, Liege."

Her footsteps died away, and Jody said, "What are you doing in Timberwolf territory?"

Lara walked to the porch railing and looked out over the Compound. Jody came to stand beside her. The yard was mostly deserted, but the Were guards stationed at the far end of the porch were close enough to hear them. Lara leapt over the railing and loped across the nearly deserted Compound to the edge of the woods on the far side. Jody was waiting, having passed her unseen without even disturbing the air.

"I left my post," Lara said, "and I have no excuse. I expected to be back before you had need of me, but I was wrong. I apologize for the error."

Jody slipped her hands into the pockets of her silk trousers and looked around the Compound. "What if there'd been an attack while I was somnolent?"

"I believed you were adequately guarded. The underground

stronghold is impenetrable. Zahn was nearby with a contingent of soldiers."

"Zahn was incapacitated. She's nearly incapacitated now, and in dangerous territory. Be careful how much you take from her."

"She's a blood servant—I thought her reserves—"

"Her reserves are more than adequate, but you—" Jody shook her head. "Your appetites are those of a newling, but your strength is that of a much older vampire. You have the power to hold her enthralled and drain her. I don't want you to do that. I need her services."

Lara laughed. "Just her *services*? Her blood is potent—the sex with her—"

Jody's hand was on Lara's throat and Lara's back against a tree, her legs dangling two feet off the ground, before she'd realized Jody had moved. Jody's pale, perfect face was close to hers, her eyes fiery beacons.

"Your place is not to question me. Your place is to follow my orders and to secure my rule. If you can't do that, I have no need of you. And if I have no need of you, well—there's no reason for you to exist at all, is there?"

Lara raged inside, desperate to fight back, and she couldn't move. Only the Alpha had ever been able to paralyze her with power, but despite the rabid howling of her wolf to strike out and the fury of her Vampire, she was helpless. Worse than her impotence was knowing Jody was right. Her service to the Vampires was her only value. The Alpha did not need her.

If I am executed, will you stand for my cubs?

Raina's plea resonated in her depths. Lara gathered all her strength and pushed back against the monstrous strength holding her immobilized. She needed to survive. She needed to find Raina. She'd said she would see to the cubs.

"Please," Lara whispered through the tiny space she'd made to breathe, her only victory despite all her efforts. She would submit if she had to, anything to answer the rising call that tore at her. Something was wrong.

Jody stepped back, and Lara's feet thudded to the ground. She tightened her thighs, keeping herself upright. "Punish me however you see fit." Her voice was hoarse from Jody's iron grip on her throat. "But allow me to continue to serve."

"I don't want to punish you." Jody gripped Lara's shoulder. "I'd prefer not to kill you. If you obey my orders, I won't have to."

"Yes, Liege."

"Tell me how you felt when you left the lair yesterday afternoon."

"I felt..." Lara didn't think Jody was asking about her sense of freedom or her joy in being able to run in pelt. Jody was asking a Vampire how she felt outside in the sunlight. Truth might be her only real weapon against Jody's remote disdain for her worth. "Warm, but not uncomfortable. Strong."

"No visual problems? No searing discomfort in your skin, sharp pains in the chest, weakness?"

"No, none of that."

"You were in full pelt when you first left?"

"Yes, Liege."

Jody glanced toward headquarters. "I need to get back. Don't discuss this with anyone."

"I won't—I—" Lara spun around, searched the Compound. Alarm reverberated in her head—an enemy, danger—an urgent call for aid. She shuddered. "I have to go. By your leave, I have to go."

"Where?"

Lara pointed to the infirmary. "There." She shuddered again, pelt streaking down her abdomen.

"Go. But remember your duty—you are Vampire first."

Lara bounded across the darkened yard and into the infirmary. She was Vampire, but her wolf ruled her now.

❖

Francesca curled up next to Michel on the royal blue brocade settee, her head on Michel's shoulder and her hand inside Michel's shirt. She stroked Michel's abdomen as she watched the monitor mounted inside the Louis XVI armoire on the far side of the room. The video feed from the private room upstairs was sharp and clear, and the audio every bit as good. Veronica Standish lay naked in the center of a king-size bed, surrounded by feeding Vampires. Luce fed at her throat, Henry from her breasts, Daniela was buried between her thighs. They fed in synchrony, their hips slowly thrusting. Veronica's face was slack, her arms thrown out to the sides in supplication, or sacrifice. Her mouth was open, but her cries of pleasure had long since died away.

"Perhaps you should instruct Luce to stop." Michel stroked the curve of Francesca's breast through the sheer silk dressing gown, fingering her tight nipple, as Francesca's hips stirred against her thigh. "They're being careful, but if they don't stop soon—"

Francesca slid her hand under the waistband of Michel's trousers and closed her fingers around Michel's clitoris. She was hard and wet and Francesca murmured her approval. "Luce is in control. Aren't you enjoying this?"

"Yes," Michel said tightly.

"Mmm. We'll let them go a little longer." Satisfied that she had Michel's attention again, Francesca squeezed for another few seconds and then drew her hand away. "After tonight, Dr. Standish is going to do anything we want her to do. Because we're going to have what she needs."

CHAPTER TWELVE

The power flooding the nursery was stronger than anything Raina had ever felt, ripping through her, unleashing her beast. She had only a second to grab her cat by the throat before the change came over her and she couldn't hold her back. She shuddered, her bones breaking and reforming faster than she'd ever experienced, the agony propelling a scream from her throat that ended in a screech of fury. Her cubs, still attuned to her life essence, shifted with her, and she pushed them to the floor behind her. In less than a second, she was crouched on all fours between her young and the beast at the door. The wolf Alpha was still in skin, but her body had the massive hulking presence of a Were in half-form—jaws jutting, limbs ending in lethal claws, trunk heavily muscled and thick with silver pelt. She might still be half Were but her eyes were all wolf. Raina had fought dozens of dominant cats, had defeated the last cat Alpha in a battle for supremacy, but she'd never been pummeled with the kind of power that streamed from this Were. If she hadn't had the cubs to protect, she would have shown her throat, but she couldn't trust this raging wolf not to tear them all apart even if she submitted.

Raina growled.

"Who let this prisoner free in my territory—with my *mate* in the room?"

Sophia murmured, "Alpha, we were just letting her—"

"I don't care! She is the enemy."

Sophia backed up hard against the counter behind her and threw Drake a beseeching look.

"Sylvan, wait." The wolf Prima pressed her hand to the Alpha beast's chest. "She's no threat."

The wolf Alpha didn't seem to hear her, her predator's gaze already locked on Raina. Ready to shift and attack. Raina bunched her shoulders and gathered her legs underneath her. If she sprang now, she might catch the wolf by the throat and tear through a vessel before the wolf had a chance to complete her shift. She had no other choice.

"Raina!" The wolf Prima stepped in front of her. "Raina, I know you want to fight. You think you have to fight. Remember your cubs. You gave me your word. You would not fight with young in danger. Who will stand for your cubs?"

A growl came from the door. "I will."

Raina swung her head to the side, narrowed her gaze. Another wolf. One she knew. The one who had hurt her. The redhead with the gun who wanted to kill her was there too. She showed her teeth and hissed. Tessa crept forward, pressing close to her foreleg. She swatted her back, and Tessa yowled in protest.

"You're not needed here," the wolf Alpha snarled at Lara. "Niki, get her out of here."

"Touch me and you die," Lara said softly, ignoring Niki and angling toward Sylvan. "What happened? Why is she cornered? You'd force a fight just to have an excuse to kill her?"

"Be very careful," Sylvan said.

"I won't let you bait her into—"

"Stop, everyone." A soft voice cut through the snarls and growls and pheromone-thick air. Sophia edged closer to Raina. "She's protecting her cubs, Alpha, just as you are protecting yours. The Prima is fine. See for yourself. *See.*"

A continuous rumble of challenge rolled from the Alpha's chest, but she broke eye contact with Raina and focused on her mate. "She could hurt you."

"She won't." Drake cupped Sylvan's cheek, tracing the harsh angle of her cheekbones, more wolf than Were now. "Remember? Niki is here to protect me. I'm safe."

Sylvan grasped Drake's arm and yanked her close, scenting her neck and face, rubbing her cheek over Drake's hair. "I looked for you and you weren't there."

Drake kissed her, stroked her chest, rested her hand in the center of Sylvan's abdomen. "I'm sorry. I didn't expect you so soon. Niki is with me. Everything is fine."

Sylvan glowered at Lara. "You cross me one too many times."

"You threaten the innocent."

"You would challenge me?" Sylvan went rigid. "Then be clear about it. Here and now. Make your challenge."

Aggressive waves of dominance permeated the room, and Sophia, unable to absorb the blast of primal energy, shifted. Her snow-white wolf circled cautiously around the posturing dominants to Raina's side.

Raina hissed, and the white wolf ducked her head for an instant, but then crystal-blue eyes met her gaze, calm and soothing. Raina tilted her head, studying the strange wolf. She was unlike any wolf she'd ever met anywhere—strong, but not dominant, comforting, but not submissive. Raina's driving urge to fight abated, but she watched the wolf Alpha warily while creeping closer to Lara. If the Alpha attacked Lara, she would have to fight both of them. Then, maybe, she would have a chance to escape. She signaled her cubs with a sharp thought. *Stay back!*

Lara glanced down, saw the huge cat at her side. Ready to fight with her? For her? She'd never had a champion—had always been the one to protect and serve. And Raina had the cubs. "Raina, no."

Raina didn't seem to hear her, and Lara braced for Sylvan's attack. She did not want to challenge the Alpha. She did not want Sylvan's rule. She only wanted to protect Raina and the cubs. In the doorway, Niki whined and shuddered, shifting to pelt. She took her position at Sylvan's right hand and snarled at Lara.

Lara reached out, felt the great cat's head under her hand. She slipped her fingers into the thick ruff and steadied herself in the cat's mighty strength. "I will not fight you, Alpha, or your second. But I stand for this cat and her cubs. I will not let you hurt them."

"If you challenge my decision, you will fight me or you will die."

"Raina is not guilty of any crime other than crossing our border," Lara said. "And you have not yet heard her reasons."

"*My* territory." Sylvan stalked forward, towering over Lara in her half-shifted form.

Lara fought power with power and let her wolf rise, unfettered and strong. She'd never experienced the exhilaration of releasing her wolf while still in skin, and her heart raced as her body partially transformed and her strength magnified. She met Sylvan's gaze for an instant, then looked to the side, not lowering her head, but not challenging with a direct gaze either. "I recognize your supremacy, Alpha Mir."

"You are an Alpha without a Pack," Sylvan growled. "What are your intentions in my territory?"

"My only claim is on this cat and her cubs."

Sylvan eased back but did not give ground. "I will afford you the courtesy of any Alpha in my territory. You are welcome in the Compound, but if you wish to hunt, I will provide you an escort."

"Thank you. I am here as warlord to Liege Jody Gates. I need to accompany her in or out of the Compound."

"Very well," Sylvan said, "but you will not travel unescorted in my land."

Lara nodded. "Accepted."

"I need to question your cat. My *centuri* will be here to bring her to headquarters in ten minutes."

"And the cubs?"

"They'll be safe here. One of the beta minders will see to them."

Sylvan spun on her heel and strode toward the door. "Sophia, Drake, leave them."

Sylvan and Drake strode out, Sophia and Niki close behind. Drake closed the door and telegraphed, *What just happened in there? Why are we leaving them alone?*

Sylvan breathed heavily, struggling to contain her wolf. *Give me a minute. And in private.*

Drake checked the hall to ensure no one was close enough to hear them. She gestured to Niki, who paced in agitated circles a few yards away. "Clear this corridor and wait for us in the main hall."

Niki whined, not happy to leave Sylvan's side, but dutifully padded away with Sophia next to her.

"Come with me." Drake led Sylvan by the hand toward an empty room across the hall. When they were inside, away from the guards and other personnel, she sat on a tall wooden stool and pulled Sylvan between her spread thighs. Sylvan would not be able to contain her wolf until she was calmer, and Drake knew only one way to settle her. Wrapping her arms around Sylvan's waist, she kissed her throat and nuzzled the hollow of her neck. She guided Sylvan's hands to her chest, pressed her clawed fingers to her breasts. "Feel me."

Sylvan shuddered and buried her face in the curve of Drake's neck. She licked her skin, rubbed her cheek over the shadow of a bite on Drake's shoulder. "I'm all right."

"Just take a minute. Let your wolf scent me, let her know I'm healthy, that the pups are fine."

"I want to fight all the time." Sylvan's voice was strained and rough. "If I'm not fighting, I want to be fucking."

Drake ran her fingers through Sylvan's thick golden hair. "Well, as long as it's me."

Sylvan laughed shakily. "Always. It's always you."

"Is this level of aggression normal for a Were with a pregnant mate?"

"Not this extreme. The mates are always irritable and aggressive, but I…I can barely restrain my wolf."

"But you did. You didn't shift in there. If you had, Lara would have too, and there would have been blood."

"There may still be."

"Tell me what happened. Why did you leave Raina with her?"

"Lara is an Alpha—she has the power to claim Alpha rights."

"Meaning?"

"The Pack owes her respect, and she doesn't need to submit to anyone, not even me." Sylvan's eyes flashed gold. "And she has claimed Raina as hers—and by doing so, takes responsibility for her. We can't reasonably chain the cat without cause."

"But Lara also agrees not to challenge you, isn't that right?"

Sylvan grimaced. "Not unless she wants my Pack."

"I will never let that happen."

Sylvan leaned back, frowning. "This is not your fight."

Drake laughed, making Sylvan growl. "This is my Pack and you are my mate. If she challenges you, she challenges me."

"You're pregnant."

"Believe me, I haven't forgotten that. And you"—Drake leaned forward and kissed her—"are my mate. This is our land, our Pack. No one will endanger it."

"Lara is not interested in this Pack. I don't think she realized her strength until just this minute. I suspected—when we were trapped underground, she partially shifted—but I've never seen an Alpha manifest so late. Something—something happened when she transformed. Her wolf survived, but she's changed."

"Do you trust her?"

Sylvan sighed. "I love her. She's been my friend, my guard, all our lives. We're blood-bonded, and she gave her life for me. I would not trust her with my mate, but I trust her to be honorable."

"She's still your wolf, Sylvan, no matter how much she's changed. We don't want to lose her."

"I'm afraid we already have."

❖

Lara waited until the door closed and she heard the Alpha and her mate move down the hall before she knelt next to Raina, putting their heads at eye level. Raina's eyes were deep green, ringed in gold, narrow and distrustful. Her ears were back, her body coiled to spring. Lara reached out, and Raina hissed but didn't move. She stroked the dark bands of fur that streaked her muzzle. "So beautiful." She let her hand drift lower, over the powerful neck. Raina's muscles twitched and she drew back her lips, showing canines that could tear Lara's arm off. Heat poured from the cat's body. "Can I see the cubs?"

Raina growled softly.

"I noticed one of them was ready to fight. Takes after you."

Lara heard a faint scratch on wood and looked down, saw the tiny cub, no bigger than Raina's paw, staring at her with challenge in her eyes. She laughed. "What's her name?" She didn't expect an answer, but a silent reply echoed in her mind. *Tessa.*

Lara bent lower until her nose nearly touched the cub's. "Tessa. Good name for a warrior."

The small female hissed and her fur rose along her back.

"Where's the other one?" Easing forward, Lara peered around Raina's shoulder. The second cub crouched a little off to the right, a good position to protect the flanks. "A soldier. Smart one already."

The great cat shivered, moaned softly, and Raina fell onto her knees with her arms extended, the cubs safely shielded in the outer curve of her body. She panted softly. "You came."

Lara tentatively brushed the damp strands of hair that fell around Raina's face, cloaking her in gold. "I said I would."

Raina flung her hair back and stared up at Lara, questions warring with rage in her eyes. "Why? Why did you bring me here? Why, if only to make me a prisoner?"

"I had no choice. I couldn't kill you."

"Why not?"

Lara slipped her fingers into Raina's hair, her need and wonder tangling her insides. She held Raina motionless and leaned closer until her mouth almost brushed Raina's. "I think killing you would have left me truly dead."

"What are you?"

"Does it matter?" Lara's chest ached, knowing her answer would drive Raina away. They were enemies as Weres, but she was not even that anymore. She was…other.

"I don't know," Raina whispered.

"I do."

❖

Veronica stirred and opened her eyes to murky darkness. She sensed rather than felt the bed was empty. No light came under the door. A row of dim lights along the baseboard provided just enough illumination for her to make out shapes. She turned on her side, waiting for her eyes to adjust. She was tired, her limbs shaky, but the lingering satisfaction of her incredible orgasms still hummed through her. She sighed and brushed her fingers over her breasts. Her nipples were hard, sensitive, almost too tender for her to touch. Her breasts were sore, and she had a fleeting image of Henry's mouth moving over her. Her clitoris throbbed, reawakening at the memory. "Luce?"

No one answered. She wondered how much time had passed. She didn't like the idea of having been helpless, almost unconscious. The sex had been wonderful—more than wonderful, incredible, the intensity of the physical release so exquisite she'd lost her breath, literally lost her mind. She didn't know how it was possible, but she wanted to come again.

She pushed up in the bed. She was naked. "Luce?"

The door opened, and a figure entered. Just as quickly the door closed.

"Dr. Standish. I'm so very glad you could join us tonight."

Veronica had the urge to pull the sheet over herself but resisted. Instead, she pushed herself upright, exposing her breasts. "Regent. Thank you so much for your hospitality."

"I trust it met with your satisfaction?"

Veronica laughed. "Oh, I would say very much so."

Smiling, her perfect face luminous in the near dark, Francesca leaned down and drew a fingertip along Veronica's jaw. "I'm so very glad to hear that. I think we're going to be very good friends."

Chapter Thirteen

Are you ready?" Lara inclined her head, listening. "The *centuri* will be here soon."

"Will they collar me again?"

"No," Lara said roughly.

Raina returned the cubs to the crib. Despite being exhausted, they both complained when she set them down. She wouldn't leave them there alone if she had any other choice. She glanced again at the small windows across the room, calculating how quickly she might shift, grab the cubs, and force her way to freedom. Alone, she might have a chance to escape the wolves. With the cubs in tow, she would have none.

"Outside that window," Lara said, "you'd have two hundred yards of open Compound to cross before you reached the stockade. It's twelve feet high and guarded at ten-yard intervals. If you made it over, the woods are patrolled by our *sentries* for five miles in all directions, and beyond that the mountains are filled with our soldiers."

"Remaining here is no safer."

Lara glanced into the crib. The cubs were huddled in one corner, uncertain but defiant. She stretched out a finger, and Tessa raked it with a claw. She smiled. "I can't imagine what it must be like to have to protect them."

"No? Then why did you come when we were in trouble?"

Lara thought about the urge to protect Raina and the cubs that had driven her since she'd found them. Maybe she was just trying to recapture what she'd lost. A fruitless, sad exercise, and not something Raina needed to know. "Habit, probably. I was one of the Alpha's personal guard, until…"

"Until?" Raina heard the despair coloring Lara's voice and, more than that, resignation. As if she had given up. Raina couldn't imagine what would have caused a warrior of such strength to lose her spirit. She remembered the fury with which Lara had fought, her power and relentless determination. What enemy could have vanquished that? "What happened?"

Lara glanced at the cubs again, then Raina. She couldn't pretend to be other than she was—she couldn't hide behind the scent of Were that clung to her when every day she became more Vampire. "I died. Only a Vampire brought me back."

"A Vampire." Raina chilled inside. Cats hated Vampires almost as much as they hated wolves. In the ancient wars, the Vampires had commanded armies of wolves that had destroyed entire Prides as the Packs claimed territory for their masters. "You were turned?"

"Yes," Lara said flatly. "Now I live—or exist—somewhere between the world I once knew and the world I awakened in."

"You fed from me out there, didn't you?" The chill inside turned to ice. All her life she had fought for her survival and the survival of her Pride. Never once had she submitted, not even when the furious need of her heat had forced her to couple or lose her sanity. She had never submitted, even then, and when the coupling had been over, she had thrown him off. She'd paid for that show of independence when he and his supporters tried to kill her, but she would make the same choice again.

"You weren't healing," Lara said. "I didn't want you to bleed to death."

"So you took my essence?" Raina said bitterly. This Vampire had taken her against her will, and for that alone she would kill her if she ever got the chance.

"Yes, and gave you some of mine." Lara shrugged. "You survived."

Raina snarled. "You expect me to thank you?"

"No. I don't expect anything."

Raina struggled with her fury, as enraged by her impotence as by the knowledge she'd been taken against her will. She still needed an ally, and this one was powerful. Until she could find a way to escape, she needed her. "I'm in your debt. What is it you ask of me?"

Lara stepped closer, her canines diamond points of light glinting beneath her full upper lip. She traced the pulse in Raina's throat with a blunt claw. "Would you give me your blood if I asked?"

Raina heated inside, her sex throbbing painfully. Her breath poured from her in sharp, hard pants. She wanted to resist, but with every passing second the urge to bare her throat grew larger. Even her heat had not stripped her control so easily. She whined softly in the back of her throat, her need a living beast inside her, shredding her willpower. "Yes. I would give you my—"

"No, you wouldn't," Lara said coldly, stepping away, allowing her thrall to diminish, watching the rage and loathing return to Raina's eyes. "You wouldn't *give* me anything. You'd let me take you, but you don't want me. Any more than I want you. I have others who want what I offer—who willingly feed me for the pleasure it brings them."

"If you desire me," Raina said, willing to do anything to keep the interest of the only being who might help her survive, "I want—"

"I don't want your lies." Lara gripped Raina's throat, strangling the words before Raina prostituted herself and truly hated her for it. "Don't. I don't want you."

Raina didn't struggle, though her cat screamed in fury. Lara wasn't preventing her from breathing, and she forced her cat to retreat. Submitting to Lara's hold, she sagged until her thighs and breasts brushed Lara's. Her nipples tightened at the contact and her pelt line flared. She didn't want to desire her, but her blood remembered, calling up the moments of ecstasy she couldn't purge from her mind. She moaned.

Lara wrapped an arm around her waist and tugged her close. Her canines were sharp against Raina's throat, and Raina whimpered again. Lara's mouth moved over her neck, velvety soft, flame hot. "I can taste your desire," Lara murmured, licking the spot she had bitten. "But your eyes don't lie. You don't want this."

She did. With every cell, with every beat of her heart, despite everything she feared and hated and knew to be wrong, she wanted the wild ecstasy of Lara's mouth on her. The place on her neck Lara had bitten throbbed, and thick tendrils of desire wended from it, wrapping around her insides like a vine encircling a tree. Lara's earthy scent filled her nostrils, recalling the forest after a hard rain—lush with life and dark secrets. Lara's skin blazed against hers, bringing her to readiness with a burst of fire. Raina gasped. "I—"

Abruptly, Lara released her and stalked to the door. "The escorts are coming. This time if you challenge, one of them will kill you."

"I won't." Raina hesitated, her cat crowding her mind, demanding something she didn't understand. "Will you come with me?"

"Yes." Lara laughed bitterly. "No matter what you think of me, you're mine now."

❖

"Come," Francesca said, holding out her hand. "You need nourishment."

Veronica pushed the sheet aside and sat up, her heart pounding with excitement and arousal. She hadn't expected to see Francesca, at least not more than a glimpse somewhere in the shadowy recesses of the club, if she was lucky. And now, Francesca was inviting her… somewhere. Where didn't matter. Francesca was the most powerful Vampire in North America, possibly the entire Western Hemisphere. Luce and the others had given her pleasure beyond anything she'd ever experienced, but the thought of Francesca and what kind of ecstasy she could bestow surpassed her wildest fantasies. She was at a disadvantage in the dim room—unable to gauge the Vampire's response by her expression—but she knew Francesca could see her. She could tell by the glint in her eyes she was watching, and she took her time rising, letting Francesca look. She brushed a hand over her breasts and down her belly. "Should I dress?"

Francesca laughed softly. "Would you prefer I led you through the club with a leash and collar around your neck?"

Veronica's thighs grew damp and her pussy clenched. "I'd prefer you do whatever you'd like."

Francesca was on her before the last words left her mouth. Francesca's mouth covered hers, her tongue molten pleasure slipping between Veronica's lips. The Vampire's breasts caressed hers as if she were being anointed with a thousand kisses from a thousand hot, hungry mouths. Veronica's thighs turned liquid and she sagged in Francesca's embrace.

"Be careful what you offer, Dr. Standish," Francesca whispered in her ear. "You would make a marvelous pet, but I think you'll make a much more important partner."

As quickly as Francesca had embraced her, she was standing across the room again. Veronica gasped for breath, so close to orgasm she couldn't think.

"Go ahead," Francesca whispered, "finish for me."

"Oh God," Veronica moaned, her fingers trailing down her belly to the delta between her thighs. Her fingers trembled, and when she brushed over her tight clitoris, her hips thrust into her palm. She searched for Francesca's face in the darkness, felt Francesca's gaze lock with hers. She stroked and pleasure ripped through her. "I'm going to come any second."

"Tell me. Is it good?"

"Oh God, yes. So good. So, so good."

She gasped, her fingers flashing as she squeezed and fondled. "I'm going to come."

"That's right, darling. You are."

"I'm coming. Coming."

Her vision tunneled and she stumbled forward and Francesca was there again, holding her as she cried out, convulsing.

When she was aware again, she discovered Francesca had wrapped a black silk dressing gown around her shoulders.

"Thank you," Veronica murmured, her limbs weak.

"You're very welcome." Francesca kissed her, slow and intimate. "You are very beautiful, Veronica."

"As are you." Veronica wanted to kiss her again but didn't want the need building inside her to show. It wouldn't do for Francesca to know she would do anything to feel her bite.

Francesca took her hand. "Come. Michel is waiting."

Veronica followed as Francesca led her through a series of hallways lit by flaming sconces. The floors were cool marble, the walls dark, opulent wood. The room the Vampire took her to might have been part of a king's castle—filled with priceless rugs, elegant furnishings, glinting silver and china settings on the low table between two brocade sofas. Michel, barefoot, lounged on one, her shirt open, her glance casually seductive.

"Come here, my dear," Francesca said, guiding Veronica to the sofa opposite Michel. "First, you should have something to eat and drink. I've provided a supplement to help restore your blood volume."

Veronica ate and drank automatically, her scientific mind wondering what exactly the pungent claret-colored liqueur was meant to do, but for the first time in her life, she couldn't bring her considerable mental powers to bear against the corporeal sensations overwhelming her. Every square centimeter of her body tingled, every impression so exquisitely sharp she could taste the air she breathed, smell the excitement in her own blood. She was reduced to pure animal instinct, unimaginably uncivilized, and some part of her reveled in this freedom. She wanted the Vampires to take her again. She wanted to relive the incredible power of feeding them. Only a lifetime of control kept her tethered to reality, enough that she kept her thoughts and her desires to herself.

"I hope it's all right with you that I visited this evening," Veronica said at last.

"Of course," Francesca said. "It's a pleasure to have you as our guest."

"You treat your guests very well."

Francesca laughed. "Henry is a delight, isn't he? And Daniela—so fresh and eager. And Luce, Luce is such a dark pleasure."

With every word, Veronica was drawn back into that darkened room, to the place where she lay helplessly beneath the feeding Vampires, a willing victim of her own pleasure. Her breasts rose and fell rapidly and her hands trembled. "They were exquisite."

Francesca drew her legs up onto the sofa, the champagne silk of her gown drawing up her thighs. She stretched one arm out along the back of the sofa until her red-tipped nails rested against Veronica's shoulder. Indolently, she drew strands of Veronica's hair through her fingers, as if she were stroking a favorite pet. "I hate to mix business with pleasure, but sometimes expediency demands it. You're aware of Nicholas's…*actions* recently?"

Veronica struggled to think through the haze of erotic thrall enclosing her. "I'm not sure I know what you mean."

"No? He didn't tell you that he planned to blow up one of Sylvan Mir's laboratories?"

"No," Veronica said vehemently. She wasn't sure if Vampires could tell if someone was lying, but she wasn't, actually. Nicholas had told her he'd planned to draw attention away from the explosion at their hidden laboratories, but he hadn't told her what he'd planned. "I understood from the news that one of the more violent animal rights groups had taken credit for that."

"Oh," Francesca said, "they have. If you believe what you hear on the news."

Veronica laughed. "Well, I won't admit to being that naïve. All the same, Nicholas is a politician, not a terrorist."

"Nicholas is a powerful man with a deeply ingrained hatred of the Weres. And I think we all know that."

Veronica gathered all of her willpower and forced herself to concentrate. She couldn't afford a misstep with Francesca. "You know that I work with Nicholas. I can't actually call him my friend. It's been advantageous for me to make use of his resources, but that doesn't necessarily mean our goals are the same."

"What are your goals, Veronica?" Francesca said, her voice a low purr. Her fingers strayed to the nape of Veronica's neck, and Veronica quivered.

"I believe the Weres represent a threat to human society, and highly evolved Praeterns will be tainted by the backlash."

"Highly evolved Praeterns," Francesca murmured. "And who would they be?"

Veronica edged closer on the sofa until her bare thigh touched Francesca's. "Vampires are not only immortal, but highly intelligent and adaptable. You control some of the most powerful institutions in the world. I would say that speaks for your superiority."

"The Weres would make very powerful enemies."

"Not if we could neutralize their ability to shift. Without that, they are powerless."

"And you think you can do that?"

"Not yet. But with enough study and experimentation, yes, I think that's possible."

"And what would Nicholas do with this knowledge?"

"I'm afraid his goal is somewhat more…radical. I don't think he will be happy until the Weres are exterminated."

"Then you and I, my dear, will very likely end up on opposite sides of this confrontation."

"It doesn't have to be that way," Veronica said, the urgency building inside her for Francesca's touch. The craving was physically painful. Her stomach knotted with need.

Francesca leaned closer and kissed Veronica gently on the mouth. "Well, of course, I'd much rather we be allies than adversaries."

"So would I." Veronica tilted her head, offering her pulse. "I very much want us to be on the same side."

"Nicholas doesn't need to know of our…friendship, does he, darling?" Francesca whispered. Silently she called for Michel, who slid onto the settee on Veronica's other side.

"No. He doesn't need to know." Veronica shuddered. She was burning.

"That's very good." Francesca gently clasped Veronica's chin and nodded to Michel. "I'm sure he has further plans for dealing with Sylvan and her wolves."

"Yes. I'll call him."

"Wonderful." Francesca smiled at Michel. "We'll be so very grateful for anything you can tell us about Nicholas's plans. Isn't that right, darling?"

"Very grateful." Michel kept her gaze on Francesca as she slid her incisors into Veronica Standish's throat.

Chapter Fourteen

Raina steeled herself to be taken to a prison cell. So far, the wolves had treated her better than she had expected. They'd tended to her wounds and allowed her to care for her cubs, but she didn't expect mercy now. Everything she'd heard about them suggested they were ruthless and brutal killers, and every skirmish she'd ever had with them along the rugged borders to the north had been a fierce fight. Neither side had taken prisoners.

The guards on either side of her did not touch her as they walked across the Compound, but they trained stun guns on her, and if she tried to break free and run, she would find herself writhing on the hard earth, her muscles locked into tetanic contractions, paralyzed and powerless, her vital essences draining from her. Lara walked just behind her, not blocking the guards' access to her, but close enough that Raina could feel the heat pouring from her, scent the pheromones wrapping around her. Lara was sending off signals telling everyone Raina was hers.

She'd never belonged to anyone before, never been owned, never been claimed. She carried no marks—had made none of her own. A mate more often than not was just a body to assuage the agonies of heat and to bring food for the young, sometimes. A mate was not a protector, a lover, or a friend. Not a comfort or a support. She would not be owned for the convenience of an easy coupling, and she could hunt for her cubs on her own. She didn't need anyone's help to survive, or she hadn't, before now. Now she accepted the unspoken claim because she had no choice and more than just her survival was at stake.

They entered another log building, this one the largest in the Compound—each level at least fifteen feet high, constructed of rough-hewn logs set on a stone foundation made of boulders as large as she was tall. Inside, slabs of stone formed the floor, and she scented the spoor of dozens of Weres as the guards led her across an enormous chamber and up a set of wide wood stairs to a landing that overlooked the great room below. Two wolves stood guard outside a pair of broad carved wooden doors with heavy cast-iron hinges and latch. Another dark-haired female, not a wolf, stood at the top of the stairs, her cool gaze moving over Raina to Lara.

"Warlord," the dark-haired one said.

"Rafaela," Lara said.

Raina stared at the female, whose insolent smile made her cat snarl irritably.

The blond wolf at the door she recognized as one who had taken her to the infirmary earlier. The craggy-faced older male with shaggy hair and a massive chest was new to her, but she recognized his dominance. She growled low in her chest when his eyes fell on her, dark and appraising.

From behind her, Lara murmured, "Raina. Keep your head down."

To be asked to lower her eyes before any Were, dominant or not, was an insult, but she forced herself to do it. Dead, she could do nothing to help her cubs. The female wolf pushed the doors open, and the guards led Raina into another enormous space with a high ceiling, mammoth exposed rafters, and a huge stone fireplace at one end. Flames leapt from a stack of logs a foot in diameter piled five feet high. Huge leather sofas and chairs with broad wooden arms ringed a thick earth-toned rug in the center of the room. To the right, the wolf Alpha sat behind an oversized dark oak desk that commanded the space. Her general stood by her right hand, her Prima on her left. A fierce and powerful triumvirate.

A rapier-thin dark-haired female with intense dark eyes sat in a deep leather chair to one side of the desk, her legs casually crossed, arms resting loosely on the armrests. A second female, coffee-skinned and sharply beautiful, occupied another chair next to her. Another figure blended with the shadows near the windows—tall, slender, radiating strength that struck Raina as more refined than that of a Were, more powerful than a human.

Raina sorted the scents bombarding her. Wolf. Human. Vampire. The dark-haired Vampire occupying center stage by the Alpha's desk radiated so much understated power Raina's skin prickled. That must be Lara's master. Raina disliked her immediately and she showed her teeth in defiant challenge.

Jody smiled softly, her gaze flickering to Lara. Her brows rose. *What have you brought us, Warlord?*

Instinctively, Lara slid a hand around the back of Raina's neck. *She's mine, spoils of the victor.*

That may very well be, but remember she is only safe as long as she has something to offer. The wolves have ultimate claim and they are our allies.

Lara curled her fingers, letting them rest over the bounding pulse in Raina's throat. The cat's life force was strong, her attitude unfazed by the number of dominants aligned against her. A brave if foolish cat.

Sylvan rose, dressed now in jeans and a dark shirt with the sleeves rolled up to the middle of her powerful forearms. "I am Sylvan Mir, Alpha of the Timberwolf Pack, and I hold rights to all the territory west of our shared borders."

Raina's chin came up. "I am Raina Carras, Alpha of the Catamount Pride, and our territory is where we choose to roam."

Sylvan smiled for a brief second. "You may claim what lands you may hold, but you have no stake in Wolf territory. You violated our borders, and the punishment for that is death."

Raina had expected the sentence, but still, the blow hit her hard. She kept her head up and her eyes on Sylvan's. A challenge would do her no good and she kept her gaze unfocused, holding her status but offering no resistance. She was still weak, and she'd have to fight the Alpha as well as the Alpha's second and probably her Prima. She would lose. Even Lara could not help her. "I petition for clemency for my young. Return them to cat lands."

"And leave them?"

"They'll have more of a chance there than here."

Sylvan folded her arms over her chest. "You should have thought of the danger to them before you brought them into my territory."

"I had no choice. I had to hide where I was least likely to be discovered." Raina barely contained her fury, knowing everything she had risked was for nothing. She'd likely never see either of the cubs again. She fought the despair tearing through her. "Wolf land was the last place anyone would expect me to go."

"Why did you flee your territory—desert your Pride?"

"I didn't…" Raina hesitated. The truth might put the whole Pride at risk. These wolves might wipe out everyone in retaliation for the cats' part in what had been done.

Lara's hand was still on her neck, her grip warm and certain.

Whatever you know, now is the time to reveal it. You will not get another chance.

Lara's soft words whispering through her mind somehow gave her a flash of hope, no matter how foolish it might be. "A group of dominants planned to kill me and my cubs to take over the Pride."

"Why should I care about a challenge? Every Alpha faces challenge. I hold my place by strength and might."

"As did I," Raina said. "But I was too close to birthing my cubs to risk a fight. If I'd lost, they would not have survived."

"They mean more to you than your rule?"

"Yes," Raina said instantly.

Sylvan's eyes were hard chips of gold, penetrating and pitiless. "Not just one, but several sought your death?"

"Five."

"Why?"

Raina hesitated. She had very little to bargain with, and once she gave up what she knew, she would have nothing left. Lara's fingers stroked her throat. Her flesh heated and she felt Lara's touch in her blood. She would have shrugged her off, but she couldn't. She leaned into the touch even though she didn't want to.

The humans are waging war on the Praeterns, although most Praeterns don't know it yet. The Pack has been attacked more than once, and the cats will soon be targets. Do you want your Pride, your cubs, to be hunted down and massacred? You could do worse than to have a wolf ally. Especially this one.

Raina took a breath, heeding the truth in Lara's counsel. Trust didn't come easily, but she'd have to risk trusting her now. "Some members of the Pride feel that the humans should be our allies. They've been working with them. I was opposed."

"Opposed to what?" Sylvan said very softly.

"Opposed to taking Weres prisoner and locking them away for months at a time."

Sylvan was over the desk and towering over Raina before Raina even sensed her move. The Alpha's rage washed over her, stifling and raw, and she gasped.

Lara pulled Raina back against her chest, one arm around her middle. "Hear her out, Alpha."

Sylvan glared at Lara before turning to Raina again. Her fury scorched Raina's skin. "You knew what they were doing to our young and you let it happen?"

"I was opposed," Raina said, the words nearly strangling in her throat. Her cat struggled to be free—wanted to strike back. "But some of our young dominants believe enough human money will bring them the respect the wolves have in the human world."

"So you let your cats become the jailers of our adolescents?"

"The Pride is large and scattered over a wide, wild range. We have always respected individual choice, allowing subgroups to govern themselves. I risked civil war if I tried to stop those who wanted to work with the humans." She shrugged, wondering just how fair the wolf Alpha would really be when faced with the truth. "And they were wolves. Your responsibility, not mine."

Sylvan snarled and her face grew heavy. The wolf Prima suddenly appeared at the Alpha's side, reached out, and stroked the Alpha's back. The Alpha shuddered and her face slowly settled. "Do you know who these humans are?"

"No—they did not contact me. They went after young dominants, males and females who were restless and eager to fight. Easily swayed by the promise of power."

"If I let you live, what can you offer me?"

Raina thought of Lara's request for her blood and knew that the Alpha would take nothing less than her blood as well, although offered in a very different way. The idea of turning over a cat to a wolf for any reason made her cat scream in rage. But at least two of her own had tried to kill her and her cubs. "I can lead you to some of those who worked with the humans. I can't promise they'll tell you what you need to know."

"We'll put together a raiding party. If you turn on us, you won't live to see your cubs again."

"I understand and accept your terms."

Sylvan turned to Niki. "Take her to a cell."

❖

Niki led Raina and Lara away, and Sylvan turned to Jody. "What do you think?"

Jody flicked a long-fingered hand. "The story sounds plausible, but there's no way to know if it's true."

Sylvan, restless and agitated, strode to the windows and pushed one open. After midnight. When she should be home curled up with her mate, or running, hunting, she was listening to tales of treachery and betrayal. Lara, her friend and trusted guard, was now a reluctant ally at best. Humans wanted to destroy her Pack, or control it. And Vampires, once their masters, were now variously friend and foe. "When did our world become so complicated?"

She spoke softly, but everyone in the room heard her. Becca glanced at Drake, her eyes concerned. Drake joined Sylvan at the window and rested her hand on Sylvan's back above the top of her jeans. Sylvan's pain and sadness made her heart ache. "These struggles reach back centuries, but since we've become visible, so have our battles. And it's the way of humans to seek to control what threatens them. But you're not alone."

Sighing, Sylvan turned back to the others, looping her arm around Drake's waist and holding her against her side. "We'll have to catch these cats Raina told us about. Until we can put faces and names to our enemies, we will be constantly at risk for attack. We can't defend ourselves against the faceless."

Jody rose and her consort stood with her. "You are in a delicate situation, Sylvan. Your borders are vulnerable. If the cats are doing the bidding of humans, they may be massing to strike. What Raina said makes sense—the cats have always lived in the shadow of the wolves, and the young ones may see an alliance with the humans as their chance to claim the public acknowledgment you've gained as well as the private power the wolves have always held. Undoubtedly, the humans have a more sweeping agenda—that lab we destroyed is proof of that."

"And the humans must have other allies among the Praeterns." Becca twined her fingers with Jody's. "Probably Vampires. And who knows about the Fae or the others."

Drake said, "We know from what the Revniks reported that humans have been involved in Were experimentation for decades. We know Vampires are somehow involved, from what Katya and Gray told us. How deeply they're involved, we can't be certain. We need more information about the nature of those experiments and we need to know who's behind them."

"The human we are holding—Martin—can help us there if we can get him to talk," Sylvan said.

"Let me talk to him," Becca said quickly. "I'm the one he called, after all. And…I'm human."

"All right," Sylvan said. "I'll have a guard escort you to his cell."

"Zahn, go with her."

Zahn materialized form the shadows. "Yes, Liege."

When they'd left, Sylvan said, "We need to send a cadre of soldiers into cat territory to round up the cats who worked with the humans, and we need to confront Francesca about her knowledge of the experimental labs."

"If we divide our forces," Jody said, "we may be opening ourselves to a two-front war."

Drake said, "But we may also speed up our discovery of who we really need to fight."

Jody nodded. "Sylvan?"

"Jody, you take Lara, Raina, and a cadre of your soldiers into cat territory. You can move faster and farther without detection than a group of my wolves," Sylvan said. "I will pay the Viceregal a visit tonight."

"Very well," Jody said. "My Vampires and I will need to avail ourselves of your hospitality tomorrow."

"We'll ready quarters for you. Any Were who volunteers is welcome to feed you."

"Very generous of you." Jody smiled and her incisors glinted. "We should take at least two of your wolves to scout for us. We'll use them as decoys to draw out the cats."

Niki, Sylvan called.

The doors opened. "Yes, Alpha?"

"Send Jace and Dasha with Liege Gates. I want you, Max, Andrew, and Katya with me."

"Yes, Alpha."

Jody took Becca's hand and joined Niki. "Remember something about Vampires, Alpha."

"What's that?"

"A predator, especially one with a large appetite, sees everyone as potential prey." Jody grinned at Niki, who snarled back.

"I'm not worried," Sylvan said. "We hunt in Packs for a reason. A lone predator, no matter how strong, will fall prey to our strength in numbers."

Jody's eyes glittered. "Only the ones foolish enough to be caught alone. Good hunting, Wolf."

"I'll see you at dawn, Vampire."

Drake waited until the room cleared and said, "Why Katya? She's still fragile. If you're going to Nocturne—"

"I know," Sylvan said. "But she's the only one who might be able to identify the Vampire—or Vampires—who were at the lab."

"Jody says it was Michel."

"We need something stronger than that to confront Francesca." Sylvan pulled Drake close. "I know it's a risk, but this is war. And Katya is a wolf. She'll stand."

"I'm going." Drake bit her lightly on the neck. "I'm not letting Francesca anywhere near you otherwise."

Sylvan sighed. "You know I never—"

"That doesn't matter. She looks at you like she wants you to fuck her." Drake snarled. "I ought to kill her just for that."

Laughing, Sylvan kissed her. "Just promise you won't tonight."

"You ask a lot." Drake nipped her lip. "But all right. Let's go find some answers."

Chapter Fifteen

Niki closed the silver-impregnated bars on thc holding cell in the underground detention center. Her eyes were flat and hard as slate. "Don't get too comfortable. We're going to be searching for your friends soon."

Raina saw no point in reminding the wolf that the cats who had tried to kill her were hardly her friends. The Alpha's second would not be swayed from her desire to see Raina dead. She paced the perimeter of the ten-by-twelve cell, her cat shredding her insides, furious to be freed. The only thing worse than being caged would be losing her cubs, so for now, she had to accept this prison. Her eyes met Lara's through the bars, and for an instant she thought she saw sympathy, quickly replaced by cold indifference. She recognized that look now—she'd seen it in the eyes of the Vampire leader lounging in the Alpha's headquarters. The remote indifference of an immortal, for whom the plight of creatures whose lives spanned only a fragment of their existence held no importance. She might have been wrong in thinking Lara would help her. Lara had no reason to care what became of her or her cubs. Lara's wolf and her cat were mortal enemies. And the Vampire who stared at her from Lara's icy eyes saw her only as prey. A thing to be devoured and cast aside.

Raina's heart filled with crushing dread. She had to make choices with nothing to guide her except instinct. She had no experience with Vampires—she barely had any with other Weres. The cats kept to themselves except when making clandestine forays into neighboring wolf territory, when game in their own lands began to disappear. The territorial boundaries that had been set centuries before restricted their hunting to land that had become inadequate as their population grew and game became a scarce commodity for a society that still relied on hunting for its main source of food. Unlike the wolves, the cats tended not to share their kills, and a large percentage of the Pride did not have regular income to supplement what they hunted with store-bought staples. Most cats preferred a solitary existence deep in the mountains to integrating into human society, as many of the other Praeterns had done. The cats were self-sufficient, independent frontier people who weren't interested in being part of the ever-advancing technological society. Those who worked at conventional jobs were usually craftsmen—carpenters, welders, masons, and organic farmers. Raina was a forester, employed by the state to preserve huge tracts of mountain growth that had nearly been deforested a century before by overlumbering and irresponsible farming practices. She was a stranger in a strange land now, and her advocate, her one ally, was even more foreign to her experience. All she knew of Vampires was that they were highly sophisticated parasites, living off the flesh and blood of others.

"I need to see my cubs," Raina said.

Niki shook her head. "You'll stay here until the Alpha decides otherwise."

"She'll need to feed them before we go on the hunt," Lara said.

"Why do you care?" Niki asked, her tone a combination of anger and bewilderment.

"For reasons you wouldn't understand."

"I'll tell you what I don't understand." Niki pushed into Lara's space, her deep green eyes shifting darker. "I don't understand why you care what happens to the leader of our enemies. You know the losses we've sustained from ambushes out on the frontier."

"Times change, Niki," Lara murmured. "Enemies become our allies, and our friends are suspect now."

Niki shook her head vehemently. "Not for me. I know where my loyalties lie." Her eyes raked over Lara, fury and aggression pouring from her. "I know my enemies from my friends."

"You think me an enemy now?" Lara smiled thinly. "That's not what you thought a few days ago when you came to my bed."

Niki snarled. "A few days ago you were more wolf than Vampire. I don't know what you are now."

"You weren't looking for my wolf when you begged me to bite you." Lara leaned close, sending tendrils of erotic suggestion snaking over Niki's skin, teasing at her senses.

Niki's skin gleamed with sex-sheen, a flair of pelt streaked down her torso. The bones in her face grew heavy and hard. "Like I said—more Vampire than wolf."

"But still you want it," Lara murmured. Sylvan's words echoed in her mind. *Niki wants you to be as you once were.* But she could not go back—none of them could. Niki had to see her for who she was now, even if it meant losing her forever.

Niki's chest heaved but her voice was steady. "You can make me want, but I will never let you bite me. I don't need what you have to offer."

"Are you sure?" Lara's hunger flared as a wave of pheromones washed over her. Niki was a dominant Were, potent and powerful in her own right. Lara's vision turned scarlet. Bloodlust gripped her mind. She battered at Niki's resolve.

"I am mated," Niki gasped. "I'll kill you before I'll submit."

"You won't win, little Wolf," Lara murmured, one hand circling Niki's throat.

Niki gripped Lara's arm, her claws drawing blood.

"Taste." Lara offered her forearm. "You remember, don't you?"

Raina pressed close to the bars, mindful of the silver that would burn on contact. "Lara, let her go."

"She doesn't want to go," Lara said gruffly, the ache to feed a hollow pit of pain consuming her. Her sex tensed and filled. She tightened her hold, drew Niki near. "Do you?"

Niki forced herself to back up, feeling as if her skin would melt from her bones. Lara's gaze was a fevered caress. "I want your bite—not you. And it's not my doing, it's yours. And now I know the difference." She broke away abruptly and stalked off.

Lara watched her go, fury and need and agonizing hunger at war with the fading remnants of the love they'd once shared. She could catch her between one second and the next, and if she set her canines in Niki's throat, Niki would give herself, willingly. In the moment, Niki would give everything—her body, her blood, her soul. But only in the mindless lust of thrall.

Shuddering, Lara gripped the cell bars with both hands, swallowing the feeding hormones that flooded her mouth, struggling with need like a thousand knives flaying her alive.

"What is it you need?" Raina whispered, Lara's pain so tangible she felt it in her bones. She ached for her, not understanding why, but unable to ignore the pressing demand to ease her suffering. She reached through the bars, hissing when light contact against one of the bars scorched her skin.

"Don't," Lara breathed harshly. "You can't help me. Don't hurt yourself trying."

"You're in pain. You need to feed again."

Lara shook her head violently, fighting the bloodlust that burned her alive. She shouldn't need more—Zahn had fed her. Jody's voice. *You have the appetites of a newling and the power of a Risen.* Lara sagged to her knees, doubling over in agony. Raina was so close. Her unique musky scent coated her tongue. She tasted the power in Raina's blood through every cell. Were blood—so potent, so euphoric. She wanted to reach through the bars and pull her close, wanted to bury herself in her throat, lose herself in the ecstasy of her flesh. "Get away from the bars. Back away from me."

"No." Raina couldn't bear her pain—she ached, her flesh burning. If she didn't ease Lara's agony, she feared she would bleed herself. She pushed her arm farther through the bars, ignoring the burn when her forearm and shoulder brushed cold steel and hot silver. "Drink. Lara, take what you need from me."

"No," Lara said, but even as she spoke she grasped Raina's arm and pressed her mouth to her wrist. Raina's pulse beat strong and fast beneath her lips. Lara moaned.

"Do it," Raina whispered, aching to feel the bright sliver of pain, wondering if the ecstasy would be anywhere near as intense as she remembered. "Bite."

Lara's canines slid effortlessly through Raina's skin and into her vein. Hot blood filled her mouth, and she injected the Vampire hormones into Raina's body.

"Yes," Raina cried, her back arched, her face transforming as her cat lunged for freedom. "So good."

Lara's cells erupted with power and life. A sea of pleasure filled her as Raina's orgasm flooded her blood with pheromones, and Lara drank. Her power, Raina's pleasure fed on themselves, growing, gathering force, transforming them both. The pain became a distant throb. Lara's belly tensed and she pressed against the bars, reaching through with her free hand to clasp Raina's neck. Raina's hips thrust with each pulse of her orgasm, in perfect synchrony with Lara's mouth on her wrist.

When the hunger was bearable, Lara pulled away.

"No," Raina gasped. "More. Don't stop."

"Enough. You have to hunt tonight." Lara's thighs quivered, and her skin dripped with pheromones. She needed Raina under her, needed to spend between her thighs.

Raina forced her eyes open and read the wild hunger in Lara's face. She might be Vampire, but her pelt had risen and her call was a Were's, stronger than any Raina had ever known. "Let me give you the rest."

"Not out of pity."

"No," Raina murmured, knowing it was true. "Not pity. Need."

"My need," Lara said.

"Mine too. Come closer."

Lara pressed full body against the silver-impregnated bars. Her flesh did not burn. She forced her hips tightly to the space between two bars. "Please."

Raina cupped her sex.

Lara's face morphed and she growled.

Raina shivered with the rush of incredible power as Lara surrendered. She squeezed, felt the hard nodes throb between her fingers, brushed her thumb over Lara's clitoris and felt the rapid flutter of her orgasm about to break free. Lara was hers to control if she chose. But now, *now*, she wanted only the pleasure. She stroked her, firm long strokes until Lara threw her head back and, throat convulsing, released over Raina's hand, coating her arm and thighs. Raina's sex contracted and she came again.

"Are you hurt?" Raina asked when she came back to herself. "The bars. They're silver."

Lara gripped the bars in both hands and pushed away, breaking contact between her exquisitely sensitive flesh and Raina's hand. Her body was unmarked, as if the bars had been nothing but steel. "I'm fine. Let me see your arm."

Raina held out her arm. The burns were gone. "When you fed from me, they healed. Is that—"

"Get some rest," Lara said roughly. She didn't know why the silver didn't hurt her, didn't know why she could heal Raina with her bite. But she knew Raina was dangerous. Raina had controlled her with nothing but a touch. She'd been helpless, mindless, lost in sex frenzy. Raina was her weakness—a deadly one. "We'll do battle before morning."

"What about you?"

"I'm fine. I'll have someone bring the cubs to you." Lara turned her back and strode toward the hall that led to freedom. Leaving Raina caged tore at her, but she had no choice. She'd given her word to the Alpha, and if Raina broke free, one of the guards would surely kill her.

"Your need," Raina called out, "doesn't frighten me."

Lara paused, looked over her shoulder. Her eyes were cold again, her smile scornful. "It should."

❖

Niki stood guard outside the detention area. She snarled when Lara stepped through the heavy iron door and closed it, slamming the lock into place.

"I should kill you for what you did back there," Niki growled.

"You've wanted to fight me all night. But we have more important duties. Your vengeance will have to wait."

"You fed from her," Niki said, loathing in her tone.

Lara smiled. "Would you rather it had been you?"

"Why the cat?" Niki shook her head, her expression confused, pained. "There are wolves who would feed you, who would be proud to feed you. You may not remember, but we do. You are *centuri*."

"Niki," Lara murmured, leaning back against the rough wood wall, "I was, before. But that wolf is dead. I'm Vampire now."

"I know." Niki raked a hand through her hair. "I *know*. But I don't want to lose you."

"You know what I'll become."

"Do I?" Niki shook her head. "Maybe none of us knows who we will be."

Lara stroked Niki's cheek, no thrall in her touch. Only memory. "You will ever and always be Sylvan's right hand. I envy you."

"I'm not who I was before." Niki gazed toward the Compound, sensing Sophia in the nursery, absorbing her strength and feeling her uncertainty wane. "Everything is different now."

"You love her?"

"More than that."

Lara nodded. "I would tell you I'm sorry about tempting you, but I'm not. I would feed from you now if you'd let me."

Niki grinned, a feral grin. "We are hunters. We will always be hunters. A hunter takes her prey when and where she can."

"You would not be easy prey."

"Not anymore."

Lara straightened. "It seems we will have a chance to hunt together soon."

The door at the far end of the hall opened, and Jody came through with Zahn, Rafaela, the captain of her Vampire guard, and Jace. Jody's glacial gaze skimmed over Niki and Lara, one brow rising. "The prisoner needs to tell us where she thinks we will find our quarry so we can plan our attack."

Lara said, "She'll need a few minutes with the cubs before we go."

Jody smiled. *Still taking care of her, Warlord?*

It won't pay to have her distracted while we hunt.

"Of course," Jody said aloud. "Get them. She can see them after we talk."

Niki said, "I'll have Sophia bring them here."

"Do that," Jody said. "And then we will hunt."

Niki said to Jace, "Guard this door. No one approaches the prisoner other than the Alpha, Liege Gates, or," she glanced at Lara, "the warlord."

"Yes, *Imperator*," Jace snapped, taking up a post next to the door. Niki loped through the hall, across the Compound, and into the infirmary. She paused outside the hall leading to the nursery. She was still aroused from Lara's thrall and didn't want to disrupt everyone within. She extended her call to her mate, and a moment later, Sophia stepped through the doorway from the nursery, a question in her eyes. "Niki?"

"You need to take the cubs to Raina. We're leaving soon."

"Of course. I'll just be a minute." Sophia gripped Niki's hand. "What's happened to you?"

"I'm all right."

Sophia smiled wryly. "No, you're not. Don't you think I can feel your need?"

"It's nothing."

"Don't tell me that." Sophia snarled softly. "Someone has been tempting my mate. Who was it?"

Niki was vulnerable to seduction without the mate bite Sophia refused to give her, but she wanted no other, would take no other. She wrapped an arm around Sophia's waist and pulled her close. "No one tempts me but you. Just a Vampire playing games."

Sophia sucked in a breath. She knew Niki was blood addicted. "Who? Lara?"

Niki buried her face in Sophia's neck and the sex frenzy settled. Her mind righted itself. Stronger now, she murmured, "It doesn't matter."

Sophia cradled Niki's jaw in both hands and kissed her. "I told you before I'm not threatened by your needs. If she—"

"No." Niki's wolf flared in her eyes. "I don't need her or any Vampire's bite. I don't want it. Just you."

Sophia brushed her fingers through Niki's hair. "Are you all right now?"

"I will be, after a few more minutes with you."

Sophia took her hand and pulled her into the room across the hall and closed the door. She pressed into her, her arms around Niki's neck. "Then make the most of them."

Chapter Sixteen

Sylvan yanked on a pair of leather pants, strapped a sheathed blade to her right thigh with a leather thong, and buckled a studded black leather belt around her waist. She slipped into a sleeveless black silk shirt that left her arms bare. Her wolf rode so close to the surface her bones and muscles were heavy, her body a brutal weapon. Drake watched from across the bedroom, her breasts drawing tight and full as Sylvan's call engulfed her.

"Your wolf looks hungry." Drake crossed to her and stroked Sylvan's chest.

"Be careful, Prima," Sylvan murmured. "I have no patience for teasing."

"No?" Drake kissed her. "Good. I like you impatient."

Sylvan rumbled and eased away to grab her phone from the dresser and shove it into her front pocket. "Then you'll be very happy later."

"Francesca's going to have a hard time keeping her hands off you tonight," Drake observed dryly.

Sylvan grinned, but her icy blue eyes showed no humor. "I'm not visiting Francesca as a friend or an ally, and I want her to know that."

"If she so much as lifts a finger—"

Sylvan bounded across the space between them and pulled Drake into her arms. She kissed her, fevered and hard. "No one will dare to touch a mated wolf, especially not the Alpha when her Prima is anywhere near."

"Just remarking," Drake murmured, nipping at Sylvan's lip. She sat on the side of the bed and pulled on her boots. The shirt she had chosen was too tight, and she pulled that off in favor of a looser one. So few wolf Weres had delivered in recent years, she wasn't sure how to judge her progress, but the fifty-day gestational period most wolves experienced seemed accelerated in her. Absently, she smoothed the plain black cotton shirt down over the fullness in her abdomen and tucked it into her black BDUs. They still fit, but not for much longer.

"You'll be too pregnant soon for hunting," Sylvan said, pride in her voice. "Then you'll have to settle into the den and let me and our wolves hunt for you."

Drake lifted her brow. "That's what you would like to think, Alpha. But I've been doing a little research, and the maternal females tell me it's perfectly safe for me to run in pelt until it's time for the pups to arrive."

Sylvan frowned. "And who gave you permission to talk to them about our pregnancy?"

Drake laughed, her heart lightening at the perplexity that crossed Sylvan's face. "You really do need training, Alpha."

"I don't know what you're talking about. If there's something you need to know—"

"I'm quite capable of finding out for myself." Drake wrapped her arms around Sylvan's waist. "Be careful tonight. If there is a fight, I don't want you thinking about me. I promise I'll step aside. I won't do anything to endanger our young."

"I know. I don't expect bloodshed, but with Francesca"—Sylvan raised a shoulder—"there's no way to know what games she plays."

"Then it's best we act before she does. Surprise is our best weapon."

The sound of the Rover pulling up in front of their private quarters signaled it was time.

"Remember this," Sylvan said. "No matter what I say tonight, the only thing that matters to me is my family and my Pack."

"I know," Drake said. "I trust you with my heart, with my life."

Sylvan's face went cold, the fire in her eyes no longer flame, but ice. "Centuries ago we fought to escape our servitude to the Vampires, and then we fought the other Praeterns to claim our lands. We will never go back—no matter who we must fight."

❖

"Bring her out," Niki said, unlocking the bars to Raina's cell.

The blond wolf and one Raina hadn't seen before, a muscular green-eyed female they called Dasha, came in to get her. Both were dressed for battle in fatigue pants, tight green T-shirts, and boots. Dasha, the more senior one, carried a stun gun. The blonde held a pair of gleaming metal cuffs in a gloved fist.

"Cuff her hands," Niki said.

Raina stiffened, showing her canines. She didn't like to be touched—even when she was coupling, she only tolerated the contact for the length of time it took to blunt her heat. Cats in general were solitary, hunting and roaming alone or with their young. They only congregated for purposes of mating or fighting. To be manhandled by an enemy sent her cat into a near frenzy. Her skin quickly slicked with aggressive pheromones. She couldn't best both of them, but her cat didn't care. She wasn't going to allow them to shackle her with silver again. This time they would have to stun her.

"No," Lara said, walking into the cell. "If we're attacked en route, she won't be able to defend herself. She's not going anywhere."

"You don't know she won't try to escape. You may trust her," Niki said, "but I don't."

Lara stepped between the two Were soldiers and Raina, blocking the stun gun Dasha held with her own body. She slid her hand around Raina's neck, ignoring the two wolves, and caught Raina's gaze. Her eyes bored into Raina's, holding her in the most excruciatingly pleasurable paralysis. Raina had never met another dominant so strong. Even the wolf Alpha had not affected her this way. Softly, Lara said, "Your word, Alpha Carras?"

Heat flowed from Lara's fingers down Raina's spine, spreading out inside her, settling her cat, soothing her in a way she'd never experienced before. And as much as she was soothed, she was excited. Her cat's pacing increased, but she didn't want to fight. She wanted something else. Her pelt flowed molten beneath her skin, her blood hummed with anticipation, her sex readied. She wanted to rub against this wolf, this enemy, this Were who stirred her in ways she didn't understand and still ached for. "My word, Warlord."

Lara's brows rose at the formal address, but she smiled. "Good." She let her grip linger, absorbing Raina's anger and something else. *Desire.* Her wolf circled restlessly, a familiar pressure building inside her to run, to tangle. But with a cat? She scented Raina's desire, the taste of her blood a fragrant memory. Bloodlust stirred her Vampire core and she let her thrall sweep out, enclosing Raina in a wave of sexual craving. Sex and blood, hunger and desire. Two driving forces she couldn't separate. She shuddered, pelt streaking her abdomen, her canines lengthening, feeding hormones flooding her throat. She wanted Raina. Her blood called for Raina's, her wolf dared Raina's cat to run, to chase, to tangle. Raina leaned into her hand, her green cat's eyes liquid with promise. Abruptly, Lara turned her face to Niki and the soldiers, escaping Raina's gaze. She wasn't the only one capable of thrall—Raina captured her with just a look. "We're wasting time."

Raina shuddered as if pulled from a dream. Her heart raced and she was wet. Full and wet and ready. She hissed in frustration—that a wolf could call her so strongly, that a Vampire could tempt her so wildly.

Lara squeezed her neck gently and released her. "Raina will not run."

Niki growled but conceded. "The Rover's outside." She paused, met Lara's gaze. "Good hunting, *Centuri*."

Lara nodded gravely. "And to you, *Imperator*."

Raina walked beside Lara, who was silent as they crossed the Compound to the waiting SUV, the two guards close behind them. Lara did not touch her, but Raina was aware of Lara's every breath. She'd only ever sensed her cubs so acutely. Even other cats in her Pride, with whom she could connect over great distances, did not resonate so deeply in her awareness. Maybe it was the blood they'd shared, and the idea did not repel her as it once did. She pushed the disquieting realization aside—she had to survive the night. Then she would find a way to gain her freedom.

Inside the vehicle, Raina sat between Lara and Dasha on a long bench bolted to one side of the rear compartment. The other wolf sat opposite her with the Vampire she'd seen in the hall outside the Alpha's headquarters. Dark hair, blue eyes, thin as a steel reed. The other one, Lara's master, sat up front with a third Vampire who drove. A small force, but that was better. They could move quickly, and they'd have to. The cats along the border were always on guard against wolf attacks, although they weren't as frequent as cat incursions into wolf territory. Now, without an Alpha to impose even a semblance of order on the small fragmented groups within the Pride, the dominant cats were likely fighting for supremacy. Raiding parties skirmishing in the mountains would have sentries posted.

Jody glanced into the back. "We'll drive as far as the area where Lara found you and cross into cat territory there. How far do you anticipate we'll need to go before we find the ones we're looking for?"

"The humans hired three or four dominants as guards. They used to hunt in this area, so hopefully, at least one of them will still be around."

"What would they do if they scented you?" Jody asked casually.

"Track me," Raina said, "until they could gather a force and set up an ambush as quickly as possible."

"They'll be looking for you, won't they?"

Raina shrugged. "They'll know I wouldn't stay in Pack land any longer than necessary. I would have been gone in another day if Lara hadn't come across my den."

"Where would they expect you to go?"

"I have loyal followers in the north, but after I was attacked, most of them went into hiding, fearing those who drove me out would hunt them next. I would go there to rebuild my forces."

Lara turned to face Jody. "You want to use her as bait."

Even running with the Rover's lights off, the moonlight was enough to show the Vampire's savage smile. "That will probably be the quickest way to draw the attention of the ones we seek. We'll send Dasha and Jace in one direction as decoys, and Raina can head north along the path they would expect her to take. We'll split their forces."

"And our own." Lara's voice had deepened, her displeasure plain. "Once they scent Raina back in cat territory, they'll send their heaviest force after her. She won't have enough protection."

"She'll have four Vampires as backup. More than enough to handle any number of cats."

Raina had counted three Vampires, but then she realized that Jody counted Lara as Vampire. To her, Lara was Were, even though she knew she wasn't completely. But she wasn't Vampire either. The remote indifference that emanated from the other Vampires was missing in her. She was fire where they were ice, she was raw power where they were elegant control. Lara tasted like life where the others radiated the dark shadow of death. Lara was…other.

Lara growled softly. "If more cats have massed in the region since Raina disappeared, she may need more protection than we can give her. It won't help us if they trap her and tear her to shreds."

"If they trap her," the Vampire across from them commented, "they'll be even more distracted. And we will have what we came for."

"Remember your station, Rafaela," Lara said with such deadly softness the hairs on the back of Raina's neck bristled.

Rafaela murmured, "I am yours to command, Warlord, if in service to my Liege."

Lara's canines flashed and the rumble in her chest grew louder. "You are mine to command as long as I live, Master of the Guard."

"As you say, Warlord." Rafaela smiled, her show of incisors a subtle taunt.

Raina instinctively slid her hand along the inside of Lara's thigh. "It's not a bad plan."

"You're not at full strength," Lara said quietly, amber flames igniting in her eyes.

The muscles beneath Raina's fingers were stone. She stroked, letting her cat's claws extend enough to puncture Lara's pants. She broke skin, her cat making her strength known. "You forget that I am an Alpha. I'm capable of doing what needs to be done."

"I won't have you hurt in power games that have nothing to do with you."

Raina stilled, wary and uncertain. She'd always been alone. Since she'd been a cub, she'd fought for her place in the Pride, fought for the position her instincts drove her to take. To lead, to protect. No one had ever stood between her and danger, and only her willingness to die to hold her place had won her the loyalty of her followers. She did not trust this wolf who fought for a Vampire, but her cat pushed on. Pushed closer, drawn by instinct over reason.

"I'll be all right," Raina said. "And you will be near."

Lara's hand covered Raina's, pressed it against her thigh. "Then I'll run with you."

Raina laughed. "A wolf in cat territory? You do want to bring everyone down on us."

"My wolf will bring the dominants, won't she?"

"She will bring every cat within fifty miles."

Jody laughed softly. "I like that plan, Warlord. After all, we might as well take advantage of the wolf you harbor as long as we can."

Lara turned to meet Jody's gaze with cool eyes. "My wolf is not going anywhere."

"We'll see, won't we," Jody murmured. "And tonight we'll see just how well she fights."

Chapter Seventeen

Nicholas Gregory was in bed, but not asleep, lying quietly in the dark on his back while his wife, Penelope, breathed softly beside him. He stared at the ceiling, distantly aware of the occasional rumble of traffic outside their town house, his thoughts on his next move in a plan he'd set in motion two decades before. That's when he'd first become aware of a transformed genetic strain his researchers had at first thought was a new mutation. Only further investigation had disclosed that the strain was very old—as old as mankind—and the subhumans who carried the mutation had been living among humans, in some cases even *interbreeding*, for millennia. His great-great-grandfather had founded the family's fortune with an apothecary shop that had grown into a pharmaceutical giant, and now Gregory Research was an international corporation involved in everything from medical research to clandestine biowarfare. Bad enough he and other Americans should have to compete for control of global markets with the rising tide of third-world nations, but to live side by side with animals and undead abominations asking to be treated as citizens? He would see them all truly dead first. He'd already sacrificed more than any man should have to in this war—his only son had been killed by Weres. And soon he would have his retribution.

He thought of the explosion at Mir Industries and hoped he had crippled Sylvan Mir's organization enough to prevent, or at least delay, her scientists from studying the subjects of his own experimentation. No one, not even the Praetern Shadow Lords he pretended to work with, really knew his long-term agenda—the eradication of every last Praetern from the face of the earth. And he wasn't alone in his desire to see the world cured of these diseased creatures. He only hoped he wouldn't have to keep up the pretense of working with the Praetern rebels very much longer. He detested their primitive behavior and uncivilized urges.

He thought of his last meeting with Francesca, the Vampire leader, and as it had done that night, his cock hardened. Evidence enough that a creature who could bespell a man of his control could not be trusted among lesser men. She and her kind were as dangerous as the Were animals, even if superficially more sophisticated. He brushed his palm over his erection and drew his hand away when pleasure jolted along his spine. Breathing hard, he ignored the pressure in his groin that demanded release. He was not an animal.

When his cell phone vibrated on the antique mahogany nightstand beside his bed, his first thought was Veronica. She had the annoying habit of calling him at home even when he had reminded her on multiple occasions not to. Her way of proving she was in control and didn't take orders from him. She seemed to think he was unaware of her little power plays, but he hadn't risen to the pinnacle of political and financial supremacy without learning to recognize—and neutralize—those who sought to manipulate him.

Fortunately, Penelope habitually took a sleeping pill at bedtime and never awakened even when he left the bed in the middle of the night. He slid the Egyptian cotton sheets aside and swung his legs to the floor, lifting the cell phone at the same time. He rose, grasped his robe from a chair beside the bed, and walked out into the hall before answering. "Yes?"

"Nicholas." The smooth baritone greeting was instantly recognizable and Nicholas was instantly alert.

"Good evening." Nicholas didn't greet the man by name, uncertain of their security. His phone was untraceable, one he carefully changed every few weeks, providing the number to only a very select few. But he didn't trust anyone else to be as cautious, even when they should be.

"I'm in my car. I think we should talk, don't you?"

The question wasn't really a question, but a command. Nicholas was usually the one arranging meetings and giving orders, but in this instance, he had no choice. A wise man recognized the power of another and didn't challenge until he was certain of victory. "Of course. Where and when?"

"I'm circling the park. I could pick you up on the corner of State and Lark in, say, five minutes?"

"I'll be there."

The call was disconnected without any other pleasantries, and Nicholas hurried into his dressing room. He slid a suit from its clear plastic dry-cleaning bag and laid it carefully over a chair back and then donned pressed boxers, a snowy white dress shirt, and dark socks. He thought about a tie but decided against it. He could be casual, considering the hour. After pulling on the pants and jacket, he slipped into dress shoes, grabbed his wool topcoat, and hurried down the wide central stairs. The door from the servants' quarters at the rear of the first-floor hall opened and his assistant stepped out. William was dressed as he might be for the start of a regular workday in conservative dark trousers, pressed shirt, and tie. His hair was neatly combed. "Can I be of assistance, sir?"

"No, thank you. I'm just going out for a few minutes." Nicholas trusted William, who had been with him for almost twenty-five years, completely—even more than his wife. Their association went beyond the professional but stopped short of friendship, of course. William was unmarried, and Nicholas had been aware for years of William's attraction to him. He didn't return the interest—he had never had any unnatural feelings in that regard, although he never discouraged William's attachment. Perhaps subtly encouraged it. Affection strengthened loyalty. He smiled and waited for William to join him, briefly gripping William's arm and leaving his hand there as he spoke. "I appreciate you being so available, but I'll be fine tonight."

"Very good, sir."

"I'll see you at breakfast, then?" Nicholas smiled as he met William's gaze.

"Of course."

"Good. Good night, William."

"Good night…sir."

William disappeared as quickly as he had emerged, and Nicholas walked out into the cold, clear night. A limousine idled at the corner, and he quickly glanced up and down the row of brownstones. A cab circled the park, but the streets were empty. He strode rapidly toward the corner, and as he approached the limo, the rear door opened. He slid into the spacious backseat of the Town Car and pulled the door closed as it sped away.

The silver-haired, patrician man across from him puffed slowly on a fragrant cigar. A privacy shield separated them from the driver.

"Senator," Nicholas said in a polite but not deferential tone, "how might I be of assistance?"

"I think we might assist each other," Senator Daniel Weston said. "You and I might have a common interest or, should I say, a common adversary."

"I wouldn't be surprised," Nicholas said, carefully not committing himself. "You and I seem to be of similar minds on many important matters of the day."

"We do. We do." The senator from New York slipped a silver cigar case from the inside pocket of his custom-cut suit jacket, opened it, and held it out in Nicholas's direction. "Try one. They're…imported. Very fine blend."

Nicholas ordinarily didn't smoke, but he took the cigar, wafted it slowly past his nose, and nodded. "Excellent."

The senator extended a gold-plated lighter, its flame flickering. Nicholas took his time lighting the cigar, allowing the smoke to circle in his mouth before he exhaled. "It's refreshing to see a man with exquisite tastes and a solid set of moral principles representing us in these challenging times. Which is why I am always happy to contribute to your campaign efforts."

Which he did—very generously too.

"I feel the same way about your efforts in the private sector," Weston said as the car glided through the night. "If only everyone I had to deal with understood the importance of handling some issues with caution. Sylvan Mir, for example—she and the Coalition for Praetern Rights are growing impatient with my committee's handling of the equal rights bill, but such things can't be rushed."

"No," Nicholas said mildly, "they can't." Weston's committee had delayed bringing the bill up for a vote for months, but Nicholas suspected he couldn't delay much longer. "But you can't expect some… individuals…to understand how a sophisticated system of government works."

Weston laughed. "Yes, well. Ordinarily a little pressure to hurry things along wouldn't bother me, but she's also growing more popular, and in politics, popularity is power."

"She seems to be winning over a substantial portion of the human population," Nicholas agreed. And that was exactly why he was trying to turn human opinion against Mir and her animals. The rest of the world needed to see them as the threat he had always known them to be.

"The unfortunate incident at her facility this morning will probably distract her for a short time," Weston mused, "but I'm not sure that's a long-term solution."

"The Praeterns do tend to be violent by nature," Nicholas observed. "I wouldn't be surprised if one of her own objected to her rising superiority and nature took its course."

"That would solve any number of problems." The senator puffed silently for another minute. "I understand this fringe group that took credit for the destruction at Mir Industries has been targeting other laboratories."

Nicholas couldn't admit to running secret experimental laboratories, but he suspected Weston had almost as many spies as he did. Undoubtedly there had been rumors. "The animal rights activists? Yes, they are getting to be a nuisance."

"I imagine it will take considerable funds to rebuild an installation like that."

"Undoubtedly, and of course, the longer it takes to rebuild, the greater the delay in finding effective ways of dealing with potentially destructive forces in our midst." Nicholas expected relocating Veronica's labs would cost him a million or two, possibly more if he wanted to get the experiments back on line in a few weeks.

"I oversee several committees that might be of assistance in facilitating the recovery of those institutions. Of course, I wouldn't be directly involved."

"I understand Dr. Veronica Standish is conducting any number of important investigative studies," Nicholas said, keeping his own distance from accountability.

"Yes. She's apparently quite capable and quite…accomplished."

"I'm sure she could explain the severity of the crisis and the importance of these studies to someone you designated."

Weston smiled. "Well then. I think we should be able to clear up these troubling matters very quickly, don't you?"

"Absolutely." Nicholas had just been paid by a United States senator to assassinate Sylvan Mir, not that he hadn't already planned to do it. But now he had protection. "If there's anything else you want to discuss, call me at any time."

"I'll see you at the fund-raiser, I hope."

Nicholas extended his hand and the senator shook it. "Of course."

❖

The Rover bumped to a stop in the shadow of an overhanging rocky ledge, and the two Vampires in the front got out. A moment later the back doors opened, and Jody stood outlined in moonlight, as silent as a shimmering blade. Raina hissed quietly. Vampire scent was so subtle, so foreign, she often couldn't tell they were near. Good when they were friends, deadly when foe.

"We're only a few hundred yards from the border," Jody said. "The Weres will cross as a group and we will follow."

Lara climbed out and Raina followed with the other two Weres. The Vampire who had been sitting across from her was gone—misted into the darkness faster than her eyes could follow. Her cat growled in displeasure, wanting to be far away from these strange dead-but-not-dead creatures.

"I'll run with the Weres," Lara said, underscoring her place with the Vampires while claiming her separateness. Her Vampire essence might be in service to Jody, but she was apart from the others.

Jody went on as if Lara hadn't spoken, silently acknowledging Lara's plan. "As soon as the cats pick up your scent, Jace and Dasha will head south, drawing at least some of the rebel group away. Hopefully, once Raina's scent is recognized, the dominants will follow her."

Raina's skin prickled, as unsettled as her cat. She'd never run with anyone before. She'd never fought with anyone before. These Vampires and Weres were all soldiers, and they worked like a trained unit. She was the loner in the group, and she wondered if she would die alone this night.

Lara slid her hand onto Raina's neck. "Remember, I can't climb as quickly as you can—at least, not trees. Anywhere else, I can follow."

"You'll be at a disadvantage on the ground. You won't be able to escape a cat. We're larger and faster and stronger."

Lara laughed. "I am a *centuri*. I have fought every kind of adversary, including some of your cats. I'm still here. They're all dead."

"Your arrogance is going to get you killed, Wolf."

"Don't worry about me, Cat. Just don't try to escape." Lara squeezed Raina's neck, a caress more than a show of strength, the kind of touch Raina had never known.

Raina shivered, but her cat settled. She'd never been so at odds with her cat before—wary when her cat was not, wanting to run from a touch her cat seemed to crave. She would have pulled away from the wolf's hold on her, but some instinct held her in place. "You don't know these mountains, and we'll be moving quickly."

"I carry your essence in my blood," Lara whispered, her breath warm against Raina's throat. "I'll always know where you are. Even if you run."

She'd thought about it—running. Once they were in the forest, on her home territory, she would know every trail, every pass, every hiding place. She could leave the Weres and Vampires far behind. She might have to fight her way to sanctuary in the north, but she would've had to do that anyhow. She had been prepared for bloody battles. But if she escaped, she'd be leaving her cubs behind. And more than that. She'd be leaving Lara alone to face a group of feral cats who would think nothing of tearing a lone wolf to shreds.

"Just try to keep up," Raina grumbled.

Lara laughed, and Raina couldn't help but lean against her. Her cat demanded the contact, and she wanted it too. Lara's body was hot and hard, and her strength had been the only hope Raina had allowed herself to feel since long before she'd been captured. Before her only thought had been surviving long enough to see her cubs independent enough to live without her.

The other Vampires shaped out of the darkness at Jody's side as if they were shadows given form. Zahn said, "The trail into Pride land is clear, Liege."

"Are you ready, Warlord?" Jody asked.

"Yes," Lara said, caressing Raina's neck one more time before removing her hand.

"We won't intervene until you signal you've found the cat Weres we want," Jody said to Raina. "Try not to kill them."

"If we don't fight to kill, we won't have much time," Raina said.

Jody smiled, a smile so cold and lethal Raina's claws tore through her skin. "Then you'd best stay alive."

"And you had better be as good as you say you are," Raina said, "Vampire."

Jody laughed, brushing Raina's cheek with a fleeting caress. "I hope you're as strong as you are brave—and foolish."

Raina snarled but her cat arched at the strange icy heat.

"Until later, Warlord," Jody murmured, and then she was gone.

Lara took a deep breath and opened herself to her wolf. In a shimmering instant, she dropped to the ground in pelt. Her spirit came alive as the crisp air streamed through her nostrils and the scent of pine forest and pungent game flooded her senses. To her right, a husky brown wolf and a slender silver-streaked white one crouched, haunches quivering, awaiting her lead. She glanced to her left where a huge mountain lion padded restlessly back and forth, her great head swinging from side to side as she surveyed the forest, her ears flickering, her lips drawn back from her powerful jaws. Raina stopped pacing and regarded Lara steadily. Lara rumbled softly and loped forward until they were nearly nose to nose. *Ready, big Cat?*

Raina made a sound like a disgusted snort, her slanting green eyes glowing with energy and power. *Try not to get lost.*

Lara, smaller by nearly half but Vampire-strong, bumped Raina's shoulder hard and skirted out of reach as a huge paw swiped at her. Drawing her lips back in a taunting challenge, she streaked off into the forest. Raina was beside her in an instant, and together, they raced into the night to hunt the hunters.

Chapter Eighteen

Drake watched the night flash by in a mad chiaroscuro of distorted shapes and strands of moonlight as Niki drove the Rover toward the outskirts of Albany, staying off the interstate and flirting with the speed limits. Sylvan wanted their business at Nocturne concluded well before dawn. The Vampire blood club at dawn was not a place any of them wanted to be—the humans and Praeterns who frequented the club came for the sex and the ecstasy of the Vampire's bite, but the Vampires had only one desire. They were hunters and the club was their hunting ground—they were there for the blood. And at dawn, with the threat of the strengthening UV rays that would weaken them all and might immolate some, they would be in a feeding frenzy. She and Sylvan and the other dominant Weres could probably fight off a handful of blood-crazed Vampires. But a few hundred? She'd rather not test Sylvan's ability to telepathically channel all the strength of the Pack.

She rode in the back of the Rover with Katya beside her and Andrew across the way. They were both agitated, which didn't surprise her. A trip to Nocturne usually put any wolf on edge. The place was a blood pit—thick with sex pheromones and the tang of fresh blood—more than enough to set off any Were's aggressive urges. On top of that, even the strongest wolf was susceptible to thrall, and for a wolf, the idea of being out of control or controlled by a stronger, more dominant enemy was worse than death. Andrew rumbled quietly, and she could sense his wolf circling uneasily, suspicious and ready to fight. She slid across the space and slipped her arm around his shoulders. He immediately rubbed his cheek against hers. His discomfort rolled over her in dark waves—more unease than just a trip to Nocturne should induce.

"What do you sense?" Drake asked. "A trap? Something the Alpha needs to know?"

"No. I—no. Nothing like that. I'm sorry." He dragged his hands up and down his thighs, his claws making light scratching sounds on his leather pants. "I've never liked going there. Most of the time, I'm driving, so I just wait in the car."

Drake knew that Sylvan used to visit the club, that she saw Francesca and that Francesca had been her lover, of sorts. She understood it, and still her wolf growled savagely. Her possessive rage broadcast to Andrew, and he shuddered. If they hadn't been in the SUV he probably would have dropped to his knees. Drake drew a breath, settled herself. Reminded her wolf Sylvan was hers and only hers. She couldn't let Sylvan walk into a trap, and Andrew was not himself.

"Is there some particular reason you don't want to go inside?"

Andrew stared at the floor between his long, lean thighs. "There was a Were, a wolf in our Pack—we used to be close. We were in *sentrie* training. Thought we'd be *centuri* together."

"Mating close?"

"I don't know. I'd hoped, but there were difficulties."

Drake wondered at Andrew's reluctance to give details. Weres were pansexual until adolescence, and some remained that way, so she doubted his vagueness had to do with gender. For some reason he didn't want her to know the Were's identity. Her silence encouraged him to continue.

"We went there one night. I don't know why. Young and stupid, I guess. But we'd heard that a lot of other Weres went there, and that the sex was…awesome." He winced and ran a hand through his thick red-brown hair. His misery was palpable.

Drake rubbed his back, staying near, letting him lean on her for safety and comfort. "I can understand the appeal. And the Vampires are very beautiful, all of them."

He shot her a look, his expression intense. "None of them come close to you, Prima."

She almost smiled, touched by the love and loyalty of the *centuri* who guarded her and Sylvan, not only physically, but emotionally and spiritually as well. These Weres would die for them without a single thought. And beyond giving their lives, they gave their hearts. Her throat tightened and she slid her hand to his neck. "What happened?"

"We…It was so crowded, so many bodies, so many sounds. The scent of blood and sex was everywhere, so potent. My wolf practically went crazy."

"I can imagine."

Andrew looked at her. "His did too."

"You said you were young. Adolescent wolves have a hard time controlling those urges."

He sighed. "We were just out of *sentrie* training, but we were still old enough."

A good ten years before, Drake guessed. She couldn't ever remember seeing Andrew with anyone, but he couldn't have remained celibate all that time. Even a few weeks without tangling was a biological hardship for a Were. "What happened?"

"We spent the night, or most of the night, with one Vampire or another. Sometimes more than one at a time. It was everything the rumors had said it would be—intense, mind-bending. We were young and strong and the only reason we stopped was the sun came up and the Vampires disappeared." His voice had taken on a tortured cadence. "When I left, I had just enough sense to look back over the night and know I never wanted it again. But he did."

"It happens quickly for some," Drake said. "The blood addiction."

"I know. I don't know if it was the blood or the sex or both, but he couldn't stay away. And I couldn't go with him."

Unmated Weres weren't possessive or jealous, and casual coupling was normal. But once mating frenzy began, wolves were viciously possessive, and Andrew was a dominant. "You must have been serious."

"I was serious enough that I would have mated with him."

"I'm sorry. What happened to him?"

"The Alpha knew—the Alpha always knows. She decided it was best if we didn't work together. Enoch's a unit chief at Mir Industries, working security. He lives off-Compound. We don't see each other much."

"If the Alpha knew you were uncomfortable about tonight—"

"No," Andrew said quickly. "My personal feelings have nothing to do with my responsibility to the Alpha and the other *centuri*. I will go where I am needed." His shoulders relaxed and his voice softened. "I'm fine, Prima. Really. I'm sorry to have disturbed you. Just bad memories."

"It's no disturbance. And…if you ever want to talk about it again, I'm here."

He grasped her hand and rubbed his cheek against her fingers, his anxious rumbling quieting. "Thank you, Prima."

She stroked his hair. "No need to thank me. You are our wolf."

Drake resettled next to Katya. They were only a few miles from the club, and Katya seemed as unnaturally quiet now as Andrew had been agitated. Drake worried that the decadent atmosphere inside the club would throw Katya back into the nightmare she'd so recently escaped. She'd been brutalized by a Vampire in the laboratories, they knew that from the bite marks on her body and what little Katya could remember, although apparently her worst torturers had been human. But Sylvan had been sure she was ready, and Sylvan knew her wolves like no one else ever could. "How do you feel about going to Nocturne?"

"I'm fine," Katya said, her gaze fixed straight ahead. Her tone was even, controlled. Her wolf seemed calm, practically dozing. She didn't seem anxious, but all the same, bringing her into the midst of hundreds of feeding Vampires and sex-crazed Weres might not be a great idea so soon after her trauma.

"If you feel threatened—"

"I can do what the Alpha needs me to do," Katya said.

Her voice was filled with pride, and Drake suddenly understood that she was judging Katya by human standards, when human motivations and fears did not apply. The fastest way for Katya to heal was to have the trust of her fellow Weres and, most especially, her Alpha. To be asked to contribute on a mission would probably do more to salvage her damaged spirit than any amount of sympathy or empathy might. "I was a little worried, but I see that I didn't need to be."

Katya shot her a glance, her brows drawing together.

Drake smiled and squeezed her arm. "I was worried it might be hard for you. You've only been home a few days." Katya started to protest, but Drake went on. "Sylvan reminded me that you are a wolf, and you would stand."

Katya sucked in a breath, her eyes shining. "Yes. I will."

Drake hugged her. "I know."

Katya's wolf basked in the trust of the Alpha and the Prima, but she wasn't worried about visiting Nocturne. From the minute Niki had come to tell her that she would be going on a mission with the Alpha to the Vampire stronghold, she'd been filled with excitement. More excitement than just a hunt. More excitement, even, than serving the Alpha. Something else. Something that came from a place she didn't understand. Her blood raced, her wolf reared and paced frantically. Her body felt alive in a way it hadn't since before she'd been captured and taken to that place. Her belly was tight with anticipation, the pelt thickening low down in the center of her abdomen. She wasn't afraid to go to Nocturne. She couldn't wait.

❖

Raina ran and the wolves ran with her. Lara was fast, as fast as most cats, and kept pace with her, loping close to her right shoulder. The other two, silent and swift as wraiths, stayed back, guarding their flanks. She'd hunted wolves before, been hunted by them, but this was different. She imagined hunting with Lara by her side, driving prey between them, circling, stalking, chasing them down. Dragging the carcass back to their mountain den to feed the cubs, teaching them to hunt, teaching them to lead one day. She snarled and shook the strange pictures from her head. Wrong pictures. Wolves. Vampires. Not friends.

Something out there, Lara signaled.

Raina lifted her snout, sniffed the air. Lara was right. Cats, half a dozen or more, coming fast. The wolf shouldn't have scented them first. But the Vampire—she didn't know about the Vampire. Wrong.

Warn your wolves, Raina responded.

I already did. Lara bumped Raina's shoulder. *What next, big Cat? Your land. You lead.*

Tell them to fall back. When the cats get a little closer, they should break off our path and swing wide to the east and then south.

Done.

Raina slowed, reaching out for a glimmer of the distinctive cat consciousness—agile and quick, clever and deadly. Closer now. *The wolves should keep to the high ground. They'll be vulnerable until they reach Sylvan's border.*

The Vampires will keep them safe.

Raina snorted.

They're allies.

For now.

Lara's eyes glinted pure wolf. *Yes.*

Raina cut sharply to the left, heading due north. Lara kept pace and Jace and Dasha fell back even farther. Raina felt the cats who bore down on them at a furious pace clearly now. Four, five, six dominants, coming fast. *We'll have to fight.*

Lara growled softly. *Jace and Dasha are heading east now. Are any following?*

Two.

Lara's canines flashed. *Then let's ambush the rest. We'll only get tired if we keep running.*

They're wild, feral cats with nothing but death on their minds.

Lara grumbled, unable to sense anything other than raw rage. If the cats they were looking for were among these, they'd have a hard time holding them off in an open fight even long enough for Jody and Zahn to take them down. She was a Vampire, even if she was running in pelt. She could sustain almost any kind of injury—at least, her Vampire part could. Fire hadn't hurt her, and she had walked in the sun. But if a cat tore her throat open or ripped her guts free, she wasn't sure how long it would take to heal. And she couldn't leave Raina unprotected. *You take to the trees. I'll draw them in. When Jody reaches us, you take the one we want. We can kill the others.*

They'll overpower you before she reaches us.

Lara snorted. *They won't. I'm not what you think.*

You don't know what I think, Wolf. Raina cuffed Lara with a huge paw, practically making her stumble. Claws raked her shoulder, not deep enough to injure, but the temper behind it was potent.

Lara dove low and nipped Raina's belly hard. *Do you want to get your cubs back or not?*

Raina hissed. *What makes you think I won't just run and leave you to the ferals?*

You won't.

❖

Michel drained her glass of port and set the crystal glass on the marble-topped Queen Anne sideboard in Francesca's sitting room. Her blood awakened with a rush, and she carefully reached out with her mind, searching for the source of the stimulation. She found it, and her heart, filled with the blood she had taken from Veronica and the nameless Weres upstairs, beat faster. Visitors. The one whose blood still lingered in her cells called to her like a secret whisper in the dark. Her incisors punched down and her stomach tightened. She must find her.

"We're about to have guests," Michel said casually.

Francesca, apparently not yet aware of their visitors, lounged on the divan sipping her wine and toying with Raymond. She twitched one sculpted brow. "Oh? It seems this is a night for visitors. What fun."

"These may not be quite as cordial as the others." Michel tilted her head toward the other sofa where Veronica dozed in post-orgasmic stupor. "It's Sylvan and a cadre of wolves. She seems—intense."

"When isn't she?" Francesca laughed delightedly and rose. Her pale blue silk robe, loosely tied at the waist, opened to reveal her voluptuous body through the sheer dressing gown underneath. She brushed one hand down over her breasts, and her nipples hardened beneath the thin fabric. "Oh, this just gets more and more interesting."

"I don't think it wise for Dr. Standish to be here when Sylvan arrives."

"No, nor the Were sleeping off his little interlude with me down the hall. Have someone rouse him and take him out the back." She bent over Veronica and kissed her. "Veronica, darling."

Veronica's lids fluttered open, her irises wide and glazed. "What? I..." She blinked several times, awareness returning more quickly than Francesca might have expected. Veronica pushed upright. "I'm so sorry. How rude of me. I'm afraid I was quite undone."

Francesca brushed her thumb over Veronica's mouth and kissed her again. "You were wonderful, darling. And I'm the sorry one. I have an unexpected meeting. I'm going to have to leave you."

"I understand." Veronica, her voice stronger and her expression composed, straightened her clothing. "It was wonderful of you to see me at all."

"Believe me, it was our pleasure." Francesca mentally signaled for Luce, who knocked at the door a few seconds later. Raymond went to answer.

"Yes, Mistress?" Luce walked in, her skin faintly flushed from a recent feeding. She'd changed into a tight white shirt and black pants.

"Please see Dr. Standish home, and take care of anything she might need."

"Of course, Mistress." Luce bowed her head. "It would be my pleasure."

"Take my limo. It's in the private lot. You can avoid the crowds in the club that way."

"Yes, Mistress." Luce extended a hand to Veronica. "Dr. Standish."

Veronica grasped Luce's hand and stood, leaning ever so slightly into Luce's side. She glanced at Michel, then Francesca. "Thank you again. I hope I'll see you again very soon."

Francesca smiled. "You will, darling."

"Good night, then."

Francesca waited until she and Michel were alone again. "Well. I expect we know why Sylvan is here. What do you suggest we tell her?"

Michel thought about Katya and the memories she had blurred so Katya would not remember their times together. She hadn't wanted Katya to know she had been the one to force her to orgasm as part of Veronica Standish's experiments, or that she had lost herself in bloodlust when Katya's blood filled her. She'd been forced to erase Katya's memory of coming to her in the woods and offering herself. Of the sex and blood they'd shared then.

She could banish the memories of the feeding, but not the bond that now connected them. Katya didn't remember and Francesca couldn't know. Katya was a weakness, and Francesca exploited weaknesses, especially in those close to her. "I suggest we volunteer nothing and remember that when this is over, the strongest will survive, and I would not put my money on the humans."

Francesca trailed a fingertip down Michel's jaw and kissed her, slow and deep. "Nor would I, darling. The only one I count on is you."

"And I, you, Mistress." Michel slid an arm around Francesca's waist and pulled her close. Francesca's body molded to hers, while upstairs, Katya drew closer.

Chapter Nineteen

Raina vaulted into a towering hickory, its broad, thick branches forming a perfect ladder for climbing and its dense leaf cover shielding her from the ground. Below her, Lara slowed to a trot in a small clearing ringed by dense holly and evergreen bushes, intentionally allowing the converging cats to draw close. Raina crouched, ready to spring, her tail swishing angrily.

I don't like this.

Don't get twitchy, big Cat. Lara shot her a look, lip curled, pelt bristling. *You'll get your turn.*

Raina hissed down at her. She didn't let others fight her battles and she couldn't sense the Vampires, didn't trust them to provide backup. Lara was alone, and no matter how ferocious she was in a fight, she was one wolf against four cats. Four larger cats.

Lara swung to her right as the first cat broke from the underbrush, a male Raina didn't recognize by sight or scent. So many of the cats were strangers, living in isolation in densely forested pockets where they carved out a living from the land and rarely ventured into settled areas or associated with other cats. He charged Lara, and Lara whipped out of his path, taunting him with a quick nip at his back leg. He roared a challenge and leapt again. Lara was fast, faster than any wolf Raina had ever seen. She crisscrossed the small clearing below almost too quickly for Raina to follow, darting in and out of the underbrush, leading first one cat and then another on a twisting, turning chase. The next cat to plunge into the clearing was one Raina recognized. He was a survivalist, the leader of a small group of Weres who congregated in the far northern reaches of New Hampshire in a fortified compound, heavily armed and a law unto themselves. He would have sold his services to anyone, and he had.

Below her, Lara spun to face the new arrival, the largest male and clearly the leader. He stalked her, seeming to enjoy taking his time. While Lara's attention was focused on him, another cat, a female, darted in and raked her claws down Lara's flank. Blood instantly soaked her pelt, but she made no sound, showed no evidence of pain. She was stronger than they expected, but there were four of them and only one of her, and they were seasoned hunters. They quickly realized the way to overpower her was to trap her between the four of them.

They pulled back and circled, slowly converging on the tiny clearing with Lara in the center, drawing the noose tighter. Raina growled softly in her throat. She wouldn't wait much longer for the Vampires who might never come. Lara darted at the big male, snapping at his throat, drawing blood, but she couldn't pull him down. He threw her off, a ferocious club to her head knocking her across the clearing. Before she could get up, two of the other cats pounced, biting and clawing. Blood soaked the ground.

Raina readied to attack.

No! Stay back. I'm all right.

Lara shook them off, circled, and slashed her canines across the throat of the female closest to her. The cat screamed, blood fountaining from her throat, and dropped to the ground, writhing from the mortal wound. Lara backed away, keeping the other three in her sights. She limped, her rear leg damaged by a deep wound that had torn through muscle, exposing the bone in her hip. Raina shuddered as fire shot through her own leg. The leader, the one they wanted, circled Lara while the others flanked her. She was trapped and losing blood rapidly. They were going for the kill. Lara was out of time.

Raina dropped through the tree branches and landed on the big male's back with a furious scream.

The underground prison was not the dank, dark place Becca had envisioned, but a well-lit tunnel fifteen feet wide with a number of cells spaced out on each side. Some were enclosed only with thick metal bars, others by heavy wooden doors set with barred portals in the upper half. The young blond Were stopped in front of one of these and turned a heavy iron key in the lock.

"Thank you," Becca said as Jonathan pulled open the door. As she started to step through, Claude, one of Jody's senior guards, followed. She stopped him with a hand on his arm. "Just wait out here."

"The Liege instructed me to stay with you."

Claude's bland expression and nonchalant tone suggested that was all the explanation she should need. What the Liege said was law. God, Vampires were stubborn, every one of them. Becca knew better than to argue—that only made her head bleed. "You have followed her orders, and now I want you to wait in the hall while I talk to this man. If I need you, I'll call you."

The Vampire frowned. "The Liege—"

"Claude," Becca said softly, "the Liege wants you to guard me, and you are. I will be the judge of when and *if* I need you to do more."

He hesitated for a long moment, then bowed his head. "Yes, Consort."

"Thank you." Becca entered the cell, and the wooden door slid silently closed behind her. The space resembled a dorm room. An open window high on the far wall, too small for someone to climb through, admitted the fresh night air. A single bed with a thick military-style olive green blanket stood against one wall opposite a small desk with a wooden swivel chair and a single goosenecked lamp. A small sink and toilet occupied one corner. A brown-haired man with a three-day beard, maybe forty, dressed in the same black BDUs most of the Weres favored when they dressed at all, sat at the desk writing on a legal tablet with a pencil. He turned when she came in, his expression wary.

"I'm Becca Land," Becca said. "I believe we've talked on the phone."

The man stood. "Martin Hoffstetter. Yes, I called you."

"Can we talk?"

He grimaced and gestured to the room. "Do I have any choice?"

"I'm not here to justify why *you're* here," Becca said. "But I think we have the same goals—I think that's why you called me. And perhaps if we can establish that to the Alpha's satisfaction, your situation might change."

"Sorry. I know you're not responsible for me being locked up." He sighed and gestured to the chair. "Have a seat."

"Thanks," Becca said. Martin sat on the bed, and Becca turned the chair to face him and pulled a small recorder from the pocket of her dark blazer. "I'd like to record this. Is that all right with you?"

"I guess it really doesn't matter what I say, since human laws don't apply here. Asking for a lawyer isn't going to do me any good."

"If you're involved with what was done to Sylvan's wolves in that lab," Becca said, "you're lucky to be alive."

"Ah hell," Martin muttered. "Actually, they've treated me fine—took care of my injuries, fed me, haven't physically abused me—but I hate being a prisoner."

"Can you tell me how you were involved in the experiments on the kidnapped Weres?"

"I was a guard." His expression pained, he stared at his hands, gripping his thighs for a long moment. When he raised his head, remorse was evident in his dark brown eyes. "Like I told Alpha Mir, our group had heard rumors of some kind of experimentation going on in secret in these labs, but we didn't have any idea that captive subjects were being used. I went in undercover, and when we realized what was happening, we wanted to get word out without endangering our people on the inside or getting the subjects killed. Our unit leader decided we should contact you."

"Why not just tell me everything right away?"

"Those of us who worked inside didn't know a whole lot—we were transported in blackout vans, didn't know where we were, and moved around so much it was difficult to pinpoint locations." He rubbed his face, closed his eyes for a few seconds. "I did the best I could to prevent the prisoners from being mistreated. We hoped someone on the outside—you or the Weres—would be able to track the prisoners if you knew they were captives."

"What about the people doing the experiments? What do you know about them?"

"I didn't have much interaction with them," he said. "I delivered the prisoners to and from the labs, but I was never there while the experiments were going on."

"Can you identify any of the individuals?"

"I might be able to pick a few out from photographs, but I don't know anyone's names. Like I said, I was way down the food chain."

"How many more of you are there undercover?"

He hesitated, as if trying to decide if what he was revealing might be harmful. "At least a dozen. Maybe more by now."

"We want to know who they are, to find out what they might know."

His jaw set stubbornly. "Look, a lot of the people in our organization would be at risk if their identities became known. People disappear."

Becca's heart beat faster. "Disappear. You suspect someone killed them?"

"We think that's the most likely explanation."

"Sylvan Mir is not going to harm people who are trying to help."

"*She* might not, but if the information got out, someone else might."

"Security here, as you might've noticed, is very tight."

He shrugged. "It's not my call."

"Then whose is it?"

"The person in charge of my unit."

Becca figured one step at a time was the best she could do—this man was not going to give up any of his compatriots if they kept him locked in this room for fifty years. "If I help you contact your unit leader, will you try to get more information for us?"

"Yes, if I can. But I want something in return."

"What would that be?" Becca had been an investigative reporter for six years and was well used to the give-and-take game.

"I want to talk to my unit leader alone. And I want your word that when you write this story, you keep our identities secret."

"I can promise you the first," Becca said. "But I can't promise there will be no mention of your organization in my report. I don't reveal my sources and your name won't be mentioned."

"I guess that has to be good enough."

"One last question—how many more of these labs are out there?"

He grimaced. "Best guess? Three."

"I'll see what I can do about getting you a phone." Becca stood, her heart sinking. Three more labs and how many more young human and Were captives being tortured?

❖

Michel watched the monitor as Sylvan and her cadre—her Prima, her second, a *centuri*, and the last, a young female—paused in front of the club's entrance. Michel studied Katya's face, the taste of her swirling through her mind.

"Well," Francesca said, stroking Michel's back as she stood beside her, studying the group. "Sylvan has come in force tonight."

"A challenge in itself," Michel murmured. "You should greet her formally."

"Mmm, yes." Francesca stroked the monitor over Sylvan's face. "Arrange it. I must change."

"Yes, Regent."

"And let them wait." Francesca caressed Michel's chest. "We are not at the beck and call of the Weres. Besides, they may enjoy the club—some of them, at least."

"I'll alert the guards to wait in the throne room." Michel kept her gaze on Katya, whose eyes glinted even in the flat gray of the monitor. "In the meantime, I'll go upstairs and greet our guests."

"Make them comfortable." Francesca laughed. "And tell them I'll see them as soon as I've completed my current business."

As soon as Francesca slipped into her bedroom, Michel signaled Antoine, one of Francesca's bodyguards.

"Yes, *Senechal*?" the androgynously handsome blond Vampire inquired. His silver eyes were set off by the merest hint of kohl beneath his lashes.

"I want you, Daphne, and Jerome in the throne room. We will have an audience with Weres shortly."

Antoine nodded. "Yes, *Senechal*."

Michel left him and climbed the winding staircase to Nocturne. She entered through a private door in the rear of the club and wended her way through the seething throngs toward the main entrance. The blood and sex that filled the air held no interest for her. What she wanted waited just inside the main entrance, where Sylvan and her wolves stood in a semicircle. Michel approached Sylvan, carefully not looking at Katya, but her blood simmered at the young Were's nearness. "Alpha Mir. What a pleasant surprise."

"I'd like to see Francesca," Sylvan said.

"Of course," Michel replied smoothly. "The Regent is in the midst of a meeting right now. If you'd care to have a drink and"—Michel swept an arm toward the depths of the room behind her—"avail yourselves of whatever else you might like…" Niki snarled, and Michel flicked a glance in her direction. She smiled. "Completely voluntarily, of course."

"Hospitable as always," Sylvan murmured.

Michel tipped her head. "We are always happy to entertain our friends."

"We're not here for a social visit," Niki snarled.

"Ah, but that shouldn't stop you from enjoying your wait, should it?" Before Niki could reply, Michel misted into the shadows. Bloodlust simmered in her depths as she watched Katya with the *centuri* move off into the crowd. Sylvan had sent them hunting. Bold of the Were, but fortunate for her. She called to Katya, a silent caress in the dark, and saw her stop, gaze around, her eyes feverish. Michel slid deeper into the dark recesses of the club. *Come to me, blood of my blood.*

She shuddered, her throat flooding with feeding hormones, and waited as Katya slipped away from her keeper and answered.

Chapter Twenty

Raina dropped onto the big male's back, digging into his hide with the claws of all four limbs. She was one of the biggest cats in all of North America, but he was bigger still. She sank her teeth into his neck, hoping to draw his attention away from Lara. She didn't want to kill him, but if she didn't, he would very likely kill one of them. Her jaws were opened wide, her long razor-sharp canines slicing through muscle and tendon, but he was so strong, so powerful, she needed all her strength and agility just to keep her mount on his back. He roared and thrashed, and she could not bite deep enough to reach the vessels in his throat.

All the same, she hurt him sufficiently to pull his focus away from Lara long enough for Lara to shake off the other two cats. Lara was slowing down, though. The ground around her was drenched in crimson, and she was dragging her injured leg. The remaining female cat lashed out at Lara, opening a gash in her shoulder, but Lara, even injured, was still faster. She darted beneath the slashing front leg of the cat Were and ripped through the cat's soft underbelly with her own claws. Blood and viscera exploded, and the cat screamed in agony. Lara clamped down on her throat, and the cat went down and lay still.

Now the odds were even. Two male cat Weres against a wolf and an Alpha female cat. Time to stand and fight. Raina gathered her legs beneath her and launched herself off the bigger cat's back, landing with a twist so she could face him again. Lara was beside her instantly, and they pressed shoulder to shoulder as the two males circled them.

How badly are you hurt? Raina asked.

I can fight.

Raina heard the strain beneath the wolf's bravado, and rage poured through her chest like acid. These cats had hurt Lara, and she wanted them dead. *Let's take the smaller one first—if we strike together we can kill him quickly. By then your Vampire friends should be here to collect the last one.*

I never said...they were my friends. Lara panted, her breath harsh rasps. *We'll have to be quick or...we'll expose our flanks to the big one.*

Raina wasn't sure Lara had enough strength left to protect herself in a close-in fight. She'd have to take him alone. *I'll distract them, you draw the smaller one away, and I'll sweep his flank.*

My pleasure.

Raina streaked for cover in the thick underbrush, and both males focused on her path into the forest. They wanted the cat, not the wolf who was more a nuisance than a threat. Time for her later. The moment they changed direction, Lara growled and charged the smaller one. He was twice her size, but he wasn't used to fighting an adversary who waged a war of attrition. She darted in and out, nipping and clawing, not doing much damage with a single strike, but drawing blood each time and infuriating him. He roared in anger and frustration, whirling from side to side, trying to keep her in sight. Several times he charged, but she wasn't where he ended up. When he swung around for the third time, Raina struck from the underbrush. She cut beneath his great head and slashed his throat open, her canines ripping through arteries and veins and severing his windpipe. He dropped, the light fading from his eyes as his blood poured out.

Raina whipped around, getting between Lara and the last cat. The leader—the one they wanted to capture. The one she wanted dead. She made short, quick runs at him, forcing him to concentrate on her. Each time she struck at his throat, he deflected her with lethal swipes of his huge paws. Several blows caught her before she could twist away, and her pelt was soon streaked with rivulets of blood.

We can't wait any longer, Raina signaled. *He'll take one of us down before long.*

We just need to hold him off a while longer. Mount him again and I'll—

The male sprang over Raina and caught Lara by the throat. She twisted and clawed at him, but he dragged her down. Screaming in rage, Raina charged him and buried her claws in his shoulder. Lara was limp in his jaws. Raina rolled beneath him and slashed at his belly. She opened a two-foot gash along his side and he dropped Lara. Roaring, he swung in a half circle, trying to bite Raina's throat. Lara lay limp on the ground.

Raina sprang away, but she couldn't leave Lara helpless. She crouched, shielding Lara and giving him a target. He gathered his powerful haunches and lunged. His body arched into the air, a beautiful, lethal missile.

❖

Becca left Martin's cell, and Claude escorted her through the prison tunnel and out onto the Compound courtyard. None of the Rovers were in sight. Max, one of Sylvan's *centuri*, stood guard by the front door of Sylvan's headquarters, and Becca crossed to him. "Have you heard anything?"

"The Alpha and the others have just reached Nocturne," the burly, craggy-faced Were said. "Lara and the others have not reported in."

Becca looked out over the darkened Compound. The flames flickered low in the fire pits, glowing coals banked against the night's damp. Beyond their small circle of light, the mountains loomed black and foreboding. She'd nearly lost Jody on the last hunt. Now they were blood-bound, and without Jody she wasn't sure she could live, even if she'd wanted to. Jody was part of her now, as essential as breathing. Becca shook off the dark anxiety burrowing into her thoughts. Jody had always been strong, but now that she'd Risen, she was even stronger. She would come back to her soon, and until she did, there was work to be done.

She said to Max, "The prisoner wants to put in a call to his unit leader. I think we'll be able to get some names from him. Possibly even an identification."

"Good."

"Do you have an untraceable cell phone?"

Max hesitated. "The Alpha should be the one to decide."

God, dealing with Weres was like dealing with the US Army—all protocol and chain of command. "I'll take responsibility."

Max's lip curled ever so slightly. Amusement or disdain, she couldn't tell. Becca smiled, wondering if he was fooled by her outward calm or if he could scent her temper. Jody always knew what she was feeling, no matter how well she hid it. But then, Jody had been under her skin since the moment they'd met. Under her skin, in her head, in her heart. Where was she?

"He says there are other facilities," Becca said. "The Alpha asked me to interview him because she trusted me to get the information she needs. I don't think we should waste time."

Max's jaw set in a stubborn line. "I'll discuss it with the Alpha as soon as she—" He cocked his head, listening, his eyes narrowing.

"What is it? Max?"

He swiveled toward the far side of the courtyard. Two wolves soared over the twelve-foot fence and landed in the center of the Compound.

Max smiled. "Jace and Dasha."

The air around the wolves shimmered and Dasha and Jace stood, sweat-dampened skin gleaming in the firelight. They strode toward headquarters and Max ducked inside. He reemerged a few seconds later and tossed them clothes as they leapt onto the porch.

"What happened?" Becca asked. "Where are the others?"

"We left them to draw some of the cats away," Dasha said, pulling on jeans. "Four or five of them came after us, but we lost them in the hills. The others went north to engage the other cats. We haven't heard from them."

Jace said, "We're going to grab a Rover and go after them."

"I want to go with you," Becca said.

Claude appeared out of the shadows. "No. The Liege would want you to stay here where it's safe."

Becca shot him a stony glance. "The Liege isn't here. And I'm going."

"Let's not waste any time, then," Dasha said.

Becca followed the two Weres across the Compound. Claude was at the Rover before her and opened the rear door for her. She touched his arm. "Thanks."

He just sighed and climbed in beside her.

Dasha got behind the wheel, and Jace turned to them from the shotgun seat. "Hold on. We're going off-road."

"I don't care how we get there," Becca said. "Just find them."

❖

Raina waited. When the big cat arched above her, front legs extended, claws ready for the strike, she jumped and crashed into his chest with the full force of her flying body. They tumbled to the ground in a roiling mass of churning limbs and snarls. His teeth sank into her shoulder, she slashed at his throat. Slaying rage emptied her mind of everything but the kill. *Kill. Her kill.*

Then the pain struck, a burning ice pick piercing her skull, and she fell.

Wake up, little Cat.

Raina shuddered and whined.

You fought well. The pain will pass.

Raina returned to awareness lying naked on a bed of pine needles. Dried blood streaked her belly and limbs. The Vampire and the human stood over her.

"How bad are your injuries?" Jody asked. "The pain in your head is the aftereffect of a forced thrall. It will fade."

"Nothing that won't heal when I shift again," Raina said, getting slowly to her feet. "Lara! Is she—"

"Alive." Zahn gestured toward the forest behind them. Lara, naked and seemingly unconscious, leaned against the trunk of a pine. Her arms were limp by her sides and her skin paper white. The male cat, naked like her, lay on his stomach, his wrists shackled behind his back with silver cuffs.

"What took you so long?" Raina started toward Lara.

"We caught the trail of another cadre of cats in pursuit of Dasha and Jace. We had to secure their rear," Jody said.

Raina only half listened. They'd gotten what they'd come for—although she hadn't gotten her kill. Yet. "I need to see to Lara."

"She needs blood," Zahn said. "I'll take care of her."

Raina growled softly. "She's badly hurt. I can give her more blood than a human. I'll see to her."

Zahn studied her for a long moment. "As you wish. Alpha." She inclined her head slightly and turned her back. "I'll stand guard."

Raina didn't thank her. Lara wasn't Zahn's. She crossed the clearing and crouched next to Lara. Her left thigh was torn open from hip to knee, muscle shredded, bone exposed. A slash across her abdomen nearly penetrated through to vital organs, and the ribs beneath her right breast were misshapen. Broken. A trickle of blood ran from the corner of her mouth down her neck. Her breathing was shallow and rasping. Blood in her lungs.

"Lara," Raina murmured. She caressed her cheek. "Wolf?"

Lara stirred and opened her eyes. "You win?"

"We won." Raina stroked her bare shoulder. "You need to shift. You'll heal faster then." She ran her fingers through Lara's hair. Her own were shaking. She'd seen cats die from injuries less serious than these. A choking fear like none she'd ever known squeezed the breath from her chest. "Please. Lara. You need to shift."

Lara focused on Raina, her amber eyes clouded with pain. "I tried. I can't."

Raina's gut clenched. If Lara couldn't shift—"Why not?"

"Blood. Lost too much blood…not strong enough."

Relief made Raina's head spin. She knelt on the ground and raised Lara with an arm around her shoulders until Lara's head rested on her shoulder. She cupped the back of Lara's neck and drew Lara's mouth to her neck. "Take. Drink."

"No," Lara groaned, her body shuddering with need.

"Take me."

Heat exploded in Raina's throat and scorched through her chest. Pain, pleasure, unbearable need doubled her over. Lara's breasts molded to hers, Lara's nipples two burning stones. Raina's belly spasmed and she cried out. Lara's arm came around her waist, a steel band holding her to the curve of Lara's body. Another surge of heat struck lower in her belly, and she came in a hot flood. Her legs deserted her and she fell with Lara on top of her. The pain disappeared. Only aching pleasure remained. She came again. She heard Lara moan, felt the thrust of Lara's hips between her legs, felt the hot wash of Lara's release anoint her belly and thighs.

Lara fed and Raina whimpered softly. Lara swallowed, the sweet nectar restoring her strength, filling her with power. She growled, wild with hunger and lust.

More. Want more.

Yes. More.

Lara fed until Raina's blood, more potent than any she'd ever had, banished her agony. She eased her canines from Raina's throat and licked the wounds closed. Panting, she lay on Raina, their bodies slick with sweat and blood and *victus*. She kissed Raina's throat, her jaw, her mouth. "Thank you."

Raina's hand fisted in Lara's hair, pulling her head back. Raina's canines scraped along Lara's throat, and then a lancing pain burned in her shoulder as Raina bit her. Forced into a furious orgasm, Lara threw back her head and roared.

Chapter Twenty-one

Michel slipped deeper into the shadows in the far corner of the club, every sense focused on her prey. Every other heartbeat faded. Only Katya's teased through her mind. Only Katya's scent fueled the hunger in her blood. A few feet away, Vampires fed from their frenzied hosts, unaware of her. But their hunger, their lust, their desperate need to fuck and feed until some semblance of life seeped into their tortured flesh hung like a decadent cloud in the air. The teeming mass of bodies blocked Katya from her view, but she felt her drawing near. Her senses, her sex, her every cell pulsed with power—the power she'd absorbed from Katya's potent Were blood, the same power she now used to compel Katya's return. Sylvan or the redheaded Were who was undoubtedly responsible for protecting Katya would notice her absence soon. She wouldn't have much time. But she didn't need much time.

Katya slipped through the slices of amber light cast by the hidden spots, the slanting beams illuminating the carved angles of her cheekbones, the straight line of her nose, the curve of her chin. She smelled like life, rich and pure. Her essence taunted Michel with promises of eternity, if only she drank her fill. Katya was young and strong, as strong as she was fragile. Michel's throat tightened and feeding hormones flooded her system. She was starving. None of the hosts she'd had earlier had so much as blunted her hunger. Her head swam with need so painful she trembled.

The darkness parted and Katya was there, only inches away. Katya reached out slowly, ran her fingertips along the edge of Michel's jaw. The touch was unlike anything she could remember in her centuries of existence. She'd fed from thousands, been touched by hundreds—but never like this. Never with a caress that carried no secrets, no seduction, no hidden agendas. Katya's fingers traced her face as if she were finding her way along an unfamiliar path she intended to travel again.

"Didn't your Alpha teach you to be careful around Vampires?"

"I'm not afraid."

"You should be."

"No," Katya said softly. "I remember you."

"You're mistaken."

Katya cradled Michel's face in both hands, stroking her as if she were blind and determined to see her. Her fingers brushed Michel's mouth, glanced over her incisors. Michel hissed quietly, her sex swelling.

"I've been searching for you." Katya smiled, her gaze slightly unfocused, as if she were revisiting some hidden memory. "I didn't know where at first, but then I felt you."

"That shouldn't be possible," Michel murmured, holding her hunger at bay. She could pull a host into thrall between one heartbeat and the next, feed from them, and be gone before they realized a moment had passed. She could fog their memory, alter their sense of time, even remove the physical presence of her bite. She could take this female now, fill herself, satisfy the gnawing hunger that slashed and tore inside her like a thousand knives, and be done with her. But she waited. If she took her, she would have to lose her again.

"I couldn't, for a while, right after I got home," Katya said softly. "I was…sick. The silver…"

Michel snarled. She'd kill Standish for what she had done.

Katya moved closer, not even an inch between them now. Her eyes stayed fixed on Michel's, the golden glow of her wolf rising behind her dark irises. "But then I felt you, and the more I felt you, the more I remembered. You were in that place."

"Only once," Michel said, unable to remember the last time she'd explained herself to anyone. Unable to remember when it mattered what anyone else knew of the truth. She brushed the long chestnut strands of hair away from Katya's throat, letting her fingers linger over the pulse she could already taste. So strong. She trembled with the need to sate her hunger.

"Why were you there?" Katya's lids lowered and she tilted her head to the side, a torpid invitation.

"Does it matter?" Michel slid her hand farther around Katya's neck. She had only to cloud her mind and she could be inside her, filling herself and flooding Katya with pleasure. She had done it so many times the pleasure was more remembered than real. But not tonight. Tonight she was electric with sensation. "Do you care why I was there?"

"You didn't hurt me."

"Then you don't remember clearly," Michel said harshly. "I bit you, I bled you. That's what I am."

Katya narrowed her eyes, studying Michel as if trying to delve beneath the ancient barriers to some truth no one else believed existed. She skimmed her fingers over Michel's mouth, unafraid, as if erasing the lies. "You could have hurt me, if you'd only taken, if you'd forced me to be a slave to the pleasure. That's what *they* did to me."

Michel snarled. "I should have killed them then. I will kill them." She kissed the fingers that teased over her lips. "I promise you."

"I'll kill them," Katya said softly.

"Yes," Michel murmured. "You are strong enough. And now you are free."

Katya slowly shook her head. "No, I'm not. They still hold me captive—in my dreams, in my nightmares."

Michel pulled her close and whispered against her ear, "And what about me? Do I visit your nightmares?"

Katya arched into her, rubbing her breasts over Michel's, tilting her head back until Michel's mouth was against her throat. "No. You come to me when I need you. You make me burn."

Michel wrapped an arm around Katya's waist, drawing her even more tightly into her embrace. She slipped her incisors infinitesimally into the hot skin of Katya's throat, and the tiny pinpricks of pain made Katya whimper. Michel growled softly. "I hunger for you."

Katya's hands came into her hair, gripping hard. "I know. I feel your hunger in my dreams. I want to fill you. I want you to make me come again."

Michel pulled her head back, her vision clouded with flame. "Do you want me to make you forget again?"

"No." Katya kissed her. Not the kiss of ownership Francesca used to remind her where she belonged, but a slow, seductive kiss that ignited the fire in her blood.

Michel groaned. "You don't know what you're asking."

"I do. I remember the second time, in the forest. I remember you inside me—everywhere. I want you. And I want to remember."

"I'll hurt you."

"No," Katya murmured, moving to Michel's throat, biting softly, opening Michel's skin. "I know what I want."

Michel jerked, her clitoris tightening. She hadn't been bitten since Francesca turned her, lifetimes ago. The Were was playing with her, and she'd have to teach her that was a dangerous game. She gripped Katya's shoulders and spun her to the wall. "Don't say I didn't warn you."

Katya gripped the back of Michel's silk shirt, her claws slicing through it. "Then bite. Take me."

Hunger ruled. Michel struck fast, burying herself in Katya's hot, pliant flesh. She covered Katya's body with hers, pressed against her and took her fill. Strength and power poured through her, more than she'd felt for centuries. She came, each pulse of her orgasm beating to the rhythm of Katya's heart.

"Yes. Yes." Katya writhed beneath her, her back bowing, her mouth open in a muted roar. Her canines gleamed, her claws raked Michel's back, flaying her skin.

Michel fed, the wounds in her back healing instantly. Katya ground against her, growling low in her throat. Michel slid a hand between them, opened Katya's pants, pushed inside. She was hot, swollen, slick. She came and kept coming with every pull at her neck.

"More," Katya moaned.

Michel slid deeper, stroked her, consumed her.

Katya's sobs broke through Michel's bloodlust, and she dragged her mouth away, sealing the wounds she had left. Only a bruise would remain. She gasped, realizing she'd lost awareness of everything around her, lost herself in Katya. She braced her arms on the wall on either side of Katya's shoulders, the weight of her body holding Katya up. Her eyes were closed, her head lolling. Michel kissed her. "Are you all right?"

Katya's arms fell limply from around her back, her breathing ragged, her heart thundering against Michel's. She moaned softly.

"Katya?"

"You're wrong." Katya's eyelids flickered open. They were dazed, liquid with satisfaction. "You don't hurt me."

"I will."

"The Alpha will know," Katya said. "If you don't take my memories, I'll tell her."

Michel nodded, a sensation filling her chest that she hadn't experienced in so long, at first she didn't recognize it. Sadness. She kissed her softly. "I know."

❖

Lara stirred to the rumble of the idling Rover. She was sprawled over Raina, both of them naked, limbs entangled. Her wounds were healing rapidly after the infusion of Raina's blood. A shadow passed between her and the moon, and she opened her eyes, instinctively sitting up to shield Raina from danger.

Rafaela stood looking down at them. "The Liege bids us to leave."

"How did you fare?" Lara peered past her. Jody and Zahn carried the bound Were to the Rover. Jace and Dasha were nowhere around. "The wolves? They are safe?"

"We tracked them almost to Pack land," Rafaela said, "and killed the cats who followed them. But there are others hunting nearby. We need to get the prisoner back to Wolf territory before we run into another group of marauding cats." Rafaela regarded Raina impassively. "And before this prisoner decides to disappear when your…guard is down."

Raina growled low and sat up. If she'd wanted to run, she would have when the other cats attacked. Should have. But if she had, Lara would be dead. Raina's cat was still battle-charged and craving a fight. And freedom. She quivered with challenge.

Lara slid an arm around Raina's shoulders, pulling her tight against her side to hold her back. "Raina has proved herself. Without her, we wouldn't have captured the rebel cat."

"All she proved was she is not stupid enough to try to escape from the Liege—and we knew she was clever," Rafaela said. "Clever and probably planning her escape right now. She has you on your back, doesn't she?"

Lara bounded up, her canines exposed, growling a warning. "You forget yourself, Vampire. I am your warlord."

Rafaela held her gaze for a second, then looked aside. "The Liege is ready. I'm taking this prisoner now. If you wish to lead, then do it."

Lara slowly closed her fist in the fabric of Rafaela's shirt and pulled her close until their faces nearly touched. She whispered, "I like you, Rafaela. But I will kill you if you touch her. She's mine."

"Are you sure?" Rafaela murmured.

Lara didn't answer. She'd claimed Raina as hers by right of capture, but she'd fed from her out of need—her need, and even now she wanted her again. Who was the prisoner?

Lara let her wolf rise, let her thrall escape. Power cloaked the glade. "I don't answer to you, Rafe."

Rafaela shuddered, her eyes glazing. Beside her, Raina whined softly and golden pelt shimmered beneath her skin. Her eyes slanted to green and her cat teased at Lara's senses.

Jody's voice ricocheted through Lara's consciousness, followed by a swift stab of pain. *You answer to me. Release my guard, Warlord. And cage your wolf before the cat shifts. I don't want to stun her again, but I'll bind her in silver if I have to.*

I can control the cat. Lara released Rafaela, whose eyes cleared instantly. "Get us some clothes."

"Yes, Warlord." Rafaela's gaze held new respect.

Lara crouched by Raina's side. "Not now, big Cat. We have to go back. You can't shift now."

Raina flowed to her feet, her muscles and bones fluid grace. Her face in the moonlight resembled an ancient carving of an animal goddess—elegant and cruel. "And if I refuse?"

Lara smiled. "Then I will have to hunt you down, which will only waste time."

Raina's cat was close—and stronger than any of them knew. When Lara had fed from her, Lara's essence had filled her. Now her Alpha strength was magnified a hundredfold, and she could shift and be gone before anyone—even the Vampire Liege—could stop her. Her cat wanted freedom. Raina ached to break Lara's hold on her, even as she craved Lara's bite. She thought of her cubs, helpless among the enemy.

In the heat of battle, she'd thought only to protect Lara, unafraid of death. But she could not willingly desert her cubs. She would return, for them. And somehow she would free them. Lara was still her only hope, but she needed to resist whatever strange hold the Vampire had on her. Need made her weak. Her gaze dropped to the punctures on Lara's shoulder, the bite she had given her. She'd clawed and slashed the cats who'd mounted her during her heats, but she'd never bitten, never taken. Never wanted a claim. She brushed her fingers over the disappearing punctures, and Lara stiffened.

"Careful," Lara whispered, the bones in her face sliding toward wolf. "If you tempt me, more than my wolf will bite."

"And if I want all of it?" Raina murmured, knowing she must fight the need, even as she hungered.

"I am not what you think."

Raina's head jerked up, the green in her eyes darkening to secret pools. "I know what you are not, and I know what you are."

Lara snarled softly. "Do you?"

"I've tasted you. I know your wolf. And I know what else lives inside you—the darkness, and the death."

"Then you should know to stay away."

Rafe appeared beside them and tossed clothing on the ground. "Are you ready, Warlord?"

"Yes. We are coming." Lara pulled on pants and a dark shirt, her eyes on Raina while she did the same. Lara slid a hand around Raina's neck, squeezed slowly. "Don't run, Raina. I would not have them hurt you."

"Not tonight, Wolf." Raina needed Lara's protection, but some force deep in her bones made it impossible to lie to her. "But I make no promises about tomorrow."

Lara smiled, no humor in her eyes. "Tomorrow means nothing to me."

CHAPTER TWENTY-TWO

"Get away from her, you son of a bitch." Snarling, Andrew shoved Michel against the wall.

Michel could have overpowered him, physically or mentally. He was a formidable Were, dominant, strong. In a near killing rage. But she was very old, and a first-made of one of the strongest Vampires in existence. She could bend his mind—break it if she chose. And if she did, the female in her arms would despise her for eternity.

"Be careful you don't annoy me, Wolf." Michel smiled slowly, running a hand down Katya's back. "I might enjoy a little more Were blood before dawn." She caught his mind, sent an image of her mouth at his throat while another Vampire rode his cock. "You might too."

Caught in the sweeping cloud of Michel's sexual thrall, Katya whimpered softly and pressed close to Michel's side. She pushed her hand under Michel's shirt, claws scoring thin tracks across her abdomen. Michel wrapped an arm around her, her gaze fixed on Andrew. If he believed she'd compelled Katya, she wouldn't try to change his mind. Katya was safer if the Weres didn't know they shared a blood connection. "She seems to be ready for more."

Andrew growled, his eyes blazing gold, fury and lust making him hard as granite. Images of the last night he'd spent in this place flashed through his memory, a collage of blood and sex and unspeakable pleasure. He trembled, sex frenzy clawing at his guts. His jaw elongated, his wolf pushed for freedom. "I should kill you for touching her."

"I should let you try," Michel said softly, "but your Alpha might object if I tore you limb from limb. And she's a guest. Some other time."

Canines erupting, he lunged for her.

Katya blocked him with her body. "No. You don't understand—"

"Oh, I understand." His words grated through thickened vocal cords. "I understand she has you in her thrall."

"I came to her willingly."

"How do you know?" He shook his head. "This bloodsucker can make you do anything and leave you believing you wanted it."

"No." Katya pressed her back to Michel's front, her wolf rumbling possessively. "I wanted her. I came to her."

"You don't know what you're saying." He grabbed Katya's shoulders. "Get ba—"

Michel gripped him by the throat and held him suspended in midair with one arm. "Careful. You don't want to make me angry tonight." Andrew's eyes glazed as she paralyzed his body, sapped his will. "I don't let anyone take what's mine."

Two of Michel's soldiers materialized beside them. One, a laser-thin male with sleek blond hair and ice-blue eyes, said to Michel, "Do you want us to take him below, *Senechal*?"

Katya gripped Michel's arm. "Please don't hurt him."

Michel turned her scarlet gaze to Katya and slowly lowered Andrew to the floor. "That won't be necessary, Adam. Show our guest outside."

The blond dipped his head. "As you command."

Andrew growled. "I'll kill you for this."

Michel smiled, tracing her finger down the column of Katya's throat. "You can try."

❖

"Niki, stay with the Prima," Sylvan said, her wolf suddenly on alert.

Drake gripped Sylvan's wrist, careful not to raise her voice and draw the attention of the Vampires milling about. "You feel it too? Who—"

"Andrew."

"What is it?" Drake shook her head, frustrated with the fragments of images and tendrils of wrath dancing just out of reach. "I can't…I sense fury and…danger. Katya—is she…"

"No," Sylvan said softly. "She's not threatened, but she's in danger."

"Don't go alone. I'm all right." Drake turned to Niki. "Go with her."

"No," Sylvan said. "Francesca's guards are everywhere, and I don't trust them any more than I trust the rest of the Risen. They'll all want to feed soon. You need protection."

"I'm only letting you go alone to prevent alerting the Vampires." Drake smoothed her palm down the center of Sylvan's chest. "Be careful, Alpha."

Sylvan smiled grimly. "I won't be long." She shot a look at Niki. "Don't leave her side."

"Yes, Alpha." Niki's eyes flashed wolf-green.

Sylvan cut swiftly through the crowd, drawn to the scent of Katya's blood and Andrew's frenzy. Their scents were distinct from all the other scents of sex and blood in the room, even though most of the other Weres were hers as well. Andrew was *centuri*, bound to her by blood, and his rage had alerted her wolf to danger. He was close to losing control, and if her *centuri* challenged a Vampire, she would have to fight in his defense. Francesca's Vampires far outnumbered her forces. Most of her wolves were enthralled and blind with lust—drawing them from their sex frenzy would divide her concentration. She was at a disadvantage in this room.

Andrew, stand down. Sylvan stepped from the crowd and casually draped an arm around Andrew's neck, facing Michel. "I see you and Katya are already acquainted."

She wasn't surprised to see Michel with Katya at her side. Jody had reported Michel's presence in the lab the night of the rescue, but Katya had not been able to identify the Vampire who had fed from her. Now she had her proof. Sylvan's wolf bared her teeth. This Vampire had hurt her young.

"I expected you sooner, Sylvan," Michel said, intentionally dropping Sylvan's title. If she was to protect Katya from Francesca's wrath, everyone must believe Katya was nothing more to her than a host. A dispensable one. "I was surprised you weren't here before I finished feeding."

Sylvan ignored the insult and the taunting challenge. "Andrew, take Katya to the Rover."

"The Vampire should pay," Andrew growled.

Michel laughed, slowly caressing Katya's throat. "And who's going to exact payment? You? I can taste your hunger. Do you want to fight me or fuck me, Wolf?"

"Someday, Vampire, I will find you alone."

"I remember watching you come while three of the Risen fed

from you," Michel said easily. "When you return, I'll invite Adam and Christine, another of my guards, to join us. I'll drain you while you fuck."

Andrew lunged, but Sylvan easily restrained him, her hand tightening on his shoulder. Calmly, she said, "Do as I say. Outside."

He shuddered under the command in her voice. He whined softly in the back of his throat, his wolf caught between challenge and his Alpha's orders. He glared at Michel and held out his hand to Katya. "Come on."

Katya's grip on Michel's shirt tightened. Michel murmured in her ear, "Go. It's for the best."

Sylvan studied Katya coolly while her wolf wanted to tear the Vampire apart. "Katya. Are you here of your free will?"

Katya shuddered under the fury in Sylvan's voice but pressed close to Michel's side, her chin up. "Yes, Alpha."

"And before?"

"Yes, Alpha."

"She thinks she is free to choose," Michel said, holding Sylvan's gaze, daring her to make a challenge in Francesca's domain. "She can't tell the difference between thrall and desire."

"So you say," Sylvan said, but she sensed no fear from Katya. "Tell me why I shouldn't kill you for betraying our alliance."

"What makes you think I have?" Michel shrugged and stepped away from Katya. "Go with your Alpha." She smiled coldly. "You were tasty, but not enough to go to war for."

Katya's chin shot up. "I am loyal to my Alpha. If you challenge her, I will stand by her side."

"I have no need to challenge. I've already had what I wanted."

Sylvan slipped her hand around the back of Katya's neck. "Go with Andrew."

"Yes, Alpha."

Katya turned from Michel, and Michel watched her go. The ache in her chest was unfamiliar, a sharp-edged pain that no amount of feeding was going to blunt. "Your wolves want what we give them, Sylvan. Why fight us over it?"

"I will not let you compel my wolves, ally or not."

Michel said nothing, waiting until she sensed Katya leave the club, safe from the Risen who were feeding mindlessly from any available host. "Dawn is coming."

"Take me to Francesca."

Michel tilted her head. "As you wish, Alpha."

Sylvan followed Michel back through the crowd to the bar where Drake and Niki waited. She kept her wolf on a short, tight leash. She wanted to tear Michel apart for touching Katya while she was imprisoned, but she'd read the truth in Katya's eyes. Michel had not compelled her this night. Katya had gone to her willingly.

Are you all right? Drake inquired, Sylvan's simmering rage forcing her wolf to pace and grumble. She eased a hand onto the center of Sylvan's back, stroked the rigid muscles.

Sylvan shuddered, took a long breath, absorbed her mate's soothing scent. Some of her fury settled. *Yes. Stay close to me when we go downstairs.*

Katya, Andrew?

Safe.

Michel held out an arm and bowed. "If you'll come with me, my friends, the Regent will see you now."

"Good." Drake slung an arm around Sylvan's waist and eyed Michel coolly. "Then we'll see if we're all still friends."

Michel laughed. "The Regent is going to enjoy you."

Sylvan growled, but Drake merely smiled. "I doubt that very much."

❖

Becca gripped the back of Dasha's seat, peering out between Jace and Dasha into the forest. The Rover's lights illuminated a narrow track, little more than a deer trail, barely wide enough to accommodate the SUV. The fortified vehicle bounced over rocks and fallen trees as they moved deeper and deeper into the mountains. Though the mountain terrain looked no different than the forests in Pack land, she felt as if she had crossed into a foreign land. Her skin prickled with foreboding. The eastern sky seemed lighter than it had moments before. They didn't have much time. "Can you scent them?"

"No," Dasha said. "They're too far away."

Jace grumbled uneasily. "I smell cat everywhere."

Becca couldn't sense Jody, either, and the disconnection frightened her. Jody had once told her she could find her if she were a hundred miles away—Becca didn't have that ability yet, but usually, even when she couldn't see her, she could taste Jody in her blood. Her absence was like missing a limb. She panicked for an instant, then forced down the fear. "Where are we?"

"Just crossing into Pride land," Jace said. "They shouldn't be far now."

"Good. It's almost morning."

Dasha looked back at her. "If they have to take shelter out here, Raina should know the location of caves where they'll be safe from the sun."

Becca nodded. Vampires kept their vulnerabilities well guarded, even from allies. The sun wasn't the only danger. Jody was still sensitive to the circadian UV cycle and wouldn't be at full strength during the day. Lara and Rafe would be even more sensitive. They'd be somnolent, vulnerable and unprotected in enemy land. "It would be best if we make sure they get back to the Compound by daybreak."

"Then we will," Jace said.

"I—"

A loud bang rocked them and the Rover screeched to a halt. Becca flew forward, taking the full force of the impact on her right shoulder. Pain lanced down her arm and her hand went numb. A screaming roar filled the vehicle, and a huge cat jumped onto the windshield with such force it cracked.

"Ambush," Jace yelled. A paw swiped through the open window and slashed the arm she threw up to protect her head.

"Becca, Claude," Dasha shouted, "there are weapons under your seat. Stay in the vehicle."

Jace and Dasha jumped out, and the air split with the crack of gunfire.

Claude pushed to the rear of the Rover. "Stay inside."

"Wait—take a weapon."

"I have no need for a gun." He smiled the arrogant smile she'd seen at least once on every Vampire she knew, and then, he was gone. The doors slammed closed behind him.

Hands shaking, Becca tore open the latch on the bench seat and pulled out an automatic rifle. She'd never fired one, but it didn't look all that complicated. A curved magazine was already attached to the underbelly. Above the trigger was a lever that she assumed was the safety. She pushed it down with her forefinger. The Rover rocked to the side as if hit by a freight train, and she fell to her knees. She wasn't waiting inside like bait.

Taking a deep breath, she jerked up on the rear door handle, pushed open the doors, and jumped out. And came face-to-face with the largest mountain lion she'd ever seen.

The cat crouched, its wild green eyes fixed on her, its lips drawn back in a feral snarl.

Becca pointed the weapon, pulled the trigger, and prayed it would fire.

❖

"Gunfire," Jody said sharply.

"A mile ahead," Lara said.

Raina rolled down the window, scented the air. "Cats, at least a dozen, moving south-southeast."

"It's a war party," Lara said, "and they're between us and Pack land."

"We're outnumbered," Zahn said quietly, slowing the vehicle. "If I cut west, we might be able to circle around them."

"No," Lara and Jody said simultaneously.

"Two wolves," Lara said. "We can't leave them."

Jody's chest tightened, fear icing her blood. "Becca is with them." She turned to Lara. "Rafe and I will engage the main force directly ahead. You and Raina circle to the east and support the wolves and Becca until we arrive."

Lara glanced at Raina. "Are you ready to fight again, big Cat?"

Raina snarled. "Every cat I defeat is one more cat I will rule. Let's go."

Lara shifted and Raina followed.

Jody pulled open the rear doors so Lara and Raina could jump out. "See that no harm comes to my consort, Warlord."

My word, Liege. Lara followed Raina into the forest, her wolf happy to be hunting again by this new Alpha's side.

Chapter Twenty-three

The recoil from the first round drove Becca back against the Rover. The repetitive *Crack! Crack! Crack!* was deafening, and the heat radiating from the housing brought tears to her eyes. Blossoms of scarlet bloomed over the big cat's head and torso, and he fell, clouds of dark earth and pine needles mushrooming from the ground around him. She imagined she felt the ground shudder. She barely had time to draw a breath before another cat landed near the bleeding body, and then another, and another. Only a few feet away. She kept her finger depressed on the trigger. She couldn't see the others, didn't know if they were alive, didn't know if she was alone.

Jody! Jody, I need you!

Suddenly the ringing in her ears was the only sound. Then came a low growl, slowly growing louder. She stared at the automatic rifle. It had stopped firing. Why was that?

An ominous rumble made her heart tremble. She blinked sweaty grit from her eyes. A cat Were, its pelt the color of autumn leaves, crept toward her, its golden eyes insanely wild, its canines and claws covered in blood. She had nowhere to run. She slid her hand behind her, groping for the door of the Rover. If she could throw herself inside and get the door closed again before the cat followed her in, she could find another weapon. She found the handle. She depressed the latch—jerked on the handle. If she could just get inside. The cat launched itself at her.

Oh God, Jody, I am so sorry. I love you—

An earsplitting scream cut the air and a missile the color of sunlight shot across the clearing and struck the cat in midleap. Another cat, lithe and muscular, dragged the attacker down, biting and slashing. Becca sagged against the Rover for the length of a frantic heartbeat, then gathered her strength, wrenched open the door, and threw herself inside. Her knees howled as she landed on the metal floor, but she ignored the shooting pain. Pivoting, she reached for the door to buy a few seconds' sanctuary.

Outside, just a few feet away, the golden cat tore through the other beast's throat and blood fountained, showering Becca with its thick warmth. And then the victor turned to her with a snarl.

Becca leapt back from the open door and scrambled for the bench. Shoving the hinged seat upright, she pawed through the compartment for a weapon. Her fingers closed around a metal grip and she pulled out a handgun. An automatic. She really needed to learn to shoot, if she survived. Rolling over on her back, expecting to feel claws tearing into her at any moment, she fumbled for the safety, couldn't find one, and prayed she hadn't missed it. Finger on the trigger, she pointed it out the open back door.

"All right, come on, damn it," she muttered. Waiting for death was so not her style.

A shadow blocked the swath of moonlight and the interior dimmed. She steadied her shaking arm with her opposite hand.

"I'd rather you didn't shoot me, darling. You should probably save your ammunition in case we run into another nuisance along the way."

Becca's breath stopped. She was dreaming, or hallucinating. "Jody?"

The moonlight returned, a few stars flickered above the tree line, and Jody was beside her, gently taking the weapon from her hand. "It's all right, you're safe."

"Are they gone?" Becca pressed against Jody's side, peering into the slowly fading dark. "There were so many. They just…kept coming and coming."

"They're all dead, or will be soon." Jody pulled Becca closer and buried her face in Becca's hair. She finally drew back, carefully cupping her face. "Is any of the blood on you yours?"

"No. At least, I don't think so. Scrapes and bruises. That's all."

Jody eased Becca toward the rear of the Rover and they climbed out. Becca ran her hands over Jody's chest, her shoulders, her arms. "Are you all right?"

"I'm fine." Jody's grip tightened. "What are you doing out here?"

"I…" Becca rested her head on Jody's shoulder. Adrenaline raced through her system, but she was exhausted. "I couldn't stand waiting. It was getting so late, I was worried."

Jody hissed, tucking Becca's head beneath her chin. "Claude will regret letting you leave the Compound."

"No!" Becca leaned back, brushed her fingers through Jody's hair. "It's not his fault. I wanted to come. Something was wrong. I could feel it."

"What's wrong is these mountains are crawling with feral cats. We've been fighting our way back." Jody shook her head. "I doubt Sylvan had any idea what was stirring along her borders. If someone doesn't control these cats, Sylvan will have another war on her hands."

"Jody, look out!" Becca gasped as the golden lion that had fought Becca's last attacker prowled across the clearing, headed straight for them. "The gun. I left it inside."

"You won't need it." Jody slid her arm around Becca's shoulder. "It's Raina."

From one step to the next, the cat shimmered into Were form. A wolf trotted out of the forest right behind her, its muzzle drenched in blood. Becca tried to see the shift, but it happened so quickly she missed the moment when wolf became Were. Lara fell into step with Raina.

"Oh my God," Becca murmured. "Raina. Raina killed the cat Were that was about to…" She steadied her breath, nodded to Raina. "Thank you."

"You're welcome," Raina said.

Jody tilted her head to Raina. "It seems I am now in your debt, Alpha."

"I'm glad you're not seriously injured," Raina said to Becca. She inclined her head slightly to Jody. She would have defended Becca in any case, but she was happy to have incurred the Vampire's gratitude. She would need to call in that debt to secure her freedom, she suspected, and from what she had seen, this Vampire was influential and powerful.

Lara said, "I sent Jace and Dasha to secure the perimeter, but we should leave soon. Another raiding party could be near, and our reserves are diminishing."

Becca looked around. The Vampires would need to feed soon, and with morning near, they could not fight a sustained battle. "Where's Claude?"

"With Rafe and Zahn at our vehicle. He's injured, but he'll recover," Lara said.

Guilt struck at Becca's heart. "He wouldn't have been here if I hadn't insisted on coming."

Jody stroked Becca's hair. "He wouldn't have been here if he'd followed my orders and kept you safe."

Dasha loped up to join them and faced Lara. "We are secure, *Centuri*."

"Good." Lara didn't bother to remind Dasha she was no longer *centuri*. The wolf Weres responded to her wolf as they always had. And with every shift, her wolf was stronger. "How many cats are alive?"

"One or two," Dasha said.

Jody turned to Raina. "What do you want to do with the injured? They are your cats in your land." She grinned viciously. "I wasn't planning to leave survivors."

Raina shrugged. For now, she had only the power the Vampire gave her. She was still too outnumbered to attempt an escape. Her cat protested, hissing angrily at the affront to her dominance, but she could not challenge. Not everything could be settled with teeth and claws, no matter what her cat demanded. "I'd like them to carry a message to the others. That I have returned and"—she smiled at Jody—"I have powerful allies."

Jody smiled briefly. "That remains to be seen, but…we might find an association to be valuable."

"Let them live," Raina said, "and leave the rest of the bodies where they are as a reminder to any other cats that we are not easy prey."

"You have good instincts, Alpha."

Lara said to Dasha, "See to it."

"Yes, *Centuri*."

Jody took Becca's hand. "We need to go. The wolves will catch up to us when they have released the prisoners."

Lara waited until Jody and Becca climbed into the vehicle before asking Raina, "Are you injured?"

"No, just a few scratches."

"You think this will make a difference to the other cat Weres?"

"Cats resent authority, avoid group ventures, prefer to live and fight alone." She shrugged. "But they also realize that to survive they need representation and protection, and if I can provide that, they will follow me."

Lara grinned. "It seems that today you've proven you can do both."

Raina regarded Lara steadily. She hadn't fought alone. Lara

had been both protector and comrade. They had fought as equals, as partners. "I had help."

"And you will again, should you need it." Lara met her gaze, saw cat and Were in equal measure reflected in the green-gold of her eyes. She would not let anyone shackle this warrior again. "We have to go back. But I promise you, you will not see bars again."

"Then I have to trust you, don't I?"

Lara took her hand, felt purpose fill her with strength. "You can."

Raina looked down at their joined fingers. She was neither born nor bred to rely on another, but she made the choice to risk her future and the future of her Pride on a stranger who had been her enemy. "Then I will."

❖

Michel led them along the familiar route through the club, down a narrow passageway behind the bar, and through the heavily guarded security door at the far end. The stone staircase on the opposite side was steep, uneven, and lit only by flickering sconces at shoulder height. Sylvan had no trouble seeing and could have made her way in the dark even had she never taken the path before. But she had been this way before, at least a half a dozen times when she had sought Francesca's company not because she desired her or the powerful orgasms Vampires bestowed with their bite, but because Francesca was powerful enough to drain her and quiet her wolf's demands for a mate. But when her mate had found her, nothing could have prevented the claiming, and now she felt nothing as she neared Francesca's inner chamber. Nothing except seething fury that her Pack was under attack and her wolves at risk. And somehow, Francesca was involved.

Drake slid her hand underneath the waistband of Sylvan's leather pants at the small of her back. *She will try to bait you into losing your temper. She will try to seduce you into believing her innocence. Tell your wolf to stand down and trust your lead in this.*

You know me too well. Sylvan brushed her fingertips over Drake's neck.

Never well enough. But fury is a useless weapon against those with no hearts. She is cold in body and mind, and you must meet ice with steel, not flame.

As you wish, Prima.

Michel stopped in front of the ornately carved floor-to-ceiling doors and looked over her shoulder. "Might I put forward, Alpha Mir, that Vampires and Weres have always been strongest in alliance, and there may never have been a time in our history when our foes were as formidable."

Sylvan regarded the Vampire silently. Michel had been Francesca's second before the Weres left the service of the Vampires to establish their own territories. Her ancestors had been generals under Michel's command. Francesca's *senechal* was a master tactician and nearly as powerful as Francesca. Perhaps the time for a new Regent was approaching, and the timing couldn't be worse. Rebellion within Francesca's Dominion would destabilize not only the Vampires, but the entire Praetern Coalition.

"I have never sought a war with the Vampires," Sylvan said, stating nothing that hadn't already been said before. She would not choose sides between Michel and Francesca unless forced to. "And the Regent knows that my first loyalty is to my Prima and my Pack. Anyone who moves against my Pack is my enemy."

Michel inclined her head. "One thing you have always been, Alpha Mir, is forthright. Not always a strength, but always a virtue."

Sylvan shook her head. "Games are for politicians…and Vampires."

Michel's eyes sparked, a brief intense crimson flare. "But there's so much pleasure in the game. You really should try it sometime."

"Tonight my business is simple. All I want is answers." Sylvan gestured to the door. "Shall we get it over with?"

"Of course." Michel opened the door, stepped through, and announced in a formal tone, "Alpha Mir, the Prima, and the *imperator* to see Francesca, Viceregal of the Eastern Territory and Chancellor of the City."

Michel stepped aside and Sylvan and the others walked in. Francesca sat on a gilded throne atop a dais at the end of a blood-red carpet that matched the lush velvet wall hangings. Her crimson gown, a shade darker than the carpet, left her shoulders bare, plunged between her voluptuous breasts, and flowed in seductive waves over her hips to pool around her ankles. Jewels glittered on her fingers and diamonds winked in her hair. A pair of Vampires dressed all in black, wearing gold sashes and ceremonial sabers, stood by her side. The Regent was displaying her power.

Sylvan strode forward in her black leather pants, combat boots, and tight black shirt, the KA-BAR military knife strapped to her thigh her only weapon. Drake on her left, Niki on her right. Sylvan stopped far enough away from the throne that she would not have to lift her head to meet Francesca's gaze.

"Thank you for interrupting your busy schedule," Sylvan said, keeping the sarcasm from her voice.

Francesca waved her hand languidly. "But of course, my dear Sylvan." She smiled at Drake before returning her seductive gaze to Sylvan. "Anything for you. You should know that by now…after all our times together."

"I won't take up much of your time," Sylvan said. "The research facilities at Mir Industries were bombed this morning."

"I did hear that. I hope no one was injured."

"None seriously. In addition, a number of my young wolves were kidnapped, held captive in an experimental lab, and tortured." She glanced at Michel. "Your second was there the night we liberated them. She fed from one of my young, against her will."

Her accusation, if proved true, called for retribution. Francesca would be obliged to let Sylvan name her price—and for such offense, the price would be death or exile.

Francesca's expression didn't change. She didn't look at Michel. Slowly, she crossed her legs, the red silk sliding up her calf to bare her thigh where the gown was split along one side from hem to hip. She trailed her fingers over her chest and let them linger over the cleft between her breasts. "Sylvan, darling, you make it sound like we've been involved in something nefarious. Why ever would we want to make an enemy out of you?"

"I don't know the answer to that. But I'd like to."

"Michel, explain to the Alpha what you were doing in the facility that night."

Michel wondered what trap Francesca was laying for Sylvan—or for her. They hadn't discussed admitting she'd been present, and she wondered if Francesca was testing her loyalty, or punishing her for Katya. Francesca undoubtedly knew she'd fed from her upstairs. Francesca knew everything that happened in the club. No matter how she answered, she ran the risk of pitting Vampire against Were, or Francesca against her. She couldn't be certain what Francesca's game was, but she could protect Katya.

"As you know, the Dominion has considerable investment in

the human business sector, so of course, we like to see how our funds are being used. I had been invited to tour the research laboratory that was working on questions of vital interest to Vampires. Imagine my surprise when I discovered, quite by accident, that one of the unrelated projects involved Were subjects." Michel was certain no one could prove she'd fed from Katya that night—Jody and her guards had not arrived until later, and everyone involved was dead or in hiding. "I hadn't been there more than a few minutes when your forces broke into the facility. I recognized one of your young, of course, and in the chaos was able to help her to safety. I'm sure Liege Gates told you I handed her over to ensure her safe passage." She fanned her hands, smiled. "I'm afraid there's no mystery at all. I just happened to be there when you arrived."

"Who invited you?" Sylvan asked.

"Why, one of the investigators—actually, one who perished in the unfortunate incident. I ran into him, I believe, at a political fund-raiser several months ago, and he extended an invitation to visit."

"Convenient," Sylvan said, "and a dead end."

Michel grimaced. "Unfortunately."

Sylvan glanced at Francesca. "And what about the attack on my laboratories? Were you aware of a conspiracy to attack the Pack?"

"Of course not," Francesca said. "Why, Sylvan, if I had been, I would certainly have alerted you. What would be the advantage of my keeping quiet?"

Drake laughed. "If you thought Sylvan's enemies might defeat her, or weaken her enough that another wolf would challenge to take over the Pack, I'm quite sure you would support the likely winner. And a Pack led by a more pliable Alpha, one you might even control, would be much more desirable than one you can't. Loyalty is not a word in your vocabulary."

Francesca pressed her hand to her breast. "I'm wounded you think so little of me, Prima. I hope it's not personal. You must know, I have no intention of compromising your…relationship…with—"

"Please," Drake said. "My mate is not susceptible to your charms, and as long as you don't touch her, I have no reason to tear your arm off. So we have no need to discuss past history."

Francesca laughed, clearly delighted. "Oh, I do like you." She glanced at Sylvan. "I imagine she's even able to meet your considerable needs in bed."

Sylvan growled and Drake casually draped an arm around her

waist. "Whoever planted the bombs in our lab had inside knowledge. Do you know how a Were might have been persuaded to betray Sylvan?"

Francesca was silent a long moment, wondering about blood-addicted Weres, and what they might do to avoid exposure or for the opportunity to host regularly. If Nicholas was using Vampires to recruit Weres, she needed to put a stop to his clandestine operations before she was pulled into an unwanted war. "It would be foolish of me to suggest you have no enemies, Sylvan. We both know that's not true. The humans would like nothing better than for all of us to fight among ourselves until we either weaken each other enough that the humans can defeat us or complete the job for them and wipe each other out." She rose and strode down the marble stairs to Michel's side. The levity was gone from her face. "I intend to protect my Dominion from those who seek to destroy us. The Praetern Coalition, if successful, will only subject us to the rule of a weaker species. If you ally with me and withdraw your support for the Coalition, I will use all my resources to discover who is behind the attacks on you and your Pack."

"And if I don't withdraw my support?" Sylvan asked quietly.

Francesca's sighed. "Sylvan, you're trying to make peace with an enemy who seeks only to destroy you. Valorous, but misguided."

"You sound very sure."

"I would hate to see you become a target for extremists." She smiled, her eyes glacially cold. "And now, with your Prima pregnant, you are so much more vulnerable."

Sylvan's wolf surged at the subtle threat, and Sylvan's control frayed. "If you—"

"Fortunately," Drake said, tightening her grip on Sylvan, "I am more than strong enough to protect myself."

Niki rumbled a low warning. "And every wolf is pledged to defend the Prima."

Francesca laughed softly. "Of course. But it pays to be cautious. Why ask for trouble?"

"You are far more vulnerable than the Timberwolves," Sylvan said, her mind clearing. "The Vampires no longer have an army. Your guard is powerful, but small in numbers. Even if you could recruit soldiers, you haven't fought a war in centuries."

"I haven't forgotten how to fight," Michel said, "and individually we are stronger than a hundred humans."

"That may be, but they have hundreds of thousands to bring against you." Sylvan waited for Drake to object to what she was thinking but felt only support from Drake's wolf. "I can pledge you an army if you bring me evidence of those who have moved against me."

"If I knew and told you," Francesca said sharply, "I would *need* an army. Do you want a war?"

"One may be coming. Who do you want to fight by your side, Francesca? My wolves or humans who would see you dead as soon as I am?"

Francesca stepped closer and extended a hand toward Sylvan's face. "My darling Sylvan—"

"I wouldn't," Drake said quietly.

Francesca smiled. "Merely a gesture of friendship." She waved the same hand toward Michel, who stepped to her side, and she slid her hand through the crook of Michel's arm. "We'll ask our sources. And if I uncover any evidence of who planned and helped arrange that attack this morning, I'll tell you."

"And who's behind the kidnapping and experiments?" Sylvan pressed.

"I might be able to help you there," Francesca said. Sylvan was right—for now, at least, the Weres were stronger allies. Michel stiffened but remained silent.

"Yes?"

"I can't prove he's involved, but I do know that Nicholas Gregory has long-standing interests in more than one research facility focused on…nonhuman studies, including the one where your wolves were held."

"Gregory," Sylvan said, unsurprised. "We'll be waiting to hear from you."

"If I learn anything, you'll be the first to know."

Sylvan said, "Thank you for seeing us."

"Of course, darling. Oh," Francesca said as if just remembering, "how is the new Liege?"

"Jody?" Sylvan shrugged noncommittally. "Stronger than ever."

"Really." Francesca's eyes glinted. "I'm so glad to hear that."

"I'm glad, since Jody has already pledged her support to the Timberwolves, and I to her."

Francesca turned her back and mounted her throne. "Just remember who holds the power, darling. Good night."

Michel led them back upstairs to the club. "I suggest you leave immediately. It's dawn."

"We will." Sylvan paused at the exit. "Katya is barely out of adolescence. She is old enough to choose who she tangles with, but if I find you've compelled her, I will kill you. And you won't hear me coming."

Michel laughed. "I look forward to you trying. Good night, Alpha Mir."

Sylvan walked out, filled her lungs with crisp night air that held the remains of neither blood nor death, and slung an arm around Drake's shoulder. "Let's go home."

Chapter Twenty-four

The sky was just lightening as the Rovers pulled through the stockade gates into the heart of the Compound. Becca resisted the urge to drag Jody toward the back of the Rover and away from the first fingers of dawn streaking through the windshield. "Are you all right?"

"Yes," Jody murmured, leaning forward to watch the sky. She was weary, as if her muscles and bones were stretched thin, but she didn't crave sleep. She craved Becca. The taste of her already simmered on her tongue. "I used to be able to tolerate sunlight for a few hours. I don't feel as drained as I did yesterday at this time. I wonder—"

"No," Becca said quickly, taking Jody's hand, ready to pull her back into the shadows where she'd be safe. This was one enemy she could at least recognize and fight. "I know you're stronger than you should be so soon, but I'm not taking any chances. I want you inside the instant this damn thing stops."

Jody smiled, still unused to being protected by anyone, and certainly not by a human. This human, though, was far from weak. Becca not only held her heart, she held her life, and each time Becca fed her, her dependence on the unique chemical makeup of Becca's blood grew stronger. Soon she would be able to survive only a few days on any other blood without losing strength, and only a few weeks without being incapacitated. Other hosts might keep her alive, but she'd be an empty shell. She brushed her fingers through Becca's hair, kissed her. "You worry for nothing."

"Not for nothing," Becca murmured, kissing her back. "For everything."

"All of my guards are Risen. Everyone needs shelter. I will see to them first."

The Rover bumped to a stop. Becca kept a grip on Jody's hand and leaned forward to speak to Zahn. "See that Jace and Dasha deliver the captive Were to whoever is in charge here. Once the prisoner is secured, post guards on our rooms. The Liege and the Risen will be going directly inside."

Zahn flicked a quick look in Jody's direction, then nodded curtly. "Yes, Consort. I'll see it done."

Becca kissed Jody's cheek. "Your guards will follow your lead. Take them inside now. Everything else is under control."

Jody smiled wryly. "You seem to have a natural talent for taking charge."

"Not anything I get a lot of practice at lately." Becca pushed the rear doors open and jumped down. Her back twinged and muscles she hadn't even known she had complained. But she felt far better than she had any right to after the events out in the forest. Jody wasn't the only one who was stronger than she had been. She threaded her arm through Jody's. "Let's go inside. I need you."

Jody's eyes flared. "Your blood calls to me."

"Just my blood?"

"No," Jody murmured. "You are my blood, my heart, my life."

Becca tightened her hold. "As you are mine."

Max strode across the compound leading a squadron of Weres, his broad shoulders stretching the fabric of his black T-shirt, his muscular thighs encased in matching BDUs. His dark eyes met Jody's, cut to the second Rover where Jace and Dasha pulled the captive cat Were from the rear. He was still naked and shackled, but recovered enough to snarl and thrash in their grip. "Good to see you back. I see you were successful."

Jody smiled thinly. "An interesting night."

"Your rooms are ready in the barracks," Max said.

"My guards will need hosts," Jody said.

"We have volunteers. They're waiting inside." Max turned to Lara, who stood with Raina by the lead vehicle. "The *sentries* will secure the prisoners."

A quartet of *sentries* armed with stun guns stepped forward.

"Only one prisoner." Lara slid her hand around the back of Raina's neck. "She comes with me."

"You'll be…sleeping, won't you?" Max asked, his voice flat, unchallenging, but shot through with steel.

Lara snarled, a deep warning growl. "She comes with me."

"I can't have a prisoner unsecured inside the Compound," Max said. "I'm sorry, but—"

Jody said, "My guards will see that Alpha Carras remains in her quarters. You are welcome to post your own security, if you like."

Max's eyes narrowed as he deliberated. "Very well. But if the cat attempts to leave the building, then she will be caged."

"Very reasonable," Jody said. "Now, if that's all, we'll go inside."

Max signaled to a young dark-haired Were with stunning green eyes. "Misha, escort Liege Gates and her company to their rooms."

"Yes, *Centuri*."

Lara sensed Raina's cat pacing in frustration, and as they fell in behind Jody and Becca, she gently squeezed Raina's neck. "I thought you'd prefer a bed in the barracks to a cell. You can see your cubs at sunfall."

"I'd prefer to be released so I can take my cubs back to my territory. I kept my word and brought you the rogue."

"I know. But protocol demands the Alpha release you."

Raina hissed. "Your Alpha does not rule me."

Lara smiled as she climbed the familiar steps into the barracks. "No one does. But if you're going to lead your Pride again, you'll need allies."

Raina's lip curled. "Wolves and Vampires?"

"We fought well together." Lara nodded to the male Were who stood at attention beside the open door to a room that held two beds set on opposite walls beneath a high window. The rough plank floor was bare. A plain dresser separated the two beds. A functional room meant for sleeping between long shifts on the training field and days on patrol in the mountains. She shut the door behind them and closed the shutters on the windows, blocking out the rising sun. The room fell into shadow. She sat on the bed and pulled off her boots. "Jody took your part out there. That will carry weight with the Alpha."

Raina leaned against the door. "I can do more good in the mountains than I can locked up here. The cats are wild, but they're fierce fighters. You saw that for yourself. I can raise a militia to help in the coming struggles."

"Why would you?" Lara asked, genuinely curious. "What do you care about the wolves or the Vampires? The cats aren't targets."

Raina shrugged. "And after you're gone? It will be open hunting season on the cats, and then the foxes and coyotes, and eventually we'll all be exterminated. The cats have lived in the shadow of the wolves for millennia, and we've resented it. But those same shadows have been long and dark, and kept us hidden too. Now we are as visible as you."

"Me?" Lara smiled thinly. "My wolf or Vampire?"

"Both."

Lara was beside her in a flash, crowding her close to the door. "Can I trust you to stay here today?"

"You said I could trust you," Raina said. "Now you will have to trust me."

So close, Lara could scent the power in Raina's blood and the heat pouring from her body. Raina was fire and strength, and she was so cold. She'd bled out there in the forest, and she was weak and cold and hungry. "The other bed is yours. Get some sleep. The Alpha will return soon."

"You're hungry," Raina said. "I feel your need."

Lara snarled, resenting her inability to hide her weakness from the cat. "I'll send for one of the wolves."

She reached past Raina for the doorknob, and Raina gripped her wrist. The tips of Raina's claws bit at Lara's skin, and her sex pulsed. "You don't want to play with me now, big Cat."

"I am stronger than any wolf," Raina said with feline arrogance. "I will feed you."

Lara brushed her mouth over Raina's neck, and Raina's taste pierced her with more than hunger. Desire, longing, a need so deep she ached. A very, very dangerous cat. "I've fed from you too many times already. My blood recognizes your blood. You would be wise to stay away from me."

"My blood recognizes yours," Raina whispered, the burn in her body too strong for her reason. She was at heart a cat, and her cat crouched, ready to pounce. Raina ran her hands up Lara's arms, over her shoulders, and down her chest. The body beneath the thin T-shirt was honed muscle and graceful curves—as beautiful as it was powerful. Her cat purred, a deep rumble of anticipation and desire. She tugged Lara's lip into her mouth, bit down. "My cat recognizes you. I want you."

Lara trembled at the scent of cat enveloping her—evergreen and earth, intoxicating and seductive. Raina was an Alpha, her call enough to bring even a dominant Were to her knees. Lara's wolf alerted, pushed through the Vampire hunger roiling her lust, and rumbled an invitation.

Raina smiled and stroked Lara's face. "Listen to your wolf. She isn't afraid."

"I'm not afraid, but you should be." Lara pressed her hands flat on the door to keep from touching her. If she moved, she would take her, pull her beneath her, feast on her. She rested her forehead against Raina's, the breath burning through her chest. Her loins ached, her bones hollowed. She craved Raina like life. Raina *was* life. "I need you." She raised her head, her vision eclipsed by flame. "I can compel you to come to me. I will, if my need grows stronger. You should not feed me again."

Raina gripped Lara's wrists, pulled her hands from the door, and pressed them to her breasts. Her nipples were hard, her breasts full. Her sex was swollen and ready. "I ran with you, I fought with you, and now I want to couple with you. I want to spend with your mouth at my throat. You can't compel me to do what I want to do."

"I'm too weak to be strong," Lara whispered.

"That's all right." Raina pulled her to the bed, guided her down, and slid on top of her. "I'm strong enough for both of us."

Raina kissed her and Lara groaned. The sound of Lara's need filled Raina with joyful power. She tore Lara's shirt down the middle and pulled her own off over her head. She stretched out on top of her, sliding her breasts over Lara's. She licked the bite she'd made in Lara's shoulder and felt Lara surge beneath her. Lara's canines gleamed in the dusky light, her eyes like beacons of fire. Raina reached between them, opened her pants and Lara's. Raising higher, her mouth claiming Lara's, she stripped them both of the remnants of their clothing and straddled Lara's abdomen. Lara's skin was hot, her pelt line a luxurious tease over Raina's distended clitoris.

"I would have you beg," Raina gasped, dragging her tongue down the center of Lara's chest and over her nipple, "but my cat is impatient to taste you."

Lara reached up, gripped her hands. Her voice was a dangerous growl. "I have little control left. I am all Vampire now, and I must feed."

"I know," Raina hissed and slid herself over Lara's hard stomach, coating her with her essence. She felt herself fill. The pressure, the need to spend, was all she knew. She leaned down again, her breasts swaying over Lara's mouth. Lara ran her canines over her nipples and Raina jerked. "Suck me."

Lara reared up, closed her mouth over Raina's breast, drew her in.

Raina's head snapped back, her mind blasted with pleasure. She was close, so close.

"I need you," Lara warned.

"I'm ready. Please. Now."

Lara wrapped her arms around Raina and twisted, pulling Raina beneath her. With her hips notched hard between Raina's thighs, her sex pressed to Raina's, she took her throat in one swift plunge. Raina came, a sharp cry wrenched from her throat, her *victus* exploding over Lara's sex. Lara drank and piercing pleasure flooded her with power. She thrust, her sex emptying in rhythmic pulsations, and surrendered to Raina's call.

❖

Sylvan and her wolves reached the Compound just after dawn. Max met them on the steps of headquarters.

"Any problems?" Sylvan asked.

"No, Alpha." He glanced toward the barracks. "Lara and the others returned a half hour ago. I provided quarters for the Vampires and guards as instructed."

"Good. How did they fare?"

"They brought back a prisoner. He's below, with Callan and Dasha standing guard. Jace was injured and I sent her to the infirmary."

"Is it serious?" Drake came to stand beside Sylvan and hooked her fingers through a belt loop on Sylvan's pants. Francesca's seductive thrall still hovered around Sylvan like a cloying mist. She wanted to wipe the memory of the Vampire's taunts from her mind. She wanted to claim her mate, skin to skin. And soon.

"No, Prima. Elena said she would be fine after her wounds were tended and she shifted."

"Good," Drake said.

"What about the other cat?" Sylvan asked.

Max grimaced. "She is with the Vampires." He looked down, then focused on Sylvan's shoulder, keeping his gaze below hers. "She's with Lara, Alpha."

"I see. You're relieved, Max."

"Yes, Alpha." He turned and strode away.

Sylvan twined her fingers in Drake's hair and kissed her. "I'll speak with Lara. Andrew will see you home."

Drake caressed Sylvan's jaw. "I'll check on Jace and the cat cubs. You can meet me at the infirmary and we'll go home together. Don't be long—I need you."

Sylvan pulled Drake close and rubbed her cheek against Drake's hair. "As soon as I can—I'll show you what you mean to me."

Drake kissed her throat. "You don't need to show me. I feel it with every breath."

"I love you," Sylvan murmured.

"I know. I love you. Go see to Lara."

Sylvan waited until Drake reached the infirmary and then strode to the barracks. At the far end of the hall, Vampires and wolves stood guard outside a half dozen closed doors. The Vampires regarded her impassively as she approached. The wolves straightened to attention. Misha stepped forward as Sylvan slowed. "All quiet?"

"Yes, Alpha," Misha said briskly.

"Where is Lara?"

Misha pointed to the room across from the one she guarded with Zahn. "There, Alpha."

The hall had no exterior windows, so Sylvan wasn't concerned about exposing the Risen to light. She also wasn't concerned about Lara's privacy. Lara was alone with a prisoner while she was compromised. Foolish, perhaps lethally so. Sylvan reached for the knob, and a human servant, a chestnut-haired male she didn't know, slid in front of her, blocking her way. "The warlord is not to be disturbed until sunfall."

Sylvan growled softly, a quiet warning. The human servant avoided direct eye contact, probably more out of protocol than respect. He was following orders, but Lara was her *centuri*, no matter what else she might be, and she would see her safe. "The cat is inside?"

"The Were is with the warlord by the warlord's request." He hesitated. "Alpha."

"The warlord has nothing to fear from me," Sylvan murmured, "but you will want to step aside now."

From behind her, Zahn said, "Let her pass."

The servant stepped aside and Sylvan entered.

A warning growl from the other side of the room had Sylvan's wolf on instant alert. A gigantic cat, glowing golden even in the near darkness, lay stretched out on the bed between Lara and the door. Sylvan's wolf snarled, her hackles rising, but Sylvan held her back. She and the cat made eye contact across the narrow space, gauging each other's strength. The cat snarled.

"You don't want to challenge me," Sylvan warned softly.

Next to the cat, Lara twitched and turned, her arm draping around the cat's shoulders. Her fingers tightened in the cat's ruff. "It's all right," Lara murmured groggily. "The wolf is a friend."

The big cat swung her head around, nuzzled Lara's neck. Lara's eyes opened a fraction and she struggled to emerge from the torpor that drained her strength and fogged her mind. She focused on Sylvan. "She won't run."

Sylvan scented the air, smelled cat and wolf, and *other*. The scents twisted, blended, entwined. The cat lay tangled with Lara in a way that was more than physical. Sylvan's wolf huffed and relaxed. The cat's tail stopped swishing, the muscles in her shoulders and powerful flanks relaxed.

"Guard her well." Sylvan turned and left.

Veronica waited until a decent hour to call Nicholas. She poured her first cup of coffee and walked out on the small curved stone balcony adjoining her bedroom. Five a.m., and the late summer sun streaked through the windows and slashed across her bed. An hour ago the drapes had been drawn and the room lit only by candles. She would have kept the room in shadows all day if it meant keeping Luce in bed with her. She blinked, her eyes watering. She hadn't slept more than an hour or two after Luce brought her back from Nocturne. She'd been exhausted, but her body had vibrated with urgency. She'd coaxed Luce to feed from her again, and the orgasms had satisfied her craving for that elusive sensation of being consumed by physical passion, but the need had been sated for only a few minutes. When she'd pressed Luce to take more, Luce had refused.

"You've had enough for tonight," the Vampire said, closing the wounds in Veronica's throat with the stroke of her tongue. "You need to replenish. And I must go. Dawn is coming."

Nothing she said could convince Luce to stay for a few more moments. Now she was alone, and the day stretched heavily before her. She'd talk to Nicholas and then try to sleep. When sundown came and the Vampires awakened, she would be strong again.

She sipped her coffee and listened to the phone ring.

"Veronica," Nicholas said flatly by way of greeting.

"Good morning. At least I hope it's a good morning."

"A busy one," Nicholas said curtly. "How can I help you?"

"I was hoping you'd tell me my new laboratory facilities are ready."

Nicholas sighed. "Veronica, I need at least a week, possibly longer. We're not just talking logistics, we're talking a great deal of money."

"I understand that, Nicholas, but we were making very good progress. Now is not the time to lose momentum."

He was silent a long moment. "There might be a way to facilitate our recovery."

Across the street a woman in black tights and a cropped tee jogged by, out for her morning run. Her blond hair swung around her shoulders, and Veronica was reminded of the golden strands that teased her throat when Luce fed. She drew her fingers down between her breasts, brushing them lightly over her nipples. They tightened and tingled. She touched her throat where Luce had taken her, and her clitoris hardened.

"Veronica?"

She jerked. "Yes? What?"

"I have a contact in the government. It's possible we can draw on that resource for funding. That would help us rebuild much faster."

"Well, I certainly hope you—"

"I think, considering your impressive reputation as a researcher, it would be better if you pleaded our case. With luck, I can set up an appointment for you today."

"All right," she said, even though she was suddenly so tired her legs shook. She needed secure, private facilities to continue her work. Right now, Nicholas was the only person she trusted with the true nature of her experiments, and she needed his considerable resources. At least for now. "Let me know when and where."

"Excellent."

"But, Nicholas, this time we need to be sure our laboratories will be secure. I can't afford to lose any more subjects. And, on that matter, we're going to need more."

"Don't worry, I'll take care of that. And I think I can safely say we won't be bothered much longer by Sylvan Mir."

Veronica smiled. Wouldn't Francesca be grateful if she could give her some truly valuable information. "Tell me."

CHAPTER TWENTY-FIVE

Sylvan closed the door to Lara's room and walked past the Were guards and Vampire servants protecting her allies. She tested the air, sorting the myriad scents—the familiar tapestry of her Pack, each individual thread familiar and distinct, at once a part of and apart from the whole. On the fringes of that unassailable whole drifted the strange new signatures of the Vampires. Faintly metallic, with undertones of stone and flame. And here and there, an even newer mixture of the pungent wild smell of Were and the cool, flinty edge of Vampire. Members of her Pack who had hosted for the Vampires and now carried remnants of the Vampire essence in their cells. Sylvan's wolf rumbled fretfully, unhappy with the nearness of those not-Pack and the taint of difference lingering on the wolves who had fed them. But Sylvan understood what her wolf could not—she ruled by primal strength and force of will, but she was not a tyrant. She would not chain her wolves in spirit or body.

Sylvan followed one particular scent, stronger than all the others, to the second floor of the barracks. No room, no place, no thought in her territory and beyond was closed to her, but she knocked quickly before opening the door. Katya sat in the center of one of the narrow beds with her back against the wall, her arms wrapped around her raised knees, her head turned toward the open window. Her face was pale in the bright golden glow of the early morning sunlight streaming in. As Sylvan closed the door, Katya jumped to her feet.

"Alpha," she said, her eyes widening.

"Stand down, *Sentrie*." Sylvan scanned the room Katya shared with Gray. "Where is Gray?"

"She's running. She—" Katya sat on the edge of the bed, her hands clasped between her knees, her shoulders stiff. "She said she wouldn't stay in the same room with me, not when I carried the enemy in me."

"Most wolves wouldn't recognize the scent of a Vampire so easily."

Katya drew a sharp breath. "The night we were rescued, there was a lot of blood—mine and some of the Vampires' too. She'd remember."

Sylvan walked to the window and glanced down on the Compound where her Pack went about the morning business. Patrols returned through the stockade gate, *sentries* climbed to the ramparts, cadets trained in the open courtyard, and beta wolves—teachers and medics and caretakers—headed for the schoolrooms and nursery tucked safely in the heart of the facility. An ordinary morning in the lives of those she had sworn to protect and keep free. When she'd assumed her father's position as Alpha, she'd thought her greatest challenge would be negotiating with the humans, who outnumbered all the Praetern species by thousands to one, to secure the safety of her Pack. She had not expected to have to fight her fellow Praeterns, but she should have. The world as they had known it had changed the day their invisibility disappeared, and when power was suddenly fluid, Praeterns and humans alike sought more.

She turned and regarded Katya. "Tell me about Michel."

Katya kept her head up, her gaze directed to Sylvan while avoiding direct eye contact. "She saved me."

"Possibly." Sylvan ignored the quick rush of anger and suspicion along with her wolf's snarl of rage. As much as she distrusted Michel, she cared more for Katya's feelings. Katya had been tortured and violated and debased, but here, among those she depended upon, she would be respected. "We don't really know what happened that night."

"I remember," Katya said. "Not the faces, not the people, but I remember her—what I felt, what she made me feel." She trembled, ran a hand over her chest and down her belly. "Touching me, shielding me." She squeezed her hand into a fist pressed between her breasts. "I still feel her."

"She's a Vampire," Sylvan said, making a statement, not an accusation. "A very powerful one."

"I know. But she doesn't compel me."

"Are you sure?"

Katya raised her eyes briefly to Sylvan's before looking away. A brave gesture. "Yes, Alpha. I'm certain."

"Why," Sylvan asked softly. "Why are you certain?"

"Because I can feel her call right now." Katya's eyes glimmered with the glow of her wolf, a strong, young dominant wolf just coming into her power. Under other circumstances she would be ready to tangle at every opportunity, but Katya's call was muted. Suppressed. But not now, not when she absorbed the seductive caress of Michel's mind into every cell. Now her wolf was alive and ready. "If she wanted to compel me, she could. But she waits."

Sylvan sighed. She could point out Michel might be playing with her, that Vampires by nature were master manipulators. Until she'd met Jody, seen her with Becca, she would have sworn Vampires cared for nothing except power. That was true with Francesca, and yet…and yet, she had played a dangerous game with Francesca, more than once. Katya was young, but she was Sylvan's wolf. "All right. I won't ask you to stay away from her, but I can't let her use you to harm you or the Pack. You understand that?"

"Yes, Alpha." Katya stood, her head up, her eyes clear. "Gray wants me gone. I can move back to the campus. I won't be a danger to the Pack if I know nothing, if I—"

Sylvan cleared the distance between them and wrapped an arm around Katya's shoulders. When Katya trembled and her wolf cowered, Sylvan's chest tightened. Her wolves submitted to her out of respect for her strength and leadership, not out of fear. She pulled Katya close, kissed her forehead. "No. You are not going anywhere. You are my wolf and I want you here. Gray will work out her problems."

"I don't want to make her uncomfortable."

"You don't," Sylvan murmured. "The memories do, and you are the light in her nightmares. You will stay for her, and for the Pack."

"Yes, Alpha." Katya burrowed her face in Sylvan's chest. Her wolf crept forward, close to Sylvan's warmth.

Sylvan caressed her back and sent comfort and welcome to Katya's wolf. "As soon as Elena clears you for full duty, you'll return to the *sentries*, but there will be times I will need you. Both you and Gray. You're the only ones who can positively identify your captors."

Katya nodded. "Anything."

"Good." Sylvan rubbed her cheek over Katya's temple. "I want you to see Elena today."

"I will." Katya pulled back. "Alpha—"

"Yes?"

"I won't put anyone or anything before my duty to the Pack."

"I know." Sylvan stepped away. "Now get some rest."

Sylvan left the barracks, the image of Katya's wolf beaten and afraid burning in her mind. Katya might think she could put duty before need and desire, but Sylvan wasn't at all sure Michel wouldn't compel her to do otherwise.

❖

Max waited for Sylvan on the steps of the infirmary. "The Prima said you were coming here."

"What is it?" Sylvan asked.

"Becca talked to the other prisoner, Martin, while you were gone. She thinks he will cooperate if we let him speak to his superiors."

"Since they say they are working on behalf of the Praeterns," Sylvan said, "let's let them prove it. Give him his call."

"Should I monitor it?"

"Can you trace it?"

He grinned, a predator's satisfied smile. "Yes, Alpha."

"Then go ahead. He can't tell them any more than they already suspect—that we have him. He can't pinpoint our location, but if you can trace them—"

"We'll scramble his call. They won't be able to locate his exact position, but everyone knows where Pack land is located."

"They don't seem foolish enough to try to breach our security, but put the patrols on alert."

"Yes, Alpha."

"And, Max—I want four guards on the Prima at all times." She grimaced, glanced at the infirmary. "And tell them to try to stay out of sight."

"Uh…yes, Alpha."

"I'm going to check on Jace." Sylvan leapt up onto the porch and went in search of her mate. Max probably thought hiding the extra protection from Drake would be as successful as she did, but it was worth a try. Maybe Drake would be distracted enough by her approaching delivery not to notice.

"How is she?" Sylvan asked when she entered the treatment room.

Elena paused in the process of cleansing the scores of slashes and bites on Jace's shoulders, limbs, and torso.

"She's been in a fight," Elena murmured. "But she should be fine as soon as I clean these and she shifts."

"It's nothing, Alpha." Jace lay on the treatment table with her twin, Jonathan, beside her. Her eyes were clear but she was pale.

Sylvan walked to the table opposite Jonathan and gripped an uninjured area of Jace's upper arm. "I understand you fought well. Anything to report?"

"The cats aren't used to tandem fighters," Jace said eagerly. "They hunt alone, one-on-one, so paired attacks take them off guard. Flank attacks open them to swift frontal strikes. We fought larger numbers all the way back and we won."

Sylvan smiled. "That's because you're wolves."

Jace grinned. "Yes, Alpha."

"She won't be fit for duty for a while," Elena said.

Sylvan nodded. "Stand down for a few days. Eat well, regain your strength."

"I'm fine, Alpha." Jace tried to sit up to prove it.

"I know." Sylvan held her down with very little pressure. "But I need my *centuri* at full strength. Two days."

Jace sighed. "Yes, Alpha."

"I'll see she rests," Jonathan said. Jace growled at him.

Sylvan glanced at Elena. "Good enough?"

"I'd prefer three, but two will do."

Sylvan brushed a strand of dark hair off Elena's cheek. "Good. Take care of my wolves."

Elena rubbed her cheek against Sylvan's palm. "Always, Alpha."

"Have you seen the Prima?"

"She went to the nursery."

Sylvan found Drake with Sophia and the cat cubs. The cubs were in pelt and seemed even bigger than she remembered. Their coats seemed thicker, the brown stripes blending into the deep gold making them resemble their mother even more. Sophia cradled one in her lap and was feeding it from a bottle.

"How are they doing?" Sylvan asked.

Sophia's eyes shone with pleasure. "They were hungry enough for me to coax them to feed."

Drake said, "I think they recognize Sophia as Omega and trust her instinctively."

"Yes," Sylvan said. "And considering that their mother is an Alpha, she's probably communicated with them enough to reassure them she will be back for them."

"They have been calmer in the last hour," Sophia said.

Sylvan leaned down and peered at the lone cub still in its crib. The male. He drew back his lips to show canines that were definitely larger than the last time he'd snarled at her. She growled, letting her wolf show, and to his credit, he held her gaze another second before crouching back and lowering his eyes. She reached in, gripped his ruff, and shook him lightly in a show of dominance. She kept him in her grip until he relaxed and arched beneath her palm. Sweeping her hand over his back, she murmured, "Hello, little Cat."

Drake leaned against Sylvan's side. "I think they have some awareness of who we are."

"He understands who *I* am now."

Drake laughed softly. "How could he doubt it?"

Sophia put the female cub in next to her brother. "They need to see their mother."

"They will," Sylvan said. "As soon as I've talked to her." She crouched next to the crib and said to the female, who crowded in front of her brother, "Your mother is safe. She's resting. You'll see her later."

The cub stared at Sylvan, her gaze skating across Sylvan's, a faint rumble sounding from the back of her throat.

Sylvan grinned. "They're a lot like their mother. They'll fight even when outnumbered."

"They'll sleep most of the day now," Sophia said.

"Have you been with them the whole time?" Sylvan asked. Sophia's eyes were rimmed with shadow.

"Yes. They don't trust anyone else."

"Get some rest."

"I'm all right, Alpha."

"I know." Sylvan stroked Sophia's shoulder. "Niki will need you too."

"Is she all right?"

"A long night." Sylvan didn't add that Niki had spent the night surrounded by Vampires. Sophia knew Niki's needs.

"I'll go to her as soon as I can."

"Good." Sylvan took Drake's hand. "We won't be leaving again today. I don't want to see Niki anywhere around until tonight."

Once outside, Sylvan grumbled to Drake, "First my Compound is invaded by Vampires, and now cats."

"It seems that Raina fought well with us."

"Yes, but she had no choice. The cats have been our enemies for as long as we have shared the mountains. It will take time to build trust."

Drake rubbed Sylvan's back. "We may not have time."

"I know." Sylvan stopped. "There are a few things I should—"

"Later." Drake signaled for a Rover, and one of the *sentries* jumped in and drove toward them. "Right now, we're going home."

Sylvan's eyes flashed gold. "I might even let you rest later."

Drake laughed. "Did I say I was tired?"

CHAPTER TWENTY-SIX

Francesca dismissed her guards with a slight nod in their direction and extended a hand to Michel. "Come, darling. Enough of tiresome politics. There are so many other…pastimes…we could be enjoying."

Michel followed Francesca across the throne room to a disguised door hidden behind the heavy brocade drapes. The ornately carved section of wall panel swung inward at a touch from Francesca, and they stepped into a dimly lit corridor with rough stone floors and polished granite walls. The narrow passageway led back to Francesca's inner chambers, and when they arrived, her bedroom was empty. Usually at dawn, Francesca's hosts waited on her pleasure, artfully arrayed on her bed like a sumptuous feast. This morning, Francesca must have given orders for them to wait.

Wary of what trap Francesca might have set, Michel crossed to the antique mahogany sideboard and poured two glasses of aged port. She held one out to Francesca. "It seems that our human friends need to learn patience. Nicholas's flawed attack brought Sylvan straight to our door."

Francesca laughed and took the glass. Swirling the dark red wine, she studied Michel above the cut-glass rim. "His tactics do lack finesse. But then he *is* only human, darling."

Michel leaned against the sideboard and sipped the port. Ordinarily she enjoyed Francesca's power games, but then she hadn't really been concerned about losing to her for centuries. After all, there were worse fates than death, terminal boredom being one. But now, she was risking more than her own death. Katya was involved. A faint pressure behind her eyes told her Francesca was mind-probing, something Michel had learned to shield against after her second or third century. She didn't often have to do it, and she was glad. Blocking Francesca took all her will and often left her weakened. Today, though, she deflected the searching force easily. When Francesca frowned, Michel sought to redirect her attention. "Perhaps bringing Sylvan to you will work to your advantage. The wolf seemed willing to support you if a fight comes."

"Perhaps. Although the alliance between Sylvan and Jody Gates could become a problem." Francesca walked to the side of her bed, put down the wineglass, and turned her back. "Untie my laces, will you, darling."

"Of course." Michel set her own wine aside and kissed the back of Francesca's neck before reaching for the ties on the back of her flowing gown. She untied the satin laces which crisscrossed from the valley between Francesca's shoulders to the hollow above her buttocks, drawing each strand through the eyelet with slow, steady pressure. As she worked, she kissed each new expanse of bare skin. Francesca moved back until the fullness of her buttocks settled into Michel's crotch. Michel had fed, and Katya's powerful blood invigorated her. Her clitoris hardened and throbbed.

Francesca glanced at her over her shoulder, her lids half-lowered, her eyes liquid heat. "If Jody raises an army of Weres, she will be a formidable adversary."

"She's never shown any indication that she wanted to rule, Regent." Michel skimmed the gown down Francesca's sides.

"Things change, don't they," Francesca murmured. She stretched back an arm and draped it around Michel's neck, tilting her head to press a kiss to Michel's throat. An instant later her incisors pierced the skin above Michel's collarbone, the pinpoints of pain releasing an arrow of lust that struck hard in the pit of her stomach.

"Sometimes they do. But sometimes, everything is exactly as it should be." Michel wrapped her arms around Francesca's waist and pulled Francesca roughly against her body. She kissed the side of Francesca's throat and the edge of her jaw and brushed her mouth over Francesca's ear. She cupped Francesca's exposed breasts and caressed the firm, cool flesh. Finding Francesca's nipples, she pinched, slow and hard. "This never changes."

"Mmm, yes." Francesca sighed, her teeth slashing shallow rivulets in Michel's throat, reminding her she could tear her throat out in an instant. "But we mustn't grow complacent, must we?"

"No. We shouldn't." Michel pivoted sharply and pushed Francesca face down on the bed. Straddling her prone figure, she clamped her thighs on either side of Francesca's hips, skimmed her hand up the center of Francesca's back, and tethered her to the bed with a hand on her neck. With her free hand, she tugged the gown to one side and slid her hand over Francesca's ass and between her thighs. Francesca's cheek was pressed against the bed, her mouth partially open, her eyes hazed.

"I still know what you need." Michel filled her in one fast, deep stroke.

Francesca gasped and arched beneath her. "I need to feed, darling, before I can come."

Michel leaned down and sucked the soft flesh at the juncture of Francesca's neck and shoulder. Francesca understood one thing, and one thing only. Power, and the dominance that came with it. Michel had revealed a vulnerability when she'd let Francesca see her feed from Katya in the club. That had been a mistake—one she couldn't undo and might not be able to avoid repeating. Even now, the thought of Katya made her blood roil while the female she fucked did nothing more than trigger a reflex need. She hadn't truly wanted anything for a very long time and was only now realizing it. Now she hungered for Katya's taste, craved the press of her body, lusted for the exhilaration of her bite. She couldn't give her up and she wouldn't let Francesca have her. "I'll let you feed in a minute. But I'm going to fuck my fill first."

"You play a dangerous game, darling,"

"Do I?" Michel withdrew almost completely and then plunged deep inside her. Francesca closed around her fingers, slick and hard. Her hips churned beneath Michel's pelvis. Michel fucked her ruthlessly, dispassionately, and Francesca's body burned like ice around her fingers.

"I'm close but I can't—" Francesca's incisors gleamed, her face contorted with lust and hunger. "Damn you, let me feed."

Michel sent out a call to Daniela, *Bring your mistress's hosts*, and flipped Francesca over, sliding her hand out and back into her again so quickly Francesca didn't have time to dislodge her. She stretched out above her and pressed her mouth to Francesca's neck. "I'll make you come. I promise."

Francesca raked her nails down Michel's back, shredding her shirt, drawing blood. "I'll make you suffer for this."

Michel laughed and pushed harder, massaging Francesca's clitoris with her palm. "I hope so."

Francesca's bedroom door opened, and Daniela led a human female and a male Were, both naked, into the room.

Michel glanced over. "Bring them to your mistress."

Daniela guided the hosts to the bed and instructed them to lie down. The male was already erect, and Michel moved to Francesca's side. Skating her fingers up to Francesca's clitoris, she said to him, "Fuck her."

He rolled between her thighs and filled her in one heaving thrust. Francesca pulled the human female, whose eyes were glazed with thrall, down next to her and struck her neck with lightning speed. The female cried out in shocked ecstasy, and Francesca groaned as she fed and orgasmed.

Michel fisted a handful of the male's thick dark hair and jerked his head back. He would be a poor substitute for the one she really wanted, but she needed the taste of wolf. Closing her eyes, she fed.

❖

At the knock on the barracks door, Max came instantly awake and jumped up naked from the narrow bed. "Report."

"Sir." The door opened and Lyn, a young *sentrie,* stepped inside. "I'm sorry, *Centuri*, but an unauthorized vehicle is approaching the west gate. Should we intercept?"

Max pulled on his pants and buttoned the fly high enough to keep them on. "What kind of vehicle?"

"A Jeep."

"How many?"

"Four passengers." She paused as he strode past her into the hall. "Humans."

He shot her a glance. "Humans? The only humans who ever come here are reporters or lost sightseers."

She shook her head as they bounded down the barracks steps and crossed the courtyard toward the west gate. "They're not tourists, *Centuri*. They're wearing camo."

"Weapons?"

"None that we could see—they might be concealed."

"They would be foolish to come onto our land armed." Max leapt up onto the barricade where Callan, the captain of the guards, stood peering toward the forest with a pair of high-powered binocs. Callan handed them to Max. "Only one vehicle. We decided to let them come close enough to attempt identification. They're strangers."

Max focused on the approaching Jeep. A male and female sat in the front, the male driving. Two figures were visible behind them, but he couldn't make out their features. "Post a unit by the gate, keep them hidden. No one fires unless the humans make a move first."

"Yes, *Centuri*."

Max swung over the rampart and dropped to the ground as the Jeep slowed in front of the closed stockade gates. He walked forward as the driver's window came down. "You're trespassing on Pack land."

The male behind the steering wheel, a bearded Asian with sharp dark eyes and heavy brows said, "We came to—" He swung his head sharply toward the passenger side as that door opened. "Andrea, you can't g—"

A woman stepped out and closed the door, facing Max across the hood of the Jeep. "We're not trespassing. We're on a recovery mission."

"And what is it you wish to recover?" Max asked. The woman looked to be about thirty, with auburn hair and sable eyes. Her jaw was strong, matching the rest of her sharp, bold features. She was a foot shorter than Max, with medium breasts beneath her khaki camo shirt, a narrow waist, and the slightest flare of hips leading to long, tight thighs. Feminine, but nothing soft about her. This woman was a soldier. Max drew a breath, sampled her scent. A bit of the sea, crisp and cool, a touch of spring leaves, rich and new. His cock hardened and his wolf raised his head in interest.

She'd been watching him, and her eyes widened slightly as if she'd read his response. A faint flush rose up her throat. Her voice was still cool and calm. "You have a prisoner, Martin Hoffstetter. I came for him."

"And who might you be?"

"I'm his commander."

❖

Sylvan wrapped her arms around Drake's waist and fit her body against Drake's back. She burrowed her face in the curve of Drake's neck, her cheek against Drake's shoulder, her crotch pressed tight to Drake's ass. "You should get some sleep."

Drake clasped Sylvan's hand and drew it up between her breasts.

She was satisfied and content, but her blood still stirred. "This is one of those times I can't get enough of you."

Pleased, Sylvan kissed Drake's shoulder. "Is there ever a time you can?"

Drake laughed softly. "Actually, not yet."

"I can sense them more now," Sylvan said, brushing her hand over the swell of Drake's abdomen. "They're strong and alert."

"They're getting impatient." Drake pressed Sylvan's fingers to her side. One of them kicked right at that moment, and she felt Sylvan jolt. Very little surprised Sylvan, nothing caught her off guard, but this had. And knowing that she could bring something new and wonderful into Sylvan's life filled her with joy. "I love you."

Sylvan pressed her face harder to Drake's neck. She feared nothing, except losing Drake. "I love you."

Drake turned enough so Sylvan could see her face. "I know you want to protect me, protect all three of us. I want to protect you every bit as much."

"Yes," Sylvan growled, "but I—"

Drake pressed her fingers to Sylvan's mouth. "Yes, I know you're the Alpha."

Sylvan bit her forefinger. "I was going to say, I'm not pregnant."

"Mmm. I stand corrected." Drake kissed her. "And I was going to say I won't insist on joining you in an active engagement. I don't want your concentration split. But not every battle is fought with teeth and claws."

Sylvan frowned. "What do you mean?"

"It's important that your enemies know you are a formidable adversary. And a mated Alpha is a strong foe."

Sylvan couldn't argue. She rubbed her cheek on Drake's shoulder. "You're right. But nowhere outside our territory is safe."

"Then we'll be careful." Drake shifted onto her back and pulled Sylvan on top of her. She arched beneath Sylvan's body, absorbing her power, exalting in her strength. "I need you again."

Sylvan kissed the mate bite on Drake's shoulder. "I was going to let you sleep, but…" She lowered her head, caught Drake's nipple in her mouth, and sucked.

Drake cried out. "I'm close."

"Wait," Sylvan murmured, kissing her way to Drake's other breast. "I want to taste you everywhere."

"Then you'd best hurry," Drake gasped.

Sylvan pushed down on the bed, kissing her way lower until she could take Drake's swollen clitoris into her mouth. Drake's hands came into her hair, pulling her close as she pushed herself deeper. Sylvan teased with her lips and her tongue, stroking and circling, dipping lower to torment and excite.

"You'll make me come in your mouth," Drake warned. Her blunt claws pressed into Sylvan's scalp. "I want to."

Sylvan growled and lifted Drake to her mouth, taking her deeper still. The taste of her unique essence aroused and completed her. Drake thrust against her mouth, and when she came, the explosion triggered Sylvan's release. When Drake finally relaxed, Sylvan nestled with her cheek against Drake's stomach, listening to the heartbeats of her mate and their young. Her heart pounded in her chest, a symphony of love and wonder.

Drake's hand tightened in her hair. "Sylvan, we have visitors. Whatever they want, tell them to go away."

Sylvan sighed. She'd heard the *centuri* approaching and waited for them to cross the porch to the door. She rolled over and said, before Andrew knocked, "Can it wait?"

"No, Alpha."

"Come in." She pushed to the side of the bed and sat up as Andrew entered.

"We have a situation, Alpha. Four humans arrived at the Compound, insisting we release the human prisoner to them."

"Any show of force?"

Andrew shook his head. "No, Alpha. Max is with them now outside the west gate."

Sylvan rose, stretched, and ran a hand through her hair. "Have Max take them to headquarters. Tell him I'll be right there."

"Yes, Alpha."

"Be sure Callan posts extra patrols outside the gates. Those of you on guard here won't be needed for an hour or so."

Andrew ducked his head. "Thank you, Alpha."

As Sylvan pulled on jeans and a T-shirt, Drake said, "It's not really fair to subject them to our coupling on such a constant basis."

Sylvan leaned down and kissed her. "I don't believe any of them are complaining. They just need time to tangle."

Drake grinned. "Perks of the job, I guess."

Sylvan kissed her again. "Get some sleep. I don't know how long I'll be."

"I'm actually going to follow your advice. If you need me, I'm here."

"I know."

Sylvan walked barefoot out to the porch. Andrew waited by the steps. "Make sure the next shift is in place here before any of you leave. The Prima will be inside."

"I'll stay until Jonathan arrives, Alpha."

She studied him for a long moment. "Then I expect you to do what needs to be done."

He averted his gaze. "Yes, Alpha."

She strode down the stairs and wrapped an arm around his neck, tugging him close. With her mouth against his ear, she said, "We are what we are, Andrew. And denying what you feel will weaken you. I know, I've tried. And I need you strong."

He shuddered in her grip, submitting to her wolf while drawing strength from her. "I'm sorry about losing control earlier."

Sylvan stepped back, keeping a grip on his shoulder. "You didn't. You protected Katya, which is what you should have done. But your rage might not have been just for her. Don't let the past rule you."

Andrew's jaw clenched but he nodded.

She ruffled his hair. "Good. Now, let's see to these humans."

CHAPTER TWENTY-SEVEN

Sylvan leapt up the stairs to her office, pushed through the door, and strode to her desk. The human facing her at parade rest had thick shoulder-length red-brown hair, intense deep brown eyes, and an unmistakable military bearing. Her expression fell somewhere between respectful and aggressive. Were she a wolf, Sylvan would have put her near the top of the order—not yet seasoned enough to assume Alpha command, but headed in that direction. An Alpha who had crossed into another's territory uninvited and making demands would have been 100 percent aggression. Posture was as important as action in the first moments of confrontation.

The air was rife with pheromones. Callan was mated, but the other two males in the room were not. The presence of a very potent unmated female had those two on alert. Max leaned against the stone fireplace, his face emotionless, his massive arms folded across his chest, his gaze riveted to the human female. A second human, a male with curly black hair, a crisp camo shirt, khaki pants, and combat boots, stood on the left side of the room, his jaw tense and his eyes angry. His focus was also the female. Callan, shirtless in faded jeans, stood next to him, his pose deceptively relaxed. His eyes, though, flickered with strands of gold as his wolf eagerly watched his prey.

"I am Sylvan Mir," Sylvan said to the female. "Alpha of the Timberwolves. We usually expect a request to cross our territory before we allow strangers on Pack land."

"And do you always imprison humans without due process?"

Sylvan smiled. There was the aggression she expected. The female was obviously angry, but her voice was cool, her posture controlled. Her scent, however, carried undertones of rage and something Sylvan doubted the human was even aware of. Arousal. Max's wolf paced, agitated and unhappy with the other males so close. Sylvan growled quietly, and Max's wolf backed reluctantly away. She regarded the female. "Due process is what I declare it to be, Ms....?"

The female's expression never changed, but a muscle in her jaw twitched. "Andrea Hoffstetter."

Across the room, Max stiffened.

"The prisoner's mate?" Sylvan asked.

"His sister, but I am here as his unit commander. You have no grounds to hold him."

"I have every reason." Sylvan gestured to the chair in front of her desk. "Why don't you sit down."

Andrea hesitated, obviously not wanting to sit in Sylvan's presence and thus acknowledge her dominance. Sylvan waited. Finally, Andrea sat. Once she had, Sylvan edged a hip onto her desk. She noticed that Andrea, while keeping her head up and her gaze forward, did not lock eyes with her. She had some understanding of how to deal with a Were, at least. Her trespass, then, was an intentional show of belligerence—or strength.

"Your brother was part of a team that held my wolves captive so they could be tortured," Sylvan said quietly. "Tell me, Ms. Hoffstetter, what would you do with an enemy who treated one of your members in the same way?"

"Martin was not responsible for those experiments. He would've told you that by now. He was there gathering information."

Sylvan leaned forward. "Why and for whom?"

The male across the room said sharply, "We're not obligated to tell you anything. You're holding a human against his will, and you have no authority—"

Sylvan cleared her desk and the length of the room in one leap and landed in front of him, her hand on his throat. She took one step forward and lifted him until his back was against the wall and his feet were off the floor. She pressed close until the length of her body covered his, her face an inch away from his startled eyes. She bared her canines and he trembled, fear hormones drenching his skin. "I have the authority to protect my wolves, against any enemy, in any place." She tightened her grip and he wheezed. His face darkened and his eyes watered. "And this is how I handle those who challenge me in my own territory."

"Please." Behind her a chair pushed back, scraping the floor.

Andrea's voice was steady but tight with strain. "Alpha, please forgive his outburst. We did not come here to challenge your authority, but to protect our team member, as you would protect one of yours."

Sylvan didn't relinquish her grip or loosen her hold. She didn't turn her head, but her voice filled the room. "Tell me quickly why I should not kill this intruder."

"Because he is not your enemy, nor am I. Our group wishes to see all of us live in peace."

Sylvan leaned her pelvis into the human's crotch until he winced from the pressure on his flaccid penis. Her voice dropped low, her words little more than a snarl. "Then you should choose your soldiers with greater care, or learn to discipline them."

"Paul," Andrea snapped. "Apologize to the Alpha."

Sylvan slowly relaxed her arm, and the human slid down the wall until his feet touched the floor. His thighs trembled against hers.

"I'm…" He swallowed, his voice rusty, as if he hadn't spoken in a long time. "I'm sorry. I meant no challenge."

"No?" Sylvan said softly. "I think you're lying." She stepped back. "But your commander has spoken for you—this time. Callan, escort this human outside the Compound walls and keep him under guard."

Paul's eyes widened. "I'm not leaving—"

"Paul," Andrea said sharply, "go with them. That's an order. We don't need bloodshed."

Sylvan smiled. "You should listen to your commander. She's wiser than you are."

Callan gripped Paul's arm. "Let's go."

Sylvan returned to her desk and waited until the door had closed again. "If you wish to secure your brother's freedom, this is what I require—the number and location of the other installations, the identity of those in charge, and information about any other Weres in captivity."

"And if I can provide this information, you'll free Martin?"

"I have no wish to imprison him, but I cannot take the word of someone who has been identified as participating in the abuse and torture of my young. I'll need proof. You can start by telling me who is in charge of your organization."

"I can't." Andrea shrugged, impatience showing for the first time. "We don't know the identity of those in charge. Our cells are separate for exactly that reason. Our instructions arrive by coded message. We exchange intelligence in the same way."

"How did your organization form?"

Andrea glanced at Max as if he were her second instead of the absent Paul.

"If you care enough to risk your life in support of the Praeterns," Max said conversationally, "then you should be willing to trust us."

Andrea sighed and nodded. "I'm not telling you anything you don't know. After the Exodus, certain groups, mostly clandestine, formed to block Praeterns from gaining recognition as citizens. Some of those groups went further than wanting to deny your civil rights—they advocated violent extermination."

"We know."

"Not all humans feel the same way. Other groups organized to counter these radical factions—men and women infiltrated some cells while others went undercover in the labs and paramilitary camps. It took almost a year for us to get people like Martin into position. We can't jeopardize their identities. First of all, they'd be killed if they were discovered. Secondly, the information they're able to pass on is vital."

Sylvan was beginning to see why Andrea struck her as more than a civil rights activist. She was a professional. "How is the human government involved?"

Andrea smiled. "Let's just say certain federal organizations have taken an interest in both sides."

"Your group is civilian, but you're not, are you?"

Andrea was quiet for a long moment. "You asked me to trust you. This information could cost me my life."

"One thing you need to learn about Weres," Sylvan said, "is we respect strength above all else. There is no strength without honor. We will not betray you. If you need to be killed, I will do it myself and you will see who takes your life."

"That's encouraging news," Andrea muttered. "Even my brother doesn't know this about me."

Sylvan waited.

"I'm a federal agent. I've been undercover since before the Exodus, when we saw this backlash coming. Your father and the others didn't suddenly decide to bring all of you into the light without preparation."

"You knew my father? He was involved?"

Andrea nodded. "I knew of him, but I was very junior at the time. I don't know the extent of his involvement in organizing the opposition to the humans-first movement."

"He never mentioned working with human law enforcement."

"I can't explain that."

"Maybe he never had the chance," Sylvan murmured. Maybe he had been killed first. But what Andrea Hoffstetter said rang true. "Max. Take Agent Hoffstetter to see her brother. Twenty minutes, supervised."

Max pushed away from the wall. "Yes, Alpha."

"Thank you," Andrea said.

"We'll see if there's reason to," Sylvan said.

❖

Sylvan hadn't slept, but her time with Drake had replenished her. She could hunt for days at a time, running without stopping, so a night or two with no sleep didn't affect her, especially when she had her mate's strength to help restore her. She used the time while Andrea spoke with Martin to call her colleagues on the Praetern Coalition, advising them that she and her Pack were stable after the recent attacks. Even among those Praetern leaders in favor of working with human governments toward peaceful coexistence, suspicions remained. Anything that threatened to destabilize the Coalition could effectively derail negotiations. Several important bills were upcoming, and if she were to be eliminated, the largest Were population in the world would be thrown into chaos, and all progress would come to a halt. She was not only the most visible of the Coalition representatives, she was the most powerful. So she reassured her Vampire, Fae, Psi, and Mage colleagues, and they all affirmed their continuing support.

Finished with her calls, she walked to the huge open windows and looked out across the Compound to the forest and mountains beyond. She had grown up in those mountains, running free and unafraid for the first few years of her life. Her mother had been Alpha then, and the Pack had been strong and unchallenged except by the occasional war party of rogue cats. She wanted her young to experience that freedom and not to be born into the eye of the storm. She wouldn't be able to give them that, not unless she took her Pack deeper into the wilderness. They'd have to leave this part of the continent and go north, where only rogue wolves and feral cats now roamed. She hadn't talked to Drake about it, and the option wasn't one she would choose unless forced to. Such a move would be construed as cowardice, and the Pack might splinter. Too many of her Pack had already assimilated into human society—

some had human mates, many held jobs in the human sector—for her to pull them away. Her rule would be challenged. The humans might declare them outlaws and hunt them with impunity. The wolves were no longer creatures of the wild as they had been a millennium before, and this was their home. The home she was sworn to protect.

A knock sounded on her door and she answered without turning. "Come."

Max entered alone and closed the door. "What would you like me to do with the prisoner, Alpha?"

"Was anything of import discussed?" Sylvan turned from the window and her musings. For now, at least, her path was clear.

"Nothing strategic, Alpha," Max said. "Martin only assured his sister he was physically unharmed."

Max's wolf prowled close to the surface, hungry and agitated, although Max looked totally in control. A lesser wolf might have accepted the superficial appearance of calm, but Sylvan sensed his unrest. His skin shimmered with the flow of pelt near to emerging.

"Is the human aware of your wolf?" Sylvan asked.

He grinned wryly. "Yes, but she pretends otherwise."

"Our populations have interbred sporadically for centuries. She may carry a distant thread of wolf, which is why she responds to you."

"And why my wolf responds to her?"

Sylvan shrugged. "She is a dominant female, and your wolf has been patient a long time. But, like every wolf, he wants to mate."

Max shook his head. "A human is no mate for a wolf."

"I thought that once myself, but our wolves will have what they want."

"She'll take her brother and go, and that will be the end of it."

"Perhaps. But be careful if you're wrong."

He nodded. "Yes, Alpha."

"Bring them to me."

"Right away."

Sylvan stood in front of her desk, and a few moments later Max brought Andrea and Martin Hoffstetter into the room. She gestured to the chairs in front of her desk, stood a few feet away looking down at them. "None of your party will leave my land until I have the information I need."

Martin looked at his sister but said nothing.

"We want something in return," Andrea said calmly.

Sylvan laughed. "And why would I negotiate with you?"

"Because you have the best interests of your Pack at heart and you need allies. We offer you that."

"You said yourself you don't trust your security. Why should I?"

"I'm not asking you to trust our security." Andrea glanced at Max, then back at Sylvan. "Only me."

"And what of your brother?"

"Martin has proved himself. You wouldn't even have known about your young if he hadn't alerted you—at considerable risk to himself." Her gaze met Sylvan's for a fraction of a second. "Some among us felt the risk was too great to alert you, but Martin insisted."

Sylvan knew what Drake would want her to do. Trusting non-Pack was against her nature and her wolf whined unhappily, but Andrea Hoffstetter was right. The Weres needed allies or, at the very least, friends. "What is it that you want?"

"A shared intelligence link with the Praeterns. We have an obligation to protect citizens, just as you have an obligation to protect your Pack. We have enemies on both sides of this divide, just as you do. We can help each other."

"I have no objection to sharing intelligence that does not endanger my wolves."

Andrea nodded. "We'd like to have someone openly associated with your Pack who can move freely among the Praeterns."

"That's not possible," Sylvan said. "Humans would be at risk here. I will not ask my wolves to restrain their natural instincts to accommodate human frailties."

"I believe you'll discover we are stronger than you think." Andrea glanced briefly at Max. "One reason I was…elected…for my post is I had prior knowledge of Weres. I was engaged to one, although I didn't realize that until after the Exodus when he came forward."

Sylvan frowned. "I would have known."

"He is a Snow wolf, in New York City with the foreign embassy."

"What exactly are you suggesting?" Sylvan asked.

Andrea smiled. "I'd think a strategic mating would provide the appropriate cover for one of our people."

"And who do you suggest I nominate for this job?"

"Max." Again she smiled. "And me."

CHAPTER TWENTY-EIGHT

Lara opened her eyes in the semidarkness and catalogued the signatures of life surrounding her. First the familiar scents of a multitude of Weres moving throughout the building, crisscrossing the Compound, trailing out into the forest. Closer, just outside the door, humans—the servants protecting the Vampires while they slept. Beyond the gates, the pungent aroma of wildlife. She detected the pulse of blood and rush of breath mingling with the scents, and her hunger surged. She lay still, searching for her own heartbeat, and could not find it.

Raina's naked back curved against her side, hot and vibrant like fresh-turned earth beneath a summer sun. Lara slid an arm around her waist, holding her even closer, shamelessly reaching for her warmth. She rubbed her face in the curve of Raina's neck, opened her mouth slightly to taste her, let her canines lightly graze warm skin. She hadn't dreamt when she was asleep; she never did anymore. She simply stopped. And when she woke, the hunger was always there. The lancing pain that filled her demanded that she feed, but even more powerful was her need for Raina. She wanted to taste her, drink her, lose herself in the hot pleasure of her. Raina was alive, Raina was life. And she—she was nothing. An empty shell. Lara drew back and a strong hand gripped her wrist.

"Don't go." Raina turned within the circle of Lara's arms, her eyes glowing golden in the near darkness. Her breasts brushed over Lara's, her thigh slipped between Lara's legs. She caressed Lara's face and slowly rubbed her thumb over Lara's mouth. When Lara flicked her tongue over the tips of Raina's fingers, Raina moaned softly. "Mmm, yes. I like waking to your hunger."

"How do you know I hunger?"

"I feel it in your body." Raina kissed her. "I see it in your eyes." She pulled Lara completely on top of her, trapping her in her embrace. She tilted her head, exposing her throat. She was wet against Lara's bare thigh. "You hunger, as do I."

"If I feed from you again, you could become addicted."

Raina laughed. "You think you are so powerful I will follow you everywhere and beg for your bite?"

Lara frowned. "You don't understand—"

"I understand this." Raina dragged Lara's head down and bit her lip hard enough to draw a drop of blood. "I choose to couple with you. I choose to feed you. And I chose to leave my mark on you. You are strong, but so is your need, and I am strong enough to meet it."

"I won't give you another chance to escape," Lara growled, her mouth already filling with feeding hormones. Raina smelled like forever, tasted like eternity.

"I ask for nothing," Raina murmured. She reached between them, cradled Lara's soft clitoris between her fingers. "I want you to feed and I want to feel your need."

"I want you," Lara gasped, bracing herself with both arms on either side of Raina's head. She ran her open mouth over Raina's throat and ever so slowly penetrated her skin, sinking into her flesh as she sank into the heat between her thighs. The first rush of blood poured through her, flooding her with life and power. Her clitoris tightened and rubbed over Raina's. She thrust, pleasuring them both. Raina released with a hard jolt, and her arms tightened around Lara's shoulders. Raina licked the bite she'd left on Lara's shoulder, and Lara surrendered to the lust and the pleasure.

She'd thought her only need was blood, that she'd only hungered for the semblance of life that came with feeding, until she'd tasted Raina. Until Raina's mouth closed on her shoulder and her bite triggered an orgasm that went beyond blood, beyond pleasure, beyond anything she'd known. She'd never felt so truly alive. She moaned, and Raina purred in satisfaction.

Forcing herself to stop, Lara closed the wound in Raina's throat and relaxed atop her, her cheek cradled in Raina's neck. She drifted, her body and soul replete.

"I never liked sleeping with anyone," Raina said softly, her fingers combing through Lara's hair. "Never liked waking with anyone nearby. But I think I would miss waking with you."

"You'll be free soon, and when you are, you won't miss this."

"Is that what you think?" Raina's voice held an edge. "Or just what you want me to believe?"

Lara kissed the edge of Raina's jaw. "You belong in the mountains, with your cubs, with your Pride. The cats need a leader." Lara sat up, rested her back against the wall. Raina lay beside her, watching her. Lara's hands tightened into fists. "I have nothing to offer you."

"That's not for you to decide."

Lara snarled. "I don't even belong to myself. I owe a debt to Jody Gates. I serve her."

"You may serve her, but she doesn't own you."

Lara jumped to her feet. Raina's blood had blunted her hunger, but she wanted her again, and the wanting was terrifying. She reached for pants, pulled them on. "Get dressed. We'll find the Alpha and secure your freedom."

Raina rose, stretched, her breasts full and lush, her body strong and powerful. Lara's throat tightened and her sex filled. She wanted her again, every way. Under her, inside her, filling her. "You would do well not to tempt me."

"And you would do well not to think you can make decisions for me."

Lara raked a hand through her hair. "You don't know what we face. You don't want any part of my world."

Raina stepped into her pants and pulled on a T-shirt. "I'll let you know what I want." Raina walked toward the door, paused beside Lara, and kissed her. "And when I want it."

Lara's wolf pushed for dominance, wanting to answer Raina's challenge, wanting to claim her. Lara tensed, denying the urge to take her.

Raina smiled and caressed Lara's chest. "Yes, we should hunt. Soon. We'll see who is the strongest then."

Lara narrowed her eyes. "You think to challenge me again?"

"Always." Raina threaded her arms around Lara's neck and leaned into her, her mouth hot against Lara's throat. She raked her canines down her neck and covered the bite she'd left on Lara's shoulder. Her hips jerked against Lara, and Lara cupped her ass, her vision hazing red. "Now."

Hoarsely, Lara murmured, "Careful. If I have you again, I have to feed."

"Maybe I want you to." Raina's canines slid deep into Lara's shoulder.

Lara's wolf howled, mad with pleasure, and Lara took Raina's throat again. She came, standing with Raina in her arms, and at last her hunger disappeared.

Trembling, Raina clung to her, moaning as orgasm rippled through her, wave after wave. She gasped when Lara withdrew and licked the bite on her neck. "I hunger too."

Lara buried her face in the curve of Raina's neck. "You make me mad with wanting."

Raina laughed. "Good."

❖

Sylvan lay awake watching Drake sleep. When she'd returned after her meeting with Andrea and Martin, Drake had been dozing. She'd crawled in naked beside her, and they'd fallen asleep wrapped in one another's arms. She'd awakened as the sun disappeared and moonlight flooded the cabin. When Drake stirred, Sylvan rested her hand on the mound of Drake's belly and kissed her softly. "Sorry. I tried not to wake you."

Drake smiled against Sylvan's mouth. "Did you sleep?"

"Some."

"Is everything all right?"

Sylvan sighed. "Everything is different, but there's no imminent danger."

Drake pushed up against the pillows and guided Sylvan's head into her lap. She stroked her face and massaged the tight muscles in her back. "What happened?"

Sylvan told her of the meeting with Andrea. "She says she will provide whatever information she can acquire about the location of the other laboratories. She thinks they'll be able to narrow the search perimeter and possibly find more members like Martin who might identify some of the individuals in charge. It's a beginning."

"Do you trust her?" Drake asked.

"She took a chance coming here."

"She came for her brother."

"She could have kept her identity a secret. And there's something else."

"Max," Drake said.

Sylvan's brows rose. "You're getting more attuned to the Pack every day."

"I think it might be them," Drake mused, indicating her abdomen. "The stronger they become, the more I…sense the individual Pack members, especially the *centuri*."

"They're linked to me by blood." Sylvan rubbed her cheek on Drake's belly. "And you to me in every way now."

Drake smiled. "Yes."

"What do you sense from Max?"

"His wolf has taken a special interest in the human female," Drake said. "It might not be a bad idea to let them spend time together. They can find out what that means, and we may benefit from another source of intelligence."

Sylvan grumbled unhappily. "The more ties we have outside the Pack, the more possibility there is for betrayal."

"I know it goes against your instinct." Drake combed her fingers through Sylvan's hair. "But we can't live in isolation. So we must find other ways to protect the Pack and our future."

Sylvan rubbed her cheek against Drake's belly. "I know."

"What about the other prisoner—the cat Were? Have you questioned him yet?"

"No. I wanted to talk to Raina first. She's with Lara. They should be rising soon."

"Good. I want to be there when you talk to her. Are you ready?"

"In a minute." Sylvan pulled Drake on top of her and kissed her. "Or maybe two."

❖

Francesca never truly slept. Even at her most somnolent, she remained aware of the heartbeats of the human servants outside her chambers, of the blood coursing through the veins of the dazed hosts in her bed. Daniela had come in a few hours ago and taken that morning's hosts away, but Michel rested beside her still. She leaned over her and kissed her. "Are you hungry, darling?"

Michel's eyes were open and fixed on the frescoed ceiling, her expression closed. "I could feed."

"We can send up to the club for someone to your…tastes," Francesca said, smiling knowingly. "A young Were, perhaps."

"Any host will do," Michel said, feigning disinterest. "I don't hunger for anyone in particular."

"No?" Francesca laughed and kissed her. "So you say."

"Blood is blood," Michel said.

Francesca stroked Michel's chest, circling her tight nipples with her nails. "Yes, but some is so much more pleasant than others."

A knock sounded on the door and Francesca frowned. "What is it, Luce?"

"I'm sorry, Mistress. Might I speak with you?"

"Come in."

Luce entered and strode to the side of Francesca's bed. Francesca held out a hand and Luce kissed it. "Forgive me, Mistress, for disturbing you, but I thought you should know that Veronica has been in contact with Nicholas Gregory. They're planning to rebuild their primary experimental installation with help from contacts within the human government."

"You read her?"

"Yes, Mistress."

Francesca rose, slipped into a robe, and tied it loosely at her waist. Crossing to the tea service Daniela had set out, she poured steaming tea into a china cup. "How strong is your link?"

"Very strong, Mistress," Luce said. "I've fed from her many times, now."

"And her?" Francesca asked indolently, regarding Luce with interest. "Has she tasted you?"

Luce smiled. "Yes, although she's unaware of it."

"You know you need my permission for a blood bond."

"Yes, Mistress," Luce said. "But I did not think you'd mind if I indulged in a slave."

Francesca laughed. "I'm impressed with your initiative."

"Thank you, Mistress." Luce smiled. "I believe she'll be quite useful."

"And as we know, quite enjoyable." Francesca waved a hand. "You should go. She'll be expecting you soon."

"Yes, Mistress." She started for the door.

"And, Luce," Francesca said.

Luce slowed, turned. "Yes, Mistress?"

"Enjoy her as often as you like. But remember, what's yours is mine, should I choose."

Luce bowed her head. "Of course, Mistress."

CHAPTER TWENTY-NINE

Lara slowed as she exited the barracks and said to Raina, "Give me a minute."

Niki waited on the porch, leaning up against a column, her expression hard and angry. She gave Raina a cursory glance, then settled on Lara. "I've come to escort you to headquarters."

Lara stepped up beside her while Raina moved past them into the courtyard. "We were on our way."

"You seem to put a lot of trust in an enemy."

"She's not the enemy."

Niki's brows drew together over eyes bright with fury. "Then who is?"

Just like Niki, Lara had thought she'd known the face of the enemy once, when the world had been simply divided into Pack and non-Pack, those to trust and those to suspect. But then the world had changed, and life as she'd known it had ended. And just like Niki, she'd felt only anger—for what she'd lost, for what she'd become, for the friends she had loved who had become strangers to her. She'd fought the pain and those who reminded her of her loss with rage, but now, looking at Niki, she felt sadness and unexpected sympathy. She clasped Niki's arm. "You know who we must fight, as do I. The power behind the experiments, the cowards who tried to assassinate the Alpha, the humans and Praeterns who plot to destroy us."

"I'm not sure I am strong enough to fight them," Niki confessed. She'd held her ground in Nocturne, despite the hunger that had clawed at her guts when the seductive tendrils of thrall had twined through her, but she'd left sick with need and sick of herself. If she hadn't had the image of Sophia to cling to, if she hadn't made a promise to the Alpha, she might have—

"But you didn't," Lara whispered.

Niki jerked. She'd felt no probing, no sweet caress of phantom hands and hot mouths gliding over her body. "How?"

"You always did broadcast strong enough for me to hear you in the next mountain range." Lara laughed softly and slung an arm around Niki's shoulders. "I can catch glimpses without trying—in fact, if you'd been with anyone other than Sophia I might have watched longer tha—"

Snarling, Niki lunged, but Lara was already five feet away. Niki snorted in disgust. "I said you were more Vampire than Were, now."

Raina leapt to Lara's side from the shadows. "And you are still just an undisciplined wolf."

"No," Lara said, stepping between them. "I'd forgotten how short her temper is." She rested her hand on Raina's back and grinned at Niki. "I *said* had it been anyone *but* Sophia…and what we want to do, or might do, is of no matter. Only what we do."

Niki grumbled, her wolf eyes tracking Lara suspiciously. But she nodded.

"And what we need to do," Lara said softly, "is work as one to defeat our common enemies."

"If the Alpha says I must fight with you," Niki muttered, "then I will."

"Good. Let's go ask her," Lara said.

Niki jumped down and led the way across the Compound, skirting the fire pits where huge cast-iron pots hung, filled with stew for the returning patrols. Lara followed with Raina by her side. She could have broken their contact, but she liked the flow of muscles in Raina's back beneath her hand. Raina was sleek and strong, and her nearness filled Lara with pleasure.

"Why do you bait her?" Raina asked.

"Niki is a dominant wolf who could lead her own Pack if she chose to leave the Timberwolves—she trusts strength, needs to be challenged, needs to fight. We have always tussled."

"And coupled?"

Lara slowed, studied the heat in Raina's eyes. "Yes."

Raina growled.

"But she is mated now, and…" Lara hesitated. "And I am a Vampire." She sensed Raina's cat pacing. "What?"

"Is there anyone here you haven't coupled with?"

"A few," Lara said offhandedly, and Raina's anger washed over her in a hot wave. "I'm a Vampire, I must feed—"

"Feeding is not the same as coupling," Raina snarled. She leapt to the door where Niki waited. "Let's go."

Lara overtook them easily as Niki escorted them to the great hall where the Alpha usually convened with the *centuri*. Tonight the *centuri* were absent, but the room was filled with power. The Alpha stood by the huge stone fireplace with the Prima seated on a carved wood and leather chair to her right. Niki moved to take her position on the Alpha's left. The three most dominant wolf Weres in the Western Hemisphere commanded so much power Lara would have knelt if she hadn't owed allegiance to another. As it was, her wolf whined unhappily and she struggled to keep her head up.

The Liege reclined in a deep leather chair angled toward the fire blazing in the hearth. Becca sat with one hip on the chair's broad arm, her hand on Jody's shoulder. Zahn stood by Jody's side, her gaze skimming over Lara as intensely as if she stood naked. Lara shuddered at the force rolling off her maker and her maker's consort—Jody and Becca were united by blood, their spirits and minds combining to project an impenetrable wall of pure control.

Lara's instincts urged her to fight or flee, but she held herself steady. Raina's fate was about to be decided, and, along with Raina's, hers. She would not let anyone hurt Raina or the cubs. She shouldn't have cared what happened to this cat—to this enemy—but despite their differences, despite the obstacles that centuries of antipathy had bred in them, her wolf had recognized her, had known her, from the first. Lara moved closer to Raina and clasped the back of her neck. Raina seemed unaffected by either the Alpha or the Liege's effortless show of strength, but she leaned ever so slightly into Lara's touch.

Sylvan tracked the gesture and then focused on Raina as if they were the only two in the room. "I have been told you fought bravely and without hesitation in support of my wolves today."

"You gave me no choice," Raina said, her chin high, "and I fought first and foremost for my cubs and my Pride."

Sylvan smiled. "Spoken like a true Alpha."

"I *am* the Alpha."

Sylvan's eyes grew hard. "How do I know if I give you your freedom that you will not lead your cats against me when you have regained your position and fortified your strength?"

"Because I never did before," Raina said, "and I have even less reason to do that now."

"You intend for us to live side by side and respect our territorial borders?"

"I didn't say that," Raina said.

"Don't toy with me, Cat," Sylvan said softly.

Lara tightened her grip slightly on Raina's neck. *Don't antagonize her. You are strong, but she is older and has the strength of a thousand wolves behind her.*

Sylvan was silent, her wolf wary, watching.

"Hundreds of years ago an agreement like that might've worked," Raina said, "but now, we have more to worry about than hunting land and room for our young to roam." She glanced at Jody for an instant, then returned her attention to Sylvan. "I was not in favor of the Exodus. Most of us with less power than the wolves and the Vampires were opposed, but that decision has been made. Now our strength lies in our unity. We have enemies, and we will be stronger together."

Sylvan leaned a shoulder against the mantelpiece. "I wish those on the Coalition could see that as clearly as you do," she said wryly.

"Perhaps you should invite more of us, and then they might."

"Not a bad suggestion. And in the meantime?"

"I intend to return to my territory, to claim control of my Pride, and to raise my cubs to live free."

"By my leave?" Sylvan said softly, challenge in her eyes.

Raina, Lara communicated urgently, *you violated Pack land. The reasons don't matter. In this one instance, your pride is not what matters.*

Raina slowly turned her head, met Lara's gaze, and said aloud, "You know as well as I, sometimes pride is all we have."

"You have more than that now," Lara said. "You have the cubs." Lara hesitated. "And, should you want it, a second who will stand for you, with you."

"That's an interesting offer," Jody said mildly. "Since you are my warlord, you can only stand for Raina if I formally recognize her as an ally."

Raina addressed Sylvan. "I propose that my cats support you against any adversary who threatens your sovereignty, and in turn, you support me and my Pride."

Sylvan turned to Jody. "Liege Gates?"

Jody shrugged without altering her relaxed, seemingly indifferent posture, but her eyes were laser sharp. "Alpha Carras kept her word and risked her life for yours and mine. I accept an alliance with her."

"As do I," Sylvan said.

Raina said, "My forces are small and it will take some time to unify my Pride. I have young to protect. I ask for sanctuary in your mountains while I rebuild my forces."

"I will extend sanctuary, but any cat who challenges a wolf on my territory will not be dealt with as a friend."

"I promise that anyone who violates Pack land will answer to me," Raina said.

Lara said, "And to me." She turned to Jody. "Will you give me leave to offer my services to Alpha Carras as your envoy?"

"As long as the alliance stands," Jody said, the cold flame in her eyes a hint of what would come if the alliance was broken.

"I will stand for her as long as she wants," Lara said, knowing she was making an oath that would cost her life if the alliance failed.

"So noted," Jody said softly.

"It seems," Sylvan said, "we have a new triumvirate. Let me be clear. Individually, we must serve our Pack, our Pride, and our Dominion, but as each stands against those who would destroy us all, we pledge to support one another. Do you so pledge?"

Raina drew her fist to her heart. "I so pledge the allegiance of the Catamount Pride to the Timberwolves and the Night Hunters."

Jody rose and clasped Becca's hand. "The Night Hunters pledge allegiance to the Catamount and the Timberwolf Weres."

Drake stood and circled an arm around Sylvan's waist. Together they echoed the pledge. Then Sylvan looked into each face. "And may we all protect and preserve those who depend upon us."

❖

Raina was silent until she and Lara reached the courtyard and started toward the nursery. The moon was high and the Compound was nearly deserted except for the guards on the gates. The wolves were hunting. "I will not have you as my second or an envoy of Jody Gates."

Lara snarled softly. "Why not? Did you find me unworthy in battle?"

"The cat Alpha rules alone, or"—Raina slowed and Lara turned back, her eyes flickering amber as her wolf raged at the insult—"with a mate." Raina cradled Lara's jaw and brushed her thumb over Lara's mouth. "I want you as my mate."

Lara jerked, her breath catching. "I—I cannot mate. You know what I am."

"Yes," Raina said, "I know what you are. I know who you are. You are wolf and Vampire—and you are mine."

Lara gripped Raina's shoulders. "I can't give you cubs."

"I have cubs. Will you stand for them?"

"I told you I would from the first."

"Will you stand for me?"

"I declared that I would to my Liege, to my Alpha."

"I know you may need to feed elsewhere," Raina said, gripping Lara's hair in her fist, raking her canines down Lara's throat, "but no one touches you. I will give you what you need. I don't share what is mine."

Lara trembled. "If I take from you all that I need, I will bind you to me for eternity."

Raina bit down, scored Lara's flesh. "That would be a beginning."

Lara pulled her close, buried her face in the curve of Raina's neck. "Raina. I love you."

"I love you." Raina kissed the curve of Lara's neck. "And I claim you. Do you accept my claim?"

"Yes." Lara pressed Raina's hand to her breast, above her heart that beat only for her. "I accept, and claim you, with my heart."

Raina lifted Lara's face, kissed her. "With my heart, with my life."

"Let's go see the cubs," Lara whispered. "And then let's hunt together."

"Yes," Raina murmured. "It is time for us to run as one."

Chapter Thirty

Raina settled the two cubs into the crib Lara had placed in the corner of the barracks room Sylvan had provided them. The privacy afforded by the closed door behind her and the ability to protect and care for her cubs had restored her sense of power and purpose. She wasn't a fugitive any longer, no longer hunted in her own land and hiding from the wolves who would see her dead just for being who she was. She stroked Tessa's golden coat, smiled as she stretched in her sleep and twined her legs around her brother.

"They look content," Lara mused. She'd watched Raina call them to skin and feed them, amazed at the simple beauty of so natural an act. Raina glowed with vitality and power, and Lara imagined she could feel a spark of life that had nothing to do with blood. Raina filled her heart. She held up her arm where the new scratches from Tessa had already faded away and smiled wryly. "I think they're getting used to me."

"That was just for show." Raina grinned proudly. "She was testing her place."

"Young for that."

Raina huffed. "Not for a cub of mine."

Lara grumbled good-naturedly. "She'll be testing *you* in a couple of years."

"I'm not worried." Raina grasped the bottom of her T-shirt and pulled it off. Lara's eyes instantly sparked red, and Raina's cat gave a satisfied purr. Lara's gaze sharpened as Raina swept her hands over her breasts and down her belly to the snap on her pants. Her nipples tightened as she slowly drew the zipper down and pushed the pants off. She stepped free and walked to Lara, twining her arms around Lara's neck and pressing close. "They'll both learn where they belong. And when they're old enough, if they want to lead, there will be plenty of cats looking for leaders."

Lara threaded her fingers through Raina's hair, tilted her head back, and skimmed her mouth over Raina's throat. Raina's pulse pounded against her lips. "I think you enjoy teasing me."

"Oh," Raina breathed softly, sliding sensuously against Lara, "I do. How much time do we have?"

"The moon is almost high and the Alpha will be running," Lara murmured, licking the spot under the edge of Raina's jaw that made Raina's hips jerk.

"We should hurry then," Raina said. "I don't want to insult your Alpha by being late to the hunt."

Lara's canines pushed down, her mouth filled, her belly tensed. Bloodlust clouded her awareness of anything but Raina. "Then perhaps you should have kept your clothes on."

Raina cupped the back of Lara's head and pulled her mouth tight to her skin, forcing the points of Lara's canines into her throat. "Perhaps you should hurry."

Lara caressed the length of Raina's back and cupped her ass, pushing her thigh between her legs. She didn't want to rush. She wanted every second to be emblazoned on her mind. She'd fed earlier and the hunger was tolerable, the bloodlust no longer insanity but anticipation of the pleasure to come. The desperation had disappeared with the welcome in Raina's eyes. "Orders, Alpha?"

"Please," Raina gasped. "I need you."

Groaning, Lara tasted her, drew her in, slowly, deeply. Raina trembled in her arms, and Lara took her, finding peace along with her pleasure.

When Raina came back to awareness, she was tangled up with Lara on the bed. Lara was naked, and they were both covered with sex-sheen. Lara lay boneless upon her, her face cradled against her throat where she had fed. Raina stretched, purred softly, and slid her hand over the carved plane of Lara's abdomen and between her legs. Lara was hot and full, slick with the remnants of their passion.

Lara stirred and kissed Raina's throat. "Are you tired? Did I take too mu—"

"Never. Are you ready again?"

"I am, but the Alpha is calling the hunt." Lara lifted up, kissed her, and pressed her hand over Raina's, stopping her teasing motions. "Later. Before I sleep. Now, let's run."

"The cubs?"

"They'll be fine with the guards in the yard. Any wolf who hears them waken will stop to check on them. They're safe here. The Alpha has declared you a friend."

"You were right, she is fair."

Lara stirred, took Raina's hand. "She is also wise. She took your advice to let the cat prisoner live so he can contact those who hired him."

"His only motivation in taking the security job at the lab was money. He values his life more." Raina had not wanted to see him killed, even though he had dishonored her and his Pride, but he was Sylvan's to do with as she chose. "I don't think he will risk angering your Alpha."

Lara smiled. "The Alpha forced him to submit without touching him. And then she let Niki have him."

Raina had stood by in silence while Niki, naked and shimmering with power, had straddled the prostrate male and buried her canines in his neck. He'd thrashed an instant then gone limp, submitting to her completely as his cock emptied impotently against her thigh.

"He knows Niki has his scent," Raina said, "and if he betrays our alliance with you, she will hunt him no matter where he hides. With my consent. And now we will have our own eyes and ears among the enemy."

Lara opened the door into the hallway. "Arc you sure you're not part Vampire? You're good at the politics of war."

"Maybe you have something to do with that," Raina said with a grin.

Lara laughed and drew her outside to the courtyard as Sylvan called her wolves to the hunt. The Alpha stood naked in a circle of moonlight cast by a brilliant full moon, her golden hair wilding around her face. Drake stood by her side within a semicircle formed by the *centuri*, Sophia, Callan and his mate, and the senior *sentries*. Beyond the gates, the jagged mountain peaks stood like obsidian blades against a mirror sky. The air was still and thick with the scent of life. Raina hesitated and Lara tugged her hand.

"Come."

Lara vaulted from the porch and shifted in midair, landing lithely and twisting to find Raina. Pulled by the force of Lara's call, Raina shifted and bounded down to join her with a feeling of freedom she had not known in weeks.

Follow me. Lara moved through the mass of wolves toward the inner circle, feeling the Alpha's call in her bones as she always had—as she had feared never to feel again. Wolves gave way, watching her and the big cat by her side as she took her place at the far end of the line of *centuri*. Andrew's wolf—a muscular brown with brilliant blue-gray eyes—nipped at her ear in greeting. She rubbed her muzzle on his neck and moved close to Raina. She was still a wolf, and she was home.

"Tonight," Sylvan declared, her voice ringing through the Compound and deep into the mountains beyond, "we claim these forests as our own by the skill of our hunters and the hearts of our warriors. Run with me and celebrate the strength of our Pack."

Sylvan shifted too fast for Raina to see, and the others followed. The Pack streamed into the woods behind Sylvan's lead.

Lara hung back, glanced at Raina.

You lead, Wolf, these are your lands.

Lara lifted her head and howled, a sound of fierce joy. Then she streaked toward the rear gate and into the protected Pack lands, and Raina gave chase. Lara was fast, but Raina was a cat and born to run. She gathered her legs beneath her and bounded over the ground, swerving off the trail into the forest as soon as they reached the dense woodland. Lara raced along a narrow trail and Raina cut above her to a high rocky summit, leaping from precipice to precipice, following Lara's scent. When Lara reached a clearing, Raina dropped down beside her, bumping her shoulder in greeting. Lara swung her head and nipped at Raina's neck, grazing her with her canines. Raina switched her tail and batted her with her front paw, then raced away. Now Lara chased her, and so they ran, first one leading, then the other, until Lara dropped down panting beneath a towering pine. Moonlight sliced through the branches in sharp silver strands. Raina curled up beside her and shifted back to skin at the same time as Lara. Raina rolled atop her and threaded her fingers through Lara's. "I love you."

Lara's eyes slowly transformed from the amber of her wolf to Vampire crimson and her hunger enveloped them. "I love you. I hunger for you, more than blood."

"I know." Raina kissed her. "Be patient."

Lara snarled but held still and Raina kissed her throat, her breasts, her belly where the fine pelt arrowed downward. She nestled her breasts between Lara's thighs and kissed the hard heat of her.

"Raina," Lara said, her tone a warning and a benediction.

"In a minute," Raina murmured and took her into her mouth, filling herself with Lara's essence, consuming her as she was consumed. Taking as she was taken.

Lara tensed, her hips rising above the pine-needle strewn forest floor. "Raina, I need—"

Raina held her a second longer, then slid upward until her clitoris nestled against Lara's. "I know what you need. What I need." She turned her head, offered her throat, and Lara took her. The pleasure was an arrow piercing the core of her, too intense to hold, and Raina shattered.

"Again," Raina gasped.

They coupled until the moon slanted downward and a distant pale heralded the coming dawn. Raina lay on her back with Lara's head on her shoulder, watching the night fade. An hour or two and Lara would need shelter. "Will you return to the city with Liege Gates at sunrise?"

"Yes," Lara said quietly. She stroked the long, muscular curve of Raina's flank. "Will you come with me? Bring the cubs?"

"For a time," Raina said softly, "until I have secured shelter in the mountains."

"There are cabins along the frontier for distant patrols. I will ask the Alpha to give you the use of one. You will be within Pack land, and our patrols will protect you."

"In a month, the cubs will be able to hunt on their own. Then, if something happens to me—"

Lara snarled and rose over her, flame eclipsing all color in her eyes. "Nothing will happen to you. You are mine. I will not lose you."

Raina caressed her face. "I can't hide, none of us can."

"I know that. And I know the cubs need to learn the mountains. But they need to learn the other world too. They will rule one day in a very different world than we knew."

"Once I have regained control of the Pride, I will come to you when you can't come to me."

Lara relaxed, settled upon her again. "Yes. I will never be far away."

"Nor I from you. I swear."

"I thought I had no reason to continue," Lara said quietly. "I thought what I had become destroyed everything that mattered." She kissed Raina. "I was wrong. You are everything that matters now. You and the cubs."

"I wasn't looking for a mate. I thought I had everything I needed." Raina pressed close until their bodies joined. "I was wrong. You are everything I need."

Chapter Thirty-one

They're active tonight," Sylvan said, her hand on Drake's belly as the shower sluiced over them.

"They've had enough waiting." Drake tilted her head back and kissed the angle of Sylvan's jaw. "It won't be long."

"I know. I can sense them reaching out to the Pack." Sylvan kissed the back of Drake's neck. "You know, you don't have to go tonight."

Drake shook her head. "This is one of the biggest political events of the year. It's not just a fund-raiser, it's the place where deals are made and votes are procured. And where laws are made or unmade. You need to be there, and if you need to be there, so do I."

Sylvan shut off the water and reached outside the enclosure for a towel. She wrapped it around Drake's shoulders and began to dry her. "Just because it's been quiet the last few weeks doesn't mean there is no danger."

"I don't think we'll be without danger until well after the legal battles are over." Drake grabbed another towel and draped it over Sylvan. "Laws might ensure rights on paper, but it takes more than a signature to change the way people feel. Or the way they act. With so many factions opposed to Praetern recognition, we're looking at a long struggle. Laws are a beginning, not an end."

"And we haven't even gotten the laws yet," Sylvan muttered.

"It's a fight, but the Coalition has the right leader."

Sylvan sighed. "Sometimes I wish we could go back to a time when all we had to worry about was securing our borders and protecting our Pack."

"I didn't know those times, but I know they're in your blood." Drake kissed Sylvan and walked into their bedroom where she'd laid out their clothes for the governor's gala. She was heavier throughout her middle, but without the classic pregnancy mound. Dressed in a shirt and pants a size larger than she usually wore, she hardly appeared pregnant by human standards. All the Weres knew the Alpha pair was expecting young, as did the Vampire upper echelons. Probably many humans and other Praeterns had heard as well. She wasn't trying to hide her state; in fact, she wanted those in attendance at the gala, some of whom were surely enemies, to see that Sylvan had the support and strength of her mate at all times. She stepped into charcoal pants with a subtle white stripe and reached for the matching jacket. "Everything you're doing now is exactly as it has been since the beginning. You are still securing your borders, only now those borders have expanded beyond the physical. You are protecting the rights and future of your Pack and our young in the legislature and in society. You are still the Alpha, and everyone looks to you to lead the way now more than ever."

"And I look to you." Sylvan buttoned her fitted black shirt and tucked it into tailored black pants. "Just promise me that you'll be careful tonight."

Drake grinned. "I'll be with you. How much safer could I be?"

❖

"You look very handsome, darling," Francesca said, taking the pearl gray studs from Michel and fastening them through the buttonholes in Michel's crisp white tuxedo shirt herself. Michel's black pants were perfectly tailored with a satin stripe down the side. Her black hair fell in roguish layers over her ears and down to her collar. Crimson simmered beneath the Mediterranean blue of her eyes. Francesca kissed the hollow of her throat. "We should leave the neck open, I think. Such a perfect reflection of what is truly beautiful. I couldn't ask for a more dashing escort."

Michel stood still as Francesca attended her in a move calculated to be proprietary, not subservient. Francesca had fed well and her face glowed. Her eyes smoldered with passionate vitality. Her sleeveless floor-length royal blue satin gown dipped between her voluptuous breasts, showcasing her milk-white shoulders and unblemished décolletage. The lush fabric dipped in at the waist and flowed over her hips and thighs in a cascading waterfall of sensuality. She moved like a dark secret, a whisper on the wind.

When Francesca finished tucking Michel's shirt into her trousers,

Michel slid an arm around Francesca's waist and kissed her. "And you, my Regent, are as beautiful as ever."

"Thank you, darling. You flatter me."

Michel smiled. "I have never needed to. You are truly magnificent."

Francesca inclined her head, hearing the truth in Michel's words. Pleased that her *senechal* had not yet grown inured to her charms despite her new interests, she slipped her hand through Michel's arm, and they walked through the underground passages to the inner courtyard where her car awaited. "It will be very interesting to see how our friends align themselves tonight."

"Yes. Much can be learned from casual conversations."

"I assume you have eyes and ears where we need them?"

"Of course. Luce is attending as part of Dr. Standish's party, and since Dr. Standish is escorted by Nicholas Gregory, we have a direct avenue to them."

"And the wolves? Do we have someone with them?"

Michel almost smiled, amused that Francesca would ask her questions to which she already knew the answers. But that was always part of her mistress's game. To be caught out in a lie was viewed as a failure of skill, as punishable an offense as the actual deceit and a sign of weakness. In this case, what the Regent really wanted to know was if Katya would be accompanying the Alpha. Michel could answer truthfully that she didn't know.

She hadn't seen Katya in the weeks since the Alpha's visit to the club—when she'd last fed from her. She had not attempted to reach her via the link they shared and had tried very hard not to think of her. Instead, she'd gone through every Were in the club on a nightly basis, hoping to temper the gnawing hunger that held her in its grip. She'd only been able to succeed enough to maintain her sanity. But with Francesca watching her so closely, and suspecting her desire for Katya, she could not go near her.

"Not for certain," Michel admitted, "but we know that Nicholas Gregory has wolves in his secret employ, and we both know Enoch is blood-addicted. I'm having him watched. If he makes contact with any of Nicholas's people, we'll have him."

"That will have to do for now. But I want a Were who answers to us." Francesca paused while Michel opened the door of the idling limo. "I'm sure you can find someone to succumb to your charms."

Katya's face flashed through Michel's mind and she quickly raised her shields. She settled next to Francesca and pulled the door closed. Francesca's hand automatically moved to the inside of her thigh and slid high enough to cup her through her silk trousers. She hardened, but she kept her voice steady. "As soon as I do, I'll be sure to tell you."

❖

Lara waited with Zahn on the sidewalk in front of Jody's town house, surveying the shadows in the park across the street, the traffic moving by, and parked vehicles for anything out of place. Zahn was the head of Jody's security, but Lara was Jody's warlord, and as far as she was concerned, safeguarding Jody was her most important job. She would lead Jody's soldiers in a fight, but even if a fight never came, the night still held danger.

"Looks clear," Zahn said.

"Yes," Lara said, watching the progress of a white van as it moved slowly down State Street toward the capitol buildings. She didn't like vans—too easy to conceal armed occupants. Simple enough for the vehicle to careen to the curb and for assassins to roll out, shooting before anyone had a chance to mount a defense. The van passed uneventfully. She checked her watch. 7:55.

"What do you think the chances are of an attack at this kind of event?" Zahn asked with the same conversational tone she might use if commenting on the weather forecast.

Lara answered in kind. "I think our enemies expect us to figure the risk of capture is too great for anyone to make an attempt at such a high-profile event. That we'd be lulled into a feeling of false safety and let down our guard. And then they'd strike."

Zahn nodded but didn't comment.

"And for exactly that reason, we have to be doubly vigilant every night, but especially tonight."

"My thoughts too." At exactly 7:58 Zahn raised her left hand and spoke into her mic to the drivers standing by where Jody's vehicles were garaged, two blocks away in a secure enclosure. "Bring the cars around."

The private lot was under twenty-four-hour guard by human servants, but car bombs were a relatively simple and effective means of assassination. Easy to assemble, easy to place—it only took a second to attach a palm-sized square of C-4 to the undercarriage of a vehicle—

and easy to detonate with a cheap burn phone. Zahn wasn't taking any chances, and Lara was just fine with that.

At eight o'clock precisely, the front door opened and Jody stepped out with Becca on her arm. Jody's ebony hair and midnight blue tuxedo with monochromatic shirt made her seem part of the night. Becca's pale ivory gown glowed against her coffee skin, a glimmering star marking Jody's dark sky.

Two Vampire guards fell in behind them as they approached the street. The limo pulled to the curb with an armored SUV carrying the rest of Jody's bodyguards right behind it. The limo idled, and Zahn walked over to open the rear door. Lara did another visual sweep of the street. These last twenty feet were the most critical if an assassin made an attempt.

"Clear," Lara said to Zahn, who motioned Jody and Becca forward. Jody handed Becca into the rear of the car but did not follow. Zahn's brows drew together. "Liege? You should get inside."

"In a moment." Jody turned and looked down the street just as another SUV rounded the corner. She smiled. "Ah. Our last guest is right on time." She turned to Lara. "Please escort the Alpha to the limo so she can ride with us."

Lara sensed her then and strode rapidly along the line of parked cars as the second SUV pulled up behind the first. The rear door opened and Raina stepped out. Lara missed a step, caught in the unexpected vortex of Raina's aura. Her blond hair was long and thick, teasing at the thin straps of a simple midnight blue dress that fell in shimmering sheets to her knees. Her heels of matching blue added to her already formidable height, and she moved with the same lethal grace she displayed in pelt. Lara swallowed the lust in her throat. "I didn't expect you tonight."

Raina smiled, her gaze raking Lara hungrily. "I received an invitation from Liege Gates this morning, asking me to attend as her ally and guest."

Lara's jaw set. "An open association with her is going to make you a target for every Were, human, and Vampire who fears her and the strength you bring to her with your cats."

"A secret alliance is of limited benefit," Raina pointed out. Moving toward the limo, she slid her hand under Lara's black jacket and rubbed her back. "I'll be fine. Besides, it's been three days. I've missed you."

Lara growled softly. "Not as much as I've missed you."

Raina laughed. "Are you hungry?"

"You have no idea."

"Later," Raina said and slipped into the backseat of the limo.

Lara leaned down to the closed window, compelling Raina to look at her. *Be careful of what's mine.*

Always.

Zahn walked around to the passenger side, opened the front door, and said across the top of the vehicle to Lara, "We've spent enough time out here already."

Lara nodded curtly and headed for the follow car. Claude was behind the wheel. "Make sure we don't get separated."

"Yes, Warlord."

Lara climbed into the back, and the vehicle pulled away. She watched the taillights of the limo, checking all approaches to each intersection as they entered. Cross streets were vulnerable points where an attack car could take out the limo or pull between them, effectively separating the limo from its protective follow car. All the drivers were experienced and trained in defensive driving, but she was happy when the short ride to the governor's mansion was over.

A crowd of reporters from TV and print media crowded the long walkway to the front entrance. There hadn't been a gathering of so many powerful politicians and Praetern representatives since the Exodus was declared. If someone wanted to cripple the Praetern initiative, this would be the place to attack.

Chapter Thirty-two

"I don't believe I've been introduced to your lovely…partner, Alpha Mir," a patrician voice said from Sylvan's left.

Sylvan clasped Drake's hand and turned to the silver-haired human who smiled at her with just a hint of condescension he no doubt thought he had hidden. "Senator Weston, I'd like you to meet my mate and Prima of the Timberwolf Pack, Dr. Drake McKennan."

His icy eyes registered the faintest surprise, as if he had not expected Sylvan to refer to her otherness in frank terms, but he graciously extended his hand with a well-practiced smile. "Very pleased to meet you, Doctor."

"Thank you, Senator." Drake gestured to the crowded ballroom where human state and federal officials, business powerbrokers, and social elite mingled with the ruling heads of the Praetern realms. "This is quite an historic event. It's been very gratifying to hear such strong support for the Coalition's goals from so many."

"Yes, we're making excellent progress in that regard." His smile stayed in place, but his eyes grew wary.

Sylvan's wolf registered the subtle rise of anger and aggression in his scent. She held back the urge to snarl. "We're hoping to see the bill reach the floor before the end of the session, isn't that right, Senator?"

"I think that's a very good possibility," he said, carefully not committing himself.

"Well," Sylvan said, "I'm sure we can count on you to do everything that can be done."

"Of course. And how are things at Mir Industries after the accident?"

"All our projects are on schedule," Sylvan said, "as the damage was far less than reported."

"I'm glad to hear that. So many of our supporters depend on the generosity of your foundation."

"Yes, I'm aware of that."

"Well, it was a pleasure to see you again"—he nodded to Drake—"and you, Doctor." He moved away into the crowd, treating others to his trademark megawatt smile.

Sylvan watched him go. "I'm not at all certain he intends to push for the vote this year—or ever."

"You might be right. But he's also a politician," Drake said, "and even if he actually supports the resolution, he may be hesitating for fear of creating animosity among his constituents or of supplying ammunition to those who might oppose his other agendas."

"I hate politics," Sylvan muttered. "You can't tell friend from foe, and alliances shift from one day to the next. No one ever says what they mean."

"No one would ever know you weren't a natural." Drake laughed softly and slid her arm around Sylvan's waist. "You may not like to play the game, but you're very good at it."

Sylvan kissed her temple. "And *you* are very good at managing me."

"I'm learning." Drake rubbed Sylvan's back. "At least you didn't growl at him. I could tell you wanted to."

Sylvan growled and Drake grinned.

"How do you feel?" Sylvan asked.

"I'm fine."

"Then why do I keep getting these twinges in my back?"

"You feel them?"

"Yes," Sylvan said. "They started just about the time we arrived."

"Nothing to be too worried about right now," Drake said, "but I suspect they're sending a message."

Sylvan grinned a self-satisfied grin. "We should give Katya a little more time to study the crowd in case something triggers a memory and she recognizes her captors. Then we should go."

"Yes. Let's finish the necessary social niceties first." Drake nodded toward the opposite side of the room where Jody, with Becca on her arm, bowed to a wildly handsome man in his early thirties with dark hair, a muscular build, and an air of power that reached Drake even across the room. "That can only be Zachary Gates."

Sylvan followed her gaze. "Yes. And Jody's father wields nearly as much power as Francesca."

"With Jody heir to all that?"

"Yes—whenever Zachary chooses to step aside, or in the unlikely event he is overthrown or meets true death."

"He looks like her brother. I don't think I ever really appreciated what it meant for them to be immortal."

"The price they pay is steep," Sylvan murmured, sliding her hand up to Drake's neck. "We will have hundreds of years together, in sunshine and in moonlight. I will take that over an eternity of darkness."

Drake kissed her. "I will celebrate every moment with you as if it were a lifetime—and that is eternity enough."

Veronica Standish couldn't take her eyes off Francesca and Michel. They were the two most beautiful individuals in the room, shimmering with sexuality and practically glowing with power. Her blood pulsed hard, straining toward the surface as if willing her to offer herself. Her breath burst from her in a rush of anticipation. Luce was nearby, just out of touching distance, and Veronica yearned to be closer, to rub against her until Luce's eyes turned to fire and she plunged her incisors into Veronica's throat. Instead, she was on Nicholas's arm, and while he had once seemed to her such a powerful ally, he now seemed pale and inconsequential.

"They all seem so civilized, don't they," Nicholas murmured, acid in his tone.

"They haven't managed to live among us for millennia without being able to masquerade as something other than the animals they are," Veronica said, feeling herself grow wet and heavy with urgency. She looked to Luce, knowing her eyes were pleading. Luce merely smiled, a flicker of her incisors sending a bolt of arousal directly to Veronica's sex. She gasped softly.

"Something interesting?" Nicholas asked, his gaze riveted to Sylvan Mir.

"Just surprised," Veronica said, trying to hide her distraction. "I didn't expect the wolf Were to bring her mate tonight. She's pregnant, you know."

"I know," Nicholas said, a slight smile doing nothing to soften the hard fury in his expression. "An unexpected bonus."

"What do you mean?" Veronica asked absently, wondering how she could get Luce alone for just a few minutes. Just a few minutes to help temper the furious need tearing her to shreds.

"Losing the Alpha pair and their mongrel get will destroy that Pack, and it's well past time that happened."

Veronica heard the words and struggled to register their meaning through the escalating need that had her heart racing and her muscles trembling. Bringing all her considerable mental control to bear, she fought to think through the lust clouding her reason. Had Nicholas just said he was going to attack Sylvan Mir? "Surely not here—"

Nicholas said, "And what better place than when you and I have such a perfect alibi? The protesters are twenty deep outside. The authorities will have plenty of suspects, and there has already been one violent attack attributed to those fanatics." He slipped his hand around her back, his palm cradling the outer curve of her breast. Her nipple tensed painfully.

"You seem very sure all of them will be—"

"Fortunately, the weapon of choice of these fringe groups has always been explosives." His smile widened and mad pleasure brightened his dark eyes. "After tonight, my dear, we will have our pick of subjects for your experiments. I have teams ready to begin procurement as soon as the Were leadership is dealt with."

"You do know what I need, don't you," Veronica said, thinking him quite insane. But at this point she didn't really care. His usefulness to her was nearing an end. And the only thing she craved more than her work was the pleasure of a Vampire's bite.

❖

Francesca surveyed the humans milling about, making plans, scheming, flaunting their pitiful power as if they had some control over their futures. Futures that were to her nothing but the blink of an eye. Still, without humans, existence would not only be impossible, it would be somewhat boring. At least they entertained her.

"What do you think of the little alliances spawning here and there, darling?" Francesca asked.

Michel shrugged. "Nothing more than I expected, although the cat is a surprise."

"Yes, she's quite beautiful, isn't she," Francesca said, eyeing the blonde with Jody's warlord. "I wonder exactly how much power she brings with her."

"The cats are fierce fighters, and if that cat can organize them, Jody and Sylvan will have a formidable army."

"Yes. An army that Sylvan has pledged us should we need it."

"Assuming Sylvan survives," Michel pointed out. "And assuming she still trusts us."

Francesca glanced across the room at Nicholas Gregory. He had been particularly circumspect that evening, actually avoiding her after the briefest of acknowledgments. "I'm afraid Nicholas may do something very foolish."

Michel laughed. "I think you can count on that."

"We may need to put Sylvan on her guard."

"Are you sure you want to spoil Nicholas's plan?"

Francesca smiled. "Weren't you the one who suggested it would be wiser to ally with the Weres than the humans?"

"Yes, but with Sylvan gone, the Coalition will break and you will have achieved your goal of delaying, or possibly destroying, the move toward assimilation."

"I have thought of that," Francesca said contemplatively. "The Shadow Lords and their followers would be in our debt, but with Jody now allied with the cats, and us without Sylvan's army, we could have an internal challenge."

"From Jody?"

Francesca searched out the handsome vampire with the midnight hair and sapphire eyes. He was so beautiful. "No, her father."

"Ah. You are right, as usual."

"Summon Luce, would you, darling," Francesca said, watching Veronica Standish shiver with bloodlust. She smiled. "Let's see what Nicholas has in mind."

"Of course, Regent," Michel said, signaling a guard to her side. "Tell Luce the Regent requires her presence."

"Yes, *Senechal*," the guard replied and melted into the crowd.

A moment later, Luce appeared and went to one knee in front of Francesca. "Regent, you called?"

Francesca extended a hand, which Luce kissed in formal greeting. "You may rise."

Luce stood. "How may I be of service?"

Francesca leaned close as if in conversation, but she had no desire to be overheard. *I wish to know of Nicholas Gregory's plans. Perhaps his lovely companion will have some knowledge.*

I believe I can find out.

As soon as you can. You may go.

Luce bowed. "Yes, Regent."

Francesca took Michel's arm as Luce made her way back to Nicholas's party. "If there's any need, I'm sure you have some way of getting a message to Sylvan that won't be traced directly back to us."

"I'll see what I can manage," Michel said coolly.

❖

"Sylvan," Drake murmured.

"Yes?" Sylvan's fury rose as she focused on Nicholas Gregory. She wanted to drag him back to the Compound and tear him to pieces. He had to be involved in the attacks on her laboratories and her young, but she had no proof. Katya couldn't recognize her captors—her memory was still clouded with the aftereffects of silver toxicity.

She would find the proof. She would continue to search for the remaining installations using the information they obtained from Andrea, Martin, and Raina's mercenaries. And when she found them, she would raid them again. If there were no captives to free, they would simply burn the buildings to the ground. And then she would deal with Nicholas.

"I think it's time for us to go," Drake said.

"Now?" Sylvan's heart leapt and her wolf surged. Her eyes flashed gold, her jaw thickened, and pelt rippled beneath her skin. She wanted her mate away from these strangers, out of danger.

Drake laughed softly and stroked Sylvan's face. "You can't shift here, Alpha. You'll terrify the humans."

Sylvan growled. "I don't care."

"Take me home."

Sylvan signaled to the *centuri* who had taken up posts around them in the crowd. "Have Andrew bring the Rovers. We're going home."

Chapter Thirty-three

Jody and Becca, along with their guards, joined Sylvan and Drake as they made their way toward the ballroom exit. Jody said, "We'll walk out with you. My tolerance for half-truths and false promises has been exceeded for one night."

"As has mine," Sylvan said.

Becca said to Drake, "You look wonderful. And a little bit…expectant."

Drake smiled. "You're perceptive. And correct."

Becca beamed. "You need anything? I'm not sure how much help I would be, but…I'm here if you need anything."

"Thank you," Drake said, squeezing Becca's hand. Sylvan and the Pack filled her life, completing her emotionally and physically, but Becca's simple offer of friendship was welcome amidst the constant strife and subterfuge. "I will. And as soon as possible, you'll have to come visit."

"Try to keep me away."

"Stay close," Sylvan murmured as uniformed attendants pulled open the wide front doors to the mansion.

Drake pressed against Sylvan's side. The rhythmic spasms in her abdomen were more regular now, but not so severe as to be worrisome. As long as they reached the Compound without delay. The crowd outside had grown since they'd arrived at the governor's mansion, and several hundred people crowded the rope barricades, forming a gauntlet along the walkway that led to the circular drive. Most were probably reporters or simple sightseers, but some were placard-carrying anti-Praetern protesters chanting *humans first* and displaying signs for HUFSI, Humans United for Species Integrity. Sylvan had her wolf on a tight leash, but Drake sensed her on the verge of attacking at the slightest provocation.

"I'm fine, Sylvan." Drake pointed down the drive to the line of Rovers and limos approaching. "Andrew and Dasha are on their way. We'll be home soon."

❖

"I only have a minute," Veronica said breathlessly, drawing Luce down a service corridor and into a dimly lit corner. "Nicholas thinks I've gone to freshen up." She slid her hands inside Luce's tailored jacket, pulled her shirt from the waistband of her pants, and stroked the cool chiseled muscles of her back. "God, I haven't been able to think of anything but you all night."

Luce caged her against the wall with her arms outstretched on either side of Veronica's shoulders. "And you think I enjoy watching that human put his hands on you?"

Veronica gripped Luce's ass and pulled her close. "I wasn't thinking of him. I was thinking of you. I'm so wet. Hurry."

Luce laughed softly and leaned forward, licking Veronica's throat very, very slowly. "What is it that you want?"

Veronica whimpered, her hips rocking. "Oh God, you know what I need. Please, Luce. Please."

Delicately, Luce punctured Veronica's skin, millimeter by millimeter, drawing out the pleasure for them both. She needed Veronica to drop all her shields, to be completely subjugated to her power, and Veronica was mentally very strong. She released a surge of feeding hormones but drew back before Veronica peaked. Veronica cried out in protest. "Are you sure this is what you want?"

"Yes, yes." Veronica writhed, hands scrabbling over Luce's back, her eyes glazed, her color high, her breath escaping in ragged gasps. "Oh my God. I'm going to come the instant you take me. Please, hurry."

Luce snarled, gripped Veronica's hair in her hand, and extended her neck. When she buried her incisors bone-deep into Veronica's jugular, she poured feeding hormones into her system, overwhelming her. Veronica snapped taut, her strangled cry of ecstasy an invitation for Luce to slide into her mind.

Tell me, what is he going to do?

An image of soaring flames, twisted wreckage, and scattered bodies jerked into view, and she knew.

❖

Niki waited with Lara and Raina just outside the entrance until the Alpha's party and the Vampires started down the wide stone steps. The Alpha led, Drake's hand in hers. Max, Jace, and the others wolves flanked them, guarding against an attack from the sides. The Alpha projected a silent air of menace and power, and bystanders pulled back as she and the Prima passed. Jody, Becca, and their Vampire guard followed close behind in similar formation. Niki fell in at the rear with Lara and Raina to ensure no threat encroached from behind. She didn't notice that Katya had dropped back from the Alpha's party until she drew alongside her. Katya stood still, a perplexed expression on her face.

"What are you waiting for?" Niki asked, taking Katya's arm as she scanned the faces nearby.

Katya turned glazed eyes to her. *"Imperator?"*

"Sentrie," Niki snarled. "Report!"

"Imperator!" Katya's stare widened. "I…danger!"

Niki spun around and for a second thought she saw a form ghost behind a pillar. Then nothing. She whipped back around. "Where?"

Lara and Raina went into battle mode, turning back-to-back to face the crowd.

Katya's face filled with horror. "The Rover."

Niki stared down the long walkway. The Alpha and Prima had just reached the drive as the first Rover, twenty feet away, slid to a stop.

"No," Niki shouted, shifting as she raced down the stairs, Lara and Raina close behind.

The wolf, the cat, and the Vampire launched themselves off the marble staircase as the world lit up and a fireball erupted.

CHAPTER THIRTY-FOUR

"Are you really sure it's necessary for me to hide?" Veronica stood at the window of the safe house Luce had brought her to the night of the gala. The winding mountain road leading up to the isolated house was barely visible in the predawn gray. No lights penetrated the murk—they were alone. She couldn't remember the details of the attack, only having awakened in Luce's arms in the rear of a limo as it whisked her out of the city. She'd followed the news reports the last few days from the seclusion of the mountain chateau, watched over by Luce and a contingent of other Vampires and human servants. "I know some rogue Were implicated Nicholas, but the news reports say there's no evidence. And Nicholas denied everything in the interview they broadcast last night."

"He would." Luce kissed the back of Veronica's neck. Veronica shivered and Luce smiled against her skin. "The Regent wants to ensure your safety, and she's right to be concerned. The law will mean nothing to the Weres now, and anyone they suspect is in danger. You are a known associate of Nicholas's—and he will be their main target."

"But I thought the only witness against Nicholas is dead."

"The Were who planted the explosives said he'd acted on Nicholas's order, and that's all the proof the wolves will need." Luce shrugged. Nicholas probably hadn't informed the Were exactly when the detonation would occur—a handy way to dispose of a witness—but the Were had lived long enough to be questioned. Nicholas Gregory had been arrogant and foolish to think the blood-addicted Were he had manipulated to do his bidding would not break when confronted by a dominant wolf like Niki Kroff. "Attacking the Pack is a death sentence."

"They can't simply kill Nicholas."

"The Timberwolves will demand justice, and Were justice is simple. Associating with Nicholas now is inviting death."

Veronica turned and threaded her arms around Luce's neck, arching her throat in a gesture so automatic now she couldn't remember a time when the promise of pleasure wasn't the center of her existence. Offering herself was as natural as the control she used to exert over others. Now all that mattered was the explosion of heat and unbearable ecstasy that was hers as often as she wanted, as long as she had Luce—or any of the other Vampires. "I suppose I should be grateful to have you all to myself for a few days."

Luce cupped Veronica's breast and ran her tongue over the pulse in Veronica's throat, Veronica's ever-present desire stirring her bloodlust. Veronica's blood pulsed hot and strong, and as long as she was careful not to take too much and saw that Veronica received restorative supplements, she could feed from her many times a day. And Veronica's need was endless. "The Regent values your loyalty and support. And she has promised to provide you secure facilities to carry on your work. There are many ways your association with us can be mutually beneficial."

"Yes," Veronica said, most of her mind focused on the instant when Luce would take her. But the part of her that still hungered for a different kind of power sorted possibilities and dismissed the advisability of working with Nicholas again. His plans had become too dangerous, his obsession putting them all at risk. And their agendas no longer intersected. She had been right to approach the Vampires, so much like humans only so much more powerful. Allying with the Vampires would afford her endless resources, and she would finally be able to neutralize the animals amongst them. "Your Regent is most kind, and I am grateful."

"A few more days with me would not be so bad, would it?" Luce murmured.

"Any time with you is heaven." Veronica writhed against her, forgetting for the moment her ambitions, forsaking her driving desire to find the weaknesses in the Were genome that would allow her to eradicate them. Now all she wanted was the bright point of pain and the oblivion of orgasm. She curled her fingers in Luce's hair and pulled Luce's mouth to her throat. "Make me come."

"Yes," Luce whispered, allowing herself the sweet satisfaction of bloodlust before reporting to her mistress that Veronica Standish was theirs.

❖

Lara stroked Raina's back as she slept, trying to reassure herself that the burns and torn muscles were gone. She leaned down and kissed the unblemished skin between her shoulder blades, then glanced across the room at the still-sleeping cubs. All those she cared about were safe. Dawn was coming, but she did not want to wake Raina, even though she might soon be lost to the day.

Raina rolled over, her eyes open and clear. "Did you think to let me sleep past your feeding time?"

Lara kissed her. "You need to rest." She gestured toward the crib. "You might be healed, but they need you strong. I need only blood."

"I'm fine, and you need more than a human servant's blood."

"You lost a lot of blood." Lara pressed her forehead to Raina's shoulder, blocking out the image of the big beautiful cat lying bloodied and broken, her body sprawled over the Alpha and her mate. So much bigger than the others, Raina had taken the brunt of the flaming debris. "I was terrified."

Raina stroked her hair. "So was I. You didn't go undamaged yourself."

"It takes more than a few shards of metal to destroy me."

Raina tightened her arms around Lara's shoulders. "You know as well as I what could have happened if one had struck your heart—"

"None did." Lara raised her head. "You must be at full strength if I have to leave. When the Timberwolves seek retribution, I will join them."

Raina's eyes hardened. "As will I."

"The law will mean nothing now, and once we strike, the humans will retaliate."

"What do we care about laws that do not recognize us to begin with?" Raina sat up. "We were attacked, and we must defend ourselves. Only if we unite all the Praeterns will we be able to survive."

Lara took her hand. "I know what you say is true, but I cannot lose you. Before you, I didn't care about surviving. Now you are what I live for."

"I am your mate and I will fight by your side." Raina kissed her. "And one day, we will win."

❖

Sophia knelt by the red-gray wolf where she lay in the tall grass staring at the Alpha's den. She stroked Niki's head and buried her fingers in Niki's ruff. *You have to eat. You need rest. Please come home.*

Niki turned her head and licked Sophia's hand. *I'm not leaving her. I'm all right.*

Then we need to do something. The Pack is agitated, even the dominants are frightened. We need you all back in the Compound. We all need your strength.

I'm waiting for her orders.

Sophia sighed and stood. *We can't wait any longer.*

Don't, Niki warned. *She is dangerous now.*

I know. But rage is often only the reflection of terrible pain. Sophia slowly approached the huge silver wolf lying on the porch of the log cabin in front of the open door, staring at her with flat gold eyes. A wave of fury struck her, nearly bringing her to her knees, but she pushed on. Icy terror streaked along her spine. Her wolf quivered, wanting to flee, but Sophia ignored the primal urge to run from a near-feral dominant. She slowly climbed the three broad wooden stairs, her head lowered. She forced herself to speak aloud through a throat tight with fear. "Alpha, we need you."

Sylvan growled. The blood that had caked her massive shoulders and back when she'd returned from the city was gone. She had shifted sometime after the explosion to heal her wounds, but no one had seen her out of pelt in three days. Her absence had thrown the Pack into a panic.

Sophia slowly sat on the top step, put her back against a post, and folded her hands in her lap. Sylvan's eyes tracked every motion.

"The *centuri* are not enough to still the alarm spreading through the Pack. You are our heart and our strength. We need to see you. Everyone needs to hear your voice."

Sylvan did not move except for a slight twitch in one ear.

"I know your pain and your rage. We all do. We all mourn." Sophia raised her head. "Do not make us mourn alone. We need you now more than ever."

Sophia had only the barest impression of the air shimmering, and then Sylvan stood above her, her eyes still wolf-gold and as cold and remote as Sophia had ever seen them. Carefully, she stood but did not meet Sylvan's gaze.

"Come inside." Sylvan disappeared into the cabin.

Sophia quickly followed, crossing the dimly lit living room to another doorway where she paused. She sensed them first—strong, quick heartbeats. Tears filled her eyes.

From the shadows, Drake said, "It's all right. Come closer. Let me introduce you."

Sophia crossed to the broad bed, aware of the Alpha watching her with the focus she usually reserved for prey.

"Meet Kira and Kendra," Drake said softly.

Sophia knelt. "They're beautiful." She laughed softly. "One silver, one black. Like the two of you."

"Yes." Drake laughed. "I wonder what that portends for sibling rivalry."

"So young to shift—so strong," Sophia murmured.

"They're healthy Were young of a powerful Alpha," Drake said softly.

Sophia met Drake's shining gaze. Drake was not a born Were, but turned, like her. And Drake's pups were perfect. "The Pack wants to celebrate with you, Prima."

From behind her, Sylvan said, "It is for me to decide."

Drake looked past Sophia to Sylvan. "It's time, Alpha. The Pack needs joy now, and they need us."

Sylvan snarled. "I won't risk any of you when I don't know who I can trust."

She turned and stalked from the room.

"I'm sorry," Sophia said, "I didn't mean to intrude—or to make her pain worse."

"I'm glad you came. She needs comforting, and you may be the only one who can give it to her. Losing Andrew is a deep wound, and she's too worried about me and the pups to hear me."

"We all bleed when one of us is lost," Sophia said.

"It's more than Andrew's death. It's that Enoch, one of her wolves, betrayed us all. Her heart grieves."

"With your permission," Sophia said, "I'll talk to her."

"Remind her of what matters—she needs the Pack as much as the Pack needs her." Drake grasped Sophia's arm, and for the first time since the single blackened and burned Rover returned to the Compound bearing Andrew's body, Sophia felt the strength of the Pack fill her.

"She has you and the pups," Sophia said, "and we will all die before any harm comes to any of you."

"I know," Drake said, "and so does she. Help her remember, so we can all heal."

CHAPTER THIRTY-FIVE

Sylvan's wolf padded into the bedroom, a huge silver beast radiating authority and effortless dominance. She nosed the crib, rumbled quietly. The pups stretched and mewed contentedly, as if sensing they were safe with her near. Seemingly satisfied, she turned to the bed and studied Drake intently.

Drake held out her hand. "I've missed you. Were you hunting?"

The wolf delicately climbed onto the bed and stretched out beside Drake, who wrapped her arm around the broad shoulders and cradled the magnificent head against her breast. Power washed over her, and Sylvan pressed against her, skin to skin.

"I was running," Sylvan whispered. "How are the young?"

"Sleeping. They shifted again for a short while."

Sylvan smiled against Drake's breast. "They are impatient young alphas."

Drake laughed. "Of course they are. They're yours."

Sylvan delicately brushed her mouth over Drake's nipple, placing a reverent kiss against the inner curve of her breast. "Ours. They'll have your wisdom, your strength."

"And your purpose and honor," Drake murmured, stroking Sylvan's hair. "Did you find what you were looking for on your run?"

"The forest pulsed beneath my pads, the clean mountain air teased over my tongue, and wildlife whispered in the underbrush. My wolf was at home."

"Mmm. All the things that define our world."

"Yes." Sylvan pressed her face to Drake's neck. "And then I called the *centuri*, and they appeared out of the forest where they had been shadowing me, to run by my side. Lara is here. And Niki and Max. Jace and Jonathan. And now Dasha—in Andrew's place."

"You ran to honor him, and remember."

"Yes."

"What will you do now?"

"I've tried to follow in my father's footsteps, to live my father's dream. To see his vision realized."

Drake waited, softly, continuously, stroking Sylvan's back.

"But while we petition to be accepted and wait for humans to pass judgment on our worthiness, the groups that want to destroy us are allowed to grow strong. Our young are violated, our territories disregarded, our strongest struck down." Sylvan raised up on an elbow, the blue of her eyes shot through with shards of gold, her wolf ever present now. "I will no longer ask for permission to live, to rule our territories, and to raise our young in safety. And I will remind those who make war against us that we are not easy prey. We have been predators for millennia, the strongest of the strong. And we still are."

"I agree that those who make war upon us cannot go unpunished, but if you strike back, they will hunt you."

"No one can beat us on our own land."

"You know I will support you in whatever you decide," Drake said, "but we must fight as wolves have always fought—swiftly, stealthily, and as one. What cannot be proved cannot be used against us."

Sylvan lifted Drake's hand to her mouth and kissed her fingers. "As I said, you are wise as well as strong."

"I am a wolf Were, Prima of the Timberwolf Pack," Drake said fiercely. "We will not rest until we have justice for our violated and our dead."

"Jody and Raina will stand with us."

"Yes." Drake kissed Sylvan and sat up. "It's time to take our young to meet their Pack."

Sylvan rose, pulled on pants, and strode to the crib. Lifting her young into the curve of one arm, she held out her hand to Drake. "Come with me, Prima, and gather our wolves for the hunt."

About the Author

Radclyffe has written over forty romance and romantic intrigue novels, dozens of short stories, and, writing as L.L. Raand, has authored a paranormal romance series, The Midnight Hunters. She is an eight-time Lambda Literary Award finalist in romance, mystery and erotica--winning in both romance (*Distant Shores, Silent Thunder*) and erotica (*Erotic Interludes 2: Stolen Moments* edited with Stacia Seaman and *In Deep Waters 2: Cruising the Strip* written with Karin Kallmaker). A member of the Saints and Sinners Literary Hall of Fame, she is also a RWA/FF&P Prism award winner for *Secrets in the Stone*, a RWA FTHRW Lories and RWA HODRW Aspen Gold winner for *Firestorm*, and a RWA 2012 VCRW Laurel Wreath winner for *Blood Hunt*. She is also the president of Bold Strokes Books, one of the world's largest independent LGBTQ publishing companies.

Books Available From Bold Strokes Books

The Princess Affair by Nell Stark. Rhodes Scholar Kerry Donovan arrives at Oxford ready to focus on her studies, but her life and her priorities are thrown into chaos when she catches the eye of Her Royal Highness Princess Sasha. (978-1-60282-858-2)

The Chase by Jesse J. Thoma. When Isabelle Rochat's life is threatened, she receives the unwelcome protection and attention of bounty hunter Holt Lasher who vows to keep Isabelle safe at all costs. (978-1-60282-859-9)

The Lone Hunt by L.L. Raand. In a world where humans and Praeterns conspire for the ultimate power, violence is a way of life…and death. A Midnight Hunters novel. (978-1-60282-860-5)

The Supernatural Detective by Crin Claxton. Tony Carson sees dead people. With a drag queen for a spirit guide and a devastatingly attractive herbalist for a client, she's about to discover the spirit world can be a very dangerous world indeed. (978-1-60282-861-2)

Beloved Gomorrah by Justine Saracen. Undersea artists creating their own City on the Plain uncover the truth about Sodom and Gomorrah, whose "one righteous man" is a murderer, rapist, and conspirator in genocide. (978-1-60282-862-9)

The Left Hand of Justice by Jess Faraday. A kidnapped heiress, a heretical cult, a corrupt police chief, and an accused witch. Paris is burning, and the only one who can put out the fire is Detective Inspector Elise Corbeau...whose boss wants her dead. (978-1-60282-863-6)

Cut to the Chase by Lisa Girolami. Careful and methodical author Paige Cornish falls for brash and wild Hollywood actress Avalon Randolph, but can these opposites find a happy middle ground in a town that never lives in the middle? (978-1-60282-783-7)

More Than Friends by Erin Dutton. Evelyn Fisher thinks she has the perfect role model for a long-term relationship, until her best friends, Kendall and Melanie, split up and all three women must reevaluate their lives and their relationships. (978-1-60282-784-4)

Every Second Counts by D. Jackson Leigh. Every second counts in Bridgette LeRoy's desperate mission to protect her heart and stop Marc Ryder's suicidal return to riding rodeo bulls. (978-1-60282-785-1)

Dirty Money by Ashley Bartlett. Vivian Cooper and Reese DiGiovanni just found out that falling in love is hard. It's even harder when you're running for your life. (978-1-60282-786-8)

Sea Glass Inn by Karis Walsh. When Melinda Andrews commissions a series of mosaics by Pamela Whitford for her new inn, she doesn't expect to be more captivated by the artist than by the paintings. (978-1-60282-771-4)

The Awakening: A Sisterhood of Spirits novel by Yvonne Heidt. Sunny Skye has interacted with spirits her entire life, but when she runs into Officer Jordan Lawson during a ghost investigation, she discovers more than just facts in a missing girl's cold case file. (978-1-60282-772-1)

Murphy's Law by Yolanda Wallace. No matter how high you climb, you can't escape your past. (978-1-60282-773-8)

Blacker Than Blue by Rebekah Weatherspoon. Threatened with losing her first love to a powerful demon, vampire Cleo Jones is willing to break the ultimate law of the undead to rebuild the family she has lost. (978-1-60282-774-5)

Silver Collar by Gill McKnight. Werewolf Luc Garoul is outlawed and out of control, but can her family track her down before a sinister predator gets there first? Fourth in the Garoul series. (978-1-60282-764-6)

The Dragon Tree Legacy by Ali Vali. For Aubrey Tarver time hasn't dulled the pain of losing her first love Wiley Gremillion, but she has to set that aside when her choices put her life and her family's lives in real danger. (978-1-60282-765-3)

The Midnight Room by Ronica Black. After a chance encounter with the mysterious and brooding Lillian Gray in the "midnight room" of The Griffin, a local lesbian bar, confident and gorgeous Audrey McCarthy learns that her bad-girl behavior isn't bulletproof. (978-1-60282-766-0)

Dirty Sex by Ashley Bartlett. Vivian Cooper and twins Reese and Ryan DiGiovanni stole a lot of money and the guy they took it from wants it back. Like now. (978-1-60282-767-7)

The Storm by Shelley Thrasher. Rural East Texas. 1918. War-weary Jaq Bergeron and marriage-scarred musician Molly Russell try to salvage love from the devastation of the war abroad and natural disasters at home. (978-1-60282-780-6)

Crossroads by Radclyffe. Dr. Hollis Monroe specializes in short-term relationships but when she meets pregnant mother-to-be Annie Colfax, fate brings them together at a crossroads that will change their lives forever. (978-1-60282-756-1)

Beyond Innocence by Carsen Taite. When a life is on the line, love has to wait. Doesn't it? (978-1-60282-757-8)

Heart Block by Melissa Brayden. Socialite Emory Owen and struggling single mom Sarah Matamoros are perfectly suited for each other but face a difficult time when trying to merge their contrasting worlds and the people in them. If love truly exists, can it find a way? (978-1-60282-758-5)

Pride and Joy by M.L. Rice. Perfect Bryce Montgomery is her parents' pride and joy, but when they discover that their daughter is a lesbian, her world changes forever. (978-1-60282-759-2)

Ladyfish by Andrea Bramhill. Finn's escape to the Florida Keys leads her straight into the arms of scuba diving instructor Oz as she fights for her freedom, their blossoming love…and her life! (978-1-60282-747-9)

Spanish Heart by Rachel Spangler. While on a mission to find herself in Spain, Ren Molson runs the risk of losing her heart to her tour guide, Lina Montero. (978-1-60282-748-6)